D1398822

BLACK DEUCE

A Novel
by
Stan D. Jensen

Copyright © 2017 by Stan D. Jensen

All rights reserved. No part of this book may be used or reproduced in any manner without written permission except in the case of brief quotations embodied in critical articles or reviews.

For information, contact the author by email at stan.1950@hotmail.com.

This is a work of fiction. The characters are the product of the author's imagination.

Original cover art by Evanny Henningsen

(This book was formatted by Once More Unto the Page Formatting)

http://omutpformatting.wordpress.com

For my mother and father.

~

"A steed as black as the steeds of night,

Was seen to pass as with eagle flight"

~Thomas Buchanan Reed

BLACK DEUCE

The year is 1978.

1. SAM JACK

The *killers* came for her that morning. A chunk of a man with dark unreadable eyes tied a chain around her legs and used a winch to drag her onto his truck. Now at midnight, Sam still couldn't get the sound of the filly being dragged across the racetrack out of his head. And there were the filly's eyes. He was brutalized by the memory of her eyes hardening to glass as the vet injected the massive dose of phenobarbital that stopped her heart. She had been a sweet filly, gentle and so fast that the first time she *worked* the *Racing Form* clockers made a point to find out who she was. And now she was dead. So were Sam's hopes.

A cloud of silky wings hung around the security light at the end of the barn, and Sam stood in the shadows beneath the slant of the shedrow roof. Sam was tall and lean, his hair blond, his eyes blue. The precise swerve of his cheekbones and a square jaw gave his face a handsome geometry. Sam showed the solemn intensity of a man who's known little but hard work and disappointment. He could discipline his body to any task, work long hours, but to make it in horse racing it took more than hard work, you needed luck, and that Sam Jack didn't have. Perils lay in ambush for those who chose racing as a career, for those who willingly made the backstretch their workshop. That morning the three-year-old filly had worked three quarters of a mile in 1:11:2. The flashy chestnut loved to run. Now she was dead. A bad step after the wire. Split sesamoids.

A breeze came up and it seemed to come from the filly's empty stall, and to Sam the breeze had on it the smell of death. He lowered his head, his lips parted. Sam tried to think, to make a plan, but when he thought of his future, his mind was a ringing emptiness.

The deep hum of solitude was broken when Sam's only other horse, Fighter Pilot, a seven-year-old gelding, came to his *webbing*. He'd run third his last time out for $3,500 claiming, a game effort, but he wouldn't run again for months. *Heat* in the knobby calcified right knee. Sam could run him again, not because he thought he could win *sore,* but because he knew there was a chance the *hard-knocking* old campaigner would get claimed and he could use the money to claim another horse to keep himself in business. But no, he could never do that to the faithful gelding. He'd never risk him *breaking down.* Fighter Pilot watched Sam, his head up, ears pricked, and went so rigid he seemed the glass-eyed work of a taxidermist.

"You always know when there's trouble, Fighter," Sam said in the gentle way he had of talking to horses. "What's your advice, should I stick my head in an oven?"

The old gelding didn't move, didn't blink.

"Just kidding, Fighter," Sam said, knowing the old gelding had a knack for picking up his moods. "You know me better than that. I'm a fighter too."

Footsteps in the dark.

Sam turned, peered down the shedrow. The soft glow of the security light created shadows, and from among the familiar shapes and forms, one of the shadows moved toward him down the row of stalls. The shadow took the shape of Clay Repp, his *gallop boy.* Clay stopped by Fighter Pilot's stall and stood swaying on unsteady feet. The fumes of alcohol. Clay was in his forties, short, spare, an ex-jockey. His small features were arranged in a face creased and furrowed like old saddle leather. Clay gazed up at Sam, seemed to have trouble finding words.

"It ain't fair," Clay finally said in a drunken mumble.

Sam briefly closed his eyes, gave a nod to agree.

"She was going to be a good one, Sam. A stakes filly for sure—" Clay stopped there, stumbled over to a railing, hung over it and retched, blowing the whiskey soup in his belly onto the ground. He staggered back to Sam, wiping a hand across his mouth, said, "At least you got a place to go Sam, a wife and little girl to go home to. That Bess is the prettiest…" Clay's words now came out of his mouth so jammed and slurred together that Sam could only make out an "Ain't fair" spoken several times.

Sam took out his billfold. In it was the five hundred dollars the killers had given him for the filly. He handed Clay a twenty. "I owe you for the last four mornings," he said.

"Hell, I should've paid you to gallop that filly," Clay mumbled and slurred again. "She was just that good—" Clay took in a noisy breath, raised his hands in a gesture of helplessness. His voice rose in pitch when he said, "There was nothing I could do, Sam. That bad step—"

"It wasn't your fault, Clay," Sam broke in, "I'm just glad you didn't get hurt." He was still holding the twenty out to the gallop boy. "Now take this."

"Thanks, Sam," Clay muttered. He took the twenty and stumbled back to the railing to unload more of what his belly could no longer tolerate.

"You can make it to your *tack room,* Clay?"

Clay jammed the twenty into his blue jeans. "Hell yes," he said, and he stood again swaying, looking up at Sam. "I'm not worried about you, Sam, you're one of the best horsemen I know. I knew it when I rode for Joshua Kincaid, back when you were only nineteen and already Kincaid's assistant trainer. We were winnin' it all, Sam. You, me and Kincaid. Kincaid was leadin' trainer right here at Lincoln Park, and I was leadin' rider until I…you 'nd me, Sam, worst luck…" Clay turned away then, still talking, and began to stumble off down the row of stalls.

Sam watched him, and just as Clay's shadow trembled into nothingness in the dark, he heard one last "It ain't fair."

Sam turned back to Fighter Pilot. The old gelding still looked stuffed and glass-eyed. Sam walked over and put his arms around the old gelding's neck. A gripping came over him, a hard clutch in his chest. Yes, Bess and little Amy waited at home, but the hard truth, the racing-plate hard truth was that horses were a drug and he was an addict. An even harder truth was that a drug overdose had the mercy to kill quickly, whereas horse racing slowly tortured a luckless man, just broke his heart and left him to suffer. There with his arms around the old gelding, Sam began to think about the church just outside the stable gate and that maybe it was time to start praying. Then it came to him, that he needed no church, that the God he wanted to pray to could be found in no other place than here, in this barn where horses slept.

2

An hour later Sam had his two-horse trailer hooked up to his 1967 Ford pickup. It was time to go.

Like all *racetrackers*, Sam knew how to travel light. In the time it takes a horse to gallop a slow mile, he had the old ford with the rusted rocker panels loaded with the few things that made it possible to live in a tack room and work in a horse barn. A roll up mattress that made sleeping on bales of straw not so uncomfortable, a coffee pot, hot plate, a tack trunk full of equipment, odds and ends. Then he was leading the old gelding through the dark to the trailer. The old gelding stepped along lightly, suddenly coming alive.

"We both know when it's time for the road, don't we, Fighter?" Sam said as he led the gelding to the trailer. Without hesitation, the old gelding walked up the ramp, his hooves clopping on the aluminum. He took his place in the stall deep-bedded with straw. Just as Sam began to swing the door to the trailer closed, Fighter Pilot looked back at him, pricked his ears and nickered. The old gelding was happy; he knew he was going home.

Sam turned the key in the ignition and welcomed the shudder of the old the truck. Tappets clattered for oil, the fan belt gave a squeal, then Sam shifted into drive and motored past the slumbering barns of Lincoln Park Racecourse's backstretch. A sleepy security guard, standing under the fluorescent light that lit the night in front of the security shack, waved him through the gate, and Sam turned north on Laramie Avenue and headed for the Eisenhower expressway. He was soon on highway 30, going west, home to Iowa, a little farm he rented just outside the river town of Camanche.

An hour passed, and the old truck rattled down the road, headlight beams bouncing ahead to light the way. Sam passed through little towns with white-steepled churches and red-brick fire houses. All were quiet and asleep beneath strings of street lamps. Just before he reached Hinckley, an animal dodged in front of the truck, a bandit-faced raccoon. Once safe in the tall grass of the ditch, the raccoon stood on its hind legs and looked back at the truck, its eyes reflecting the headlights like bright discs. Sam hardly noticed, he was staring through the windshield remembering his father.

Sam's earliest memory was of sitting on his father's lap and winding his gold pocket watch, the fine Patek Philippe engraved with *Silhouette, Winner of the 1953 Chicago Gold Cup.* Silhouette was one of Henry Jack's greatest accomplishments. He'd taken an incorrigible horse no trainer wanted, and with the hands of a gifted horseman transformed him into one of the great *handicap* horses of his time. "Baffle them with kindness" was Henry Jack's method of dealing with rogue horses, and this philosophy of training made him one of the most successful trainers in the country...until the gambling became a sickness and he was suspended from racing for life.

Now came a tornado of memories whirling through Sam's

mind. Police detectives threatening his father with prison if he didn't talk. The grand jury investigation. The name of a bookmaker, Antonio Belichio. Long nights when his father peered out into the dark from behind curtains as if waiting for an unwanted someone to arrive. Sam finding his father in the barn dead, holding a revolver in his right hand. Sam on his knees beside his father begging him to be alive, to please take a breath, even though there were two holes in his head: one a small black-burnt hole, the other a bloody crater. A boy screaming so hard and so long blood vessels burst and flooded both his eyes to red.

The tires of the Ford truck hummed against the asphalt and insects spattered against the windshield. Now and then a car passed, and headlights briefly revealed the torment of a man still remembering. Sam tried counting backward from 100 aloud to interrupt his thoughts, but the memories kept coming, flashing like newsreels before his eyes. The police ruled Henry Jack had committed suicide. Sam knew his father hadn't, that someone had stolen the Patek Philippe watch off his father's body, that his father was never without the watch he was so proud of, that his father was left-handed and so his father couldn't have shot himself the way the police said he had, that his father loved him and would never leave him, not this way, not like a coward. Sam telling the police about the dapper little Italian who had talked briefly to his father outside a grocery store just days before the suicide: Antonio Belichio. He told the police about the slick-haired little Italian's eyes and how they were the mean eyes of a snake. Sam hearing his mother tell him they were moving back to Davenport, the farm was lost, no way to keep it. The night he ran away from home and hitch-hiked to Lincoln Park Racecourse's stable gate…and then there came the image of a mother who never came looking for a boy who wasn't yet sixteen years old.

Sam shook his head, a violent motion, and he slowed the old truck down and pulled off to the side of the road. He leaned forward, and with a dull thud put his forehead on the steering wheel. He tried to build the sounds in his throat that would release the pressure, the grief in his heart. He couldn't make a sound, all the groans and sorrows remained unuttered and festering, and he was remembering again. He had the gold watch in his little hands, sitting on his father's lap. A kind man, so much gentleness. "Baffle them with kindness" was the philosophy by which Henry Jack also raised his son, the little boy who adored him. His father's face pressed to the top of Sam's head, through blond hair his father's soft mutter "I love you, Sammy, I love you more than horses."

Sam's heart heaved in his chest and he suddenly looked up, a feverish brilliance in his eyes. Then, with a hard jolt, he realized he had no idea where he was and the whirl of memories began to slow. During the trauma of remembering things best forgotten, he vaguely recalled taking a turn, then maybe another, and he shouldn't have taken any. Highway 30 was a straight shot to Iowa.

Sam pulled the truck back onto the road. In the glare of the headlights, a dead leafless tree looked like a struggling man reaching toward heaven with arms outstretched. Then a stop sign loomed out of the night and there was a bar there at the crossroads. The neon light perched on the ramshackle building's roof read *Noah's*. Sam pulled in and brought the truck and trailer to a stop. He sat there in the dark, the newsreels flickered to a stop. He took a deep breath, pulled himself together.

Sam needed coffee and directions. After turning off the truck, he got out and closed the door behind him. A creek twisted through the open field beside the bar, and along it bullfrogs grumbled.

Sam walked by the trailer, his boots crunching on gravel. After hearing the old gelding munching hay from the hay net, Sam walked up to the building past a dozen parked cars. When he entered the bar, it was like walking into a brown fog of whiskey and beer. In the low-ceilinged room were men crowded together, arguing, laughing, and telling tales, and there wasn't an honest face among them. These were brutal men with mouths that cursed and belittled anything good and decent. The women there were the painted kind that naturally follow such men. A silent alarm went off in Sam's head. When Sam was a boy, bullies avoided him because he was strong and unafraid, but Sam knew he didn't belong here, not in a bar that made it easy to believe that hell really did exist. He was about to back his way out, but saw the coffee pot on the counter beneath the shelves of liquor bottles that gleamed in the low lights. Sam walked to the long marble-topped bar and sat down on a tall chrome-legged stool. The bartender was an older woman with lips smeared red and hair dyed black and roped into a mound on top of her head. Tufts of whiskers sprouted from her chin, her dark eyes were like bits of coal in the folds of her face.

"What'll ya have, handsome," she said.

"Coffee," Sam answered.

"You'll like my coffee," she said, a smile slanting her mouth, "I got my own blend, a wildcat in every cup."

The bartender left briefly, returning with a steaming cup that gave off an aroma somewhere between coffee and roofing tar. She set the porcelain mug down on the marble bar with a click.

"Careful, it packs a wallop," the bartender said.

Sam took in a drink, swallowed. His throat seized up, his eyes got wide. "Wow," he said in a strangled voice.

"My coffee can wake the dead," the bartender said giving a cackle. Then the door to the bar opened behind Sam, and the folds of the bartender's face twisted into a look of fear. With a croak, she said, "Son-of-a-bitch...not him, not tonight."

The room had suddenly gone silent and Sam looked over his shoulder. Now standing in the room was the biggest man he'd ever seen, a hulk dressed in a black pin-striped suit and shoes that gave off a shine even in the low bar lights. On his huge square head the man wore a black fedora, and from beneath the wide brim, his eyes glittered out of a boxer's punch-scarred face. On one of the man's thick fingers was a diamond so large it looked like a crystal from a chandelier. He walked over to the bar, the old wooden floor complaining with each step he took. He sat down two stools over from Sam.

"Hello, Bill Baker," the bartender said.

"Shot of whiskey, Irene," Baker rumbled, "and don't give me that cat piss you serve these rubes."

A stir went through the room. Men leaned toward each other, exchanged whispers, then looked back at Baker. Slowly, conversations started back up. Danger came off Bill Baker like sparks from a downed high-voltage wire. Here was a man who broke the bones of other rough and brutal men and left them scattered behind him. Irene put a shot glass in front of Baker and poured him a shot of Crown Royal. Sam picked up the coffee mug, braced himself, and chugged the mug empty. His throat seized up again, his stomach rolled, and his eyes took on a caffeine-overdose shine. He stood up to leave.

"You lost, mac?" Baker rumbled at Sam.

"Maybe you're the one lost," Sam shot back. "And my name's not mac."

Baker's face warped into something like a smile. "Feisty, I like that," he said. Baker was a dangerous man trying to be friendly. He picked up the shot glass and emptied it in a quick swallow, then went on, "I know you're lost because that's your horse trailer out front with Iowa plates and your truck has race track stickers all over the windshield."

"How do you know—"

"And look at these bums," Baker waved a big hand toward the men sitting around the tables, "a guy like you hasn't got business with losers who'd gamble their teenage daughter away for a three-dollar trifecta ticket...hell, not a damned one can tell a thoroughbred from a cow."

Baker's eyes suddenly focused into a dark corner of the room. He seemed to grow fangs. From out of the corner a man suddenly sprang up out of his chair and ran for the front door. The flapping of a suit that looked cut from billiard table cloth made him resemble a startled pheasant. Once out the door, the man left behind a room gone silent again.

"Bill, you won't hurt Freddy, will you?" Irene, the bartender said, the bits of coal in her face now big as chunks.

Baker's face expanded, contracted. "He took the bet, and he's going to pay me...one way or the other your scumbag of a bookmaker husband is going to pay me."

"Please don't hurt him, Bill," Irene said in a frantic breath.

"Freddy's probably half way to Peoria by now," Baker

answered, "and anyway, I want to talk to my new friend here about horses. But you tell Freddy I want my money…you tell him I want it by noon tomorrow."

"I'll tell him, Bill," Irene said.

When Baker looked back at Sam his anger was gone. "So, mac," he said, "tell me about your racehorses."

"Racehorse, singular, I'm down to just one."

"What's his name?"

"His name's Mac," Sam said.

Baker threw his head back, growled a burst of laughter, said, "Don't take offense, I call guys I like mac, it's just a habit. Now what's your horse's real name?"

"Fighter Pilot."

Baker's heavy jaw dropped open and he slammed his open hand on the bar so hard it rattled the liquor bottles on the shelves. "He's a runner, that one. I've made a lot of money betting on that horse." Baker waved at Sam to come closer, patted the stool beside him. "Sit down here, tell me about yourself. What's your name?"

Sam moved over two stools, sat next to Baker. "I'm Sam Jack," he said.

Baker put out his hand. "Glad to meet you, Sam."

When Sam shook Baker's hand he had the feeling he was about to lose his arm to the elbow in Baker's meaty thick-fingered grip.

"You're right about me being lost," Sam said. "How do I get back to Highway 30?"

"Your way north. You'd be better off catching 38 west, it's just up the road."

"Thanks, now I've got to be go—"

Baker interrupted, said, "You just let me know when that horse of yours is ready to win again. I'll bet for you too, make it worth your while. You can always get a message through to me by way of The Deacon. You know who The Deacon is, mac?"

"I know *of* him. But, Bill, I'm no gambler."

"You one of the good guys, mac, one of the honest ones?"

Sam didn't have time to answer. The door behind Baker

slammed opened, and Freddy, the man who'd run out the front door looking like a startled pheasant, had a shotgun pointed at Baker's head.

"Bill!" Sam shouted and dived off the stool.

Baker swung his arm back, a powerful motion, and his arm hit the barrel of the shotgun just as it went off. The whole room seemed to explode. The blast put a ragged hole in the ceiling and bits of plaster fell to the floor in a clatter. Dust and gun smoke swirled. Freddy dropped the shotgun as Baker threw him up against the wall. From seemingly nowhere, Baker had a switchblade in his hand and he now held the point of it to Freddy's throat.

"I ought to bleed you like a hog," Baker said.

Irene screamed, "Andy and Frank, don't let your pa get kilt!"

Two men rose from the tables, both bent-nosed bruisers, and that's when Sam reached down and picked up the shotgun. Sam worked the slide handle to eject the empty shotgun shell and chamber a new round. The two men stopped in midstep, exchanged glances.

"Let's all just get a grip here," Sam said in a quick shout, holding the shotgun in his hands so it pointed at the ceiling.

Irene had ducked down behind the bar. The only thing Sam could see of her was ropes of dyed black hair bobbing back and forth.

"Don't shotgun my boys, mister," Irene wailed. "And, Bill, don't go killin' Freddy."

Now the only sounds in the bar were those of a whimpering Irene and Freddy snorting with fear. Freddy's eyes bulged in his pale bony face, and he stood on his tiptoes, trying to get away from the point of the switchblade. On Baker's face was a look Sam had never seen before. Baker's eyes had the hard shine of a man incapable of pity, and he was grinning a ferocious grin, the grin of a killer.

"Is this how you treat your new partner, Freddy," Baker said, "shoot me in the back with a shotgun?"

Freddy blinked. "What?"

"If you haven't got my money, I now own fifty-one percent of this dive."

Freddy blinked again, could only repeat himself: "What?"

Irene got brave and stood up. "For the love of God, Freddy, just say yes."

"Yes," Freddy obeyed.

Baker tipped his head back and roared laughter, his whole body in spasms as he said, "I love breaking a bookmaker more than sharks love blood." Then Baker let Freddy go, and Freddy stood trembling, still blinking in confusion. Baker put the switchblade back in his coat pocket and reached a hand out toward Sam. "You can give me the shotgun now, mac."

"All yours," Sam said, handing it over.

Baker looked at Freddy's two sons, said, "You two shit heads sit down." They did just as Baker ordered and Baker turned back to Sam. "Mac, you're a handy guy in a tight spot. Thanks for the help."

"Didn't do it just for you, Bill," Sam answered. "If they were going to kill you, they wouldn't have left a stranger alive long enough to be a witness at a trial."

"Ain't that the truth," Baker said. "Get yourself out of here, mac, and remember The Deacon, he always knows how to reach me."

Sam didn't waste time on goodbyes, he made a straight line for the door and then hurried through the parking lot. Parked beside his rig was a red Cadillac convertible. Before he got into the truck, he went to the trailer's open window to look in at Fighter Pilot. Sam reached in and rubbed the old gelding's neck, and at Sam's touch the old gelding turned his head and looked at Sam with bright eyes that communicated that which needed no words to be understood. Sam loved horses, and horses loved Sam right back.

Five minutes later, Sam took a left onto Highway 38 and headed west to the Mississippi River and Iowa.

2. BESS JACK

In the dark, just before dawn, Bess lay sleeping, curled up on her side, her cheek buried in the softness of a pillow. She didn't see the lights of Sam's truck stream through the bedroom window in shafts of yellow that fanned and shifted across the walls, or hear the Ford's fan belt squeal as Sam came down the lane and brought the truck to a stop in front of the barn. Bess was a shining, slim, black-haired beauty. She was feminine in every curve of her body, in every note of her voice. In a short dress, she could make men stutter, make men stare. Bess was a flower in the perfection of spring bloom.

While Sam put Fighter Pilot away in a stall, saw to the old gelding's feed and water, Bess dreamed. In this dream, she finally told Sam how she felt, that she wasn't happy being without him, that she needed Sam to stay home, that she needed him there to talk to, to tell her dreams to, to share her dreams with. That she needed him there to be a father to little Amy. In her dream, she finally managed to take the sound of flutes and harps out of her voice, and make that voice stern when she told him he had to give up the racetrack, give up horses. Now she dreamed of Sam bowing his head and telling her that he was sorry he'd ever hurt her, and yes, he was home to stay. Bess was twenty-seven years old, but in a sweet way she was still a naive young woman who believed she lived in a world where there was a doll for every little girl, a bike for every little boy.

Then there was a noise and Bess was awake, reaching to turn on the lamp on the nightstand. When she saw Sam in the sudden glare, standing there in his worn jeans and patched shirt, her lovely violet eyes eclipsed her face. In a burst of reckless joy, she was up out of the bed, running to him in a light, dancing step. Bess threw herself into Sam's arms, kissed his face over and over, then once so hard and long on the lips that it left her lips reddened and plumped. The stern girl in her dream was gone, she was a puppet made of yarn in his hands.

"Oh, Sam, you're home," she said over and over, the words like a happy song on her tongue. Then a sudden thought frightened her and she pressed both hands to his chest, looked up into his face. "Is everything alright? What's happened?" In a breathless urgent way, she said, "Tell me, Sam."

"It's the filly—" Disappointment suddenly took away Sam's ability to speak.

Bess held her fingertips to her mouth briefly, then in barely a whisper said, "What happened?"

"I had to put her down," Sam said.

Different emotions pummeled Bess. The filly was gone, taking with her all of Sam's hopes and every cent they had, but Sam was home, he wasn't in some dusty backstretch tack room, he was home. She watched in silence as Sam took off his shirt and hung it over the back of a chair. The sight of him caused in her a surge of hatred for horses and the sport that showed no mercy. He'd lost weight, she could see his ribs, and she knew the horses had eaten, but that he hadn't.

"There's cold chicken in the fridge, and Mother brought a pie—"

"No, Bess, I'm too tired to eat," Sam interrupted, his eyes red from exhaustion.

"When did you sleep last?"

"Everything's a blur, I'm not sure…I didn't get much sleep yesterday, and the day before I was too excited about the filly working three-quarters for the first time. So maybe three days ago."

"Oh, Sam—"

"And then I got lost this side of Aurora and I'm still not sure exactly where I was. The outskirts of hell, I think."

Bess twined her arms around Sam's neck, laid her head on his shoulder, gave a little sigh, then said, "I'm so glad you're home. Amy will be so excited to find you here when she wakes."

In the next minutes, they were lying together in the dark.

"Dad will give you a job at the store," Bess said.

"Don't, Bess, not now," Sam answered.

Sam turned toward Bess, cupped his hand to the side of her face. Her skin was smooth and soft like a satin ribbon. Sam lived a life without luxury, save for one, a wife who adored him. When Sam sat up and slipped her nightgown off, the feeling of fabric brushing her skin sent a tingle through Bess from her head to her toes. She could become excited just by watching Sam comb his hair, and now that his hands were on her, she began to tremble and thrill to his touch. She kissed his chest, smelled the smell of him, found relief and reassurance. Sam was home, Sam was in her arms. Bess exchanged unhurried kisses with Sam, and when he placed himself between her open legs, she closed her eyes and lights began to flash behind her lids. How remarkable Sam was, this man with the rough, calloused hands that were always so tender and gentle when he touched her. Words tumbled from her mouth, tumbled out of her heart and soul, words that told him how much she loved him and wanted him. Then Sam's hips began to work, and her pleasure was so sharp she suddenly couldn't talk, the only sounds she could make were little moans, little cries, and the soft sweet sounds only playful kittens and happy young wives can make.

3. CHARLES KEENE

The black 1939 Mercedes 540K pulled up to the stable gate. The hood of the nearly eighteen-foot long Roadster seemed to stretch beyond barn three, and under it, an inline eight-cylinder engine hummed a tune of power and German engineering. From the driver's seat of the two-seater convertible, Charles Keene smiled a Hollywood-bright smile at the uniformed security guard and tipped his straw Panama hat. Sprawled in the seat next to him was a blond in a red dress. She was passed out. Her right leg hung out the window and a red spike-heeled shoe dangled precariously from her toes. The security guard, a pudgy, dough-faced man, had become accustomed to such a sight when it came to Charles Keene, and a reflection of the security guard smiling could be seen in the mirror-like finish of the Mercedes. The guard waved Charles Keene through to enter the backstretch, and an impressive roar came from under the classic car's hood. Chrome wire wheels flashed, the engine's roar traveled through chrome outside exhaust headpipes, and Charles Keene was off to barn seven to see to the training of his father's horses.

Charles brought the Mercedes to a stop in front of his barn, and got out. His shoes were by Ferragamo, a pair of brown and white cap toes. His white shirt, rolled up to the elbows, was by Armani. Alligator suspenders by Belinni held up his perfectly creased Zennella slacks. His wide-brimmed straw Panama shaded his perfectly tanned, Hollywood-handsome face. He'd been out all night partying, but looked as if he could step onto the set of a fashion photoshoot in Milan. Charles started for his shedrow office and moved in a manner befitting a man of style and elegance. Charles Keene didn't merely walk, he glided.

Outside his barn, Mary Linwood was giving the four-year-old-filly Tigress a bath. Mary wore her long wheat-colored hair in a ponytail and set in her face was a small up-turned nose and two wide-set blue eyes. Mary was Tigress' groom, and Tigress was going to run Saturday as one of the *morning line* favorites in the 89th running of the Margret Mitchell Stakes. Mary waved to Charles and Charles stopped.

"Good morning, Mr. Keene," Mary called out, smiling.

Kevin Strand, the *hotwalker* who held Tigress' *lead shank,* looked over his shoulder and smiled and waved too. "Hello, sir," called the freckle-faced boy.

Tigress, a sturdy bay roan built for speed, swung her head around and also looked her trainer's way. Everyone, including horses, loved Charles Keene.

"Good morning to you," Charles called back.

Then Charles turned to look at the blond still passed out in the passenger seat. A sweet and gorgeous girl, he thought to himself, and vowed then to help with her hopes of getting into the movies. He'd call his friends at the Phillip Morris Agency in Hollywood and get her a good agent to kick off her career.

Charles walked under the barn's slanting roof. His shedrow mirrored his good taste. Shining were tack boxes, webbings, and racing plaques, all in black and stenciled with the gold initials KRS: Keene Racing Stable. The shedrow hummed with activity, but at the sight of Charles, grooms, gallop boys and a gallop girl, hot walkers, and his assistant trainer, Vance Reed, stopped what they were doing and waved. Smiling, they all said their good mornings to Charles. Charles removed his hat, waved it at everyone and smiled a smile that lit up his entire side of the barn. Everyone took a moment to watch him. There was something about Charles Keene that made everyone who saw him feel good about themselves, he had a way of making everyone feel as if they were important too.

"I have to make a few calls, Vance," Charles called down the shedrow. "I'll be with you to watch the next *set* go to the track."

"Very good, sir," Vance answered. "Tigress galloped smooth as your Rolex watch this morning."

"Very good."

Charles walked into his office and closed the door. Behind him he could hear a sudden outbreak of noise and activity as the shedrow returned to its normal routine. His office looked like a small version of an office a Wall Street mogul would have strutted over. Oak paneling, a mahogany desk, carpeting and comfortable leather chairs and sofa. Win photos covered the walls and on a long shelf silver trophies gleamed. Charles sat down, intending to call the Phillip Morris Agency for...for who? He suddenly couldn't remember the lovely blond girl's name. He smiled to himself, thought of how delightful it had been splashing around with her in the hot tub and how wonderfully she'd performed on satin sheets. Still smiling, Charles took the keys out of his pocket and unlocked the bottom drawer of his desk. He needed a bit of energy to get through a busy morning. He took out a small box, sat it on his desk and opened it. He removed a clear-glass vile of cocaine. He was about to go through the ritual of using a small mirror, a credit card and small brass tube, but instead used a finger to close off one side of his nose. He held the entire vile up to the other nostril. He snorted loudly and half the vile disappeared up his nose in a snowy little blizzard. His eyes widened, his pupils went to pinpoints. He leaned back in his chair. In that suspended moment, it was as if he could see all of it, the beauty of all the oceans and continents, the beauty of humanity, the beauty of every racehorse all the way back to the Turk, the Arabian, the Barb...and he now remembered the girl's name. She was Laura, Laura Richmond. A sudden pain ripped through Charles' chest. The pain disfigured Charles' face and he grabbed his chest with both hands. Then Charles Keene's good heart exploded and he was dead.

4. JOSHUA KINCAID

Joshua Kincaid stood in the shaft of midmorning sunlight that came into his barn through the open double-wide doors. He had his eyes closed, breathing in the familiar smells of hay and horse. Into his seventh decade, he was still a vital man though arthritis made knobs of his finger joints and put a curve in his back. Some days the arthritis was so bad the curve in Joshua's back made it look as if he'd lost something and was searching the ground for it. Joshua's face was lined and creased by the years, but his was a pleasant face in which his eyes always seemed to be shining with laughter. He was the manner of man children ran to and hugged, and in a room crowded with people, his lap would be the lap puppies and kittens would find their way to. He'd been with the horses all his life, starting out as a stable boy and in his early teens becoming a jockey in his native Ireland. As a jockey, he was acknowledged as fearless, able to *skim his boot along the rail* with the best riders in Europe. Then, in his early twenties, when keeping the weight off his five-foot-ten frame became one of the few battles he couldn't win, Joshua came to the United States and began to train horses. He was an immediate success. He trained thoroughbreds for the likes of Eldon Smyth's Rolling Rock Stables and Emily and Edwin Brandt's Southern Oak, the latter being one of the largest and most successful breeding farms in the country. They'd called Joshua fearless when he was a jockey, and as a trainer, all who knew of thoroughbreds used one word to describe

Joshua Kincaid...brilliant.

The colt in the first stall of Joshua's wide-aisled twenty stall barn, called to him, a lip and nostril quivering call for the old horseman's attention. Joshua turned, opened his eyes and a smile curved the lines and creases of his face. He'd retired from the races but not from thoroughbreds. That he could never do. He bought and sold horses. He'd bring them here to nurture and train at his farm on Hart's Mill Road in Clinton, Iowa. Joshua stepped over to the colt, and as Joshua rubbed the colt's neck, he glanced back out the double-wide doors, out across the green of his farm, and what he saw caused his heart to leap. There she was...Emily.

Emily came walking toward him through the thick green grass of the main paddock. Her green eyes sparkled like emeralds, a smile magnified the loveliness of an already breath-takingly lovely face. Emily had flowers braided into her long auburn hair. She wore the wedding dress Joshua had seen her wear on the day she married Edwin Brandt.

Joshua took in a sharp breath, then blinked, and Emily was gone.

Emily, the reason Joshua had remained a bachelor all his life, the reason he now felt a pain in his heart. When Joshua thought of all the sorrows Emily had suffered these last years, his hands dropped away from the colt. Joshua closed his eyes and allowed the arthritis to do its work and now he was bent nearly in half.

The sound of footsteps from behind him.

Joshua opened his eyes, hoping for the miracle that Emily would really be there, but instead saw a pair of Kroop boots. He straightened slowly, painfully, and when his back creaked he found humor in the thought that he was in need of oiling. He now looked into the blue eyes of a young girl in a riding helmet. A frown was on Marcy Winchell's small pretty face. Joshua could read horses, could read people, and now he read Marcy's frown.

"And what might ye be lookin' at?" he snapped, the lingering lilt of Ireland in his voice.

"Are you okay?" Marcy asked.

"No, I'm not okay," Joshua answered. "Stop talkin' to me

horses so much with yer whip. How many times have I told ye, talk to a horse with yer hands…yer hands, girl."

"That colt is—"

"Too much for you."

"I wasn't going to say that," Marcy said.

"I came to be in Iowa to get meself away from all the hubbub and nonsense, and I end up fighting every morning with a wee girl who thinks every time I close me eyes to enjoy a bit of peace that I'm having a stroke."

"You are going to have a stroke, if you don't calm down," Marcy said.

Irritation knitted Joshua's brows together, but he couldn't keep his nose from twitching, couldn't keep the twinkle from his eyes. A smile put dimples in Marcy's cheeks.

"Oh, I forgot to tell you, Josh, that I saw Sam Jack's truck and trailer parked by his barn when I came down Willow Lake Road."

"What? Truck *and* trailer?" Joshua said.

"Yep. I wonder how the filly he bought from you is doing?"

Joshua began to rub his elbow, that joint that worked at predicting trouble as a barometer can predict weather. He looked down at the pattern of hoof prints all around him on the ground, the pattern found all along the path of his life, then worry gave him a push toward the phone on the desk of the tack room.

"Thanks for telling me, Marcy," Joshua said, walking away, still rubbing the elbow, "I'll be giving Sam a call, then."

Joshua had just swung open the tack room door, a room paneled in knotty pine and smelling of leather and saddle soap, when the phone rang. Joshua picked up the phone, held it to his ear, said, "Sam?"

"No, this is not Sam," came a voice vaguely familiar. "This is Bentley Keene, and I'm calling for Mr. Joshua Kincaid."

"Mr. Keene," Joshua said brightly, "this is Joshua, and how good it is to hear from ye. How's that rascal Charlie?"

A long silence.

Joshua finally said, "Hello, are ye there, Mr. Keene?"

Bentley's voice was rough when he said, "Mr. Kincaid, my son passed away this morning."

Shocked, Joshua took a step back as if he'd taken a punch. He gathered himself, said, "Oh, Mr. Keene, I'm so very, very sorry. I had no idea—"

"No need for apologies, I'm on an errand of business, there will be time for grief later. I want you—" Bentley's voice abruptly collapsed in midsentence.

A long silence again.

Joshua said, "No kinder man have I known than yer son, sir. He was a joy to one and all who crossed his path."

"Thank you, Mr. Kincaid," and Bentley's voice was strong now, with pride in it, "your thoughtful words are much appreciated. But this call is, as I said, about business. In my life, Mr. Kincaid, my wife and son, have always come first, and a close second are my horses. Let me get to the point, I want you to come out of retirement and take over the training of all my thoroughbreds."

Now it was Joshua who was responsible for the long silence. Arthritis pulled on him, worsening the curve in his back. He was looking at the tile floor of the tack room. "Mr. Keene, it is with regret—"

"Three calls Mr. Kinkaid, and one knocking at my door," Bentley interrupted. His voice broke when he said, "My son hasn't been dead three hours and yet they keep calling and come to pound on my door, asking to train—"

"Mr. Keene, I'll speak to ye plain," Joshua broke in. "Ye've watched racing from yer grand box seat in the clubhouse, insulated by your millions, but it's a brutal sport, maybe the most brutal of all, and those who've called on ye may seem as wolves, but they are, each one, fighting to survive. To train for a man such as ye, is the dream of many."

"Then you'll take my horses?" Bentley said.

Again, Joshua was responsible for a long silence. It was Bentley's voice, the subtle plea in it, the obvious pain, that moved Joshua. Then he thought of Marcy Winchell's report that Sam's truck *and* trailer were parked outside his barn this morning. Slowly, Joshua straightened, the curve nearly disappearing from his back.

"I accept, Mr. Keene."

"A three-year contract for Sixty thousand a year, plus ten percent of everything the horses win. Last year, Mr. Kinkaid, my horses earned nearly two million dollars."

"A generous offer, and I accept," Joshua said. Then he uttered a softly spoken, "But..."

"But?" said Bentley.

"I'll need two or three weeks to tie up some personal matters here."

"But Tigress runs in the stake Saturday, and while my assistant trainer Vance Reed is a fine young man, he's in medical school, is going to be a dentist, and has classes and can't be here to saddle horses in the afternoon and that includes Saturdays."

Joshua's nose twitched, the twinkle was in his eyes. "In the fine sport of baseball, Mr. Keene, there is a term they use...*pinch hitter.*"

5. SAM

It was just after ten A.M. when Sam stirred from a sleep as deep as that of bears in winter. Groggy at first, his mind cleared and functioned at the smell of food. He was up and out of bed in a quick hop. He slipped on a shirt, a pair of pants, and moved toward the kitchen in quick steps. When he got to the doorway, he paused. His father-in-law was at the little wooden table in the center of the sunlit room.

Ezra Van Cleef had small puffy eyes and a complexion the color of pie dough. His thin oiled hair lay across his bald head in long flat strands. Being short and chubby, the brown suit he wore made him look like a stuffed sausage. How a man like Ezra had sired such a girl as Bess puzzled Sam. Ezra seldom laughed and the sound of others having fun always seemed to displease him. He was a selfish man, and like most selfish people, he thought he was the only one who ever suffered and had real worries. Ezra owned and managed Van Cleef's, the fashionable department store in downtown Clinton that his father, Palmer Van Cleef, began in 1905. Van Cleef's was an imposing five story brick structure and in it could be found all the things that brought people to shop there from all the surrounding Iowa counties and Illinois counties just across the Mississippi. Ezra ran his business with notable ability and with faultless efficiency. Van Cleef's was a hugely profitable business.

Bess was at the stove frying up eggs, ham and hash browns.

She wore a white blouse, cutoff jeans and was barefoot. The sunshine through the kitchen windows made her long black hair all the more glossy. She suddenly reached for something on a high shelf. The way her body stretched and her feet arched when she stood on her tip toes made Sam draw a quick breath. He felt the lure of her curves. That's when Bess turned and saw him. Her violet eyes bloomed endlessly wide.

"Good morning, sleepy head," she said, singing the words in different notes like only she could do.

Now Ezra turned and saw Sam, and so did little five-year-old Amy who sat at the table with her back to the door. Amy, always bubbling with fun, let out a series of shrieks that sounded like an entire playground of five year olds playing cowboys and Indians. She was up and out of her chair, and Sam knelt and swung his arms open. Amy threw herself at him so hard it nearly knocked him backward. Amy clutched at Sam, wiggled happily, kissed him all over the face.

"Daddy! Daddy! I'm so glad you're with us!"

"How's my big girl?" Sam said, looking into his daughter's clear blue eyes.

"Billy Wilson pulled my hair in class yesterday," Amy reported, "and Miss Beecher told him to stop but he wouldn't!"

Sam grinned, said, "And then what happened?"

"Miss Beecher made him sit in the corner, and then at recess Billy told me he was sorry and he wants me to marry him someday!"

"Did you say yes?"

"Daddy! I said no!" Amy answered, her voice breaking into giggles, "I'm going to marry you remember?"

With that, Sam stood up, laughing as he did. Bess was waiting, on her face the smile she only smiled for him, the one that always caused in him a surge of affection. She gave him a quick kiss before going back to the stove where the skillets sizzled. Sam watched her. No woman had a lovelier sway to her hips than Bess did when she walked. Then Sam looked at Ezra. Ezra didn't smile, didn't speak. He looked at Sam with disapproval in his small puffy eyes.

"How are you, Ezra?" Sam said.

Ezra didn't answer. He had the odd habit of showing all his front teeth whenever Sam said anything. Finally, after Amy sat back on her chair and Bess gave him a darting frown, he said, "Fine. I'm fine."

"Well, that's good to hear," Sam said. "How's Myrtle?"

Myrtle also puzzled Sam. How could a woman who was the female version of her husband be the dam of a beautiful filly like Bess? The word adopted passed through Sam's mind, and so did the word kidnapped. Ezra never answered Sam's inquiry about Myrtle. He just stared at Sam in the way he did to make his employees fidget. Sam only smiled at him and sat down at the table.

"You snore when you sleep, Daddy, and it's really, really loud," said Amy, picking up her fork to finish a half-eaten fried egg.

"I do not," Sam said, pretending to be insulted.

"Do to," Amy answered. "Mommy and I went in and watched you sleep for a while before grandpa came. You snore loud!"

"You watched me sleep?"

"Yes, and I so wanted to give you hugs and kisses, but Mommy wouldn't let me, she said I'd wake you, and I said, I'd be really careful, but she still said I couldn't, so she and I just sat and watched you sleep."

"I love you, Amy," Sam said, and reached over to briefly tangle his fingers in her long blond hair.

"Oh, Daddy, I love you too. I love you so much I cry sometimes when you're away with your horses." Amy stopped then, looked at her father a long moment. "Do you love horses more than you love Mommy and me, Daddy?"

"No," Sam blurted.

"Grandpa says you do," Amy answered.

Sam looked up, leveled the hard shine of angry eyes at Ezra. Ezra looked back at him, showing his front teeth, breathing heavily with the old anger. Ezra wanted an argument, he was ready and waiting, but Sam didn't take the bait. There was always bickering and arguing when Ezra was in the house, always laughter when he wasn't.

"Daddy, I heard the ghosts again last night," Amy said.

"Ghosts?"

"Yep, they're back. You couldn't hear them?"

"I sure didn't."

"But, Daddy, they were in you and Mommy's room. I heard them knocking against the wall and making funny noises like someone was hurting them."

Sam and Bess exchanged quick wide-eyed looks, and Sam was grinning when he said, "There are no such thing as ghosts, Amy."

"But, Daddy, I think they follow you around, they only come when you're home."

Stockings, Amy's white-footed black tomcat came slinking into the kitchen. When Stockings saw Ezra, the cat arched his back, hissed, and darted back into the living room.

Sam looked at Ezra, smiling broadly. "Animals are amazing, aren't they, Ezra?"

"So, that horse is dead?" Ezra said. "The one you spent every dime you had on?"

Sam felt a twinge in his chest, saw the chestnut filly flash over the racetrack, then tumble into a tangle of flailing legs. His mind suddenly wordless, Sam said nothing. He picked up a fork and speared a sausage from the plate of food Bess sat down in front of him. Ezra searched and found another nerve.

"There's a job open in my warehouse—"

"No," Sam said through half-chewed sausage.

"What, you think you can do better? You didn't even finish your sophomore year in high school."

Sam made no response, didn't bother to tell Ezra that the only education he'd ever wanted was one gained in a horse barn. Now the two men glared at each other.

"How are you going to pay the rent on this place if—"

"Have I ever missed paying you the rent? Have I ever even

been one day late?"

Ezra's doughy face stretched and pulled. "You're killing them and you know it," he said raising his voice.

Sam felt every muscle in him tighten. But he held his temper, and, like it always did when Ezra brought up the "killing them" topic, the shame came over him, the odd shame over not being ashamed of living closer to horses than he did his own family.

Amy looked at her grandfather blinking, then with the clear soft eyes of the innocent looked at Sam and asked, "Who are you killing, Daddy?"

Sam looked at his daughter, into the sweet little face, and couldn't find words to answer her.

Ezra said, "You can start in the warehouse tomorrow—"

Then the phone rang to interrupt, and after Bess answered it, she turned to Sam and said, "It's Joshua, Sam, he says it's important and needs to talk to you."

2

When Sam turned off Hart's Mill Road onto the lane of Joshua's farm he passed a broad white sign with raised green lettering that read Blarney Stone Farm. Sam saw Joshua standing outside one of his barns, the barn nearest the half-mile training track, and he gunned the old Ford to make the tappets clatter. The truck fish-tailed and left behind billowing dust along the gravel road. Turning off the lane, toward the barn where Joshua stood, Sam really gunned the pickup. Belt's squealed, tires spun, and Sam aimed the truck right at Joshua, coming to a skidding halt just feet away from where Joshua stood. Sam was laughing when he swung open the pickup's door and got out. No matter how close he came, he could never make Joshua jump or flinch. Joshua stood with his hands on his hips, just shaking his head.

"Ye know, ye *loose horse*, one of these days ye'll misjudge and run me old ass over."

Sam grinned and walked up and hugged the old horseman. Joshua put his arms around Sam and hugged him back.

On June 1, 1966, at 4:30 in the morning, Sam stood on the sidewalk outside Lincoln Park's stable gate. Long-legged, his hair bristling like a yearling colt's, he held his battered suitcase in his hands. He'd hitch-hiked from Iowa and now when the headlights of a truck turning off Laramie Avenue blinded him, he held a hand up briefly to shield his eyes and squint. The truck stopped, a window rolled down, and in the predawn dark, he and Joshua Kinkaid exchanged a long look. Each measured the other, and both measured correctly. "Do ye walk *hots,* then?" Joshua asked. Sam nodded yes and got into the truck. Sam's career as a hotwalker for Joshua lasted for only two horses. His career of grooming horses for Joshua started that first morning after Joshua watched Sam help a fumbling groom put *rundown bandages* on a horse that was to *breeze.* With quick, knowing hands, Sam made sure the bandages weren't too tight or too loose. Sam was gifted, Kincaid was horseman enough to see it, and Kincaid gave Sam the meanest of the mean to *rub.* There wasn't a horse Sam couldn't handle in Kincaid's barn, and when Joshua asked Sam one morning how he did it, Sam told him: "You baffle them with kindness, Mr. Kincaid." It didn't take long for everyone under Joshua's shedrow to discover where such a boy as Sam had come from, that he was Henry Jack's son. After that, all who knew the fifteen-year-old understood why such old eyes looked out of his young face. The backstretch of a racetrack is no place to try to keep secrets. All had heard about Henry Jack, that he was a good man who'd made the mistake of gambling with the bookmaker, Anthony Belichio, and all came to know the horror story of how Sam had discovered his father's body. Joshua kept close watch over Sam, expecting Sam's mother to come looking for him, and when she didn't, Joshua cursed her to hell and made for Sam a special place in his heart.

Pigeons floated in the air above the two men, then settled on the peak of the barn's roof to roost. Sam and Joshua stepped back from each other.

"Sorry about the filly, Sam," Joshua said.

Sam only nodded, stuck his hands in his blue jeans, looked down at his boots. For the time it took the three colts in the main paddock to race from one fence to the other, the two men kicked at pieces of gravel, shook their heads, muttered about luck.

"So, will ye help me out, then," Joshua said, "and go to Lincoln Park, run Keene's shedrow until I can make it in to take over?"

"Be glad to," Sam answered. "How long do you think you'll be?"

"Two, three weeks at the most. Once I'm there full-time, I'd like ye to run me farm here. I'll send ye horses, young ones to bring along, old ones to repair. And I'll pay ye an honest wage with dividends that will keep yer father-in-law at bay."

Sam nodded, watched the three colts frolic in the big paddock. His eyes focused on one colt, a solid black colt with no markings. When the colt moved, he moved with the easy grace that captures a horseman's imagination. Sam's eyes stayed riveted on the colt, and now the colt broke into a run. The colt's *action* was poetry only a horseman could understand, his every move rhymed with the movement before it.

"Who is he?" Sam said, still watching the black thoroughbred.

Joshua followed Sam's gaze to the paddock, acting as if he had to be told what Sam was talking about: "Which one?"

There was a bright heat in Sam's eyes when he looked at Joshua. "You know which one."

Joshua smiled, nodded, said, "Fool's gold, give him no thought."

Sam looked back at the colt, rubbed his nose, looked back at Joshua and changed the subject by asking, "So how many *head* do you have here now?"

"I could have a hundred if I wanted, I get calls all the time, but right now there's thirteen in all. Three three-year-olds, five two year olds and five yearlings."

"Good help?"

"I've got three good hands. All young, eager to please."

Thinking of the new life he was committing to on a farm, Sam hid his disappointment behind a blank expression. In that place inside him, that place where the love of racing burned white-hot, he heard a distant bugle play *Call to the Post.* Clouds drifted across the sky, casting shadows on the earth, and Sam forced a smile.

"Sounds like a deal to me, Josh," Sam said. "When do I need to be at Keene's barn?"

"Tomorrow morning," Joshua answered.

6. BESS

The Ford truck bounced and rattled down the lane, Sam's arm out the window waving good-bye.

"See you soon," Bess called out, caroling her words happily.

Amy waved too, but the pink glow of her little girl cheeks was streaked with tears and she sniffled. She only understood that her daddy was leaving again to be with the horses, and two or three weeks without him seemed a lifetime to her. Bess couldn't have been happier; the sooner Sam was out of sight, the sooner he'd be back, switching places with Joshua. In just a short time, the world would be a perfect place. Sam would have his horses and she would have her Sam.

After the truck was out of sight, disappearing up Willow Lake Road, heading for Highway 30, Bess and Amy walked back into the house. Amy still sniffled.

"I don't like horses anymore," Amy said.

"He'll be home soon," Bess said.

When Bess and Amy walked into the kitchen, Bess' mother, Myrtle, was sitting at the table. She was a stuffed sausage in blue. Like her husband, she never missed a chance to say anything negative about anyone, and was always the first to give credence to the evilest rumors about neighbors and strangers alike. When she turned to look at Bess, the fake flowers on her little hat nodded and quivered.

"He's a dreamer, nothing but a dreamer," she declared. "He's the kind of man who'll always be just one horse away from all his problems being solved, one horse away from all his dreams coming true.

And I stress the *his.* "

"Mother—"

"He doesn't care a twit about you and Amy—"

"Stop talking about my daddy that way," Amy interrupted in a shout, her cheeks turning red. She went stiff with anger, she clenched her little hands into fists. "I hate you and grandpa. You're mean, mean, mean, and I don't like you anymore."

"Amy Jack," Bess said, horrified, "you apologize to your grandmother right now."

"I will not," Amy raged, and ran to her room.

Myrtle had an odd habit of clucking like a chicken when she was upset, and she now sat clucking away, the little flowers on her hat bobbing about as if she was picking at seeds and bugs in a barnyard. "I won't stand for it, I won't let her get away with talking to me that way. Find me a switch."

"There'll be no switch," Bess said calmly and sat down in a chair at the little table.

"She's just like him, you know," Myrtle clucked, "wild, undisciplined. What kind of child are you raising?"

"The kind of child who loves her father," Bess said, looking at her mother with anger in her lovely eyes.

7. SAM

Just as he reached Morrison, Illinois, Sam heard a thump under the hood, then a slapping sound, and he looked in the rearview mirror to see the truck's fan belt twisting and bouncing on the highway behind him. The timing was perfect, a Shell station was just half block away, and a young mechanic with hair the color of July corn tassels and grease under his fingernails replaced the belt. Sam was driving east again in less than half an hour. He made only one other stop to eat a quick bite at a diner just outside Aurora. The waitress, a plump, gum-chewing forty-something, batted her heavily mascaraed eyelashes at Sam and gave him her much used "Coffee, tea or me" line. Sam laughed, ate the special, a hamburger-greasy goulash that wasn't bad after a few shakes of pepper. Then Sam was on the road again. It felt odd to Sam not to be pulling a horse trailer.

It was dark when the security guard at Lincoln's Park's stable gate waved Sam through. Sam motored slowly past the barns. His headlights made shadows leap and sway under the shedrows. He parked his truck by barn seven. Sam walked through the night, heard the rattle of a long chain and looked to see the Rottweiler that stood sentry over barn eight. The big short-haired dog raised his head, and from deep in his throat came one rumbling growl, a warning to Sam that he would tolerate no strangers near the horses he guarded. When Sam stepped under the Keene shedrow and stopped, he heard the chain rattle again as the dog laid back down.

Then came a moment of stillness, and in it nothing stirred.

Being away from horses left Sam with a feeling of being empty, void of purpose, but standing there in the nighttime solitude of the shedrow, Sam felt his soul return to his body, felt in the company of horses a peace that the rest of the world never allowed him to have. From the back of a nearby stall came the sound of a horse pulling air into its lungs then releasing it in a slow snort of contentment, and from around the low-watt security light outside the feed room came the faint buzz of insects, the rustle of moth wings. Sam gazed down through the shedrow, and flashing and gleaming even in the dim light were webbings across every stall front, racing plaques hanging beside every stall door, tack boxes where grooms kept the tools of their trade. The Keene racing colors of black and gold were everywhere, an emblem of pride, an emblem of wealth. In this moment, the harsh memory of his own recent failures made Sam feel that he didn't belong, that he was most certainly in the wrong place, and then in the next moment he reminded himself that he did belong, that this was, if only for the next few weeks, *his* shedrow.

From far away, Sam began to hear it. Softly at first, then coming nearer to hum in his head. A song, a song he heard only when he was happy and with horses, a wordless, nameless song of saddles and bridles.

"Who's there?" came sharply from out of the night.

Sam turned, and a face, just off-white, seemed to float before him in the dark. It was a man with a gray beard and wearing a baseball cap.

"I'm Sam Jack."

A smile made it through the thick gray beard. The man put out his hand. "I'm Oscar Holley, Sam. I'm the night watchman."

"Nice to meet you," Sam said, shaking the offered hand.

"I was told you were on the way," Oscar said. "I'll unlock the office for you."

Once the office door was unlocked, Oscar flipped on the lights and shadows were driven under the desk, behind the sofa, into the four corners of the room. "There you go, Sam, and I'm to

give you this set of keys." Oscar held out a ring from which
dangled several keys. Sam took the ring, held the keys in his hand.
"Those unlock everything. Feed rooms, office, tack rooms,
everything, and now I'm going to top-off water buckets." Oscar
walked away then, said, "Good to have you here, Sam."

"Thanks, Oscar," Sam said.

Sam walked into the office, looked around, took in the quality
of the leather chairs and sofa, the wide desk and other furnishings.
He counted twenty-seven trophies on the shelf behind the desk,
glanced at the win photos that covered the walls to his right and
left, then turned around and for several minutes gazed at the large
white board mounted on the wall by the door. The board, with its
black parallel lines, was marked up with an erasable marker: every
horse's name, twenty-four of them, was neatly printed, and noted
in the grids that followed was what each horse had done day by
day for the past week and what they'd do in their training
tomorrow morning. Sam nodded, liked the organized feeling the
board gave him, and sat down behind the mahogany desk. He
opened the center drawer: a *condition book*, races marked with the
names of the Keene horses. He put the condition book down,
opened one of the desk's large drawers: folders, the name of a
horse on the tab of each. He pulled out a folder labeled Tigress,
laid it on the desk and opened it. Inside the folder were Tigress'
Racing Form charts and *past performances,* also her Veterinarian
records, her *shoeing* records, and notes about her made in Charles
Keene's handwriting.

Not until after 3:00 A.M. did Sam finish reading through the
folder of each of the Keene horses. Sam had a curious mind, could
remember without effort, and when he walked out into the
shedrow, he knew the history and details of every horse in the
barn.

2

At 4:45 Sam awakened from a short snooze on the leather sofa in the office. He heard a car, saw the beams of headlights flash and careen off the barn. Then the headlights went out and came a car door closing. Vance Reed walked out of the cloaking darkness and under the shedrow. He glanced down the line of stalls, then looked at Sam now standing in the office doorway.

"Morning," Vance said, and Sam repeated the greeting back.

Vance walked up to Sam with his hand out. "I'm the assistant trainer," he said, "and I'm going to assume your Sam."

"You assume right," Sam said as the two men shook hands.

Vance was young, only nineteen, but looked fifteen. He had the clean healthy look of a high school athlete. His face was constructed of wide cheekbones, dimpled chin and broad forehead. His sandy hair was neatly combed. He wore a polo shirt and khaki slacks.

"We start at five sharp," Vance said. Then went on: "So you ran Joshua Kincaid's shedrow, back when he was leading trainer here in Chicago in the '60s?"

"I started out as a hotwalker for Joshua back in '66, groomed horses for him for two years, then ran his *shed* until he retired."

"He's still a legend around these barns, a great horseman, and anyone who could work for him that long deserves respect."

Sam frowned. "What?"

"No offense, Sam," Vance said grinning, "but Kincaid's irascibility is still a topic of discussion, especially by the people he fired from the job you held for years. You really must know your stuff."

"Irascibility?"

Something in Sam's calm voice caused Vance's grin to disappear. "Only repeating what I've heard," he said, "and I hope I'm not starting off on the wrong foot here."

"Joshua Kincaid taught me everything my father didn't have time to."

Vance lowered his head, said, "I've heard people talk with great respect about your father too, Sam."

"Thank you," Sam said. "And just so you know, Joshua was, and still is irascible, but only with nitwits and incompetents."

Vance was grinning again. "I'll remember that, Sam." Then Vance changed the subject: "Did Bentley explain that I only work mornings, that I'm going to Loyola?"

"No, no one said a thing, but that's fine with me. You won't be here in the afternoons then?"

"I'll be gone by eleven," Vance said. "I hope you don't mind saddling the horses yourself."

"I'd actually prefer to saddle them," Sam said. "What's your major?"

"Dentistry."

The light in the tack room beside the office was on, and Oscar, the night watchman, could be heard rattling around. Now the aroma of strong coffee drifted to where Sam and Vance stood. People began to arrive, taking form from out of the dark. Young and old, men and women. There came black faces, white faces, brown faces. As people drifted by on their way to the coffee, Vance stopped them and introduced them to Sam. Sam shook the hands of eight grooms, five hotwalkers, and one gallop boy and one gallop girl. At the sound of voices came a stirring from the line of stalls, and horses began to bob their heads in and out over their webbings, nickering and calling. There was a sharp thud as a horse struck the side of his stall with a hoof. When Mary Linwood told Sam she was pleased to meet him, Mutineer, the seven-year-old gelding in the first stall, stuck his head out, looked at Mary, his groom, and began to dig with a front hoof.

Mary, a bright-eyed tomboy in faded blue jeans, looked toward the gelding and talked to him like he was human: "I'll be right there, just let me get some of Oscar's good coffee before it's gone." As she walked toward the smell of coffee she used a rubber band to do her long wheat-colored hair up in a ponytail. Over her shoulder, she gave Vance a playful grin. "You better get some of Oscar's coffee too, Mr. Jack, 'cause you don't want any part of what Vance brews. It's like drinking DMSO."

Vance laughed, so did Sam, and Vance said, "That Mary, she's something."

Just then, at exactly 5:00 A.M., the lights in the shedrow came on. Sam blinked in the sudden glare. For him, the sight was magical, like that moment in the *Wizard of Oz* when the movie goes from black and white to color. The shedrow gleamed and glowed, was alive with human voices and the sounds of horses. Sam felt a rush of excitement to be back in this place untouched by the industrial revolution, where man still worked with the horse just as he did in centuries past. Suddenly, everything that had been distant and unattainable for Sam, was near and familiar.

"Did you see the *board*, Sam?" Vance said.

"I did," Sam answered, "and other than a few changes I want to make, I'm going to let you go about the morning as usual. I want to watch, catch the rhythm of things."

"Everyone here knows what they're doing, Sam. Professionals, every one of them. That, and we all really love these horses, and we love the Keenes too."

Sam smiled, nodded, was pleased.

"Just one thing, we are short a gallop boy. John Cheever left us for a new job in Kentucky last week. thought I'd let you or Joshua do the hiring"—Vance smiled broadly—"just as a professional courtesy."

Birds called out from their hiding places in the rafters, and from down the line of stalls came the hum of a busy shedrow just starting the morning. Vance walked away then, talking to the grooms who rubbed the horses that would go to the track first, and Sam put a hand over his heart. He wanted to make sure there was still a beat there, for he had the feeling that he had died and gone to heaven.

8. Bentley Ward Keene

Bentley stood in the doorway of the master bedroom of his fashionable Chestnut Street townhouse, looking back at his wife. In good health, Ruth weighed not ninety pounds. She was a delicate woman, like a little bird, and while even in her youth she'd never been a great beauty, she was the only woman Bentley had ever loved. Since the news of the death of their only child, their son Charles, Ruth had wept herself into a near catatonic state. She lay ridged beneath the covers of their bed. Her pale lips trembled and twitched, and from out of a face that looked like wadded tissue paper, her eyes peered back at Bentley like those of an anguished little wren. Bentley dare not say where he was going. The mere mention of horses was one of the few things that would bring Ruth out of her silence and send her into a fit of tears and spasms. Bentley feared that one more such fit would shatter the delicate little woman into pieces that could never be put back together.

"I shall be home shortly, my dearest," Bentley gently said. He glanced at the white-uniformed nurse sitting straight-backed on a chair in the corner of the room. "Miss Greene, your nurse, will be with you at all times."

Bentley could see a slight movement of the pale trembling lips, but Ruth made no sound. Bentley held his fingers to his lips, and like he always did, blew her a kiss before closing the door and leaving. He walked down the hall, carpeting padding his footsteps. Bentley was only five-foot-six, yet held himself so straight he looked taller. In him was the pride of a dozen ordinary men, the business knowledge of a dozen Harvard MBAs, and about him was the unmistakable air of importance, this man of finance and industry, this man of vast wealth. This air of importance was magnified by a full head of neatly barbered white hair, his impeccable taste in clothes, and a noble, strong-featured face that wouldn't have looked out of place sculpted into Mount Rushmore. He began to descend the staircase. Halfway down he stopped, looked back over his shoulder into the gloom of the hallway he'd just left behind. When Ruth was happy, he was happy. When Ruth was sad, he was sad. He loved her with every chamber of his heart, and at this moment, the ache in every chamber was almost more than he could bear. He proceeded on his way, and at the door, Foster, the butler, a tall man with a receding hairline, was waiting to hand him his cane.

"Thank you, Foster," Bentley said, taking the cane with the gold horse-head handle. He stood beneath an imposing empire-style chandelier. Sixteen gilt-bronze swans supported sixteen flame-shaped lights. "I won't be long. Help Miss Greene keep good watch." He paused to look into the butler's dignified face. He put great stress into his next words: "Open no windows on the second or third floor, and stay vigilant, make sure Mrs. Keene doesn't either. Do you understand why?"

"I do, sir," Foster answered, and in the always formal-deep voice there was the slightest quiver.

"Very good," Bentley said.

Foster reached and took hold of the great brass handle that opened the eight-foot-tall solid oak front door, and Bentley stepped out into the morning sunshine. Ancient magnolia trees, their branches gnarled and twisted, threw shade on either side of the brick-paved sidewalk. At the curb, his white Rolls Royce Silver Wraith waited. His chauffeur, Randolph, liveried in black jacket, jodhpurs, polished knee-high black boots and short-billed cap, waited with the elegant auto's back door open. His cane tapping on bricks, Bentley hurried to the car and got in. When the door closed behind him, the interior of the Rolls held him in a comfortable grip of fine leather and finished walnut.

"To the barn, Randolph," was all Bentley had to say.

With swept-back fenders and *The Spirit of Ecstasy* ornamenting the massive stainless steel grill, the Rolls Royce entered the backstretch. Bentley suffered the pressure of a dreadful grief, but was thankful that once inside the stable gate he felt an immediate easing of at least some of the business pressures he lived with. He didn't allow his lawyers and advisers, his accountants and investment bankers to invade this world of the horse. In this place of shedrows, he wanted no talk of properties, forecasts of production, or talk of investments in the New York, London, or Tokyo Exchange.

"If the car phone rings while I'm visiting the horses," Bentley said to his chauffeur, "tell them I'll call back, just take messages. Of course, if it's Foster, nurse Greene or my wife, come get me at once."

"Yes, sir," Randolph answered.

When the Rolls came to a stop by barn seven, Bentley let himself out of the backseat. He took several steps and stopped. His grip on the gold handle of his cane tightened. Out of the corner of his eye, he'd caught the glimpse of brown and white cap toe shoes, a white panama hat, his son's smiling face. Past episodes now formed in the vapors of Bentley's memory: Charles saddling a horse, the click of Charles' stop watch, and in that moment he could hear Charles laughing. It was all Bentley could do not to scream his grief, to call out his son's name, to tell him to stop this foolishness, that he couldn't be dead, that he had to stop playing this cruel joke. Bentley felt his throat spasm, yet more emotion to build. Then he saw a sight that stopped the torture of memory. Going to the racetrack was one of his horses, a colt named Matchbook, and Bentley's bruised and battered heart began to rise.

9. Sam

After Vance told Sam there was a need for another gallop boy, Sam called the stable gate and had Clay Repp paged to barn seven. Clay was the former jockey who'd been working Sam's filly when she went down. Clay arrived at Sam's shedrow minutes after hearing "Will Clay Repp please report to barn seven" over the backstretch loudspeaker system. His weathered, unshaven face looked like harness leather with bristles on it. He wore blue jeans, a plaid shirt, and twirled a whip in his right hand. When Clay saw Sam, the deep lines and creases around his eyes and mouth bent into a smile of surprise.

"I knew you wouldn't stay gone long," Clay said, shaking Sam's hand, "and you've come back in style."

"I'll only be here for a few weeks," Sam explained. "Joshua Kincaid's taking care of some personal business before he comes in to take over the Keene horses."

The first horse Clay took to the track was Matchbook. The colt stepped along in an athlete's free and easy way of moving, his plated hooves sounding like tap shoes on the asphalt road that ran the length of the racetrack's outside fence. Sam and Vance followed the colt, Sam looking the colt over. When Sam looked at a horse and watched them run, he thought in rhythms that made music of motion, and thought in numbers, the time and distance covered, and while observing the dictums of confirmation, he thought in the abstract term of heart—because, like all horsemen, he knew no other word to describe what it was he looked for—when he judged whether a horse had what it took to be a runner.

Before coming to the *gap* where horses came on and off the track, Clay stood in the irons and shifted his weight back and forth. Sitting back down on the colt, Clay looked back at Sam.

"Sam, hold this horse," Clay said. "I need to tighten the girth another notch, I think the colt was holding his breath when I tightened it before."

Sam took hold of the reins, and Clay jumped down off the colt. He flipped an iron up over the saddle and out of the way, then pulled up on the straps of the leather girth to tighten it, making a small grunting sound as he did. When Clay cocked his leg and looked over his shoulder at Vance, Vance boosted Clay back into the saddle, giving him a *leg up.*

"Thanks, guys," Clay said. When he stood in the irons this time, shifting his weight, he said, "Oh, yeah, that's better."

"So, what are we doing with this colt, Sam?" Clay said.

"Take him—"

"Do you mind if I join you?" came Bentley Keene's voice.

Sam, Vance and Clay turned toward Bentley. Bentley stood smiling at the three men and the colt. He stood very straight, both hands resting on the gold handle of his cane. Sam had seen Bentley Keene before, mostly in the winner's circle getting his picture taken with his winning horses, and now as he looked at the white-haired gentleman, he felt the full weight of Bentley's commanding presence.

Vance spoke first. "Mr. Keene, I'm so glad to see you." Then grief warped Vance's face. His voice dropped, becoming soft when he said, "I'm so very sorry—"

Bentley took in a quick breath, held up a hand to stop Vance in midsentence. "I know you loved Charles, Vance, everyone did. But not now, for now let's just talk about horses." A heavy silence passed, Vance got control, introduced Sam and Clay. There were handshakes all around. Now Bentley looked the colt over, said, "This is Matchbook, isn't he running today?"

"I *scratched* him," Sam said, "but let me tell Clay here what to do with him this morning, then I'll explain to you why."

"Of course," Bentley said.

Sam turned back to Clay. "This colt likes to *run off* as soon as he's turned to gallop. I want to stop that. Take him the *wrong way*. When you turn him and he goes to run off, take hold of him, turn him back around, and go another quarter mile the wrong way. Keep doing that until he stops trying to run off and gets the idea that he needs to wait for you to tell him what to do."

"That might take all morning, Sam," Clay said, "or maybe even all week."

"It won't, he's a smart colt," Sam answered.

"How far should I go, if and when he behaves?" Clay said.

"I want to take the speed out of this colt," Sam answered, "so take him slow, and let him go as far as he wants to."

"Gotcha, Sam." Clay turned to look at Bentley. "Nice to see you, sir."

"And you too," Bentley answered. "And what was your name again?"

"Clay, Clay Repp, sir."

Clay gave the colt a nudge with the heels of his boots and the colt hopped into his next step, showing how eager he was to get to his work. When the colt stepped out onto the track, Clay brought the colt to a stop so the colt could have a look around. The colt didn't stand quietly. He threw his head up, stepped sideways, tried to break off, but Clay got Matchbook turned back the wrong way. Now Clay had the colt moving at a trot along the outside fence. The colt's plated hooves pushed down into the loam and then kicked it up, scattering sand and dirt behind him. Bentley, Sam and Vance stepped up onto bleacher-like steps that allowed them to see over the tall white-plank outside fence. It was a typical morning. Horses were being galloped, worked, ponied, and trainers and other owners were standing on the several sets of bleacher-like steps that lined the backstretch fence at intervals. All were there to watch their horses and see the action.

Sam said, "Let me explain about this horse, Mr. Keene—"

"Call me Bentley, please."

Both men smiled and Sam said, "Bentley, this colt has run three times in his life, all three sprints, going three-quarters. He's led the way in all three races up to the quarter pole and then stopped. The best he's done is a fifth, beaten six lengths."

"What do you plan to do with him, Sam?" Bentley asked.

"There's a *maiden allowance* going a flat mile a week from tomorrow."

"Sam, I never interfere with the training of my horses, I let my trainer call all the shots, but if the colt stops after running a half mile, what makes you think he'll run a full mile?"

"Matchbook's by Parliament, out of the good mare Snowshoe. Parliament won the New England Handicap going a mile and a quarter and the New Port Handicap going a mile and one-half. Snowshoe was a stakes-placed mare going *long* on the grass. Matchbook is bred to run all day. I'm going to bring him up to the race with long, slow gallops and no works. That should take the early speed out of him, and hopefully he'll show all that saved energy in the stretch and come from behind when it counts."

The sound of fast-pounding hooves interrupted the conversation, and Sam, Vance and Bentley watched three horses working on the rail. The three thoroughbreds bounded and swooped by like dancers across a stage. Bentley turned back to Sam.

"I like your logic, Sam," he said. "And I really like the fact that you have real knowledge of this colt on the very first morning running my barn."

"I spent most of last night going over the charts and past performances of all your horses, Bentley. Charles left notes on each horse that were especially helpful at bringing me up to speed."

At the mention of his son, Bentley briefly closed his eyes, then looked off across the racetrack. Suddenly, he was smiling. With wonder in his voice he said, "My word, that certainly didn't take long. Look at Matchbook."

Sam's eyes swept over the track, seeking Clay and Matchbook. He found them in the distance: Clay sat on Matchbook

by the outside fence in front of the empty grandstand. The colt
stood quietly, ears flicking back at forth, and Clay was leaned
forward patting him on the neck. Then Clay nudged the colt with
his boot heels and the colt broke into an easy *rocking-horse* gallop.
Clay stood in the irons, took a long hold of the reins. Clay and
Matchbook put in a slow two-mile gallop. Several times
Matchbook tried to break off and run when another horse went by
him, but when that happened, Clay tightened his hold, forcing the
colt to bow his neck and keep to an easy gallop. When they came
off the track, Sam, Bentley and Vance were waiting.

"Well?" Sam said, tilting his head back to look up at Clay.

Clay gave Sam a one-word answer, "Cadillac."

"Will he go long?"

"This colt'll run all day, Sam," Clay answered, leaning
forward to pat the colt on the neck again. "He enjoyed himself this
morning."

Sam took hold of the reins and led the colt back toward the
barn. The muscles in Matchbook's shoulders and quarters were
pumped up like any athlete's would be after training. He'd proven
to Sam in just one morning that he was a colt of energy and fire.
Clay kicked his boots out of the irons and let his legs dangle. This
let the colt know his work was done, that he could relax.

Vance said, "I'll see that the two-year-olds are ready, Sam,
they always go out in a set."

Matchbook's groom saw them coming, and hurried out to
take the colt from Sam. The groom led the colt under the shedrow,
and before he led the colt into his stall, Clay dismounted. Once in
the stall, Clay removed the saddle and slipped the bridle over the
colt's ears so the bit dropped out of the colt's mouth. The groom
was ready and slipped the colt's halter on, then looped a lead shank
through the brass fittings on the halter so the chain came across the
colt's nose. He fastened the lead shank to the brass ring under the
colt's chin. The groom handed the shank over to a waiting
hotwalker.

"Good job," Sam said, having watched the smooth teamwork.
"Matchbook *ties up* so keep him moving."

"Yes, sir," the hotwalker answered, letting the colt step along in a lively prance.

"Vance," Sam called out, "that filly Evening Song still acting up when she *tracks*?"

"She's been a problem, Sam," Vance answered.

"Don't send her out with the other two-year-olds. Let's send her out with that six-year-old mare Voodoo Queen, maybe the mare can teach the filly some manners by example. And Vance, if that works, move Evening Song into the stall next to the mare. You understand where I'm going with this?"

"Sure do, Sam," Vance answered.

"Have Clay get on Evening Song too."

"Done deal, Sam," Vance said as he hurried down the shedrow.

When Sam turned around, Bentley was leaning on his cane, a smile doing pleasant things to his face. "And I understand where you're going with all that, too, Sam," he said. "And I must say, I like the way you think."

Sam's smile was sudden, bright, like the flash of a camera flashbulb. "Thanks, Bentley," he said.

With that, Bentley's chauffeur came around the barn at a brisk walk. Bentley saw him coming, understood the urgency in his manner, said, "I'm off, Sam. I probably won't see you again until Tigress runs Saturday in the stake." Bentley reached and shook Sam's hand. Then, as he walked away with quick steps to meet his chauffeur, he said over his shoulder, "Keep up the good work, Sam. I already have great confidence in you."

Sam watched Bentley and his chauffeur disappear around the corner of the barn, then turned to see a sight that made his pulse loud in his ears. Coming toward him, under full tack and with helmeted riders on their backs, were three of the best looking two-year-olds he'd ever seen step out from under a shedrow.

2

It was 10:30, the morning work was done and the horses were eating. Horses munched from their feed tubs a mix of oats and sweet feed. Also in the mix was Calf-Manna, flax seed, electrolytes and vitamin supplements. By each stall hung a hay net stuffed with timothy, clover and alfalfa. Most everyone had left, only one groom was still busy, raking in front of his horse's stalls. The shedrow sparkled from the attention of dedicated grooms who took pride in their barn and the horses they rubbed. Sam sat down on the desk, dialed a number on the phone, and pressed the earpiece to his ear. While the phone rang, a robin landed just outside the office door, looked in at Sam, chirped, then flew off in a snap of wings. Sam's call was answered on the fifth ring.

"Hello," came Joshua's voice.

"You are going to love this barn," Sam said with a ring of excitement in his voice. "I've never seen a better-looking bunch of horses under one shed in my life. And the balance is perfect. Three stakes horses, four two-year-olds, and the others are allowance horses and high-priced claimers. The cheapest horse in the barn runs for a *tag* of twenty thousand, and he's won two races this year already."

"Ye sound like a boy in a candy shop with money to spend," Joshua said with a laugh. "What do ye think of the gelding, Mutineer? He's eight years old now, isn't he?"

"He's seven, Josh, and he's...I can't think of the right word...magnificent? He's one of the biggest horses I've ever been around. He has to weigh near twelve hundred pounds, and he's so *kind,* just a big pussy cat. A gallop girl gets on him every morning and can do anything she wants with him. I think he's the best handicap horse on the grounds."

"When's he run?"

"The Chicago Handicap is a week from this Saturday."

"And there's that good filly Tigress. She moves like a dancer among the club-footed."

"You should have seen her work today. She *blew out* for Saturday's Margret Mitchell Stakes in 36:1. It was like she was shot out of a cannon."

"Fernando DaSilva rides the Keene horses, doesn't he?"

"On everything, he's the leading rider at the meet."

"What's the other stake horse, a five-year-old mare, I think?"

"Voodoo Queen, but she's mostly for the grass, she won't start until the meet opens up at Suburban Downs next month."

Then Joshua said, "Keene called me."

A fly skittered in the sunshine that came in through the open window behind Sam, its wings tiny flickers, and Sam blinked, asked, "What did he have to say?"

"He called to thank me, that I couldn't have sent a better pinch hitter. He's already decided ye're some kind of horse genius."

Sam laughed, a pleasant sound. "That's nice to hear. He's a gentleman."

"That he is," Joshua said.

Sam's tone changed, saddened: "I feel so sorry for his loss."

"Tragic, yes, but Charles died as all horsemen hope to die...still owing the feed man."

Sam voiced his agreement, then changed the subject, asked, "How's Fighter Pilot?"

"I moved him over here and he likes his new stall, loves the company. He thinks he's the king o' the paddocks. Pretty sure those are *chips* in that knee, Sammy."

"That's why I brought him home."

Then, sounding in a hurry, Joshua said, "Keep up the good work with Keene's horses, Sam. I'll be there as soon as I can, but now I've got to go, I've a flight to catch."

"Flight?"

"I'm flying down to the Carolinas; Emily Brandt wants me to come see her at Southern Oak." Images flashed in Sam's mind. A mile-long avenue of ancient moss-draped oaks, a great columned house glowing white in the sunlight, white-fenced paddocks stretching to the horizons and in them thoroughbreds. Then, in the dark of night, a barn burning, orange-red flames seeming to reach to the moon, the screams of horses, the figures of two men running into the barn, into the roar of the swirling flames.

Sam said, "Mr. and Mrs. Keene are going through hell, but the tragedies Emily Brandt has suffered these last years, I don't know how she's lived through it all. That fire brought her whole life crashing down around her, and now she's living as a recluse…such a shame. I remember the last time I saw her, it was in the paddock at Suburban Downs…stunning, so beautiful. You remember, Josh, you were there too."

Sam paused, waited for Joshua to say something, but there was only silence on the other end of the line. This silence lengthened, hardened. Finally, Sam said, "Josh?"

There was a click in Sam's ear, and Joshua was gone.

3

Sam parked the truck on 36th Street in Cicero, and walked toward the bar on the corner. The Knotty Pine was a favorite of racetrackers, a place where owners worth millions talked about horses with hot walkers who made one hundred dollars a week and lived two or three to a dorm room above a horse barn. When Sam walked in, he had to work his way through the crowd to get to the bar. "Excuse me," he kept saying, and people, turning to look, recognized him and said back, "Sam, it's good to see you. Good luck with the Keene horses." News travels fast on the backstretch of a racetrack.

At the bar a seat was open, and Sam sat down next to Clay Repp. Behind the bar, above the rows of liquor bottles, was a large oil painting of Seabiscuit in a heavy gold frame. A revolving Budweiser Beer sign streamed a swirling design of high-stepping Clydesdales against the walls. When Clay turned to look at Sam, he almost fell off the stool. Sam caught him by the shoulder, steadied him. On the bar in front of Clay were empty shot glasses and beer bottles.

"Isn't it a bit early to be so hard at it?" Sam said.

"I'm just getting' started," Clay slurred, smiling a drunken smile.

The bar was rowdy around them. Friends slapped each other on the back, told jokes, rocked with laughter, and pestered each other with advice.

"Had dinner yet?" Sam asked.

"Yep," Clay answered, "and here goes desert." He picked up a shot of Seagram's, threw it down, and chased it with a guzzle of beer. He once again turned to Sam, a drunken smile on his face.

"We've got a busy day tomorrow," Sam said.

Clay frowned, tried to keep himself from weaving back and forth on the stool. "I'll be at the barn at five, and I'll be sober. Have I ever let you down?"

"No, you never have," Sam said, and reached into his pocket and put a five-dollar bill on the bar. "Get me a shot of what you're having, and a beer. I'm going to call Bess."

"Nurse!" Clay called out. "We need more medication down here!"

Through a side door, a tall man with a shining bald head hurried in and in a voice loud enough to be heard above the crowd said, "Does anyone know who won the last race?"

There were three jockeys sitting at the table nearest the door, just behind where the man stood. In unison, the three answered him by shouting, "We did!"

The man turned around, stared bewildered at the laughing riders, and then bolted back out the door. The entire bar burst into a roar of laughter at this old joke known by all racetrackers, and Sam, laughing along with everyone else, made it into one of the phone booths against the wall. He stuck a hand deep in his pocket and pulled out a fist full of quarters. He dialed the number and started to drop quarters at the instructions of an operator. The phone only rang once.

"Hello?" Bess answered.

"Hey, honey," Sam said. "Wanted to call and let you know the first day went great."

Bess teased Sam, said, "Not sure I should be happy about that or not."

She giggled. Sam laughed.

"How's Amy," Sam asked.

"She's at the store with Grandma, a new dress, I think." Bess changed the subject, said, "Joshua came early this morning for—"

"He told me, Fighter Pilot's over at his place now."

"I miss you," Bess said. "The next two weeks are going to seem like a year."

"It'll go quick," Sam said, and there was something in his voice he couldn't hide.

Bess and Sam talked until Sam was out of quarters, then Sam hung up, opened the door to leave the booth but paused when he heard his name. He recognized Fernando DaSilva's voice. DaSilva had sat down with the three jockeys sitting by the side door, not two steps from the phone booth. DaSilva was a thick-necked, dwarfish man with stiff short black hair and dark shining eyes. He was a top rider, tough, known for his fierce physical strength.

"I show up at Keene's barn to work the good filly this morning," DaSilva said to the other riders, "and there is this man in patched blue jeans and a shirt bought from a Salvation Army store telling me how I should work her, that I should not let her work too fast. Me, this man is telling me, how I should work a filly I've won five races on. I say to myself, what trailer park did Mr. Keene find this man?"

DaSilva burst into laughter, but the other three riders sat quietly, looking toward the phone booth behind him. DaSilva stopped laughing, then turned in his seat to look up into Sam's face.

"Hey, jock," Sam said, and smiled.

Clay Repp slammed a hand down on the bar, threw his head back and snorted laughter so loud everyone in the bar turned to look at him. Now Clay pointed a finger at DaSilva, said in a drunken squawk, "Fernando, you dumb son-of-a-bitch, you might be able to *switch sticks* faster than any jock I've ever seen, but you're no horseman, and you never will be." Clay swayed precariously on the stool when he pointed to Sam. "That man there, the man you just made fun of, is the best horseman who'll ever give you a leg up. And you aren't fit to lick his boots, you stupid son-of-a—"

Clay lost his balance and fell head first off his stool. He lay in what looked like a pile of old clothes with arms and legs sticking out of it. DaSilva laughed at him, but he was the only one, and when he realized it, he abruptly shut his mouth. No one who knew Clay Repp, who knew what a *race rider* he'd once been, thought the scene was funny. A legend had become a drunk, and people exchanged glances, shook their head, and remembered who Clay Repp once was. A mutter went through the bar, a few groans. Sam helped Clay get to his feet.

Carl Burns owned the Knotty Pine. He was a good-natured man with a pock-marked face and ears that stuck out so wide from his head that flight seemed likely in a strong wind. Carl stepped up to Sam, picked up the five-dollar bill Sam had put on the bar and put it back into Sam's shirt pocket. Carl whispered: "Can you get Clay out of here and home, Sam? I'll get you some help if you need it, and when you come back, dinner's on me."

Sam had his arm around Clay, holding him up, but Clay now pushed Sam away.

"I been thrown out of better places than this," Clay slurred, "and by god, I'll leave on my own fuckin' two feet."

Clay lurched toward the side door, looking as if he would fall with each step. Sam was right with him, ready to prevent any more head-first dives to the floor. Clay swung the door open, then stopped, looked back at DaSilva with anger twisting the creases and furrows of his face. "This gringo knows," Clay said, pointing at himself, "that the day'll come when you come crawlin' to beg Sam Jack to ride his horses." Then, no longer restraining his voice, Clay yelled, "This gringo knows!"

DaSilva smiled a mocking half-smile at Clay, then gave a

quick glance around the bar. When he saw everyone was watching him, he lost the smile and gave a self-conscious cough. Clay and Sam left, and as they made their way down the sidewalk toward Sam's truck, the red light of sunset stained the tops of the trees a rosy red color. Sam guided Clay as he staggered and fought to keep his balance with every step.

"It all happened so quick, Sam," Clay said, as Sam opened the passenger side door to the pickup. "It was like an avalanche. I got married, my wife gave me a beautiful baby boy and I had money, a house in Oak Park, two cars…"

Sam helped Clay sit down in the truck, and Clay looked up at him with eyes that had the yellow color of old varnish, the sick eyes of an alcoholic. "And then it happened. I was ridin' the third race, the day after my son was born, and a *hole* opened up on the rail. Do you know what happened when I saw that hole open up, Sam?"

"No, Clay," Sam said, "what happened?"

"I hesitated, Sam, that's what happened. I couldn't see the hole no more, I could only see the faces of my wife and new baby boy and could only think how much they needed me. I hesitated, wouldn't take the risk of going to the inside, and the hole closed up. I took the safe way and went around and got beat a neck…a neck, Sam. I should've won that race by five."

"It's all over, Clay, it's in the past," Sam said.

"All over?" Clay answered. "It's not all over, Sam. I see that hole open up every night in my dreams. I see all the holes open up, and I see me hesitate over and over again, afraid to take the risk, until I can't look at myself in the mirror…until just the thought of me wearing racing silks makes me want to puke…I turned into a chicken shit, Sam. A *no-ridin'* chicken shit."

Clay slumped forward, put his face in his hands, and Sam closed the door and walked around to get into the driver's seat. Sam slipped the key into the ignition and Clay dropped his hands and looked at him. The sick yellow eyes were now wet and swollen.

"And then I thought if I had a couple drinks before I rode,

that it'd help, but it didn't. And the rest happened so quick, like an avalanche, and the horses were gone, the cars were gone, the house was gone, my wife was gone, and my beautiful little boy was gone. All gone, Sam…all gone."

Clay sank back into the seat, still looking at Sam. "Do you know who broke Mutineer's maiden, Sam? Do you know who won the Suburban Park Juvenile, the hundred grander on Mutineer?"

Sam blinked, thought, remembered: "You did, Clay."

"And Mr. Keene didn't even know who I was this morning…didn't even know who I was."

Clay slowly leaned his head against the window, tried to keep his eyes from falling shut and sputtered a few more words. Then he passed out.

Sam sat there behind the wheel, staring at Clay, and in that moment understood how loneliness and alcohol could destroy a man. Sam inhaled a long deep breath, then exhaled it and started the truck. Clay was living in a tack room in barn three, and when Sam pulled the truck up to the barn, a uniformed security guard was walking by. Sam got out of the truck, called to the security guard.

"Hey, can you help me get this guy to his tack room?"

The security guard, a man with a round face and a freckled nose, walked over to the truck and looked in. "Oh, sure I'll help," he said. "Clay's a good old boy, I help him make the last few steps home most every night."

10. ANTONIO BELICHIO

Antonio Belichio sat in the back seat of a black Cadillac with heavily tinted windows. The Cadillac was parked across the street from the Knotty Pine. He was a small man, thin, into his seventies, but looked to be in his fifties. He combed his thick gray hair straight back so it fell like a curtain to his shoulders. His nose was big, like that of a Roman emperor, and he would have been handsome but for the eyes. His eyes were strangely elliptical, like that of a snake. He'd survived all his close friends: Capone, Nitti, Luciano, and as these friends died off, his modest bookmaking operation in Cicero became an empire that stretched from Chicago to New Orleans, from Omaha to Detroit.

Belichio stirred in the backseat. He took a Cuban cigar, a Cohiba Esplendido, out from the inside pocket of his tailor-made black suit, and pushed a button on the door console to crack a window. The man who sat in the front passenger seat turned around and held out a lighter. Belichio bit off the end of the cigar, spit the small junk of tobacco into his hand and put it in an ash tray. He leaned forward, and when the lighter's little flame lit his strange eyes and made them glow, the hand that held the lighter trembled. Belichio held the cigar to the flame, puffed, and smoke filled his lungs. He smiled a secret smile. He liked the fact that even the strongest and meanest of men were afraid of him. When he leaned back, he blew fragrant smoke toward the cracked window, and the man with the lighter turned back around. He and the man behind the wheel of the Cadillac were so big that their broad shoulders almost touched.

Belichio pulled on the cigar again, the cigar flared red, and while he savored the mild spicy flavor of aged tobacco, he watched as Sam and Clay came out of the Knotty Pine and disappeared around the corner.

"I had business with that tall boy's father," Belichio said, smoke rolling out of his lungs and mouth.

"Business business, boss?"

Belichio didn't need to involve himself in the murders that struck fear into gamblers and kept them paying their losses, he had an army of *bone breakers*, like the two men in the front seat, willing to do anything he told them to do. But Belichio liked being involved. What gave other men nightmares, only entertained the man with the cold, unforgettable snake eyes.

"Yes, business business, but it wasn't any fun, not like the fun we're going to have tonight with this piece of shit who thinks he doesn't need to pay his gambling debts. Henry Jack didn't beg for his life, didn't piss his pants, didn't shit himself, he just looked me in the eye while I gave the order for a bullet to be put in his head. The last thing he said was 'Please don't hurt my family.' I respected Henry for that, and thinking about it now, I'd have to say that Henry was actually a good man, an unlucky man, but good…and brave, very brave."

"Didn't his kid walk in on you, boss?"

"The kid ran into the barn right after the gun was planted in Henry's dead hand. We were only a few yards away, and I was smoking a cigar just like this one, but the kid didn't see us, he just threw himself at his father and started to shake him like he was trying to wake him up. And scream," Belichio's face split into a wide grin, "you should have heard that kid scream."

"What you got planned for this guy we're pickin' up tonight, boss?" asked the man behind the wheel.

"We strip him, hang him upside down, stick a pipe in his ass and fill the pipe with gasoline," answered Belichio, puffing away at the cigar. "Of course, before the gas goes into the pipe, we give him plenty of time to cry and beg. That's part of the fun. But the real fun comes when we light the fucker up. You really haven't heard a man scream or seen a man wiggle until you've seen a man with flames shooting out his ass...it's a sight to behold."

"What's this guy's name again, Boss?"

"Fernando DaSilva," Belichio said.

2

Belichio stood by himself in the warehouse, his hands clasped behind his back. There wasn't a wrinkle in his black suit, his white shirt was spotless, his tie in a perfect double Windsor. He stared at what remained of Fernando DaSilva, the flesh and bone of him that hung by one leg from the chains and meat hooks. The body still smoked, and the thick stench had driven the two bone breakers away. Out of the corner of his eye, Belichio could see them move in the shadows, just out of the light, hear one of them repeatedly gag. As big as the two of them were, DaSilva had put up an amazing struggle when he finally understood exactly what was going to happen to him. The two men had been all out to get him tied with chains and then hung spread-eagle from the two meat hooks.

"So much power in a small package," Belichio muttered.

When Belichio took two steps closer to DaSilva, the heels of his polished black shoes clicked on the cement. He tilted his head sideways to look into DaSilva's upside down face. DaSilva's features were crooked, oddly wrenched. The jockey had dislocated his own jaw while screaming and shrieking after the burning started. In his agony, DaSilva had chewed through his lower lip and blood dripped from his mouth into the blackening gluey pool underneath him on the floor. Between DaSilva's legs he'd been roasted and burned until this part of him was unrecognizable as human.

DaSilva's death fascinated Belichio. He didn't want to leave, just wanted to stare and feel the thrill of remembering the struggle of it, the horrendous and magnificent physical struggle DaSilva put up. The jockey only hung by his left leg because he'd managed to do the unthinkable, to break the chain that held his right leg. Belichio looked at DaSilva's right upper leg, the tough dense muscle, and marveled at the strength that had once been there. And then Belichio's face split into an ugly grin. It happened like it always happened when he witnessed a struggling death. He could feel it in his pants, the pulse and throb of an erection.

11. JOSHUA

Joshua rented a Ford at the airport in Charleston, a small two-door Escort. There'd been a delay at O'Hare in Chicago, another short delay in Atlanta, but he'd finally made it to Highway 61 and was headed to Southern Oak...and to Emily. The highway followed the Ashley River, and the waters of the river sparkled and gleamed through the heavy growth of oak and cypress trees that lined its banks. The car's four-cylinder engine puttered down the highway, then came a sweeping bend in the road, and there it was, the tall double-swing iron gate to the farm.

Joshua slowed, turned into the entrance, and atop the imposing red-brick columns were the monumental bronze horse heads that remained forever in the memory of all who saw them. With wind-swept manes and arching necks, the bronze horses looked down with fiercely knowing eyes upon all who entered the grounds of Southern Oak. Joshua gazed up at the pair as he drove by them, then looked down through the long avenue of live oaks. The sprawling branches of the century-old oaks arched over head like the beams of a cathedral, allowing only thin shafts of sunlight to enter and touch the ground in golden dapples. Shawls of Spanish moss draped the heavy gnarled branches. There was a muffled quiet beneath the dense canopy of leaves that even the rattle and clunk of the rental car couldn't disturb.

Halfway down the avenue of oaks, Joshua stopped the car and got out. He took a long look around, and his heart dropped. He could hardly believe it was the same farm he'd known, a farm thriving and prosperous. The paddocks were weed-tangled, and some of the planks of the white fences were warped and broken. Everywhere there was peeling white paint. Joshua felt it then, the sorrow that dwelled at the great farm, and even in the light of day he saw ghosts there among the shifting shadows beneath the oaks, ghosts of horses saddled long ago, and the ghosts of the people who had saddled them. A weariness came over him, and to make it worse, an electric pain shot out of his lower back, and the pain bent him over. Getting back in the car was an ordeal.

Joshua turned to the right on the circular flagstone-paved drive in front of the house. He parked the car at the foot of the white-marble stairs that led up to the broad portico. Joshua got out of the car and stood looking up at the great antebellum plantation house. Designed by the famed 18th century architect Emile Gallier Dufort, the house was built between 1796 and 1799 and stood as a monument to the once powerful Arceneaux family. Eight four-foot-thick plaster and brick columns soared up to support the huge pediment carved from cypress, and tall windows lined the first and second story. The front entrance was double-doored, and each of the imposing mahogany doors was mounted with a bronze lion-head knocker.

Just as Joshua began to walk up the steps to the portico, he glanced to the right. Off in the distance the bricks of the once grand eighty stall broodmare barn were charred black, and sticking up from inside the walls were the beams of the roof that had collapsed during the fire. Joshua looked away, briefly clenched his eyes closed, tried not to think about things that hurt to remember. But the memories had started to come and he saw himself walking through the barn where lived some of the bluest of the blue-blooded broodmares in the country, where lived the progeny of one of the great sires of modern times, Southern Lord. In his memory, Joshua could see the bright eyes of the thoroughbreds standing in their stalls: Kalahari was there, Columbia, Blue Nile, Crisis, Confederate Gal, Nana Sahib, Executrix, Imperial Rome, and so many more...with their foals, all dead.

Joshua walked up onto the portico, took hold of the heavy ring that a bronze lion held in its mouth, and used it to knock. The deep, heavy sound echoed through rooms beyond. Came the sound of footsteps, and both doors swung open. The butler, wearing spectacles and formal livery, stood in the center of the doorway. He was black, slender, of medium height, and his hair was gray and cut short. His face was wide and polished.

"Good afternoon, Mr. Joshua," the butler said in a drawl, delivering even this simple greeting with great dignity.

"Robert, it is good to see ye," Joshua said. "How is she?"

"Miss Emily has instructed me to tell you that she will not see you until after you see the other twin."

"Twin?"

"The colt Miss Emily sent to train at your farm has a twin."

"She never mentioned—"

"Those are Miss Emily's instructions to you, Mr. Joshua. You will find the other twin in the *horses-in-training* barn, it was untouched by the fire."

With that, Robert stepped back and swung the doors closed, leaving Joshua standing on the portico blinking and in wonder. After a collection of seconds passed, Joshua stepped down the stairs and began to make his way along the road that led to the barns. An evening breeze caused strange banging and creaking to come from the burned-out barn. Joshua wouldn't look at it, and with a low mutter asked God how He could have permitted such a tragedy to happen.

A small tractor with a harrow attached was parked alongside the horses-in-training barn, next to a four-stall starting gate, and Joshua, the arthritis in his back forcing his head down, noticed the single set of hoof prints that came out of the barn, and the single set returning. Curious, he followed the hoof prints along the path that led out onto the carefully harrowed training track. He stopped in the center of the track, the surface soft but not deep beneath his feet. He followed the set of hoof prints that came out onto the track with his eyes until they disappeared, then shifted his gaze to where the hoof prints reappeared again down on the rail. Joshua uttered a small sound of disbelief. The horse that made these tracks was running...really running. He guessed at the length of the stride to be nearly thirty feet, then called himself "Daft." He walked over to the hoof prints, and now walked the length of the stride measuring it by the length of his own.

"Just short of twenty-nine feet," Joshua muttered, then recalled the longest stride ever recorded as being the twenty-eight-foot stride of Gladiator, the European champion.

Joshua slowly turned his head and stared into the darkness beyond the gaping entrance to the horses-in-training barn. His heart began to pound when he thought of the horse that must be waiting for him there.

Joshua walked up to the barn and the open iron-studded oak doors towered above him. Twenty-four stalls lined the wide aisle. The iron-studded doors at the other end of the barn were open too, and Joshua could see the flaming red of the setting sun. The smell of oats and hay welcomed him, and Joshua began to walk down the aisle. Above him, swallows maneuvered through the rafters. As he passed stalls, he swung his head from side to side searching, and found nothing. Then he came to the stall in the corner of the far end of the barn, across from the feed and tack rooms.

Light from the setting sun came through the tall open doors in shafts of scarlet and gold, and Joshua stood in the shifting evening light peering into the stall. The sound came of hooves moving in straw, and Joshua's eyes adjusted and he could see the dark shape of the colt in the deep shadows. He opened the stall door, and the colt stepped toward him, emerging from the darkness. The colt's great liquid eyes caught the sunshine and reflected it back at Joshua in diamond points of light. Joshua stared into the diamond light, felt that profound power few horses can hold over men, and it seemed to the old horseman that the entire world had come to a standstill. Joshua slowly straightened, the curve disappearing from his back. He felt lightheaded, then reminded himself to breathe. For the rest of his life, Joshua would remember every millisecond of this first meeting.

Joshua stepped back out of the stall, secured the door, and

hurried down the wide aisle. He stopped only once, briefly. It was as if the colt had a gravity of his own that pulled on Joshua to come back. But Emily was waiting, and Joshua left the barn.

Clouds of blinking fireflies rose up from the weed-tangled paddocks, and the long shadows of the coming night seemed like fingers reaching out to clutch at the great house. When Joshua got to the front doors he didn't bother to knock. He threw open the doors and rushed into the great hall. A spectral half-light and the smell of dust greeted him. The dust was so thick Joshua began to cough. Then he raised his eyes. At the top of the sweeping staircase stood Emily Aurora Arceneaux-Brandt.

"I've never seen anything like him," Joshua said, struggled through his coughs.

The woman at the top of the stairs was not the auburn-haired beauty Joshua remembered. Emily was frail, shrunken, in her eyes the vacant look of an old woman broken by grief and solitude. The realization of this now replaced the thrill Joshua had felt over the colt, and the enormity of the pain Emily had endured these last years caused Joshua to feel sorrow in the marrow of his bones. Suddenly, it took all his strength not to react, to let this sorrow overwhelm him. Joshua watched Emily in silence as she gazed at the oil painting of her husband, Edwin Brandt. The painting was a life-sized portrait by the French portrait painter Etienne Auguste Moreau. Edwin looked out of the painting, a robust, handsome man with piercing steel-gray eyes.

Emily said in a soft drawl, "He excelled at everything he did, except for handling money. Edwin was too trusting and unlucky. Not one of the horses was insured, and the fire took the very best but one. That night when Edwin reached the barn, flames had swept through most of the stalls. He rushed in and managed to save the broodmare Sudan. The last time I saw Edwin alive he was running back into the flames with William at his side...our brave boy William at his father's side."

Emily now shifted her gaze to the portrait of her son that hung on the wall across the great hall opposite his father. Also by Moreau, the painting was of a beautiful boy, sparkling in his youth.

Father and son exchanged looks through the spectral light of the great hall.

Joshua recovered himself, said, "I've thought of you so often, Emily. My sympathy—"

"We have no time for that," Emily interrupted, her voice flat, now cold as stone.

Joshua understood, picked his next words carefully: "The mare Sudan is the dam of—"

"Sudan died giving birth to the twins. She was too old to take such punishment, but she was all I had, in her I put all my hope."

Emily had an uncanny ability to select broodmares. She knew the secrets of the blood, what line of thoroughbreds to cross with another, and in the farm's glory days, the results consistently kept other breeders in awe and Southern Oak among the top breeding farms in the United States. Twenty-five years ago, she'd devoted herself to the task of finding Sudan, the last living mare sired by the champion Eurasian. This was no easy task. Because Sudan had never produced a foal, the mare had been sold several different times, but Emily was determined, and after a year-long search, finally did find the mare. Sudan was discovered at a carnival where she was used as a pony to give rides to little boys and girls. Her name at the carnival was Patches, and when the mare was brought to Southern Oak, everyone laughed, and continued to call her by that name. The mare was small with poor conformation. She'd been retired from racing still a *maiden,* never having won a race. But Emily insisted on breeding her to the farm's leading stud at the time, Cosmopolitan. She argued that the mare's blood, not the homely little mare herself, would produce a foal worthy to be a son or daughter of the great Cosmopolitan. After receiving the best veterinary care, the mare was declared *in foal*, and the laughter over the mare's appearance only increased. Her belly became so big that the weight made her sway-backed, and when standing, she had to do so with her legs spread wide. The mare walked with such a waddle, that the sight even made Emily smile. Then came the early morning that Emily was awakened with the news she'd been impatiently waiting for. Patches was giving birth. By the time

Emily made it to the broodmare barn, most everyone who worked at Southern Oak was there looking into the mare's stall. They'd all come to enjoy a good laugh, but as Emily stepped through the crowd, there was no laughter. When Emily finally looked into the stall, she understood why. Standing at his dam's side, already nearly as tall as she was, was the grandest foal ever seen on the farm. From that day, the little mare was no longer called by her carnival name, and when the name Sudan was spoken, it was spoken with reverence. Her first foal was given the name Southern Lord.

"The twins, their dam is Sudan. And their sire?"

"Judgement, the last son of Cosmopolitan still standing at stud."

Joshua pinched his chin in thought, said, "He wasn't much of a racehorse."

After hearing this from Joshua, Emily lost the vacant look. She stared down on Joshua and her eyes seemed to gather up all the light in the great hall and the light made her eyes shine like emeralds.

"I've had to deal with doubters my entire life," Emily said, "and to them, I said the same words I'm about to say to you, Joshua...blood dominates." Now Emily's voice rose, stirring the dust of the terrible years and filling the hall: "I knew you'd follow the colt's hoof prints, that even if you doubted me, you wouldn't doubt his hoof prints, that his hoof prints would tell you what I already knew from the day the colt was foaled...that the blood of greatness is in him."

Without another word, Emily turned and stepped back into the hall behind her. Her form briefly wavered, then the shadows seemed to absorb her and she disappeared spirit-like into the darkness.

Joshua stood there at the bottom of the staircase breathing in the dust of the great house, the dust of neglect. Then, behind him, Robert closed one of the heavy front doors, and stood holding open the other. Joshua understood that he was being asked to leave. He walked out onto the portico and Robert followed him. Both men stood in silence for a long moment, looking down through the avenue of oaks. It was Robert who broke the silence.

"Mr. Edwin was a good and decent man, Mr. Joshua," Robert said, the last of the evening light reflecting on the lenses of his spectacles, "but he squandered a fortune that took five generations of Miss Emily's family to accumulate. It's all gone, all the money, and there are bankers and tax liens to satisfy."

"I had no idea it was that bad," Joshua answered, and briefly rubbed his right elbow.

"Josiah Krump, an antiques dealer from Charleston, is coming to look among the furniture and paintings of this great house. He is willing to pay cash. Miss Emily intends to raise over two hundred thousand dollars, and this money will be given to you."

Joshua jumped, astonished, said, "Me?"

"You will run the twin you have on your farm twice, and being the colt he is, he will be beaten badly twice, and then before the third *start* you will switch the colts, and you will wager all of Miss Emily's money to win."

Joshua's jaw dropped. "'Tis a *ringer* ye're asking me to run?"

"I'm not asking you, Miss Emily is," Robert answered, the whites of his eyes bold in his dark face. "Two hundred thousand will not save this farm, but two hundred thousand wagered at twenty-to-one, will."

Joshua turned away from Robert, looked off to the east and frowned into the coming dusk. He could feel Robert watching him, waiting. Joshua had first seen Emily in the paddock at Empire State Race Course in New York nearly fifty years ago. He was training for her father, Phillipe Arceneaux, and she was there with her father to watch one of the farm's fillies run in the Brooklyn Oaks. He was twenty-six, she was only sixteen, a lovely red-lipped girl with long auburn hair, and after one look into Emily's emerald-green eyes, Joshua was madly in love. He'd attempted courtship, but then Emily met Edwin Brandt, and Joshua was doomed to the life of the broken hearted. Since Joshua first looked into the emerald of Emily's eyes, he'd not for one heart beat ever stopped loving her. Even now, as she was, he loved her, and she knew it, knew that after long years of being helplessly and hopelessly in love with her, he could never say no to the plan that would save her and Southern Oak.

Robert said, "The colts are identical, solid black, no markings."

"That colt—" Joshua's voice diminished to a croak. He cleared his throat, a harsh guttural sound, then he turned back to Robert, said, "That colt I just saw is over a *hand* taller and at least one-hundred-fifty pounds heavier than the colt I've got on me farm."

"You can deal with that," Robert said flatly.

"But what of the tattoos? I can't deal with the tattoos."

Robert took off his spectacles, wiped them, replaced them, said, "Only one colt was registered with the Jockey Club. By all records, Sudan had one colt. The tattoos are identical."

"Emily has been plotting this since the colts were foaled? How could she possibly know? And the tattoos, how—" Joshua stopped himself, said, "No, don't tell me how you got the tattoos done, I don't want to know. But what of everyone else who's seen the colts together, and what of the vet who was there when the twins were born?"

"There is no one else, there was no vet, I alone, Mr. Joshua, am left to serve Miss Emily."

"Ye gallop and work the colt?" Joshua said.

"I was ten years old when I first came to Southern Oak looking for work. I cleaned stalls, then at twelve, began to *get on* horses. In my twenties, Mr. Edwin insisted I come to this great house as his valet, then later I was made Butler and supervised a household staff of twelve. But I never stopped riding...you don't just stop loving to ride thoroughbreds."

"Aye," Joshua said with a nod. "Once the horses get their hold on ye, there's no giving them up, and I understand what Edwin saw in ye, Robert, that such a house as this should have a man such as ye to run it, a man with yer dignity. Over the years, when I thought of Southern Oak, I first would think of Emily, then think of ye."

"Help Miss Emily, Mr. Joshua," Robert said, and there was urgency in his voice.

It was dark now, and Joshua looked up to where two of the tall windows of the second story stood out in the night as oblongs of yellow electric light. He thought of her beyond those windows, the woman of ivory and rose petals who was always before him in his dreams.

"Of course, I'll help her," Joshua said, and his words had the softness of a caress. "She's always known she can depend on me."

Joshua shook Robert's hand, then stepped down off the portico and walked to his car. For a long moment, he gazed up into the clear night sky, looking from star to star.

"And what name do the colts share, Robert?" Joshua asked.

"Black Deuce," Robert answered.

12. SAM

Tigress was only to walk the day before the Margret Mitchell Stakes, but the sturdy bay roan was so wound up and full of herself, that Sam decided she had to do more than walk or he'd risk allowing her to hurt herself. One of the grooms saddled the stable's pony, a stout golden palomino named Herbert, and Sam used the calm nine-year-old gelding to *pony* the four-year-old filly. Tigress frisked alongside the pony at the end of the lead shank Sam kept a short hold on, and Herbert tolerated her antics, giving only the occasional snort of disapproval. Tigress enjoyed her riderless romp around the racetrack, and so did Sam. He spent most of the time laughing at the fun-loving filly. When he brought Tigress back from the track she continued to bounce and frisk, but in a way that had nothing of self-destruction in it. Sam stood watching her groom, the ponytailed Mary Linwood, give her a bath. Mary squeezed a sponge full of warm soapy water so that it ran down the filly's face, and the filly shut her eyes and licked at the soapy water with her long twisting tongue.

Sam stood watching the filly with his shoulders squared and his arms folded across his chest. From the shedrow came a blend of sounds: the thud of hooves, the hollow clunk of a muck basket being set down, the creak of saddle leather, the voices of people and horses. A smile made Sam's face glow. The wordless, nameless song of saddles and bridles was playing in his head. Then Carol Vincent, a jockey's agent, walked up and stood beside Sam.

Carol had a tangle of long brunette hair and clear hazel eyes. She was a head-turner in blue jeans. She was agent for Taylor Howard, one of the leading riders at the race meet.

"Mornin', Sam," Carol said.

The song in Sam's head stopped, and he turned, said, "Well, good morning, Carol."

"I've been hearing rumors—"

"Carol, it's almost nine o'clock," Sam interrupted, a smirk tipping his face, "you're not the first agent to show up and tell me about DaSilva being MIA."

Carol gave Sam a smile, a show of white and perfect teeth. "I just want you to know that Taylor is *open* in the Margret Mitchell."

"I've always liked Taylor," Sam said, "he's good on the front end, knows pace."

"He'd love to ride Tigress," Carol said.

"I'll keep Taylor in mind, if DaSilva doesn't turn up."

"What more can I ask?" Carol said, still smiling. Now she changed the subject and lost her smile: "It was tragic about Charlie Keene, what a great guy. I've heard his mother, Ruth, isn't doing well at all."

"There are some things you never get over," Sam said.

Carol nodded, cleared her throat. "You know I grew up on the backstretch—"

"I know, both your mother and father were grooms for my father."

"A more gentle man never lived, Sam," Carol said in a voice suddenly small. "When I was a little girl, he let me ride his pony around the shed all the time."

Sam glanced away from the filly, gave Carol a steady look. "Like I said, some things you never get over, and it only hurts to talk about them."

"I never believed it was suicide, Sam, nobody who knew your father believed that." Now Carol hesitated, took a deep breath, said, "Tony Belichio—"

Something inside Sam snapped, he raised his voice, shut Carol off in midsentence: "Don't ever...*ever* say that man's name in my presence again."

Carol's cheeks flushed red. "Sorry, Sam," she said.

Sam turned back to watch the filly. He felt nauseated, as if his breakfast had gone rancid in his stomach. An old scar had been opened, becoming a fresh wound, and Sam remembered himself as a boy, waking from a sound sleep sobbing and thinking of his father. Now pain flooded his heart, and for a long moment Sam had the feeling he couldn't catch his breath, that he was drowning. Without another word, Carol walked away. Sam looked down at his boots, began to collect himself, and before Carol got to the corner of the barn, he was in control again.

"Carol," Sam called.

Carol stopped, looked back at Sam.

"Tomorrow," Sam went on, "if DaSilva is a no-show in the Jock's Room, *name* Taylor on Tigress."

Carol smiled at Sam, not a broad happy kind of smile, but a small sad tight-lipped smile. "Thanks, Sam," she said.

13. EMILY AURORA ARCENEAUX-BRANDT

Emily sat resting in an over-stuffed lounge chair by the fireplace in her bedroom. Her dim eyes were set in the hollows of orbital bones that looked far too large for her withered face. Her complexion was as gray as the ancient gown she wore. She had on her wedding dress, the same gown that had once been her mother's, and before her, her grandmother's. The long gown of silk, satin and lace was worn threadbare at the hem and edge of the sleeves. Emily wore it nearly every day. With her eyes closed, Emily escaped her sorrow by allowing memories to alter reality, to scramble time. It was suddenly her wedding day. The great columned house was dazzlingly white in the spring sunshine, the over six hundred wedding guests waited seated in rows beneath the oaks. A senator was there, the governor, a large gathering of political and industrial captains. Well represented were the women of Southern society. When Emily stepped out onto the portico, all these guests stood and the orchestra began to play Mendelssohn's *Wedding March*. Violins and cellos blended to a lovely sound. It was all so real, so unbearably beautiful, and she could see Edwin waiting for her so dashing and handsome in the shade of the oaks…Edwin waiting for her in the shade of the oaks.

Now another memory interfered, and the flames of a great fire made long quick shadows in the night. Emily gave a gasp, opened her eyes, and though the flames receded, the hard reality of the present returned so suddenly that the shock of it caused her fragile heart to labor in a wild rhythm. Pain shot up into her left shoulder and down her left arm: Excruciating, torturing. Emily's chest heaved as she struggled to gather enough breath to call out.

"Robert," she said in a voice breathless, frightened, barely able to be heard.

But Robert did hear, and he was there with the little nitroglycerin pills. He placed one under her tongue, and when her struggling continued, he placed yet another. The pain and torture quieted, receded, and Emily caught her breath.

"Thank you, Robert," she said, her voice but a whisper.

Robert stood before Emily in the straight and formal manner expected of a butler serving in a great house. He was never familiar, always maintained the customary space between servant and the served, and no matter how extreme Miss Emily's emotions became, he never lost his composure. Robert was a man of unshakeable dignity, of unshakeable nerves, a man who was only strengthened by difficulties and uncertainties. He didn't ask Miss Emily if he should call the doctor, he'd given up on that months before when her small issues with pain began to be large issues.

Emily's face suddenly changed, brightened, and in a voice now stronger asked, "Is William, my little Billy, home from school yet, Robert?" Emily's hope lasted only briefly and her face changed back into a sorrow-lined mask. She touched her lips with the trembling fingers of a vein-knotted hand, muttered, "What am I saying? Of course he's not home from school, William is never coming home again."

"Mr. Krump will be here on Tuesday of this next week," Robert said, diverting the conversation.

Eyelashes fluttering, Emily made a mental adjustment, said, "And Joshua returns when?"

"Next Thursday he'll return to pick up the colt and the—"

"Yes, yes, yes," Emily interrupted, not even wanting to hear the word money.

In the silence that followed, only the ticking of the gilt-bronze clock on the marble mantel of the fireplace could be heard. Robert stood waiting in this silence, and Emily's eyes began to flicker. She beheld nothing around her, saw only the past, dwelling on that day when the violins and cellos played, that day when lilies and orchids lined her path out to where Edwin stood tall and handsome, waiting beneath the oaks.

Robert now played the trump card he used to break the spell the past held over the mistress of Southern Oak. "If there is nothing else, Miss Emily," he said, "I'll turn the colt out in his paddock."

Emily looked up at Robert, stared, came back from days lived long ago. "Yes, please do, Robert. I haven't much longer to sit by the window and spend my afternoons with him, he'll be gone soon."

Robert bowed, then left the room. Emily now tried to stand, but her heart labored and she fell back into the chair. She didn't try to move again until she felt her heart return to a steady beat, and that took a quarter of an hour. By the time Emily made her way to the window, the colt was already in the paddock nearest the house where a single live oak spread its shade. When Emily saw the colt, her eyes sparkled like emeralds, and she stretched her hand out the open window, out toward the blaze of the colt's presence.

14. SAM

Lincoln Park Racecourse held racing dates for a spring and fall meet. Because of the Chicagoland weather during these times of the year, the paddock was enclosed on the ground level of a two-story building at the end of the grandstand. Broad plate-glass windows allowed people to look into the paddock with its line of stalls and sand-surfaced walking ring. A set of stairs against the far wall descended from the Jock's Room on the second floor.

A large crowd gathered around the paddock for the Margret Mitchell Stakes, and as the fillies were led by, people talked back and forth, sharing nonsense and knowledge while they looked the horses over. Some people were there to gamble, some just out to enjoy a beautiful day and the sight of thoroughbreds. Before entering the paddock, each horse made a stop to allow the *Identifier,* a bespectacled woman with short-clipped sandy hair, to flip up the horse's upper lip and compare the tattoo there with information from the horse's papers she had organized on a clipboard.

Sam had chosen to walk over with Tigress and not sit in the Club House with Bentley prior to the race, and as Mary, Tigress' groom, stopped to let the Identifier do her inspection, the filly became impatient. Tigress threw her head, kicked out with both back legs and sent several racing fans, who'd ventured too close, scrambling to avoid flying hooves. This caused action from a security guard.

"Step back there," the blue-uniformed guard said, holding his arms wide as a signal to the crowd, "let the horses through. Make way for the horses, ladies and gentlemen."

Sam stepped up to the filly's right side, took hold of the reins, said "Easy big mare," and the filly looked at Sam with bright eyes, quieted and let the Identifier do her job.

Mary grinned at Sam, said, "She's on tilt, Sam. Today she's going to make those other fillies look like Shetland ponies."

Sam smiled, then said, "Keep her moving, Mary, the valets haven't come down yet."

Mary led the filly to the walking ring, her ponytail bobbing with each step, and fell in with several other fillies being walked. The filly gave a snort and broke into a nimble prance. Sam made his way over to stall seven where Bentley waited. Bentley stood with his cane planted in front of him, both hands resting, one on top of the other, on the gold handle. He was dapper in a black cashmere blazer, gray slacks and a large red bowtie. When he saw Tigress, his smile lit up the paddock.

"Sam, this is going to be such fun," Bentley said excitedly. "And, oh my, but Tigress does look spectacular."

Sam shook Bentley's hand. "She does, Bentley."

"What about our rider DaSilva?" Bentley asked, suddenly frowning.

"All I know is that he didn't ride yesterday or check into the Jock's Room today, and that nobody, even his agent, has heard from him."

"Odd," said Bentley. "But I think this Howard is a good rider."

"Taylor knows how to win races," Sam answered.

"I should also tell you, Sam, that Joshua called. He asked if it would be alright if he trained one outside horse along with mine. I told him that wasn't a problem, and he said he'd be bringing a colt over from Iowa in the next day or two."

"Fine," Sam answered, "I'll have a stall waiting, and I have something to tell you, Bentley."

"Oh?"

"Matchbook did so well yesterday and again this morning with long gallops, that I entered him in a maiden allowance going a mile for Monday. The race *went* and he *got in*."

"Excellent," Bentley said, "I'm anxious to see if you're correct about his ability to *go long* after being sprinted."

Sam smiled. "Yep, we'll see."

Just then the valets, wearing green uniforms and caps, came down the stairs with their rider's tack, and Sam waved at Mary to bring over the filly. While Sam and the valet saddled her, Tigress stood quietly, ears pricked, keenly aware of everything going on around her. She blinked her amber-colored eyes, looking at Sam, Mary, Bentley and the valet, and at the crowd that peered at her and the other fillies through the broad plate glass windows.

The jockeys came down the stairs. There were bright silks, small faces beneath riding helmets, the flash of polished boots. Taylor Howard walked over in his customary swagger. He had a manner of self-assurance about him that lacked any arrogance. Taylor first shook Bentley's hand.

"Thank you, Mr. Keene," Taylor said, "for letting me ride your filly today."

"You're most welcome," Bentley said.

Taylor turned to Sam, shook Sam's hand, a firm grip. "I appreciate this, Sam."

"Get the money, Taylor," Sam replied, then went directly to business. "The filly from New York, Shazam, is pure speed, and they shipped in her regular New York jock to ride her."

"I know Gustines," Taylor said, "he can *horseback*."

Sam nodded, said, "I talked to an agent I know out East yesterday and he said Shazam doesn't like to be hit left-handed. Three starts ago she finished a badly beaten seventh, all because the jock hit her left-handed and she *bolted* to the outside fence."

"Got it, Sam," Taylor said.

"Tigress has speed, but not the speed Shazam has. Shazam can throw a twenty-one and change at you, and a forty-four, so no speed duals, remember we're going a mile. We've got the seven hole, Shazam's in the number three, so if she wants the lead, let her have it, lay back on the outside of her. The rail's deep, right?"

"It's been deep all meet," said Taylor.

"Good, so when you turn for home and make your move on the outside, I want you to keep Shazam pushed down in that deep going, and make it so tight on that jock that he can't use his right-handed stick. We know he can't hit her left-handed, and if you deny him his right stick, you'll beat him. No filly is going to outrun Tigress today under a *hand-ride,* not the way she's been training, not in her own backyard...today this is *her* racetrack."

Bentley couldn't contain himself, he bubbled, "Oh, this is going to be great fun!"

The Paddock Judge, a squat little man with sideburns, gave his command: "Riders up!"

With his left hand, Taylor took a cross in the reins and grabbed a fistful of the filly's mane, and with his right hand took hold of the saddle. When he cocked his leg, Sam gave him a leg up. Taylor came down lightly on the filly's back, then began to tie a knot in his reins. Taylor looked down at Sam.

"Keep Gustines down in the deep going," Taylor said, "and don't let him use that right stick."

Sam smiled up at Taylor, said, "See you in the winner's circle."

A bugler, standing down the track just outside the winner's circle, now played *Call to the Post.* The brassy notes came through the air sharp and ringing. This caused a surge of voices to come from the grandstand and clubhouse, and a swarm of gamblers to drift toward the Tote machines. The chatter from the stands increased in volume as the horses stepped onto the racetrack, and the bugler now played *The* Horses *Are on the Track.* The horses paraded before the stands, a pageant of beautiful fillies.

Sam and Bentley walked out of the paddock with the other trainers and *connections.*

"I want you to join me in my private box, Sam," Bentley said, "it offers a great bird's eye view."

Sam stopped, gave the white-haired, impeccably dressed Bentley a smile, then held his arms out and looked down at himself. Sam's blond hair was glossy and his face freshly shaven, but he wore blue jeans and an old plaid shirt with the sleeves rolled up. Now Sam, his smile widening, reached out and gave the lapel of Bentley's cashmere blazer a playful tug. Bentley gave a start.

"Oh my," he said, "I've made you uncomfortable, I should have been more thoughtful and worn slacks and a shirt...maybe even a pair of dungarees."

Sam tossed his head back, gave a quick laugh, said, "You in blue jeans, Bentley? About as likely as finding Eskimos in Jamaica."

Bentley tapped his cane on the asphalt apron, joined Sam in laughter. He rocked and swayed in the manner of the delighted, and in that moment Sam saw Bentley as one of those rare people who laughed from the soul and with all his heart.

"Let's just stand here by the fence," Sam finally said, "we can watch them come running out of the turn. Going a mile on this track makes that part of the race worth seeing up close."

On Lincoln Park's five-*furlong* oval, the mile races were started just before the far turn. Horses dropping into the turn right out of the gate made the start of these mile races a spectacle.

Bentley sobered, looked longingly toward the clubhouse, then his attitude changed and he smiled broadly. "I haven't watched a race from the fence in a good long while," he said. "In fact, it's been so long I really can't remember the last time."

"Good, today you get to see horses the way they were meant to be seen, not from the point of view of a bird or on a TV screen, but right here at track level."

Bentley gave a quick nod, said, "Let's pick out a good spot right on the fence."

The announcer's voice now came over the public-address system, a rich and clear voice: "The horses are at the post! At the post!"

Sam and Bentley stood by the outside fence, looking off across the track, watching the horses being loaded into the gate one by one. The crowd quieted to a murmur of anticipation.

The announcer: "They're all in. The flag is up...."

The sound of the bell ringing and the gate slamming open came across the infield.

The announcer: "...and they're off and running in the eighty-ninth running of the Margret Mitchell Stakes!"

The murmur of the crowd now exploded into a roar of voices, and the field of twelve horses was running. When the tightly bunched field swept through the turn and into the stretch for the first time, there were five horses across the track, and the twelve thoroughbreds came like a thundering charge of cavalry arriving on a battlefield. There was the crack and pop of whips, the shouts and curses of jockeys.

Bentley gave a jump, waved his cane. "Are you seeing this, Sam? I'd forgotten how much fun racing can be from a spot on the fence."

Sam grinned, kept his eye on Tigress as the field went on by the stands the first time.

The announcer: "And through the stretch for the first time, it's Shazam in front by a length, Tigress running second under a hold..."

Bentley was red with excitement. "Under a hold, Sam. Under a hold."

Sam glanced at the tote board. "twenty-two flat. They're flying."

The announcer: "Into the backstretch, Shazam keeps her lead by a length, Tigress is right there second, coming on is Trilogy..."

Going into the far turn again, Taylor moved on Tigress, cutting Shazam's lead down to half a length.

"That's it, Taylor," Sam said, raising his voice. "keep that other filly down on the rail."

Coming into the stretch, Taylor had Tigress right alongside Shazam, the two fillies neck-in-neck. The fillies ran by Sam and Bentley in a pounding of hooves, and there was bumping and contact as one rider tried to get out of the deep going and the other rider was determined to keep him in it. Taylor kept it so tight on Gustines, that there was no room for Gustines to effectively use his whip right handed.

Sam swung his fist, shouted, "That's what I call race riding."

"Run, Tigress," Bentley shouted, waving his cane.

The announcer: "It's Shazam on the inside, Tigress on the outside, and inside the sixteenth pole Tigress takes a half-length lead!"

"We're going to win it," Bentley shouted.

The announcer: "Tigress in front by half a length, Shazam second, but on the outside here comes Trilogy with a rush!"

In the middle of the racetrack, the filly Trilogy was making a late run. Taylor moved Tigress away from the inside to meet this new challenge. Tigress dug in gamely, responding to a left-handed stick, and when Trilogy came to her, Trilogy *hung* on the outside of Tigress and couldn't get by her. Tigress was in a drive for the wire.

The sound of cheering from the stands now expanded, swelling to a thundering roar.

The announcer: "Tigress in front, Trilogy is done, but coming back on the inside is Shazam…"

When Taylor moved Tigress to meet the new challenge, it gave Shazam room to come off the rail and out of the deep going, and her rider, Gustines, began to hit her right handed and she responded, giving him a burst of speed.

The announcer: "…and with just yards to go it's Shazam on the inside, Tigress on the outside…"

Sam and Bentley had their voices raised to shouts.

The announcer: "…both fillies are all out! And here's the wire! On the inside, it's Shazam by a nose! What a finish in the eighty-ninth running of the Margret Mitchell."

Bentley's excitement vanished, he shook his head a little in shock. "I thought we had it won," he said, hoarse from shouting.

Sam said, "Bentley, I'm going to see how the filly comes back and I want to talk to the jock."

"Fine, Sam," Bentley answered, "I'm going to watch the replay in the *Racing Secretary's Office*, meet me there after you're done, I'll give you a ride back to the barn. If our rider would have just done what you told him to do, to keep Shazam down on the rail, we would have won that race."

Sam didn't answer, he hurried off to where the riders brought the horses back for the unsaddling. Tigress was already there, out on the track in front of the paddock, and Taylor had already slipped the saddle from her back. The filly was wet with sweat, she was blowing hard, her chest rapidly expanding and contracting as she pulled air into her lungs and blew it back out. Sam gave her a searching look and watched her step off as Mary led her away. When Sam looked at Taylor, the jockey averted his eyes.

Sam said, "That was one hell of a ride, jock."

Taylor swung his head up quickly in a flash of anger, but one look into Sam's face and he understood Sam wasn't being sarcastic. "Thanks, Sam," Taylor said, "I thought I had—"

"The filly on the rail *put away*," Sam interrupted.

Taylor nodded. "I thought she was beat, and that other filly was coming fast on the outside, I just couldn't let her get by me."

"We learned a hard lesson today, Taylor…we learned Shazam is a real racehorse."

Taylor stood looking up at Sam, his saddle in his arms. "What that filly did, coming back that way…you just don't see horses do that, once you're by them, you're by them and it's over." Taylor's valet took his tack from him, and Taylor and Sam walked back toward the paddock. "I'll tell you something else, Sam," Taylor said, putting his hand out. "It's a pleasure to ride for a trainer who really understands. Please make sure Mr. Keene does."

Sam shook the rider's hand. "I'll make sure he understands," Sam answered.

"And tell him I'd really like to ride the filly back."

"I will."

"Thanks, Sam," Taylor said as he started to walk away, "I'll stop by the barn in the morning to say hello and see how the filly is."

"Just one thing you did wrong," Sam said to make the jockey turn and look back at him. "Don't pull my horses up so quick, take your time with them after the wire, let them *gallop out*."

Taylor smiled, nodded, said, "You got it, Sam." Then he

headed for the stairs that went up to the Jock's Room.

Sam found Bentley in the Racing Office, and as they walked out to the parking lot, Sam explained the race to Bentley and Bentley understood.

"It makes perfect sense," Bentley said, "and after watching the replay, I'm very pleased with our filly's performance."

"Taylor wants to ride Tigress back," Sam said.

Bentley held up a hand, said, "That's totally up to you. Remember, I only come to see and enjoy my horses, I don't come to make decisions. You ride anyone you like. You've proven in just a few days that you're a very capable horseman."

Sam smiled, and Bentley waved in the direction where Randolph, his chauffeur, was leaning against the Rolls Royce. Randolph saw Bentley and got into the car. He had to wait before pulling out of the parking space. A black Cadillac with heavily tinted windows was going by. Sam didn't pay attention to the black car when it rolled past, even when someone in the backseat of the Cadillac flicked ash off a cigar through a back window partially rolled down. It wasn't until the Cadillac was by him that Sam caught the spicy aroma of the Cuban cigar, and like a particular song can, the smell took him back to another time and place. There came a violent clenching in Sam's gut.

15. ROBERT TODD

Robert closed the door to Emily's chambers and stood there in the hallway for several minutes. When Emily didn't call for him, remained quiet, he knew she had settled into her after-lunch routine of looking through books of old photographs. She would soon sit by her window and spend the remainder of the afternoon watching the colt after the colt was turned out in his paddock. Now Robert stepped down the hall and descended the sweeping staircase. Once in the great hall he stopped, listened, waited to hear the great house speak to him in creaks and groans, knocks and taps, waited to hear the sound that was proof to him that the great house was not just a cold collection of rooms. But the great house was still, the sound that balanced delicately on the edge of silence did not come, the sound of the great house inhaling and exhaling, breathing as if it was a living thing.

Robert turned and looked through the tall open doors of the library. He had the sense the room was waiting for someone. A clock ticked, a book lay open on a desk, long moiré drapes hung at an open window. Robert would not allow himself to notice the heavy dust and cobwebs. Alone, he was only able to keep the kitchen, Miss Emily's chambers and his small room in the third-floor servant's quarters clean. Taking care of the twin colts these last years had put a great strain on him, but he was determined that this great house should not fall. Dust may be heavy in the air, but the Bayshore Corporation would not make these rooms into a clubhouse, the paddocks would not become a golf course. When Robert thought of such things, he felt an outrage that caused him to clench his jaw until his teeth throbbed.

Down through the avenue of oaks a breeze stirred leafy branches to make shadows dance beneath the ancients, and the long moiré drapes at the open window in the library stirred. It was then that Robert heard the sound he'd been waiting for. The great house seemed to draw a breath, and then spoke to Robert of visitors. There came the closing of a car door. Robert's aristocratic manners were no act, he was a gentleman, and he brushed off the arms of his black jacket, straightened his white bowtie, gave a quick pull at the bottom of his black vest to remove the wrinkles. He was as prepared as he could be. He was about to experience one of the most difficult ordeals of his life.

The hammering clunk of one of the heavy bronze door knockers echoed through the house. With a measured step that had in its cadence the dignity of a king, Robert proceeded to answer the door.

"Good afternoon, Mr. Krump," Robert said, the sudden sunlight flashing on the lenses of his spectacles. He stepped back, swung the door wide, gave a small bow, "Please come in."

"You think this is a good afternoon?" said Josiah Krump. He spoke carefully, with the slightest trace of a slur. "I hardly think so, not for Emily Brandt anyway."

The tone was set for the afternoon Robert had been dreading.

Josiah Krump was one of the most important antique dealers in the country. He had acquired a great knowledge of fine paintings, European decorative arts, and had written a book on French porcelain. When Josiah Krump entered the bidding rooms of the esteemed auction houses of Christie's and Sotheby's in New York, those auction houses laid before him a red carpet. Josiah spent hundreds of thousands of dollars for fine objects, and sold them for two or three times what he paid for them to wealthy international clients who depended on his expertise and good taste. Yet, Josiah Krump's life had not been an easy one. He had no wife, no family, no friends, and when he was a boy, his father had worked at Southern Oak but been fired for leaving open the gate to the yearling paddock. Not once, but three different times he was responsible for yearlings being pursued across the Carolina countryside. The third time he left the gate open, one of the escaped yearlings had been hit by a truck and killed. After his dismissal, Josiah's family had lived in wretched poverty. It was the years of the Great Depression, and jobs were non-existent. To Josiah, this alone justified his hunger for justice and revenge, but there was more.

Josiah had suffered a stroke five years ago. He'd retained his memory and shrewd business mind, and after extensive physical therapy was able to recover his ability to walk, though he was left with a limp. But what Josiah couldn't recover caused him to become a twisted and bitter man who wanted to punish the entire world. What Josiah couldn't recover was his face. The stroke had disfigured him. The left side of his face appeared to be melting, and the deformity was such that little children often ran away crying when they saw him. And now Josiah Krump stood on the portico of the Arceneaux mansion, thinking of his father, of the poverty he'd known as a child, of the cruelty of stroke, of his great opportunity for revenge. When Josiah looked at Robert, his left eye glittered with malice from out of the side of his face that appeared to be melting off his skull.

With a lurching walk, Krump entered the great hall.

Robert closed the door behind him, turned, said, "It's a hot day, Mr. Krump, could I get you some refreshment. Perhaps a cold lemon—"

"Where is Mrs. Brandt?" Krump said, giving Robert no chance to finish.

"Miss Emily won't be joining us," Robert answered, "I'll be showing you through the house."

Krump sneered, a grotesque knot forming on the affected side of his face. "I came to deal with Mrs. Brandt"—he flicked his wrist, waving Robert off—"not her darky servant."

Robert made not a twitch, invincible in his good manners. "Miss Emily is unwell," Robert said, "and will not be joining us."

"I'd be unwell too," Krump snorted, "if my finances were in the condition her's are in."

Krump glanced up at the ornate plaster medallions on the twenty-five-foot coffered ceiling and had to crane his neck to study the chandelier that hung in cascades of crystal above him. So covered with dust and cobwebs was the chandelier that only an occasional wink of light escaped the hundreds of prisms. Still, Krump recognized it as French and by Baccarat. Next Krump glanced at the matching pier tables facing each other across the great hall. Even under layers of dust he recognized the style and craftsmanship of Duncan Phyfe. He glanced at other objects, at the gallery of paintings, and his breathing changed; he began to breath in short gasps. When Krump looked back at Robert, his eyes were hostile with greed.

"Show me everything," he said.

Robert first led the way to the library where Krump looked over Medieval illuminated manuscripts collected in the nineteenth century by Emily's great grandfather, Julien Arcenauex, and couldn't stop touching and inspecting the five-foot-tall Malachite urns that flanked the doorway. Even under years of dust the bright green of the urns was dazzling.

"These urns," Krump said, "are Russian, late eighteenth century, and are exquisite." A phlegmy rattle came from his throat, then he coughed, looked at Robert, demanded: "Go get Mrs. Brandt, I must know the provenance of these urns, where, when and from whom they were acquired."

"No need to bother Miss Emily, I can tell you about them."

"You?" Krump said, his face screwed into a sneer. "You're one generation from picking cotton, what could a darky possibly know about fine decorative arts? Can you even read?"

Robert didn't react to Krump's verbal assault. He remained stiff and unfazed, and Krump, staring at Robert in a brief silence, became infuriated over his inability to affect Robert's dignified composure.

"Talk then," Krump finally snapped, "tell me about these urns."

"They came to this house after World War II," Robert explained calmly. "Miss Emily's father was invited along with other wealthy Americans to come to Russia by Stalin himself to buy items that had once belonged to Czars. Stalin's government was in dire need of cash. Phillipe returned with these urns and other items that filled an entire shipping container. These urns were once in the reception hall of the Czar's Winter Palace in Saint Petersburg."

"Did Phillipe bring back any Faberge?" Krump said, saying the name of the Russian Court Jeweler as if speaking of the holiest of the holy.

"There is a collection of snuff boxes and cigarette cases, various other articles, including two different silver flatware services and a samovar that bears the Romanoff Imperial Eagle."

Krump drew a sharp breath, stared at Robert with glittering eyes. "Show me the Faberge, but before you do, show me the painting."

"*The* painting?" Robert answered.

"Don't play games with me," Krump said, his lopsided face warping into a ghastly scowl. "You know which painting I speak of."

Robert remained silent for a moment, chin up, standing very straight. Then he turned on his heels, and in a calm, unhurried voice said, "Follow me to the drawing room, Mr. Krump."

Robert opened the double wide doors to the drawing room, and dust swirled in the air. Not even he had been in this room for years. Krump stood for a moment gazing into the gloom, then lurched by Robert as if being chased by wolves.

"Lights, you fool," he said in a shout, "turn on the lights."

Robert flipped a switch, but not an electric light came on.

"Can't Brandt even pay her electric bill?" Krump said.

Robert didn't answer. Krump was using humiliation as a weapon and Robert refused to be wounded by it. He walked over to the tall windows and pulled back the brocaded drapes. He tucked the heavy material behind huge gilt-bronze tiebacks. Dust billowed in the air, an explosion of tiny flickers in the sunlight.

Now a golden shaft came through the window, and caught in its brilliance was the painting above the fireplace. Krump uttered a small cry, held his hands out toward the painting, his fingers working like the legs of spiders.

"I must have this painting," Krump said.

From across the centuries, Camille Juliette Duval-Arceneaux gazed out of the painting with hauntingly beautiful emerald-green eyes. Emily's great-great-great-grandmother, Camille was the founding matriarch of the Arceneaux family fortune. Never documented, but much believed, she had been the lover of King Louis XVI of France. After the ill-fated king was guillotined, she fled France for America, taking with her a fortune in jewels gifted to her by Louis. In 1795, she married Hugo Alexis Arceneaux. Hugo was young and ambitious, but it was Camille's money that built this great house and established Southern Oak as one of the South's wealthiest pre-Civil War plantations.

Krump finally calmed. He took a linen handkerchief from his coat pocket and wiped at the spittle that dribbled from the drooping side of his mouth.

"I'm feeling a bit light-headed," Krump said in a breathless voice.

Robert walked over and removed the large white sheet that covered one of the chairs that stood before the fireplace. More dust clouded the air, and both men coughed.

"You idiot," Krump said, his voice muffled by the handkerchief he held over his nose and mouth, "are you trying to asphyxiate us both?"

Krump sat down in the over-stuffed armchair. He indulged in a long look at the painting.

"Once the plantation was established," Krump began to explain, "Hugo Arceneaux, at great expense, commissioned the English portrait painter Adrienne Saxon White to come from London to paint Camille. White and Don Diego Velazquez are the two greatest portrait painters in the history of Western Art." Krump fell silent and with spidery fingers once more reached out toward the painting. "White goes beyond the beauty of line and form, he catches the very heart and soul of his subjects…"

Krump leaned forward, was not the master of his emotions, and it was now that Robert saw there were tears in the dealer's eyes. Krump's voice squeaked and croaked when he said, "Don't you see? Even the ignorant monkey you are, don't you see? Camille lives and breathes, she is not dead…she lives and breathes."

Robert remained silent, refusing to respond and feed Krump's anger. His concern was that Krump was working himself into illness.

Krump said, "This knowledge is wasted on you, but White spent half a year painting this portrait, probably sipped sherry in this very room, laughed and talked here with Camille and Hugo. Then, on his return voyage to England, White caught pneumonia and died." Krump turned and looked at Robert with oddly shining eyes. "This is the last painting painted by one of the greatest portrait painters in history."

"It is not for sale," Robert said bluntly.

"Three hundred thousand dollars," Krump said. "I have it as Mrs. Brandt requested, in cash in the trunk of my car, and if you do not sell me this painting—"

Krump suddenly stiffened, arched his back, trembled, appeared to be having a seizure. Robert took a step toward him, but the critical moment passed, Krump collected himself, continued, "If you do not sell me this painting," his voice slowed and there was a threat in it, "I will buy nothing from Mrs. Brandt, not today, not ever. See how many other dealers will bring large sums of cash to bargain with an uppity nigger."

Robert faced Krump with a wide clear gaze, refusing to acknowledge what he'd just heard. At this moment, Robert could only think of the great responsibility Miss Emily had given him, that she had given him complete control over what should be sold to Krump. All that Krump had told him about the painting, Robert already knew, just as he knew the history of all things to do with Southern Oak, and Robert had to decide whether to sell or not to sell *the* painting he considered the very heart of the great house.

Robert stood motionless in a rare crisis of indecision.

Then Robert felt something fan his cheek, and now the dust stirred at his feet, and he heard a sound that trembled on the edge of silence, that to him was the sound of the great house drawing breath. Robert waited, listened. When the breath was released, Robert heard the great house softly sigh. Robert's eyes were suddenly very bright behind the lenses of his spectacles.

"The painting is yours, Mr. Krump," Robert said.

16. SAM

It was 3:32, Monday afternoon, and Sam was in the shedrow office, his feet up on the desk, phone to his ear. He was feeling in high spirits. Bentley had been unable to come watch Matchbook run his first race at a mile, Ruth had gone through a difficult night, and the difficulties had carried on into the morning. In this condition, Bentley wouldn't leave her. The news Sam was giving Bentley about Matchbook was brightening Bentley's day.

"Matchbook ran third, Bentley," Sam said, grinning as he talked, "only beaten half a length for all of it."

"You were right about the distance, Sam," Bentley chortled, "a great improvement, marvelous."

"Clay Repp, the colt's gallop boy, deserves a lot of praise. Clay got the colt to settle down in the morning, and that had a lot to do with my decision. Clay's a good *hand*."

"He is indeed, I liked the way he handled the colt that morning when I came out to meet you. Who rode the colt this afternoon?"

"Taylor Howard was *open,* I named him on."

"Please, tell me more about the race."

"Matchbook and Taylor broke sharp from the gate, and Taylor reached and took hold of him right away. The colt threw his head a few times, but Taylor got him to relax and he settled into fifth, about eight lengths out of it, then turning for home Taylor swung him to the outside. Matchbook made a great run, but it was a lightning fast track, the speed carried today, the two speed horses never came back to him…only half a length, Bentley."

"How did the colt come back?"

Sam looked out the door, saw Matchbook's groom, the red-haired Billy Wallace, leading the colt down the shedrow for another pass around the barn. "He's fine, we'll run him back in a couple of weeks."

"What did Taylor say about him?"

"The jock said he's a useful colt, that he'll win some races for us."

"Any news about DaSilva?" Bentley asked.

"Not a word. It's a missing person's case now, the police are involved."

"Oh, my, I hope nothing has happened to that young man."

"Me too," Sam answered.

"Excuse me for just a moment, Sam," Bentley said. Bentley held the phone away from his mouth and Sam could hear him talking to someone else. "I'll be right there, Miss Greene," Sam heard Bentley say. Then Bentley was back on the phone. "I must go, Sam. I know we have horses running this week, but I probably won't make it to the track until Saturday…I'm so looking forward to watching Mutineer run in the big handicap."

"The gelding couldn't be doing better," Sam said. "And, Bentley, if there is anything I can do to help you in any way, please don't hesitate to ask. I hope Ruth begins to feel better soon."

"These are difficult times, Sam. The funeral's tomorrow, just a small family affair, and you're already doing a great deal for Ruth and me, you're taking care of our horses. After knowing you these few short days, I know the horses we love couldn't be in better hands…and I mean that."

The two men exchanged "Goodbyes," and Sam hung up the phone. He started to dial his home phone, he wanted to tell Bess all about Matchbook. When he called her Saturday night, she'd been thrilled over Sam's description of how well Tigress had run. Sam only had three numbers dialed when he heard a truck pull up outside. He hung up the phone, got up from the desk and walked out into the shedrow. Joshua had just pulled in with his International Loadstar box truck horse van. He got down out of the cab.

"Got a present for ye," Joshua said with a wink.

"I'm anxious to see this colt," Sam said.

Joshua opened the side doors, and Sam helped him pull out the ramp and raise the guardrails. After this was done, Joshua straightened, put a hand to the small of his back, rubbed at it.

"Getting old isn't for the faint of heart," he said.

In the next minutes, Joshua opened the door to the stall in the van and led the colt out. The colt paused in the doorway, looked about bright-eyed, sniffing the air noisily with wide nostrils. Joshua let the colt take his time, then when the colt was ready, he led him down the ramp. Joshua walked him around in a circle, letting the colt stretch his legs.

"Solid black, not a mark on him," Sam said. "And he's put together nicely, just a bit small."

"A wee bit," Joshua answered. "Have ye a stall made up for him, then?"

"I do," Sam said. He gave a shout: "Billy, are you done with Matchbook?"

Billy Wallace called back. "I Just put the colt away, Mr. Jack."

"Then do me a favor," Sam said, "and take this horse from Joshua, walk him a few times around the barn and put him in the empty stall all the way at the end. Put fresh water in his water bucket and hang a hay net for him."

Billy hurried out from under the shedrow, his red hair the color of copper wire in the sunshine. "Sure thing, sir."

Billy took the shank from Joshua and began to lead the colt away.

"Another thing, Billy," Sam said, "easy with all that Mr. and sir stuff."

Billy gave Sam a short, quick smile from over his shoulder, and Sam and Joshua watched the colt until Billy disappeared with him around the corner of the shedrow.

Sam turned back to Joshua, said, "I recognize that colt from that day on your farm, you called him fool's gold."

Joshua didn't answer, gave instead a nervous fidget. Something wasn't right and Sam picked up on it.

"You okay, Josh?"

Joshua ignored the question said, "This colt's ready to run, just *blow him out.*" Then Joshua began to rub his elbow. "Get in the cab, Sam," he said, "I need to talk to ye, and want no one else to hear."

Once in the cab, Joshua's nervous fidgets increased. Eyebrows twitching, he glanced at Sam, into his face, then looked away to stare out the windshield. He said nothing while he took several deep breaths. Sam frowned, studied Joshua, concerned. It was strange to see Joshua behave with uncertainty.

"What's wrong, Josh?" Sam said.

"The colt has a twin," Joshua began, an odd crackle in his voice. "Solid black he is, and a good hand taller and at least a hundred and fifty pounds heavier." Joshua turned and looked at Sam now, fixed him with his Irish eyes. "And, Sam, God put every ounce of those pounds right where they should be on a horse."

"What—"

"Grand this colt's twin is, the likes I've never seen before. He has the look of diamonds in his eyes."

"Josh, settle down," Sam said.

"These twins are out of Sudan, by Judgement, the last son of Cosmopolitan standing at stud."

"That breeding alone is enough to make—"

"Twins, exactly alike but for a bit of height and weight. Twins exactly alike only one is but an average colt, the other has diamond eyes. Twins out of Sudan, but only one colt was registered. Twins with the same tattoo. Twins, the average colt to run and get beat twice, then switched with the colt with diamonds in his eyes."

Sam processed all that Joshua had explained, then said, "A ringer."

"I'm going to help Emily save her farm. I have no choice, me heart is dictating I must do this. I've loved the woman for more than forty years. Two hundred thousand bet on a horse starting for the third time after getting beaten badly in his first two tries…it will be a fortune, and a fortune is what Emily needs."

Sam looked away from Joshua, sat quietly with his hands in his lap.

Joshua tilted his head to look closely at Sam, said in a small voice, "Will ye help me, Sammy?"

Sam took a deep breath, let it go slowly, then looked back at Joshua, his blue eyes steady into Joshua's Irish eyes. "You found me as a boy standing outside the stable gate with only an old suitcase to my name," Sam said. "After others drove by that morning without giving me a second look, you stopped and took me in, gave me a job, shelter and food. Though you never said it, I knew after just a few short weeks that you loved me, and that's what got me through those long nights when the nightmares came and all I could see was the body of my father lying there in the barn…did you really think I would say no to you? That I wouldn't bleed red blood trying to do whatever you asked me to do? Josh, take me to the Sears Building right now, up to the roof, and if you want me to, I'll take one hell of a running start and try to get you the moon."

Joshua opened his mouth to speak, but couldn't seem to make his voice work. He turned away from Sam, looked out the driver's window, and Sam opened the door and got out of the truck. While Sam walked toward the shedrow, Joshua started the horse van, turned it around and drove away.

2

It was late evening, and a storm was coming from the west. From out of the line of dark billowing clouds, thin bolts of lightning twitched and kinked, flashing briefly in the darkening sky. Thunder boomed, and sparrows, picking at grain spilled by the feed room door, flew up into the rafters. Sam stood by the black colt's stall, leaned up against the webbing, watching nature unfold its fury. Next to him, the colt had his head out over the webbing. When the front hit the barn, it came with a gust of wind and there were creaks and groans in the rafters. Then came the rain, heavy sheets of it, so heavy Sam imagined fish swimming through the air. That's when Sam thought of the word shark, and that he'd heard someone use the word recently: "I love breaking a bookmaker more than sharks love blood." In that moment, Sam could see Bill Baker's face take shape from out of the dark swirling clouds of the storm.

Sam straightened so quickly that he bumped the colt's muzzle and the colt jerked his head away, retreated into the back of his stall. A plan for betting Emily Brandt's money took shape in Sam's brain before he was two steps away from the colt's webbing, and it was a plan that fit into a prayer he'd prayed over and over since his father's death. Sam's prayer was for an opportunity, an opportunity for revenge. Baker would know how to do it, use Emily's money to break Belichio.

Standing there in the shedrow, the wind tangling his hair, a trick of mind caused Sam to suddenly smell the aroma of spicy Cuban tobacco, and if anyone had been there to see him, the wild look in his eyes, they would have thought Sam Jack had lost his mind.

3

The track was labeled *sloppy* for Tuesday's races, and Sam and Vance Reed—whose classes had been canceled for the afternoon—stood by the finish wire watching the field of horses splash down the backstretch of the third race. The *three and up allowance* race, non-winners of two races since April 20th, had attracted a solid field of nine, and these proven runners weren't disappointing the fans: eight lengths covered the field, it was a battle royal of veteran thoroughbreds doing what they loved to do. The two speed horses were locked in a dual, and they set fractions of 22:4 for the quarter, and 46:2 for the half. Because of the hard rains, every time the horses put down a hoof they were going right down to the bottom, the very foundation of the racing surface. It was like running on water poured over cement. Now as the field swept into the far turn, a horse made a move from out of the pack behind the speed, saving ground on the rail and moving up to third. Except for the two horses in front, the field was so covered with mud that it was impossible to see numbers on the saddle towels, or see the colors of silks.

"That's Bamalam, isn't it, Sam," Vance said, excitement in his voice, "moving up third on the inside?"

"No, that's not Taylor," Sam answered. "I know the way he *sits* a horse...that's not him."

The track announcer: "Through the turn, It's Cumberland Road and Sunflare, side by side, and on the inside making a run is"—even the announcer using binoculars was having trouble identifying horses—"I believe that's Wolfhound on the inside..."

The speed horses came into the stretch nose to nose, drifting off the rail as they *switched leads,* and the horse making a run on the inside made a move to run up into the opening hole on the rail. But now a horse rocketed out of the pack to come up on the outside of the front runners and keep them from drifting. After some bumping, the hole closed on the inside before it was open. The jockey on the outside horse executed the move with precision. He'd maintained a straight course. It was the speed horses that came out, caused the bumping, and then altered course back to the inside. The rider on Wolfhound had to *stand up* and *check* his horse so hard that the thoroughbred threw his head up and opened his mouth so his teeth looked like piano keys.

The track announcer: "Wolfhound denied racing room on the inside! Bamalam charging with a quick burst of speed on the outside!"

"Now that's Taylor," Sam said, swinging his arm and snapping his fingers. "Come on with that horse, jock, come on with that horse."

Three horses came down the stretch nose to nose. Taylor was using his right-handed whip, and each time Bamalam's head came up, Taylor swung, hitting Bamalam *in stride.* Taylor was in perfect sync with his horse, and like it always did, it thrilled Sam to see a top rider going about his work. The crowd in the grandstand and clubhouse were on their feet, and the sound their merging voices made roared in Sam's ears. Sam was still snapping his fingers and shouting. Inside the eighth pole, Sunflare *spit the bit* and it was just Cumberland Road and Bamalam driving for the wire.

The track announcer: "Sunflare is out of it! They're in the final sixteenth! Cumberland Road is desperate to hold the lead! Bamalam right alongside in a furious battle! It's Cumberland Road and Bamalam, nose to nose! It's Cumberland Road and Bamalam, it's Bamalam and Cumberland Road. Here's the wire! A dramatic finish…it's…"

In their drive for the wire, both horses moved swift and faultless in their strides, running with the grace centuries of breeding had given them.

The track announcer: "…too close to call! It's Cumberland Road or Bamalam in a photo finish!"

"I think we won it, Sam," Vance said, raising his voice happily. "I think you *broke your maiden* with the barn today."

Sam watched Taylor as he pulled up Bamalam, letting Bamalam gallop out and come to a slow stop on the backstretch. Taylor and Bamalam were covered with slop. Taylor removed the pair of goggles over his eyes, let them dangle around his neck with several other mud-spattered pairs, then turned Bamalam and came back around the clubhouse turn in an easy jog. Where the goggles had been was the only clean place on Taylor's face. Taylor didn't even glance at the winner's circle or the tote board, he kept going, back to where the losing horses were unsaddled in front of the paddock.

"No, we didn't win it," Sam said, shaking his head. "Taylor knows; he doesn't need a photo to tell him anything."

Vance put his hands on his hips and swung his shoulders in a small tantrum. "Damn it," he said. "I hope you win one soon, you don't have that much longer to stay with us. We run two tomorrow, and both have a shot, and then there's the big race Saturday...Mutineer won't let you down, Sam."

"We'll win one soon," Sam said. Then, putting aside his disappointment: "Would you hurry down and tell Taylor he did a great job. I'll meet you back at the barn in a bit, I've got some business to take care of."

"Sure thing, Sam," Vance answered.

17. THE DEACON

No one knew the bookmaker's real name, he was just The Deacon. He always dressed in black and carried a *Bible*, though why he carried it was another of his secrets. The only time anyone had ever seen the *Bible* open was when The Deacon accidently dropped it. The Deacon was bald, and the features of his oblong face were strangely exaggerated. The lobes of his ears hung loose and fleshy, his nose looked like the Horn of Africa, and the cleft in his broad chin was so deep a razor couldn't reach bottom. The clump of hair that grew out of this cleft appeared to be the nest of some animal that had made The Deacon's chin its home. The Deacon was blind in his right eye, and that eye had the shine of a gray marble, at its core a faint circle of iris. Once you saw The Deacon, you never forgot him.

The Deacon was famous for two things. The first was that no bet was too big. He'd once taken a one hundred thousand dollar bet to win on Sing Song in the Bermuda Stakes at Caribbean Park in Miami. Sing Song had run seventeen times in his racing career and had won seventeen races. The day The Deacon took the *plunger's* bet, Sing Song ran last. Even more impressive was the second reason the Deacon was famous. The Deacon was the only man Bill Baker was afraid of.

There on the third floor of the grandstand, where he could always be found by gamblers, The Deacon stood out away from everyone else. He heard footsteps behind him and swiveled to meet them. The messy, long-haired man who approached was bettor 219. All bettors were assigned a number, and behind that number was another number with a plus or minus in front of it. The minus numbers were always followed by more numbers, a date and time representing when the gambler needed to payoff. All this information The Deacon kept in his head. Nothing was ever written down for the IBI—the Illinois Bureau of Investigation—to find. The Deacon presently had the information of 456 bettors in his head. If the professors of the mathematics department at MIT could have looked inside The Deacon's head and seen what his brain could do with numbers, the calculations he could do instantly, they would have been humbled.

The long-haired man stopped, looked around with quick, jerky movements of his head, then put his hands in his pockets, said, "In the ninth, the four horse, five hundred to win—"

"219, minus 2,210, 5/12/78, by 1:00 P.M," The Deacon interrupted in a cold mechanical voice.

"But—"

The Deacon interrupted again by repeating himself, then swiveled away so his back was to 219.

219 said, "Please don't come to the house, I'll have your money."

The Deacon swiveled back to look at 219. His good eye narrowed, and in an eerie way that could make anyone shiver, the gray marble eye spun slowly in its socket. 219 said nothing else, just hurried away with his hands in his pockets.

Other footsteps approached, and The Deacon swiveled to meet them. A young man came toward him, and the face beneath the blond hair registered as number 97. But in The Deacon's head, behind a large minus number, and a date and time long expired, was the word deceased. The Deacon's gray marble eye gave one quick spin, then stayed twisted in its socket so only a small arc of iris was visible in the corner of his eye. The Deacon was able to make *book* only because he *kicked up* a percentage to Antonio Belichio. It was a stable relationship, and the protection he received from Belichio against other crime bosses was good for business, but 97, Henry Jack, was a sore spot. Belichio had gotten in a hurry, terminated 97's account without giving The Deacon a chance to collect. As the young version of 97 approached him, The Deacon's mind was deftly doing a calculation that had nothing to do with numbers. He quickly calculated no danger. The young version of 97 stopped in front of The Deacon, looked into the twisted gray marble eye, then stared into The Deacon's working eye.

"I'm Sam Jack and I need to get in touch with Bill Baker. I need to get him a message ASAP."

The Deacon moved not a finger. He stared back at Sam with his working eye. Sam put a hand over his mouth, gave a quick cough, looked all around him, then back at The Deacon. Sam started to repeat himself.

"I'm Sam Jack and I'm looking for—"

"Bill Baker?" The Deacon interrupted, an odd vibration in his mechanical voice. "I don't know any Bill Bakers."

Sam stared at The Deacon, a long silence passed, and in that silence, the twisted gray marble eye straightened, focused cloudy investigation on Sam. Sam pulled air into his lungs, released it so his chest heaved with impatience. Sam turned, started to walk away, said over his shoulder, "I'll get hold of *mac* at Noah's, Irene will know—"

"Know this," The Deacon interrupted, "you don't get in touch with Baker, Baker gets in touch with you."

Sam stopped, turned around, faced The Deacon. "Tell Bill—"

"I've got all the information I need," The Deacon said.

Sam walked away, and as he did, The Deacon registered Sam as number 457. Numbers began to appear behind 457, numbers transferred from behind 97. The Deacon began to calculate, adding and multiplying, and the number behind 457 became a large number that grew larger because of time and *juice*. When the calculations finally ceased, The Deacon's gray marble eye spun slowly, then stayed twisted in its socket once again.

Came the shuffle of approaching footsteps, and The Deacon swiveled to meet them.

18. SAM

Late Thursday morning, Sam sat behind the desk in the shedrow office on the phone with Bentley.

"Mutineer blew out in 36 flat," Sam said, "and came back bouncing. Clay said he had a lot of horse under him."

"Saturday can't come soon enough," Bentley replied. "I'm so very excited about the handicap...I'm excited about how well all the horses are doing."

"Haven't won you a race yet," Sam answered, a note of disappointment in his voice.

"Not to worry," Bentley insisted, "you've got at least another week before Joshua comes in, and all these seconds and thirds we're running will soon put us in the winner's circle."

Sam moved on to a new subject: "I wanted to talk to you about the filly Danube."

"She's the little bay three-year-old?"

"Right. She's been running for a *tag* in the maiden filly races, showing a little speed, but getting beat double-digits."

"She hasn't been doing well for us," Bentley said. "Do you have a plan?"

"The maiden fillies for twenty-five thousand claiming are tough races, a lot of nice fillies on the grounds. The *open* three and up non-winners of two in a lifetime for fifteen to eighteen thousand claiming is coming up a lot easier. Yesterday it was won by a four-year-old colt who's had twenty-two lifetime starts and ran for eighty-five hundred last time out."

"Run Danube where you wish, Sam. *Drop* her down."

"I think she'll show her speed against those cheap horses, that she'll go right to the front and run away from the colts and geldings chasing her."

Bentley laughed then. "I almost feel badly for little Danube, being pursued by all those boys. She better be quick."

Sam laughed along with Bentley said, "I put her *in* for Saturday already, Bentley."

"Very good," Bentley answered, "Talk to you soon, Sam. Good-bye."

"Bye, Bentley."

Sam got up from behind the desk, walked over to the training board, and picked up the magic marker. He pulled the top off the marker, and at the bottom of the list of horses printed: black colt. The magic marker squeaked as he put a G for gallop on Friday and a *W* for work on Saturday. He stood looking at it for a moment, then erased everything he'd just written. Sam had just sat back down behind the desk when Clay Repp walked into the office. He took off his helmet, ran his fingers through sweat-damp hair.

"Damn, Sam, Mutineer worked good. He's exactly like I remember him as a two-year-old. Just a happy horse who flat out loves what he does. He looked back at me today, at about the quarter pole, like he was saying 'are you going to let me run or what?' He was so willing to do so much more, and I think he was pissed at me when I pulled him up in the 36 you wanted."

"He looked back at you?"

"Oh yeah, just like he did when he ran in the Juvenile. Just before the three-eighths pole he looked back at me, and boy, when I *clucked* to him and let a notch out on the reins, he turned into a rocket ship. I've never been on a horse that pushes as hard as he does. When he really goes to running, he gives this grunt every time he pushes off with those hind legs, at least he did when he was a *baby*."

Sam slanted his mouth into a sly smile. "Doesn't sound as if you like Mutineer much," he said.

Clay tossed his head, laughed. "He's just a great horse, so much personality." Now Clay frowned, said, "Why didn't Taylor show up to get on him?"

"I've got my suspicions why," Sam said.

Clay grinned. "You know those *pin heads.*" Then Clay sobered, changed the topic: "That black colt I *shedrowed* today...something odd about him. He looks the part, but he's so skittish, and...I don't want to disappoint you, but I don't think he's much of a racehorse."

"He's in new surroundings, he'll be okay. We need to get him okayed by the *starter* tomorrow, and on Saturday I want you here early, say around four...I want to work him five-eights."

"Sure thing," Clay answered.

"We should *school* him in the paddock tomorrow too."

Carol Vincent, Taylor Howard's agent, was suddenly in the door. She had a condition book in one hand, and Saturday's *overnight* in the other. Carol looked into Sam's face but carefully avoided direct eye contact. Carol was nervous, and Sam took note of it, was positive he knew why.

"Mutineer got the seven hole," Carol said.

"Good as any," Sam said.

"Danube got in too, the three post in the fifth, and so did that new black colt. He's in the first, coming out of the ten spot."

Clay looked at Sam, surprise on his face. "The new colt's in Saturday?"

Sam glanced at Clay, briefly straight in his eyes, and Clay understood. He dropped the subject of the black colt.

Carol handed Sam the overnight and he scanned the horses in the handicap. Taylor was named on Mutineer, and he was also named on the California ship-in, Obedient, the probable betting favorite. Obedient was trained by Ben Foltz. Foltz trained for several Hollywood movie stars and had enough horses in training to fill a racing card all by himself. Sam looked at Carol and smiled.

"Now I know why Taylor didn't show up to work Mutineer...you going to *spin* me, Carol?"

"I know I gave you the *call,* Sam, and I'm sorry about Taylor not showing this morning, but I didn't know Foltz was going to *name us on.* Foltz usually rides DaSilva—"

"You don't need to lay a story on me, Carol," Sam broke in. He put the overnight aside and his smile became a grin. "If you can't spin your friends, who can you spin? You can ride who you want, and anyway, I've got a backup rider."

"Who?" Carol asked.

"Same jock who broke Mutineer's maiden and won the Juvenile on him at Suburban."

Clay's mouth dropped open.

"I can't remember that far back," Carol said.

"Clay Repp," Sam answered.

Clay's eyes looked ready to pop right out of his head.

2

Carol was gone, and Sam was hitting the top of the desk with both his open hands, laughing happily.

"But, Sam," Clay said, the quick sharp notes of his voice told of his shock, "I haven't ridden a race in years."

Sam calmed, folded his hands together, said, "When I tell you to work a horse in 36, the horse works in 36. Not 36:1, not 35:4, but 36. You haven't lost that clock in your head."

"But Sam, I'd have a tough time tacking"—Clay hesitated, looked up as if to consult the ceiling—"a tough time tacking *20.*"

"20 is fine, Mutineer carries 23."

Clay looked out the door to where the old gelding had his head out over the webbing. Mutineer had hay sticking out his mouth as he slowly munched a snack. Mutineer had his eyes set on Clay. It was like the old gelding knew he was being talked about.

"Wow," Clay said, turning back to Sam and recovering from his shock, "I feel like a kid on Christmas…thanks for having confidence in me, Sam."

"Bentley lets me do what I want with these horses, and I'll

always do what's best for them and best for Mr. and Mrs. Keene. So, unless Obedient scratches, I think what's best for Mutineer is for me to put a rider in the saddle who knows him, who's won races on him."

Clay sat quietly, looking up at the trophies on their shelf, then looked back at Sam. "I've been thinking about a comeback for a while now, but I wanted to get my drinking under control first, didn't want to make a fool of myself by asking an agent to take my *book* and have them laugh at me. I swear, Sam, I never dreamed of asking you to ride me on one of these horses...the Keene horses just seemed out of reach."

"I watched you do a miracle with Matchbook in one morning," Sam said, "and have watched you do miracles on other horses for years. There's not a rider in the jock's room of this racetrack who looks better on a horse than you do, not a jock I'd trust more with a good horse. Today, when Taylor didn't show, I was actually glad. You know how most riders are, their mind is on speed, and I was afraid Taylor would let Mutineer go too fast. Last night I had a dream, I dreamed Taylor let Mutineer blow out in 34 and change—"

"The old gelding could have done that easy this morning," Clay interrupted. "He was just waiting for me to move my hands. He's a good old horse, Sam...he'll win Saturday."

Sam smiled, nodded, put his hands behind his head and leaned back in the chair. "I know he's going to win, I know he's going to win just like I know the black colt is going to get beat by twenty lengths."

19. CLAY REPP

On Saturday, just before noon, Clay walked up the stairs to the Jock's Room with a gym bag that held his tack. Arthur Keats, the Clerk of Scales, sat behind the desk at the door. Keats, a ruddy-faced middle-aged man whose once blond hair was mostly gray, looked up when Clay entered. He looked so surprised he seemed about to sneeze.

"Good Lord Almighty!" Keats said in a loud voice. "Behold you unbelievers, it is the second coming."

Clay smiled awkwardly and after he signed in, Keats grabbed him by the hand and shook it.

"It's good to see you back in the irons, Clay," Keats said, smiling broadly.

"Thanks, Art," Clay answered.

Now several valets, busy polishing boots and saddles spread out over long tables, began to shout out their hellos. One valet stood looking at Clay, his hands on his hips. Rudy Sharpe's face was a mass of wrinkles, but shining out of that face were friendly blue eyes.

"Who is that, Art," Rudy said, "a new *bug boy*?"

"The only bug in here is the one up your ass," Clay shot back.

Clay dropped his gym bag and opened his arms, and he and Rudy, his valet for fifteen years before he stopped riding, exchanged rib-breaking hugs. Rudy stepped back, looked Clay up and down. A grin pulled his wrinkled face wide.

"You're tacking twenty," Rudy said, "you fat son-of-a-bitch."

"You nailed it," Clay said.

"I saw you named on in the handicap, and I've got a spot for your stuff over here in the corner." Rudy snatched Clay's bag from the floor and led the way, said, "This is just like old times, Clay, you on a good horse in the big race."

Rudy got Clay settled in, and then Clay walked through a door into the jock's kitchen. A man in his sixties was busy working over the grill and watching over steaming pots on the stove. There were two jockeys sitting at the counter, putting enough food away to feed ten people, and a group of riders sat at a table, cards in their hands, concentrating on their game of racehorse rummy.

"Hey, George," Clay called out, "fix me a pork chop sandwich."

"I know that voice," George said. When George turned around and spotted Clay, he did a double take, then a grin made his white teeth standout in his black face. "My god, that is Clay Repp." Now George began to shake his head and his grin turned into a frown. "You're too old to ride, get the fuck out of my kitchen." George looked at the jockeys sitting at his counter, pointed a wooden spoon at them, then pointed the spoon at Clay. "You boys, you help that old man who just came wandering in here, it's obvious he's got the Alzheimers."

"Shut the fuck up, George," Clay fired back, "and get me that sandwich, I haven't had a good pork chop since the last time I ate right here in this kitchen."

George came hurrying out from behind the counter, wiping his hands on the short white apron tied around his waist. He exaggerated licking and smacking his lips. "You got to give me a kiss first, Clay," George said, giving Clay his best pervert-in-the-schoolyard look, "a great big kiss, you good-looking mother fucker."

George began to chase Clay around a table, and Clay, dodging and darting just out of George's reach, started yelling for help. Everyone in the room roared laughter, even the jocks playing rummy at a dollar a point.

The Clerk of Scales came into the room, Art Keats said, "God damn it, George, stop trying to fuck poor Clay and get me some of that beef stew I smell."

George stopped chasing Clay, looked at Keats, said, "Come on, Art, this boy ain't rode a horse in the afternoon in a long time, you know he needs his *seat* fixed."

"Maybe so," Art said, sitting down at a table with two jockeys, "but I need me some of that stew…chop, chop."

And just like that, Clay Rep was welcomed back to the Jockey's Room.

2

Clay sat at a table and ate his pork chop sandwich. He'd almost forgotten what it was like, the jock's room. The restless energy, the loud laughter, the occasional arguments, the conversations about horses, the way jocks slapped each other on the back and laughed while they teased George the cook. When one of the riders coming and going around him stopped to shake his hand and welcome him back, Clay smiled happily and told them how much he appreciated their good wishes. When the first race went into the gate, Clay watched the black colt run and get beat the twenty lengths Sam had predicted. The black colt finished last. Why Sam had worked the colt just that morning was of no concern to Clay. When you worked for a horseman like Sam, you never questioned how he trained his horses, you just rode them to win in the afternoon.

After watching the black colt run, Clay wanted to get away from the noise and activity of the main jock's room, and he told Rudy he was going to lay down in the *sleeping room* for the next three races. In a dark room with several sets of bunkbeds, Clay climbed up into a top bunk and closed his eyes. He hadn't had a drink since last night, and then only a long swallow to empty the last bottle of vodka in his tack room. Lying there, he felt a tremor go through him. When he thought of seven more races without a drink, anxiety made his stomach roll. Then thoughts of Mutineer, and the big chance Sam had given him, caused an excitement that made everything else he felt unimportant.

Clay got up in time to watch Danube run the best race of her career. The three-year-old filly led every step of the way, the colts and geldings chasing behind her, and she just got nosed out at the wire. Another second for Sam, and while the filly's performance was only proof that Sam knew where to place horses and how to use a condition book, Clay knew Sam was growing tired of seconds and thirds. After the sixth race, Clay stripped and sat in his corner with a towel around his waist. The muscles across his shoulders and in his legs were hard and strong, and his hands were scarred and calloused in odd places...the hands of a jockey.

Way before the seventh race left the paddock, Clay was dressed and ready to ride. White nylon pants, polished Kroop jock boots, the black and gold Keene racing silks. He studied himself in the mirror, and he saw not a deeply lined leathery face, but the fresh pink face of a boy of sixteen. He stared into the sparkling brown eyes of the boy he once was and to himself said, I remember you, you were a good rider, and I could sure use your help today. The boy in the mirror smiled and nodded, and Clay swore he heard the boy say, I'll be there when you need me, Clay. Clay felt a rush of emotion, and the young face vanished beyond the shimmering flood that blurred his vision. Clay wiped at his eyes, and it was then that he heard someone clear their throat, heard the unpleasant sound of snickering meant to belittle.

Clay turned around, and across the room, three young riders he didn't even know were looking at him grinning. There was no friendship in their grins. One of the riders, a boy with a mouth too small for his big square teeth, suddenly pretended to fall off the trunk he was sitting on. He lay there on the floor, his arms and legs waving in the air as if he couldn't get up. Clay recognized himself drunk and on the floor at the Knotty Pine. It was then that a boot sailed by Clay's head, a hard-thrown boot that hit the young rider on the floor with a loud smack. The young rider scrambled to his feet, but knew better than to challenge Rudy Sharpe, to even say anything that might make the old valet even angrier.

"You *no stock* pieces of shit," came Rudy's voice from behind Clay, "ain't any of you fit to clean this man's tack."

Clay turned and smiled at Rudy, said, "Easy there old timer, you'll pop an artery."

Rudy glared at the three young riders, breathing hard through his open mouth, and they moved further across the room, looking over their shoulders to make sure Rudy wasn't on the attack. Rudy twitched with anger as he watched them retreat.

"The one I hit with the boot is Don Bloom," Rudy spit his words, still seething, "he's on the three horse in the handicap. He's a *white-knuckle rider,* so bounce him off the rail if you get a shot, make the mother fucker's ass hole pucker."

A grin tightened Clay's face, and it was then that a surge of nausea hit him. When he put a hand over his mouth, he began to shake so badly he swore he could hear his own bones rattle. Clay struggled briefly with the shakes, then got control of himself and glanced around, looking for anything with alcohol in it. His eyes settled on a big bottle of Scope mouthwash that Rudy kept for his riders. Rudy followed Clay's line of sight.

"That's for the *flippers,*" Rudy said, "it's to wash away the taste of puke. It's not for a jock to drink, a jock trying to make a comeback."

A long cramp gripped Clay's bowel, and the nausea increased. "Just talk to me, Rudy, get me through the next few minutes. Once I'm down in the paddock, I'll be alright."

Rudy nodded, began to talk, grinning as he did. "Did I ever tell you the one about the six-legged horse who needed a three-legged jock to ride him? Well they had to look all over the world, and finally found a three-legged jock riding giraffes at a racetrack in Africa..."

Clay was already smiling, and Rudy fired jokes at him over the next few minutes that kept him smiling and laughing even though he'd heard every one of the jokes a dozen times. Somehow, in the four years he'd been gone, every one of Rudy's jokes had become funnier. In no time it seemed Clay was going down the steps to the paddock, and just as he predicted, he became so focused that his hands had steadied and the nausea became unimportant, all he could think about was Mutineer. As Clay's valet, Rudy had helped Sam saddle Mutineer, and now as Rudy and Clay walked by each other in the paddock, Rudy whispered, "You're not just a jock, you're a race rider, and don't forget it."

Clay fixed his eyes on Mutineer, and as he walked up to where the old gelding was saddled and waiting for him, Mutineer lowered his head and dug at the ground with a front hoof. With Race-hardened muscles working beneath his chestnut coat, Mutineer gave off a coppery shimmer. There was about the old gelding an air of power, as if inside him was an engine with pistons and cylinders. Clay came to a stop by Mutineer, and he and the old gelding began a wordless conversation, an ancient conversation repeated over and over across the centuries between horses and riders, a conversation older than any racetrack, older than any saddle.

Bentley interrupted the exchange, and like he was coming out of a spell, Clay turned to Bentley and blinked.

"I'm so pleased you're riding my horse today, Clay," Bentley said, shifting his cane to his left hand and offering his right.

Clay took Bentley's hand and briefly shook it. "Mutineer means a lot to me, Mr. Keene. I won't let you down, sir."

Sam said, "I don't need to tell you how to ride this horse, Clay."

"We'll make our run late, Sam," Clay answered.

Sam nodded, said, "There's lots of speed, it'll back up."

The paddock judge, a stout, pop-eyed man, gave his familiar command: "Riders up!"

Sam gave Clay a leg up, and Mary Linwood, Mutineer's groom, led the gelding away to join the line of horses leaving the paddock. Mary's ponytail bounced as she stepped along. To Clay, the ten-minute post parade seemed to last an hour, but only once did the nausea become almost too much. It was when the pony boy, Cal Davis—a tobacco-chewing cowboy from Oklahoma—handed Mutineer over to an assistant starter to be loaded into the gate. Just as Clay pulled down a pair of goggles over his eyes, he leaned over in the saddle and gave a short retch. Neither Cal Davis or the assistant starter even noticed, but Don Bloom on the three horse did.

"You're lookin' a little green around the gills, old man," Bloom called out.

Clay ignored Bloom, only had time for his horse, and once in the gate, he twined his fingers into the reins, grabbed a fistful of Mutineer's mane and set himself.

The bell rang, the gate slammed open, and the field was away.

In a great bound Mutineer left the gate, and in the next few strides the speed horses, three of them, were up ahead, spread across the track, kicking dirt back at the rest of the field. Jockeys yelled, there was the pop of whips, the slapping of reins. The other horses were around Clay and Mutineer only briefly, then they were racing away, and now Clay let Mutineer settle into an easy stride that left them in last place. All Clay's weight was balanced on his toes in the irons, his elbows were to his knees, his head still, his back parallel to the ground. He held the reins in a long hold. The clock in Clay's head started the moment he left the gate, and everything he did he measured in the tick of that clock. Clay and Mutineer glided over to the rail, and Clay felt nothing of the nausea, didn't think about any of his troubles, what tomorrow held, he only thought of the here and now, about being on Mutineer in the mile and one-quarter Chicago Handicap. The clock in Clay's head told him the speed horses had run the first quarter in 22:4, and now the half in 45:4. Clay calculated that fifteen lengths separated Mutineer from the two horses in front, and he felt a smile working his lips...the speed would burn out fast at this pace.

Through the stretch the first time, Clay was vaguely aware of the murmur and cheers that came from the grandstand and clubhouse, then the speed horses came out of the clubhouse turn and reached the three-quarters and Clay registered 1:10:2. One of the speed horses had already dropped out of it, and now as he and Mutineer straightened out for the run down the backstretch two other horses put pressure on the lead horses. Beneath Clay, Mutineer coiled and then uncoiled, again and again, with a grace that involved tendons, ligaments, and muscles big and small. With the half-mile pole behind them, the old gelding looked back at Clay for the first time, pricking his ears, but Clay sat still in the saddle and didn't move his hands, keeping a long hold of the reins.

"Not yet, big horse," Clay said above the snapping of black and gold silks, the muffled pounding of Mutineers hooves, the deep roll of Mutineer's breathing.

Down the backstretch, Mutineer began to pass tired horses, two of them, then another, and the old gelding grew impatient to run, jerking his head up and down and pulling on the reins. Clay leaned back in the irons and didn't change his hold. The reins bit into his hands, his arms began to burn. Clay talked to Mutineer, telling him to hold on, it was almost time, and the old gelding seemed to listen and settled. Now at the three-eighths pole, Mutineer pricked his ears and turned his head just enough to look back at Clay again.

"Now!" Clay shouted. He slapped the reins at the old gelding, threw a new cross in the reins, got low in the saddle. "Yaaaaaa!"

The old gelding pinned his ears, and when he next pushed off with his rear hooves, Clay heard him give a hard grunt. Not the high-pitched grunt of a two-year-old learning to be a racehorse, but the deep ferocious grunt of a racehorse at the top of his game. Mutineer went from idle into drive in two powerful strides. Clay and Mutineer blew by other horses, and Clay saw a blur of bright colored silks, saw riders pitching and moving on their horses, heard hard snaps as riders worked their horses over with the whip.

Then came the three-sixteenth pole, and there was nowhere to go.

Clay couldn't get Mutineer to the outside, there were horses already there, one of them Obedient, the six-to-five favorite, with Taylor Howard belly-down, race riding for all he was worth. And now the wall of horses in front of Clay and Mutineer was coming back fast. Clay had no choice, he went to reach for Mutineer, to check him to avoid *clipping heels,* but now the inside horse of the wall began to tire badly and come off the rail. Clay threw a new cross in the reins, gripped it with both hands to get a better hold of Mutineer's head, and began to push on the old gelding, asking him to lengthen his stride and run even harder. Clay shouted at Mutineer and with his whip still in the down position tapped the old gelding on the shoulder. Up through the saddle Clay could feel Mutineer's heart speed up, and the old gelding lowered his head and delivered a burst of acceleration. Giving a ferocious grunt each time he pushed off, Mutineer was all out, was giving Clay everything he had, and in the next three strides Mutineer took Clay to that place of risk and danger. The old gelding powered his way up into a hole not big enough for a child's pony. Clay's boot skimmed the rail, and as he passed the horse on the outside of him, there was the loud click of irons striking each other.

"Crazy fuck!" Clay heard a rider shout and saw the number three on a saddle towel.

And then they were clear, only an empty racetrack and the wire was ahead. In that moment, Clay loved Mutineer more than he'd ever loved any other horse, and with the love of the sport inside them both, the love of riding and running in their hearts, Clay and Mutineer hit the wire to win the Chicago Handicap by five lengths.

The clock in Clay's head stopped at 2:01:3.

Clay let Mutineer gallop out a long distance after the wire, not pulling the old gelding up until they were halfway down the backside. Clay breathed heavily from his effort. Once he had Mutineer stopped, he turned the old gelding so he faced the grandstand and clubhouse. The cheers and shouts had diminished after the wire, and at this distance the sounds from the big Saturday crowd were murmurs that rose and fell. Clay sat listening and thinking about what he'd just done. The inside had opened up and he hadn't hesitated. Beaming happily, Clay gave a wordless shout...*He hadn't hesitated.*

All Clay did was lean forward and lift the reins with both hands, and Mutineer turned and began to jog back the way they'd come. The old gelding knew his way to the winner's circle. The other horses hadn't gone as far as Clay and Mutineer and were already back in front of the paddock being unsaddled. When Clay entered the winner's circle, he looked up at the stewards, the racing judges, high in their stand above the finish wire, and raised his whip to salute them. He felt himself glowing, glowing with the fluorescence of the brown-eyed sixteen-year-old in the mirror, the teenage boy he once was. Approving voices rose up all around Clay and Mutineer in the winner's circle, and the fans that crowded around the winner's circle behind the white-plank fence filled the air with noise. While the announcer called out that Mutineer was trained by Sam Jack, owned by Keene Racing Stable and ridden to victory by Clay Repp, a fresh volley of cheers and applause came from the grandstand and clubhouse.

"No stick and only three ticks off the track record," Sam said happily, smiling the broadest smile Clay had ever seen him smile. "You never once uncocked your stick, you hand-rode this horse all the way."

"I didn't need to hit him, Sam," Clay answered. "Every time I asked him, Mutineer gave me everything he had to give."

Mutineer's groom, the blue-jeaned Mary, clipped a shank to the bit and began to bring Mutineer around for the track photographer to take the win photo. She talked happily to the old gelding, telling him she loved him and what a great horse he was.

Bentley was bubbling. "Congratulations, Clay. What a jockey, what a racehorse!"

Clay repeated, "What a racehorse," and leaned over and hugged the old gelding's neck.

Bentley said, "Sam, I never interfere with your decisions, but if you were to ask this jockey to ride *first call* for me, I would be delighted. I'd love to see him ride every horse I own."

Clay looked down at Bentley, his mouth open, his eyes wide.

Sam said, "You heard it, Clay. Will you ride first call for Mr. Keene?"

At this moment of supreme joy, Clay looked at the crowd of fans surrounding the winner's circle, searching for two faces: the faces of his wife, Doris, and his little boy, Tommy. He could only hope the hope that somehow Doris had seen that he was named on Mutineer and had come out to the track to watch him, bringing little Tommy. Clay sought their faces, and when he couldn't find them the disappointment was sharp, but then he was smiling happily down at Sam who stood looking up at him with one hand on Mutineer's quarters.

"I'd be honored to ride first call for Mr. Keene, Sam," Clay said. Then he looked at Bentley. "You don't know how much this means to me, sir."

"Oh, I think I do," Bentley said with a wink.

Bentley reached up a hand toward Clay and Clay leaned over and shook it, then Clay shook Sam's hand, and now everyone, including Mutineer, looked into the lens of the photographer's camera.

The first rat Clay saw was on the scales.

Mutineer had been unsaddled, the crowd was drifting away, and Clay had the saddle in his arms, ready to weigh out for the Clerk of Scales. Now that the adrenaline was wearing off, he felt the sickness in him rising, the nausea trying to reach the back of his throat. Art Keats was smiling at him, and Clay abruptly stopped short of the scales and stared down at the gray sewer rat. Clay looked back up at Art, a look of shock on his face, but when he looked back down at the scales, the rat was gone.

"What the hell?" Clay said. "Did you see that rat, Art?"

Art only laughed. "Get on the scales, jokester, let's go, let's go."

After Clay stood on the scales, Art looked up at the Steward's box, and waved his program, signaling to the racing judges that Mutineer had carried the correct weight. When Clay stepped off the scales, he handed the saddle to Rudy. Then he, Art and Rudy got into a station wagon parked on the outside fence near the winner's circle. Art got into the front seat with the driver. Clay and Rudy sat in the backseat.

"Just like old times," Rudy kept saying, his wrinkled face in a grin.

"Did you see that rat, Rudy?" Clay asked.

This registered with Rudy, and suddenly his grin was gone.

The station wagon came to a stop down by the paddock, and Clay, Art and Rudy got out. It was while Clay walked through the paddock toward the stairs that he saw the second rat, and then the third, and then a hundred. By the time Clay got up the stairs to the jock's room, he was hysterical, and he ran to his corner and looked all around him wild-eyed and sweating. That he was shaking and sick meant nothing, it was the rats that had him freaked out, and now spiders appeared, big black hair-legged spiders. There in his corner, the rats turned into yellow-eyed monsters that chattered at him, spitting bits of foam from their mouths as they did. And the spiders, huge hand-sized spiders, began to crawl toward him across the ceiling, and now the rats were running up his pant legs and Clay began to whirl helplessly, spinning in the middle of the attacking rats and spiders. And the horde of frights kept coming, the fanged and hairy horrors, and Clay was screaming like his lungs might burst, driven to insanity by fright.

"Help me, Rudy...Art...George. Oh, God, help me."

George the cook came running, and with one look, said, "It's the DTs, somebody call an ambulance." George grabbed Clay. "Help me, Rudy," George said, wrestling a struggling Clay to the floor, "help me hold Clay down, if we don't, he'll jump right out a fuckin' window."

And the rats chattered and the spiders crawled and Clay screamed.

20. SAM

Sam was in the white Rolls Royce with Bentley, parked by the barn. They'd just returned from Berwyn General Hospital. Randolph, the chauffeur—always stiff, formal, silent unless spoken to—sat in the front seat behind the wheel. He gazed straight ahead, out the windshield, responding as he always did to Mr. Keene's conversations: as if he heard nothing, as if he was deaf.

"I'm not sure what they gave him," Bentley said, turned in the backseat talking to Sam, "but I was relieved that he was calmed when we got to the emergency room. The scene described by his valet was harrowing...poor Clay."

"Your generosity is amazing, Bentley," Sam said.

Bentley looked down at the floor, saddened, said, "Many believe that men like me breathe a different air, that I'm not subject to the same calls of nature as everyone else. But that's not true, Sam, we're all the same, each and every one of us, and I'm more than familiar with alcohol and drug abuse. My boy, Charles..." Bentley's voice faded away, a strange glow came to his eyes, then he turned back to Sam: "This New Hope Recovery Center I'm having Clay transferred to is a marvelous facility. In thirty days he'll be a new man, and I hope your mind hasn't changed about riding him first call, I know mine hasn't. At this point I doubt we'll ever see Fernando DaSilva again, and Clay will need us, he'll need these horses to complete his recovery when he's released."

"First call it is," Sam said.

"Isn't it amazing that Clay got all that run out of Mutineer without ever hitting him with the whip?"

"It is amazing...but good jocks like Clay do amazing things with horses every day."

"Indeed, indeed," Bentley said, "and now I should be off. Have a good remainder of your evening, Sam, and I'm thrilled about Mutineer."

Sam got out of the car, looked back at Bentley before he closed the door. "I have one thing to say before you leave, Bentley, and that's to tell you that we're not all the same...I've never in my life met a man as good-hearted as you."

With that Bentley nodded, grinned, and Sam closed the door. With the smooth roar of a high-performance engine, Bentley was swept away by the Rolls Royce.

Sam walked under the shedrow. Mutineer was long back from the detention barn and in his stall. The old gelding had been to his water bucket, and when he came to his webbing, water dripped from his muzzle. He looked at Sam, blinked, then looked down the shedrow to where the pair of barn swallows who had built their nest above the feed room were scolding a big orange tomcat. The tomcat sat on his haunches in the middle of the shedrow, looking up at the swallows with great interest. Mutineer was behaving like it was any other evening, that he hadn't, just that afternoon, run the race of his life. Sam walked over to Mutineer, knelt in front of the old gelding, and took the bandages off both his front legs. There was a strong smell of liniment. Now Sam slowly ran his hand down each leg from knee to ankle. Sam replaced the bandages and was smiling when he stood up.

"Not a trace of *filling* or heat," Sam said to Mutineer.

Then Sam heard the phone in the office ringing. He fumbled briefly with keys, then swung open the door and answered the phone.

"Hello," he said.

"Congratulations," came Joshua's voice.

"Mutineer is one hell of a racehorse," Sam said.

"That he is," Joshua answered.

Sam next explained what had happened to Clay and the two men talked about it, then Joshua said, "Clay's tough, he'll come back strong, but we need to talk of other business...we have some planning to do. I've got a bag full of money, and a new horse here."

"When did you get back from the Carolinas?"

"Last night. It was a long but thankfully an uneventful trip."

"Glad to hear it. You know I've run the colt once already."

"Run him again next week, but there is a problem. Emily's taking for granted that I know how to bet this kind of money and not affect track odds. I know how it should be done, but don't have—"

"Leave that to me, I know someone."

"Who?"

"I think the less you know about *who* the better off you are."

"I believe that to be true. Well, run the colt again, and then I'll come and get him. After that, we'll be changing places soon, I'll be there with the Keene horses and ye'll be here running the farm. Ye can wait two or three weeks and then bring me the good colt. How's that for a time schedule?"

Sam glanced down the shedrow. The sudden thought that he'd soon be leaving the Keene horses made him wince and remain silent.

"Sam? Do ye like that time schedule or not?"

Sam broke his silence, answered, "Fine, it sounds fine to me, Josh."

2

Sam and Joshua had talked on for a short time, then Sam left the barn. He headed for the Knotty Pine and dinner. It was Saturday night, *the Pine* was busy, but Sam finally found a parking place two blocks down the street from the bar. He stepped out of the truck. In a tall elm tree Crows squawked the same warnings and complaints over and over, and without thinking or looking, Sam stepped into the street. There was the screech of tires and Sam threw himself backward, sprawling himself flat against his truck, his arms spread wide. The chrome grill of a red Cadillac convertible, with the white top up, had come to a stop just feet away from him. Sam looked behind the wheel of the car and recognized the face of the man dressed in a gray vested suit. The car rolled forward, the passenger's side window rolled down to the sound of a buzz.

"Get in, mac," said Bill Baker.

Sam glanced around to see if there was anyone he knew watching. When there wasn't, he got into the Cadillac.

Baker's lips parted in a grin. "What's wrong, mac," he said, "you don't wanna be seen with me?"

"You almost ran me down," Sam said.

"You almost run down Kincaid all the time," Baker answered.

Sam turned, looked squarely at Baker. "How would you know that?"

Baker's grin widened, and there was nothing friendly in it. "Because I know everything about the people I do business with." Now Baker's grin dissolved, and he gave Sam an intense stare: "And don't forget that, mac."

Sam stared back at Baker. "Call me Sam."

"Sure thing, mac."

Baker hit the gas, and after a short squeal of tires, the Cadillac rolled down the street.

Baker said, "Talk to me."

"I'll have a horse running in the next month, and I want to make a large bet."

"Large? How large?"

"Two hundred thousand, all to win."

Baker had taken a turn to go west on Ogden, and then a turn to go north on Austin. Now he pulled the Cadillac into a Mexican restaurant's parking lot. He parked in the back. A red neon sign glowed in the dusk of the evening: Senor Taco.

Baker looked at Sam, studied him in silence, then said, "Where the fuck did you get that kind of money? The last time I saw you, you were lost and pullin' a broken-down claimer in a beat-up horse van."

"That's none of your concern."

In the voice of a man capable of great violence, Baker said, "Oh, but it is my business. The only way you can make a bet like that is to have cash."

"You don't take credit cards?"

Baker's voice lowered, in it a warning: "Don't fuck with me."

Sam looked out the car window, thought about just getting out, but dismissed that thought. Joshua needed him and there was revenge to be had. He turned back to Baker, said, "Alright, no more jokes. I'll have cash, all two hundred thousand in cash in a couple of weeks."

Baker's eyes lit up like the muzzle flashes of two revolvers. "How do you know I won't take that kind of money and leave you dead somewhere."

"Because this is only the first horse," Sam said, lying. "There'll be more."

A look of amusement replaced the threat of danger in Baker's expression. "Well, if you haven't turned into a golden goose." Baker rumbled a low laugh. "Strange, but when I saw you in Noah's that night, I knew there was just something about you, and when you helped me out—"

Baker suddenly lunged across the seat at Sam, and the look on his face could have driven lions away from a fresh kill. He pinned Sam in the corner, his hands all over him, searching to see what he might be carrying. The last place he searched was Sam's crotch, and he gripped Sam there, squeezing, and Sam uttered a gasp of pain.

"Bring a gun with you, mac?" Baker said, and he put his face close to Sam's. "I remember how handy you were with that shotgun back at Noah's."

Sam's eyes blurred and when they refocused, he could see the hair in the black holes of Baker's nostrils. Baker breathed heavily through his open mouth, blowing breath into Sam's face and Sam turned away from it.

"No, I don't have a gun," Sam answered.

"You better not be fuckin' with me. Now tell me what the fuck is going on here."

Sam tried to move, but couldn't. He let out a small cry when Baker squeezed his crotch harder in a vice-like grip. Baker brought his face even closer to Sam, so close that his lips almost touched Sam's cheek. Baker's breath seemed hot enough to peel skin. When Sam spoke again, his voice was notched up higher than normal: "You said you liked breaking a bookmaker more than sharks love blood."

"What bookmaker you wanna break?"

"Belichio."

Baker let go of Sam, sat back into the driver's seat. A stony quiet came over both men, then Baker said, "You could hurt Belichio with a bet like that, but you're not gonna break him." Baker drummed his fingers on the steering wheel, then went on: "Sorry I got rough with you, mac. Hope you understand, and I hope you understand that you've got my interest."

"Good," Sam answered, and reached down and rearranged himself, pulling on his blue jeans. "How do we bet that kind of money and not affect track odds?"

"You spread it thin, bet it at the last possible minute so the books don't have time to *lay it off.*" Baker was smiling now. "Belichio has betting tied up all through the Midwest. I can spread the money across a dozen states with a hundred different bookmakers who work for that snake-eyed *wop*." Curiosity was in Baker's voice when he asked, "Why do you want to fuck Belichio?"

Sam didn't answer right away; it was like someone had him by the throat. When he did answer, the beat of his heart banged in his ears. Sam said, "He murdered my father."

Baker said nothing to this, he reached into the inside pocket of his jacket. The huge diamond on his hand flickered, a gold watch chain that stretch across the front of his vest gleamed. He took out a pen and small notepad. He scribbled on a sheet of paper, tore the sheet from the pad, handed it to Sam. "Here's the number to call when you've got the money."

Sam took the paper, folded it, put it in his pocket.

Baker started the car, pulled out of the lot, said, "So this has something to do with that bum you ran the other day...Brandt's horse, the one Kincaid brought?"

"I'll give you the horse's name when I give you the money," Sam answered. Then he asked, "What's it going to cost, you arranging all this?"

"Half of everything," Baker answered, "and Belichio only pays up to twenty to one."

"So, I get back two million max?"

"Take it or leave it."

"I'll take it."

In the next few minutes, Baker pulled the Cadillac up next to Sam's truck. Sam opened the door, then looked at Baker. The night had come, and the dashboard lit Baker with a green light. The green light made the ridges and hollows of Baker's face into a Halloween mask.

Baker said, "You do understand that you're gambling more than money here, right, mac?"

Sam didn't respond, he got out of the car, and the Cadillac drove away. Sam stood next to the truck watching the Cadillac's red taillights until they disappeared. Blood pulsed up through the arteries in Sam's neck, putting a painful pressure in his head that made him dizzy. Sam felt like a man on a high wire who's made the mistake of looking down.

3

Mutineer's win in the Chicago Handicap was just the start of a perfect week for Sam and Keene Racing Stable. Voodoo Queen surprised everyone on Tuesday. Sam was only getting a prep race into her for the up-coming opening day Ruffian Stakes at Suburban Park, a mile and one-sixteenth turf event, and wasn't expecting much out of the mare in the seven-furlong allowance race on the dirt. But the mare *fired* and won. Taylor Howard rode her, and he said to Bentley in the winner's circle, "Mr. Keene, this mare just mowed 'em down!" Then on Wednesday a colt named Highland Lad won his non-winners-of-three-in-a-life-time condition, and also on Wednesday the three-year-old filly Queen of Hearts broke her maiden first time out. Then on Saturday, Matchbook ran in a maiden allowance race going a flat mile and won in high style by seven lengths. Everyone was talking about Sam Jack.

Sam stood with Bentley by his truck in the horseman's parking lot behind the racing office. Matchbook had just won, and cars were leaving the lot in a rush to beat the traffic coming out of the main parking lot where the fans parked. Laramie Avenue and Cicero Avenue would soon be snarled in bumper-to-bumper traffic.

Bentley tapped his cane on the asphalt, said, "I'll be in London on business next week, Sam, and with Joshua scheduled to take over from you next Friday, I won't be seeing you again for some time."

"I'll try to keep our streak going, Bentley," Sam said. He wanted to smile, but with the talk of leaving he found it impossible. Sam continued: "It's been a pleasure to work with your horses, Mr. Keene."

Sam offered his hand, and Bentley took it, said, "Oh, we're not parting company yet. I'm taking you to dinner tonight. I want to celebrate our five-for-five week."

Sam took a look in both directions. Cars were already in a snarl of slow-moving traffic at all exits.

"But look at this traffic, Bentley," Sam said, "it'll take us an hour to get out of the parking lot. I tell you what, why don't I buy you dinner instead of you buying me dinner."

Bentley hesitated, tapped his cane, said, "Well, if you insist. Where will we go?"

"Do you like gumbo, and I mean the real Cajun-style gumbo?"

"I've a genuine taste for it, but outside of the French Quarter, where do we find such fare?"

Sam pointed at his truck, said, "Get in."

Bentley turned to where Randolph waited with the Rolls, and in sign language understood only by the chauffeur and Bentley, told his driver to drive back to the barn, that he'd meet him there after having dinner. When Bentley opened the passenger door to Sam's truck, Sam was busy gathering *Racing Forms* off the seat where Bentley would sit. Bentley, smiled, waited, then, when Sam waved him in, the short little man took a big step up into the truck.

"You still haven't told me where we're going," Bentley said, settling into the seat.

"The track kitchen," Sam said, putting the key in the ignition.

Bentley blinked and his white eyebrows began to climb up his forehead.

"Don't look at me that way, Bentley. Lucien Thibodaux runs the kitchen and Saturday means seafood gumbo."

Bentley smiled, nodded, said, "Drive on, Sam."

Sam started the truck. New holes in the muffler and an odometer that read 212,978 miles, caused a racket to come out from under the truck. When Sam put the truck in gear and drove off, he left a cloud of blue smoke behind him. Tappets clattered, the fan belt squealed, and Bentley, every bit a gentleman, acted as if he didn't notice. He sat back and enjoyed the short ride to the track kitchen. When Sam brought the truck to a stop and turned it off, the cloud of blue smoke caught up with the truck and made Bentley cough. Bentley still said nothing. He got out of the truck and he and Sam walked into the brick building between barns ten and eleven on the backstretch of Lincoln Park.

Sam opened the door for Bentley, and as Bentley walked into the kitchen he said, "Matchbook looked like a young Nureyev today. He's such a graceful animal."

"Taylor was right, he's going to be a useful horse," Sam answered.

The track kitchen was a place where racetrackers not only ate, but also entertained each other with tall tales and good humor. When Bentley and Sam were noticed, there was a pause in the chatter around the tables as people turned to look at them. Bentley and Sam took their place in line to get their dinner cafeteria-style. Bentley smiled at several of the people turned his way, then in a pleasant greeting meant for all he said, "Good evening, everyone."

The response was a deluge of welcoming voices:

"Good evening, Mr. Keene."

"Hello, sir."

"Nice to see you, and congratulations, that Matchbook is a nice colt."

"I bet on Mutineer, Mr. Keene, I knew he'd win the big one."

"Queen of Hearts, I think she's going to be a good one, Mr. Keene."

"Nice to see you, sir."

And then someone at a back table called out, "Congratulations, Sam…five-for-five this week!"

Then someone else said, "Yeah, no more excuses, Sam…loan me twenty bucks!"

With that came hoots of laughter, and everyone went back to eating and telling jokes and stories about horses that couldn't possibly be true. Bentley leaned close to Sam, said, "That was so nice of everyone."

Sam smiled, said, "I've done three things in the past couple weeks I'm proud of. The first is that I was able to saddle some winners for you, the other two things are that I got you out of your box seat in the clubhouse to watch races from the fence and got you to eat dinner in the track kitchen."

"I'm surprised you haven't insisted I walk hots," Bentley said happily.

"I was picturing you in a riding helmet," Sam said. "With Clay gone we need someone to work horses."

"I'm so pleased Clay is doing so well."

Sam said, "It's a relief knowing he's in a place like New Hope and is trying so hard."

Sam and Bentley each took a tray and pushed it along the tubular rungs that ran the length of the glass case behind which food was served up both hot and cold. The kitchen area was bright with appliances, chrome faucets, tall coffee urns and stainless steel serving dishes. Burgers sizzled on a grill attended by a woman wearing a hairnet and a long white apron. A calendar from Hall's Turf Supplies hung on the back wall. Lucien Thibodaux was there. Lucien was rotund, wore a spotless white shirt and had clean hands.

"Hi, Sam," Lucien said. "And, Mr. Keene, it's nice to see you in my kitchen. What can I get for you gentlemen?"

"Two gumbos, Lu," Sam answered.

"Rice?"

Sam looked at Bentley and Bentley said, "I'm having what you're having."

"Rice in both, Lu," Sam said.

Lucien ladled up two big bowls of gumbo thick with shrimp and crab claws. Then he dished up a serving of white rice using an ice cream scoop and put the rice on top of the gumbo. He handed the steaming bowls over the glass case to Sam and Bentley. Bentley's eyes got big, and he looked up at Sam smiling.

"This looks delicious," he said.

"It's even better than it looks," Sam said.

Lucien was grinning. "Enjoy, gentlemen."

Sam paid the cashier and he and Bentley sat down. Sam and Bentley talked seriously about some things and laughed about others while they ate, and several people stopped by the table to say hello. The gumbo was quickly gone, and then Sam was driving up to his barn to drop Bentley off where Randolph waited with the

Rolls Royce.

"That will not be the last time I eat gumbo in the track kitchen," Bentley said. Then he turned to offer his hand to Sam. "Again, thanks to you, Sam, for all you've done for my horses."

"My pleasure," Sam returned, shaking the offered hand.

"Goodbye," Bentley said, then reached and opened the door.

There, with the door handle still in his hand, Bentley paused, turned back to Sam to give him a questioning look. The questioning look quickly turned to a look of impatience. Bentley said, "So, you're just going to let me leave?"

"I don't understand."

"Sam, in business, timing is everything," Bentley said. "This is the moment you should be selling yourself to me. You should be attempting a *hostile takeover* so to speak; you should be telling me how you could do a much better job with my horses than Joshua Kincaid."

Sam shook his head side-to-side. "I'd never *submarine* Josh."

"But this is about money, this is about what I can only guess to be your greatest ambition, to train nice horses and have stability in your life."

Sam said nothing, just shook his head again.

Bentley settled back in the seat, looked out the windshield of the truck, then turned and looked straight into Sam's eyes. "There's something you need to know, Sam...Joshua's not coming back."

"What?" Sam said, his eyes widening.

"Joshua called me several days ago, and explained that he's happy on his farm, and won't be coming back to the races."

Sam stared at Bentley, for a time couldn't think, then said, "He never mentioned any of that to me."

"I asked him not to. I wanted to see what kind of man you really are, and this little drama we're engaged in right now is telling me much."

"Bentley, I—"

"A three-year contract for sixty thousand a year, plus ten percent of everything the horses make, it's what I offered Joshua, and it's what I'm offering you."

Too much to take in, Sam's mind jumped in all directions and he couldn't concentrate.

Bentley went on: "If you accept, there is one thing I insist on."

Sam blinked. "What?"

Bentley grinned. "You simply must stop living in the shedrow office."

Laughter tumbled out of Sam and Bentley.

Bentley said, "Have we struck a deal?"

Smiling his biggest smile, Sam said, "We have a deal."

Sam hadn't turned the truck off, and the wind changed and oily blue smoke came into the cab. Bentley took out a handkerchief and coughed into it. "There is one more thing," he said, giving another small cough, "I think it's time for a new truck."

"But I like this old truck," Sam said, grinning.

"You don't have to get rid of it, just get a new one, so the next Saturday night you give me a ride to the track kitchen for gumbo, you won't poison me with carbon monoxide."

Sam's grin widened, but a sudden thought jolted him and his grin fragmented. He was grave when he said, "I need to say something, Bentley."

Bentley frowned, studied Sam, said, "What would that something be?"

"Looking back..." Sam paused, a sense of unease taking him over. "I'm not so sure Joshua ever intended to come and train your horses. I think maybe he planned—"

"Maybe he planned?" Bentley interrupted cheerfully. "Sam, there's no doubt in my mind that Joshua Kincaid planned...and that everything has now worked out just as he planned it to."

Sam relaxed, smiled, thought of the crafty Irishman, then looked Bentley full in the face, said, "I'm grateful, sir."

"And I'm grateful to you, Sam. You're a good man, and I know I can trust you with my horses." Bentley tapped his cane on the floor of the pickup, continued by saying, "And I'm also grateful for Joshua Kincaid's ability to carry out a good plan."

Both men were laughing again.

Then Bentley was in his white Rolls Royce and gone. Sam finally turned off the engine, got out of the truck, and walked over to the barn. He went into the office and made a call.

"And who would this be?" Joshua answered.

"You sly old fox," Sam said.

The phone call lasted nearly half an hour, and in that time, not once did Joshua admit to anything. Sam hung up smiling and half-believing Joshua's professed innocence, but then remembered why Joshua was so dangerous...he could make anyone believe anything. Now Sam stood in front of the office, looking down through the shedrow...*his* shedrow. Mutineer was the first to come to his webbing and look at Sam. Then came Voodoo Queen, Tigress, Matchbook, and soon others of the twenty-four Keene horses were at their webbings. And Sam could feel it, the end of the familiar, and the beginning of something extraordinary.

21. BESS

When the phone rang, Bess was at the sink, washing the dinner dishes, and Amy was swinging from a tire attached by a rope to a branch of the elm tree in the backyard. Bess dried her hands on a hand towel, then picked up the phone on the fourth ring.

"Hello," Bess said. Then while listening to Sam's excited voice her red lips grew wide with a smile. The more she listened the happier she became. She was so happy for Sam that when she spoke her voice went up and down like a song: "Oh, Sam, this is wonderful! All your hopes are coming true!"

Bess continued to listen to Sam explain all that had happened, and the more he talked the more she wanted to hug and squeeze him. She suddenly realized this was one of the biggest moments in Sam's life and that she could only share in it long distance. The smile left her face. She wanted to be there with him, to see the way the excitement and joy made the features of his face move and change. Now she missed him so much her delicate pink nostrils began to quiver. She missed watching his hands while he shaved, missed scrubbing his back in the shower. She missed the little knot that was his navel, missed the way his hair took the color right out of the sunlight.

Bess blurted, "When can Amy and I come to be with you?"

Sam's answer caused Bess to squeeze her eyes closed. Now her long curving lashes touched her cheeks. Sam began to explain how busy he'd be with all the Keene horses, how Mrs. Brandt's colt was taking up so much of his time, and how he didn't like the idea of she and Amy living in the big city, how he especially didn't want Amy to go to school anywhere near Chicago.

Bess stopped listening, reminded herself that Sam did love her, that he'd proven it the first time they'd been alone parked in his truck. After Sam realized he could do as he pleased with her, he hadn't become frantic to undress her, hadn't rushed to get her out of her blue jeans. He'd taken his time to kiss her over and over, short sweet kisses and long kisses, taken his time to whisper things to her no boy had ever said to her before.

"Give me time to settle in, Bess," Sam went on. "Please understand that I need some time, then in a few weeks you and Amy can come in for a visit."

"Sure, Sam," Bess said, "we'll come and *visit*."

"Thanks for understanding, honey."

"I'm so happy for you, Sam," Bess said.

Then came the "I love yous" and the "Goodbyes" and Bess was hanging up the phone.

Bess sat down at the little table in the kitchen. The brightness went out of her eyes, leaving them flat, remote. She sat there long enough for the sun to shift lower in the sky and the light through the windows to change the colors around her. Her eyes told the story of her discouragement, her privation, disappoint, her sorrow. Sam was her perpetual joy, her perpetual heartache, and that he could be both these things was tearing Bess apart.

22. SAM

Sam ran eight horses during the last two weeks of the Lincoln Park meet. The Keene horses won three more races, had two seconds and three thirds. The only Keene horse to not *hit the board* was a three-year-old filly named Mississippi Miss. Sam blamed himself for her poor showing. He used a bug boy on the filly, thinking the talented but small three-year-old would benefit from the five-pound apprentice allowance. He'd also used the bug boy to work the filly two mornings before the race, but the filly had worked too fast, and come race day she ran *flat,* getting beat over ten lengths. Sam was anxious for Clay and the clock he carried in his head to get back in the saddle.

Two of the wins were the filly Danube. Coming off the second she ran against colts and geldings, she broke her maiden ten days later in the same race, a non-winners of two in a lifetime for a tag. She came back twelve days after that and beat the same weak field of claimers again. The other win was a five-year-old allowance horse named Excommunicator. A stake horse at two and three, the five-year-old had lifetime winnings of $492,546, and though he'd developed foot problems as an older horse, he was still useful and Sam couldn't wait to get him on the turf course at Suburban. Bentley was particularly sentimental about Excommunicator, the five-year-old was his wife Ruth's favorite horse.

The eighth horse Sam ran was Mrs. Brandt's black colt. He

ran a dismal ninth, only beating one horse. Joshua came and got the colt two days later. Joshua also brought a briefcase, a briefcase Sam passed on to Bill Baker. The black colt ended up on a farm where children with special needs came for day camp, and the gentle colt became a favorite there. No one questioned why the colt's upper lip had been tattooed on the inside over and over until it was a solid color of black-purple.

Shipping a stable of twenty-four horses isn't a task without its challenges. But all of Sam's people—grooms, hotwalkers, exercise boys and girl—happily worked a long day on Thursday to get the horses moved. Vance, Sam's assistant trainer, was everywhere, watching over everything, and was invaluable. Vance was competent and cheerful, and in the last weeks Sam had grown to appreciate Vance more and more. With the hammer of the diesel engines that pulled the two horse vans, with the clank and clunk of feed tubs and water buckets, with the laughter and sweat of his shedrow crew, the horses were finally settled into barn one on the backstretch of Suburban Downs, the customary Keene barn. Just after Sam thanked everyone for all their work and the pizzas he'd ordered for the barn were delivered by Nino's Pizzeria, a truck from Westgate's Garden Center pulled up. While everyone drank Coca Cola and ate slices of pizza, two men from Westgate's hung ten huge baskets of geraniums from the eyehooks screwed at regular intervals into the eaves of the barn's sloping roof, and placed two large planters overflowing with colorful blossoms at either end of the barn. The two men also cleaned up the grassy area in front of the barn, and on a four-foot-tall brick pedestal already there, they placed a heavy cast iron *lawn jockey* painted in the Keene racing colors. By evening, the Keene side of barn one at Suburban Downs looked right out of a storybook.

Just after eight o'clock, Sam finally left the barn. The familiar nameless, wordless song of saddles and bridles was playing in his head when he got into his new white F150 Ford pickup truck and drove off toward Arlington Heights. His new studio apartment was in the Ambassador Villas, right off Euclid Avenue.

2

Sam and Bentley stood at the end of the shedrow, watching Voodoo Queen come toward them. The mare moved easily, flicking her tail as her groom, Robbie Nelson—a 30-year-old with short sandy hair that bristled like a brush—stopped to let her take another drink of water. The mare didn't drink this time, she played with the water, using her lips to splash it around.

"She's stopped drinking, Robbie," Sam said to the groom, "you can take her around once more and put her away."

"Okay, Sam," Robbie answered. He walked the mare by where Sam and Bentley stood, and just before he and the mare disappeared around the corner of the barn, he said over his shoulder, "I still don't think she deserved to have her *number taken down.*"

It was Sunday, opening day at Suburban Downs, and Voodoo Queen had run second in the Ruffian Stakes, but the rider of the horse that ran third lodged an *objection,* a *claim of foul,* and Voodoo Queen's number had come down. She was placed third by the stewards.

"I agree with that young man," Bentley said, "I think the stewards did the mare wrong."

"The *head-on replay* showed what happened," Sam replied, "that Taylor shut the door hard on that California ship-in, Hollywood Honey. It's a fine line between race riding and being dangerous, and Taylor put at least a toe over that line."

Bentley suddenly began to smile.

"What are you so happy about?" Sam said, a trace of disbelief in his tone.

"I'm always pleased when my horses run good. Voodoo proved she's still to be reckoned with."

Sam nodded, smiled. "She's a stone-cold runner. In my opinion that New York mare who won is the best distaff grass horse in the country."

"Do you think if Taylor had kept a straight course we could have held on to second?"

"Taylor wouldn't have almost put that California jock over the rail if he thought he had a lock on second. In Taylor's defense, that jock had no business going to the inside of *one* horse, it was a bad move and he got what he deserved." Sam let notes of humor slip into his voice when he said, "That California jock *stood up* like he popped out of a toaster. Taylor's a race rider, got to give him credit, he only thinks about getting his number hung up, does what it takes, and worries about his number coming down later. The stewards might give him *days* for what he did…*might*."

Bentley looked at his wrist watch, there was the gleam of gold, and he said, "I must be off, and Sam, it's Tokyo this week, so I probably won't see you until the first part of the following week."

"Alright, Bentley, travel safe."

"Indeed," Bentley said, and then was in the Rolls Royce and gone.

Sam watched the groom put Voodoo Queen away, then Robbie waved to Sam and left the shedrow going the other way. A Miller Brothers Feed truck was parked at mid barn, a long flatbed, and two men were making a delivery. Bales of hay and straw crackled and thumped as the two men stacked the bales in the feed room. Then came a familiar voice:

"Hey, Sam."

Sam swung around and there was Clay Repp.

"Clay!" Sam said, happily surprised.

Sam grabbed Clay by the offered hand and shook it. Clay looked ten years younger. His eyes were surprisingly clear and bright, his face no longer had the look of saddle leather. Clay glowed with health. A close shave gave him a polished look.

"Has it been thirty days?" Sam said.

"Not quite, but I'm doing so good and begged them so long and hard to let me come back to work, that, well…here I am."

"You've been missed."

"You and Mr. Keene—" Emotion stopped Clay and he

swallowed hard. Gratitude was in his voice when he continued: "You and Mr. Keene have been so supportive. To know there were people who really cared…it meant so much."

"The beginning of a new life," Sam said.

"That's right. I'll always be an alcoholic, but I'm twenty-five days sober and going to stay that way."

"That's the spirit."

"New Hope has a really good follow-up and support program. I'll see my doctors and counselors twice a week, and they're always on call for me. That's what I want to talk to you about, about getting to those meetings downtown. My first meeting's tonight, and I could use a ride."

"Clay, I'll take you downtown any time you need me to." Sam paused, put his index finger in the air to signal the arrival of an idea. "But wait, I can do better than that. I've still got my old truck, why don't I give it to you to use."

Clay looked up at Sam blinking, said, "Is it Christmas?"

"And I moved all your things over from the other side of town, got everything set up in a room over in the dorms."

"I won't forget this, Sam."

"Now, when do you want to start riding?"

"Right away. I worked out every day in the gym at New Hope, so I'll be here tomorrow morning."

Sam gave Clay a quick up and down appraisal. "You look *light.*"

"I've kept watch on my diet, and you'd be surprised how many calories are in Seagram's and Budweiser."

Both men laughed in a reserved way.

"Evening Song runs Tuesday, but why don't you get on horses for a couple mornings, and we'll start you back on Wednesday. I'll name you on Emily Brandt's colt."

"I remember the colt, the solid black one."

"Joshua's bringing the colt back to me this evening, he's had him back at his farm for a few weeks. The colt had a couple of problems, Josh straightened those out, and Josh tells me the colt is a completely different horse now." Sam smiled broadly when it

came to him what he'd just said, then repeated: "Believe me, the
black colt is a completely different horse."

3

Sam was standing by the large planter filled with flowers at the end
of the shedrow when Joshua pull in with his International Loadstar
horse van. Joshua waved and brought the van to a stop near the
grassy area in front of the barn. Sam walked out to meet Joshua,
heard the driver's door open and close. Then Joshua came around
the front of the Loadstar. The first thing Sam noticed was how bent
Joshua's back was. He was so stooped it looked like he was
searching the ground for something. Next, when Joshua looked up,
Sam saw how tired Joshua looked. His face was pale, waxen, and
there were deep grooves at the corners of his eyes and mouth.

"Josh, you look exhausted," Sam said studying the old man.

"I'm fine," Joshua said, "or at least will be, as soon as I turn
this colt over to ye."

Sam frowned.

Joshua began to open the two side doors to the van, talking as
he did: "Every time we talked about this colt, I knew by yer tone
that ye weren't quite believing what I was telling ye—"

"I know he's a good colt, Josh," Sam interrupted.

Joshua paused to look at Sam before he swung the second
door open. "*Good,*" Joshua repeated not hiding his sarcasm. "All
I've told ye, and ye label this colt *good.*" Joshua swung the door
open, and as Sam helped him slide out the ramp and put up the
plywood guard rails, Joshua said, "Well, ye're about to find out
why I look the way I do, why I haven't been able to sleep for
weeks, why I'm up two or three times a night."

"Why are you up two or three times a night?"

Joshua pointed up into the van, said loudly, "To check on
him. To make sure he's alright. That he hasn't somehow hurt
himself, that he hasn't got colic, that he's not—"

Sam put his hands up as a signal for Joshua to calm down. "Whoa, take it easy."

"Ye take it easy," Joshua snapped back.

Then Joshua hurried up the ramp into the van. Sounds came from inside the van: Joshua speaking in a low voice, an answering nicker, the slow shuffle of hooves. Then the colt was standing in the van's double-wide doorway, and Sam looked into the diamond light.

Sam felt his pulse accelerate.

The black colt glowed with the blue luster of a true ebony racehorse, and as Joshua led the colt down the ramp, the flow of the colt's walk was so graceful it was sensuous. Sam looked on, knowing he'd never seen a thoroughbred so beautiful. Joshua walked the colt in a circle around the cast iron jockey on the brick pedestal, then brought the colt to a stop. The colt's perfection was startling. It was as if he'd been carefully constructed by artists and engineers, a rendering in flesh and bone of exact angles and perfect shapes. The colt was so fit, all his muscles stood out in high relief, and his tendons looked like steel cables. Sam kept looking the colt over from his velvet muzzle to the sleek hair of his long tail, it was as if he couldn't see enough of him, as if he couldn't look away.

"Well?" Joshua said.

Sam finally looked at Joshua, said, "He's—"

"He's going to keep ye up at night too," Joshua interrupted. "Tell me what ye see, start from the ground up."

"He's got nice sized feet, not too big, and he stands square, not toed in or out."

"The pastern?"

"Short, a good forty-five-degree angle."

"Cannon bone?"

"Straight to the ground and not too long."

"Knees?"

"Nice flat knees, good forearms, broad and deep chested, and his shoulder's solid with a forty-five-degree slope. Handsome head, wide between the eyes, a strong graceful neck."

"Top line?"

Sam studied the colt again, answered, "It's deceiving. His shoulders and quarters are so muscled it makes his back appear short, but it's not, he's got nice length to his back."

"Aye."

"In fact, he's so well balanced, you don't realize how big he is until you step up close to him. He's an easy eleven hundred pounds and I'd guess just short of seventeen hands."

"Right on all counts."

Sam went on: "When he walks he brings his legs forward nicely, and there's good space between his hocks when he moves."

"A free and easy way of moving he has, and he runs like that too. The wee girl who's been getting on him for me said he's like riding a cloud."

"A small girl?"

"He's a kind colt, smart, smarter than any I've ever been around, and that's why I'm telling you to *daybreak* him and run him. Don't bother with schooling in the paddock or gate, he's good to go. Anyway, if too many people see him, you'll cut the odds we get in half."

From under the shedrow, came the sound of Voodoo Queen and Evening Song calling back and forth. The colt heard. He bowed his neck, pulled a great draft of air into his lungs, and released it in an explosive snort. The colt swung away from Joshua, then stopped, holding his head high with his ears pricked, looking toward the barn, smelling the air with dilated nostrils. In that moment, Sam and Joshua saw nothing else in the world but the colt, he filled their eyes. The evening breeze lifted the colt's mane and tangled his long tail.

"There is magic in this colt," Joshua said, looking at Sam with overly bright eyes, "and I am under his spell."

"I can feel it too," Sam said.

"Nothing that wears racing plates can beat this colt," Joshua said. "Ye tell the jock to *send* him, that this colt can throw a twenty-two and a forty-four without taking a deep breath."

Sam looked at Joshua, cocked his head.

Joshua squinted at Sam, fixing him with a harsh look. "Have

ye ever known me to misjudge a horse?"

Sam shook his head no.

"Then do as I ask, tell the jock to send him right out of the gate."

Sam had the stall at the very end of the barn ready for the colt, but replaced the webbing he'd put up with a webbing Joshua had brought. The webbing was done in Emily Brandt's colors, a green silhouette of a live oak on a white background with Southern Oak printed in an arc above it. Joshua also handed over the Brandt racing silks to Sam. The silks were in the same pattern as the webbing. On the front of the white silks was a small green live oak tree over the heart. On the back, Southern Oak was stitched in green lettering in an arc above a large green live oak.

Joshua and Sam left the colt to munch hay, and were now in the office. Sam put the Brandt colors on the desk. Joshua stood looking down at the silks, picked up a sleeve, rubbed the material between his fingers, then let the sleeve drop. Joshua looked up at Sam.

"There's a lot of history there," Joshua said. "These colors really belong in a museum. These are the silks Bobby Stewart wore when he rode Southern Lord to victory in the International Handicap at Empire State Racecourse. That day Southern Lord, *top weight* at 131 pounds, beat La Plata, the Argentine champion, Saxon Knight, the British Derby winner, and the Eclipse Award-winning champion, Insurrection. That International is considered *the* greatest handicap race in the last fifty years."

"I'll take good care of the colors," Sam said.

Joshua nodded, said, "If the colt's good in the morning, enter him as soon as you can."

"There's a race Wednesday for three and four-year-old maidens."

Joshua nodded again. Then it seemed gravity began to work on his back, and he was suddenly bent in half, looking at the floor. He cleared his throat several times, began to rub his right elbow. Sam watched him, waited. When the silence lengthened, Sam became uncomfortable in it.

"Just say it, Josh," Sam finally said.

Joshua looked up at Sam then, and when he spoke, his voice dropped, becoming grave: "Remember Francis Wheeler?"

"I do, he trained Memphis, one of the greatest three-year-old fillies of all times."

"That's right. That filly near drove Francis insane. If he wasn't in her stall, he was in a bar somewhere drinking himself stiff. A great horse can do that to a man…you can't stop worrying about them, can't stop being near them. Ye give up everything else just to train and be with that horse."

"I can handle it," Sam said.

Joshua stopped rubbing his elbow, and his Irish eyes were steady into Sam's when he said, "Can Bess handle it?"

Sam flinched. "That came out of nowhere."

"Take care of yer horses, Sam, but don't forget yer family."

Sam frowned. "Has Bess said something?"

"No," Joshua answered flatly.

Sam looked down at the Brandt racing silks, then back up into Joshua's eyes and didn't blink when he said, "I'm dealing with some bad people, and you know why. I can't even imagine bringing Bess and Amy into the middle of this right now."

"It'll be over soon."

Sam nodded.

Joshua turned down Sam's offer of dinner, and was soon in his van, headed back to Iowa. For the first time ever, Sam was glad to see Joshua leave.

4

One mosquito buzzed in the apartment, and Sam, unable to sleep, looked over at the clock. It was 2:17 A.M. Tuesday morning. Sam closed his eyes, and in the darkness behind his lids began a staggering rush of images. From the flurry of people, places and horses, he held on to Bess. He wanted Bess to be there. He wanted to smell the wonderful clean smell of her, wanted to feel the touch of her hands, the warm squeeze of being inside her. He saw her now with the loveliest bloom to her cheeks, the bloom that always came over her after the sweat and tumble of sex. But Bess wouldn't stay clear in his thoughts. Bill Baker projected in his brain, so did Belichio, so did the colt. Anxiety put a knot in Sam's chest. The colt had gotten in for Wednesday, the first race, and Sam had called Baker to let him know that the bet should be made. Clay was going to meet Sam at the barn at four o'clock to work the colt. Suddenly, the buzz of the mosquito seemed to be coming from the center of Sam's head. Sam looked at the clock again, it was 2:18.

Within half an hour, Sam was in his truck driving past a security guard at Suburban Park's stable gate. Sam parked the truck and started for the shedrow office. The early morning was cool and a thick fog mixed with the darkness to make it difficult to see. Around him, the backstretch was still asleep, there wasn't a whisper of voices, only a soft wind in the rafters of the barns. Then Sam had the feeling he was being watched—an attack of paranoia and guilt—and he stopped and looked around. Through the fog, dark shapes formed and presented themselves. A different anxiety came over him, not the acute kind that had stirred him from his bed, but the chronic kind, the kind that drains away strength and is a perpetual companion. Sam traced this new anxiety back to the first time he laid eyes on the colt.

A voice startled Sam, made him jump.

"You're up early," said Oscar, the night watchman. After flipping on a switch in the tack room beside the office, Oscar stood in a shaft of yellow light, scratching at his gray beard. "I just made a fresh pot of coffee, come and have some."

Sam walked toward the smell of the coffee, said, "Oscar, you're a lifesaver."

Sam soon had a big mug in his hand. He sipped at the steaming brew. "Damn, Oscar, you make good coffee."

"Thank you, sir," Oscar answered. "The secret is to leave some of the previous pot as stock to mix with the fresh pot…that, and never clean the pot."

Sam smiled. "Oscar, I'm giving you the rest of the night off…go on home, get some sleep."

"Well, thank you," Oscar said, rubbing at his eyes. "I was having trouble keeping the peepers open."

Oscar talked on with Sam for a few minutes, then shuffled off into the dark and was gone. First Sam saddled Herbert the pony, then he gathered tack for the colt: saddle towel, pad, saddle, girth, girth pad, yolk, bridle with a ring bit. As only a horseman can, Sam carried all this down to the colt's stall, plus still managed to hold onto a fresh mug of coffee. Sam laid the tack down on a bale of straw. Before sitting the coffee down, he took a long scalding gulp, then walked over and flipped on the light in the colt's stall.

Black Deuce had been lying down and now seemed to unwind his long legs with a complicated grace as he stood. He shook off the straw, then came to his webbing. The colt's nostrils widened, quivered with interest as he took in Sam's smell.

After Sam put rear rundown bandages on the colt, he put on the tack. Now he stepped back looking at Black Deuce and felt a rush of boyish excitement. "I can't wait to see you run," Sam said.

A voice in the dark.

"I need coffee," Clay Repp said as he took shape out of the fog.

Sam pointed at his mug, and Clay picked the mug up from where it sat on the bale of straw. He took several long swallows, smacked his lips and set the mug back down, said, "I know Oscar's coffee when I taste it."

"I made that," Sam said.

Clay grinned. "Bull shit."

Both men laughed, and Clay went on: "You sure you don't want to wait till later to work this colt? It's downright foggy out on the track."

"As long as you can see the poles and the rail, we'll work him," Sam answered.

Sam had taken care of the colt since the colt's arrival at the barn. He'd walked him early the day before, before anyone had shown up for work at five, and had mucked his stall and fed him. Nobody had been in the stall with the colt but him, and nobody except for Mary Linwood had given the colt a second look. When Sam caught Mary looking in at the colt, he'd called her down the shedrow to talk to her about packing Excommunicator's feet with *mud.* Mary's only comment about the colt was: "What did Joshua feed that colt back at the farm?" Sam had ignored Mary, talking to her instead about Excommunicator's feet. But now Clay stuck his whip into a back pocket of his blue jeans and ducked under the webbing. He stood in the stall, and with one look at the colt, his demeanor changed.

"Holy shit," Clay said with an odd pitch to his voice, the pitch of someone who's trying to express excitement and disbelief at the same time.

Sam said nothing, went on with business as usual. He dropped the webbing and led the colt out of the stall. When the colt moved, muscle flexed and stretched beneath a coat that shown like black satin. Clay came around to the colt's left shoulder and with his left hand took a cross in the reins and grabbed a handful of mane. With his right hand, he reached up and gripped the pommel of the saddle. Next Clay cocked his left leg and Sam gave him a boost up. Clay sat down lightly in the saddle. While he tied a knot in the reins, Clay looked down at Sam with a question in his eyes. Sam only glanced up at Clay, but this was enough, and Clay understood and said nothing more.

Sam said, "Take him once around the shedrow. I'll be waiting out front on the pony."

"Sure thing," Clay said as the colt stepped off.

Fog lay thick over the racetrack, and Sam felt spits of rain on his face as he led Clay and the colt the wrong way in a jog. Hooves thudded against soft dirt. Halfway down the backside, Sam slowed the horses to a walk and then turned to come back the right way in an easy gallop. Clay stood in the irons, and the colt floated along beside the pony. The colt snorted now and again, and when the colt came to the grandstand, the exit and security lights of the massive steel and glass structure reflected off his coat in silver highlights that changed patterns as the muscles in his quarters and shoulders pushed and pulled.

"Break him off at the three-eighths pole," Sam said. Rocking in motion with the pony, he leaned over in the stock saddle and unsnapped the lead shank from the colt's bit. "Let him go in :36. I'll be waiting for you after the wire, shout if you need help."

There was humor in Clay's voice when he answered, "You'll hear me loud and clear if I need help."

Sam brought the pony to a stop after the wire. Clay and the colt cantered away toward the Clubhouse turn, and Sam watched them until they were only a fading silhouette in the fog and the dark. Looming behind Sam, the Clubhouse and grandstand seemed hollow and strange, strange as all places meant for crowds are strange when they stand empty. Sam sat on the pony listening and straining to see, but his eyes gave him nothing. Now and again he could hear hooves, but the sound came through the fog distorted and he couldn't make out exactly where Clay and the colt were. He sat on the pony and waited.

The pony was the first to hear.

The pony pricked his ears and turned his head to look up the stretch. Now the sound of fast-moving hooves echoed in the immense glass cave of the grandstand. Just as Sam turned to look, the colt burst out of the fog, leaving the mist swirling like gray smoke behind him. He ran with his head low, pulling hard on the reins, and each time his hooves reached for the racetrack and snapped back up under him, he was airborne. There was such power in the thrust and push of the colt's *action* that Sam expected to see steam come out of the colt's nostrils. Sam choked with excitement and understood his life would never be the same, that his life would be divided into a before and after the morning the colt worked in the fog. When the colt went by him, his mane and tail still snapping in the wind, Clay was bent in half trying to pull the colt up and Sam could see the bottom of Clay's right boot. Clay's feet were *on the dashboard.* Urging the pony into a run, Sam took off after the colt and Clay. By the time he caught up with them, Clay had the colt geared down to a long loping stride.

"I couldn't see," Sam said, bringing the pony up beside the colt, "so I didn't even bother to take out my stopwatch, but I know that was no :36. What did the clock in your head say?"

Sam leaned over in the saddle, and with a metallic click, attached the lead shank to the colt's bit. The colt was wide-eyed, his ears pricked back and forth, and he pulled air into his lungs and blew it back out in loud blasts. Sam led the colt back the wrong way, staying up against the fence.

"I could give you a number, Sam," Clay said, still a bit out of breath, "but it'd only be a guess. I've never been on a horse like this, he doesn't just run, this colt explodes over the ground."

"Give me the number."

"First, understand I never really let this colt run," Clay explained, beginning to talk easier. "I changed holds when I dropped him to the rail and he just took off. When I reached for him, he came back to me, but he was still running so fast. I just sat still and kept him under the best hold I could."

"Give me the number," Sam repeated.

They were past the clubhouse and grandstand, and Clay raised an arm and wiped the sweat from his face with the sleeve of his shirt. The colt jogged alongside the pony in an easy bounce.

Sam lost patience. "The number, Clay," he said sharply.

"Thirty-four and three."

Sam turned his head quickly. "You couldn't slow him down—"

Clay stopped Sam in midsentence by holding up his right hand. Sam saw the new blisters.

"You should wear gloves," Sam said as they went through the gap to go back to the barn.

"Gloves are for pussies," Clay shot back.

Sam put his head back and hooted laughter.

5

Wednesday morning, when Sam walked under the shedrow at 4:20 A.M., he was surprised not to smell coffee coming from the tack room. Then Oscar called to him from the other end of the barn.

"Sam, I'm down here by the black colt's stall."

Sam's blood pressure spiked. "What's wrong?"

"Just come down here," Oscar called back.

With a quick step, Sam hurried down the shedrow. At the sound of voices, horses stirred in their stalls and came to their webbings. They stood tall and shadowy, watching Sam with gleaming eyes as he rushed by in the dark.

"Is the colt alright?" Sam said in a near shout.

"Yes, he's fine," Oscar answered, "but something strange happened about an hour ago."

Sam flipped on the light in the stall and the colt, standing at the back of his stall, lifted his head and nickered. Straw snapped and crackled under the colt's hooves as he stepped up to his webbing. Sam's head moved quickly this way and that as he gave the colt a quick scan. Then with darting glances, he looked all around the colt's stall.

"What strange thing happened?" Sam said.

Oscar scratched at his gray beard, explained, "I was standing by the feed room there," he pointed toward the middle of the barn, "and I'll be damned if some guy didn't walk right up out of the night and flip on the light in the colt's stall to have a look at him."

"Who the hell was it?"

"When I yelled, he flipped the light back off, and I didn't get a good look at him. But he was a ballsy bastard, he didn't run off like you'd think. He stood there until I was just a few stalls away then just walked off and disappeared in the dark. I would have called you, even got track security, but I didn't want to leave the colt long enough to make any calls, so I've been sitting right here on that bale of straw waiting for you to show up."

"Good job, Oscar," Sam said. "Can you describe the man at all?"

"He was bald, had on dark clothes, and it was strange…"

"What was strange?"

"What he held in his hand."

Sam stared at Oscar, waited.

"Sam, I think it was a *Bible*."

Sam's heart gave a hard thump. "Oscar, you did good. Go on down and turn on the shedrow lights, I'll stay here with the colt."

"Yes, sir," Oscar said and walked off toward the other end of the barn.

Standing there in the glare of the stall's electric light, Sam looked out into the darkness. What the hell have I got myself into, he said aloud to himself. He thought about how much money two hundred thousand dollars was, how Joshua and Emily Brandt were depending on him, how he was now engaged in a dangerous game with Bill Baker and Anthony Belichio. Sam was sure it was The Deacon who'd come calling on the colt. Sam's gut twisted and writhed like a twenty-foot snake pinned to the ground by a pitchfork, and then he looked back at the colt. The colt put his handsome head out over the webbing, and Sam, feeling some relief at just being able to touch the colt, began to rub and scratch the colt's neck. The colt groaned with pleasure. Then all the lights flashed on down through the shedrow, and Sam saw Vance and Mary talking to Oscar. Oscar suddenly raised his arm and pointed at Sam. Vance and Mary hurried his way, not running, but with elbows pumping like those of speed walkers.

"I'm an idiot," Sam mumbled, thinking he should have told Oscar to keep quiet about the incident.

"Sam, is the colt alright?" Mary called out.

"Yes," Sam answered, "and let's not make a big deal out of this."

Vance said, "You don't think someone drugged the colt, do you, Sam? I mean the colt's in today, and the story Oscar told is a strange one…and I don't believe in coincidence."

Sam stepped away from the colt, and Mary and Vance walked up and didn't hesitate: they ducked under the webbing and looked the colt over and then they both walked around the stall kicking aside straw to see if they could find anything that didn't belong and shouldn't be there. They both carefully looked over the colt's feed tub and water bucket. Then the two were standing beside Sam.

"Should we scratch the colt, Sam?" Vance said.

"No," Sam answered quickly. "The colt's acting fine, everything is okay."

Vance gave Sam a long look, said, "Sam, you're sweating."

"Really sweating," Mary said, frowning.

Sam looked down at himself. Beneath his arms his shirt was ringed with dark sweat stains. Sam wiped at his face with a hand. When he looked at the hand, his fingers were wet.

"Are you okay, Sam?" Mary asked.

Sam nodded, but by the expressions on Mary and Vance's faces, they weren't convinced.

6

For Sam, the remainder of the morning was a meaningless blur. The only event he clearly remembered was talking to Clay after the rider *shedrowed* the colt.

"Feel alright to you?" Sam asked.

"He was every bit the colt I got to know yesterday morning," Clay answered.

Sam nodded, said, "This afternoon, when the gate opens, I want you to send this colt, and I don't want you to stop riding him until he hits the wire." Sam leaned toward Clay, his face coming close to Clay's, his eyes drilling into Clay's. "Do you hear me, jock? You *send* Black Deuce."

23. BLACK DEUCE

Black Deuce watched the sparrows flit back and forth in the rafters of the *holding barn*. He liked sparrows, he liked them ever since the day he awoke from a nap beneath the tree in his paddock to find one perched on his quarters. The little bird had looked at him with tiny bright eyes and chirped a cheerful little greeting. Black Deuce understood from that time that sparrows were like butterflies, they meant no harm, and weren't at all like the bumblebees that deserved his wary respect. The sparrows suddenly took flight from the rafters with a rush of their feathered wings and he watched them dart away. Black Deuce was jealous of sparrows, he wished he could fly too. But he was a thoroughbred, and unlike sparrows, had to contend with fences and stalls.

Black Deuce put his head out over the webbing, and looked up and down the barn's wide aisle. He looked among the people coming and going for someone he knew. He missed Robert, the man who nursed him from a bottle when he was little and taught him the bridle wasn't the device of torture he first thought it was. And he missed Emily. From her bedroom window, Emily had been his ever-present companion on long afternoons in his paddock. After Joshua had taken him away from the farm, he thought often of Robert and Emily, and sometimes when he thought of them late at night when he was alone in his stall, a strange trembling in his heart would make it impossible for him to sleep.

Black Deuce suddenly pinned his ears. He thought he

recognized Marcy Winchell come into the barn, the girl who galloped him at Joshua's farm. The colt didn't like the gallop girl, didn't like the way she jerked on the reins and made the bit saw painfully at his mouth, didn't like the way she rocked her weight in the saddle in a way that put him off balance when he galloped and ran, didn't like the way she always hit him with the whip. Robert had never been mean to him, though Robert had felt heavy in the saddle and frustrated his wanting to run with the leverage of a martingale. Robert had only let him run once, with little restraint, and that was on the morning of the day Joshua had first come to visit him on the farm.

When the girl he saw wasn't Marcy Winchell, Black Deuce pricked his ears and looked for Joshua. When he couldn't find him, he was disappointed, but his biggest disappointment was when he couldn't find Sam. It was Sam who touched him with the gentlest of hands, it was Sam who spoke to him in a voice that sounded like a soft brush felt against his coat.

Horses were led by Black Deuce's stall, and he watched them stepping lightly. A bolt of excitement shot through the colt and he backed away from his webbing, whirled in his stall on nimble legs and gave a call that burst from his throat. This brought Mary Linwood, the groom who was *running* him that day, to the webbing.

"Hey, hey, hey," Mary said. "You settle down. We'll be leaving for the paddock soon enough."

Mary went back to sit on a folding chair. The colt gave a quick snort to show his displeasure. Over the last days whenever something new and exciting happened, Sam had always been with him and he wanted Sam there now. Somehow the colt understood there were more things that Sam would teach him and ask him to do. The colt went to his webbing and watched and waited for Sam.

2

Ten minutes later came the announcement over the loudspeakers for the horses in the first race to come to the paddock, and Black Deuce's world went spinning into chaos. Chaos was not new to him. He'd gone through chaos on the day he'd tried to suckle from his dead dam, the day he was separated from his brother. He'd gone through chaos on the day Robert introduced him to the lead shank, introduced him to a saddle, on the day Robert first got on his back. But those days of chaos weren't nearly as complicated and astonishing as were these events happening now.

The walk with Mary along the pony path to the paddock had been without incident, but now the identifier gripped his upper lip to see his tattoo, and did it so quickly it left him shocked into standing still as a statue. Then he entered a world of noise, noise created by more people than he'd ever imagined existed. The way people rattled their *Racing Forms,* waved around their programs, talked and laughed as they crowded against the paddock fence put him in a near state of hysteria. The colt exchanged long looks with the other horses, seeing in some the reflection of his own panic, yet in others a calm that left him baffled. Then a sudden gust of wind blew a *tip sheet* out of the hands of a racing fan and it came at him, hanging in front of him like a kite. He reared, striking at the piece of paper with his front hooves, his eyes rolling in fear.

Then Sam was there.

Sam took the shank from Mary and began to lead the colt around the saddling ring. Black Deuce walked by beds of flowers bright with colors, walked beneath the heavy branches of stately elms. And Sam talked to him, and in his voice were the soft brushes. If not for Sam being with him, the colt would have used every source of power he had to try and escape. But Sam was there with his voice, handling him with knowing hands he knew he could trust, hands that gave him confidence, and the colt began to calm.

Now Black Deuce was under a tree being saddled by Sam and Rudy the valet. When Rudy reached under the colt to pass the girth to Sam, the girth slapped the colt's belly. This slap brought the colt out of his calm, angered him, caused air to rifle out of his nostrils in a loud snort. The colt's eyes flared, and he stepped sideways on agile legs, trying to maneuver Rudy so he could kick him.

"Easy, Deuce," Sam said, and the colt listened and settled. Now Sam looked at the valet and his voice was hard: "No need for that."

"Sorry, Sam," Rudy answered, "but I'm a bit pissed. Couldn't you have put Clay on a good horse, something *live*? I mean, this is his first mount since—"

"Rudy," Sam interrupted, "if you weren't my friend—"

"But I am you friend," Rudy said, now grinning, "and I'll buy you dinner tonight if this hundred-to-one shot finishes better than last."

"That's a bet," Sam said, smiling.

Black Deuce shifted his weight nervously from hoof to hoof. A trainer saddling another horse in the race was looking at him, a bright intensity in his eyes, and the colt wondered why this trainer's interest in him was so great. Now the colt watched the jockeys come into the paddock. Each carried that which he feared and hated...a whip. In helmet and Emily Brandt's white and green racing silks, Clay came up and shook Sam's hand. Clay's eyes were clear and sharp, the eyes of a race rider.

"The colt looks good, Sam," Clay said and tapped his own leg with his whip.

At this movement of the whip, Black Deuce's legs seemed to uncoil like springs and all four of his hooves came off the ground. The colt's eyes rolled to white in his head. Mary struggled briefly with the colt, her ponytail swinging back and forth, but soon had him in hand.

"Whoa, big horse," Clay said. "I remember from the other morning that you don't like the stick."

"You remember my instructions?" Sam said.

Clay nodded, smiled, answered, "Yep, and I can't wait to turn this colt loose."

With this, Rudy walked away frowning and looking at Clay like Clay had lost his mind.

Black Deuce kept his eyes on the whip in Clay's hand and was glad Marcy Winchell wasn't riding him today. With Marcy holding a whip, it was only a matter of time before the hitting would start. Black Deuce began to blink rapidly, looking around to see if Marcy was anywhere near.

The paddock judge gave the command: "Riders up!"

Sam gave Clay a leg up, and now Clay sat very straight in the saddle, as if his backbone was a steel rod. Clay tied a knot in the reins, a double loop through the middle, and Mary led Clay and the colt away to take their place in the line of horses leaving the paddock. Some of the racing fans stayed by the paddock fence to watch the horses leave for the track, and some hurried off to stand in line at the mutual windows. Came the sharp ringing bugle notes of *Call to the Post.*

"Well, aren't you behaving like a gentleman all of a sudden," Mary said to the colt.

With Sam following behind him and Clay sitting so easily in the saddle, Black Deuce was almost comfortable. Now and then the colt would look back at the whip Clay carried. The gusting wind tossed the branches of the tall elms so that shadows made shifting patterns on the walking ring in front of him. The colt watched them, remembering how he'd once romped and played with his shadow in the paddock back at the farm, always trying to escape it. But shadows weren't all play, there were times he ran across his paddock and felt angered when he couldn't outrun it. After he'd come to realize the shadow beside him was of his own making, he often wondered about this anger, but had never come to understand the anger and why not being able to outrun his shadow caused it to come.

The colt now found himself on the racetrack and Mary unsnapped the lead shank from the bit. When Mary turned him over to a waiting pony girl, the colt felt the feeling of chaos return. The post parade was a nightmare. Sam wasn't there to comfort him and Mary was gone too. They'd been replaced by strangers, a pinto pony and a red-cheeked pony girl. Then the colt noticed the huge presence of people in the towering grandstand and clubhouse. There were faces and faces, then even more faces, swarming and swirling, and the noise the people made, the merging of all their voices, put the colt into something like shock. The next thing Black Deuce knew he was being loaded into the starting gate.

In the same instant the bell rang, the doors opened in front of him with a slam and Clay was yelling at him: "Yaaaaaa!"

In the colt's second stride from the gate a horse bumped him hard and forced him into another horse. This bewildered the colt, and he was further bewildered by the yelling, cursing jockeys, and the horses that seemed to have him surrounded. From far across the infield the roar of the crowd in the grandstand and clubhouse reached him, distracted him, and he turned his head to look. The whip waved beside his head, never touching him, but causing him to look forward again into the direction he and the other horses were running. Just the sight of the whip caused a terror in the colt and he lost coordination, was unable to control where he put his hooves down. Now the other horses kicked dirt back at him, and it stung him, blinded him, and to get away from the dirt he ducked back and forth, threw his head in the air. Then he felt the bit working at his mouth, and it startled him when there was no pain, just a firm pull, and he knew it was Clay, telling him what to do. When he did as Clay wanted, he found the other horses were running on the inside of him and he was away from the stinging, blinding dirt. When the colt came to the turn, he felt Clay shift his weight, and the colt naturally switched to his *left lead*. Midway through the far turn, the feeling that all was chaos left him, and he settled into stride and it came to him that not once had Clay hit him with the whip.

Coming into the stretch, the colt did what Clay asked and switched back to his *right lead*. And the colt was amazed. Clay didn't throw him off balance by rocking his weight back and forth in the saddle. Clay sat poised above his withers, and with every move the colt made, Clay moved with him so together they were coordinated in their motion. Now the colt knew exactly where his hooves would touch the race track, and for the first time in his life, with a rider on his back, he felt free to really run. Clay threw a new cross in the reins, got low in the saddle, and Black Deuce took hold of the bit. When Clay waved the whip beside his head, the colt was unafraid, somehow understood that Clay was asking him to run even harder.

Within the wide arc of the colt's ribs, embedded in eleven hundred pounds of muscle and bone, the colt's heart began to hammer, valves and chambers working with the precision of a diesel engine. The colt threw himself forward, clenching the bit, and when he heard Clay shout again, the colt felt the irresistible need to please Clay by running still harder and faster.

The engine opened to full throttle.

The colt *flattened out,* his hooves reached still further, and the anger the colt had never understood while he raced his shadow now turned into a will to outrun other horses, now turned into a will to win. As the colt passed the last horse in front of him, he felt with every stride that he was lifting away from the racetrack, and he was seized by joy, for it seemed to Black Deuce that he was just like the sparrows, that he was flying.

Then after the wire, Clay reached for the colt, and the colt obeyed the tightening of the reins and began to reduce speed until in the clubhouse turn he was going at a long lope. When Clay finally stopped him on the backside, the colt stood there lathered and blowing, and beneath his sweat-darkened coat a vast network of veins and arteries stood out. The colt worked the bit in his mouth, still excited, still wanting to run, not wanting the joy of it to be over. Then Clay leaned forward, gave a gentle tug on the left rein, and the colt broke into an easy jog to go back to the winner's circle.

Black Deuce felt another rush of excitement when he saw Sam waiting for him out on the track, and when Sam walked up to him and spread his arms wide, the colt stopped and Sam hugged him. The colt felt one moment of alarm when Sam put his face against his neck. Sam talked to him in low mutters, and there were ripples and chokes in Sam's voice the colt didn't understand, but then Sam stepped away from the colt and snapped a lead shank on his bit and began to walk him into the winner's circle. When next Sam spoke, the colt knew all was well.

"Make way for the big horse," Sam said as he brought the colt to a stop for the win photo.

It was then that Mary let out a whoop. She was looking at the time of the race posted on the tote board. "Look at that, Sam. 1:09:2," Mary said.

Clay said. "And the colt damned near got knocked off his feet at the gate."

"I saw that," Sam said, looking up at Clay in the saddle, "and damned near had a heart attack."

When everyone looked toward the track photographer, the colt did too, and the colt's eyes caught the sun light and reflected it in diamond points of light.

Mary took the shank from Sam and after Clay dismounted and removed his tack, she led the colt out of the winner's circle. The colt's senses were sharp, as if he could taste, smell, feel everything around him, as if he could hear every sound. The world was a huge place, this he now knew, and more exciting than he'd ever dreamed. The crowding around of people didn't bother him now. He gave no notice to the rattling of *Racing Forms* or the waving of programs, and when fans leaned over the fence to look at him as he walked back through the paddock, he returned their look with the diamond light in his eyes. Outside the paddock, just a short way down the pony path, the colt suddenly bowed his neck, began to prance, and swung around to look back. He could hear a distant bugle play *Call to the Post* and he could see the horses form into line to leave the paddock for the next race. In a single afternoon the colt had been transformed, never again would he be the same, for in him the spirit of his kind had been awakened, never to be forgotten.

"Come on now, Deuce," Mary said, and once more began to

lead the colt down the pony path, "you'll get your chance to do all this again real soon…I promise."

When Mary led the colt into the *detention barn* area, there was a group of sparrows lined up on the white fence, and they twittered and hopped and ruffled their feathers. When Black Deuce turned his head to look at the sparrows, something very much like a smile moved through him.

24. SAM

Sam left the winner's circle and went straight back to the barn. Once in his office, he closed the door, sat down at his desk and made a call. The phone rang once.

"How'd he run?" Joshua said, his voice squeaky with tension.

"He won by twelve lengths in 1:09:2."

Joshua's voice leaped: "Aye!"

"Money showed on the tote board in the last minute and dropped his odds to sixteen to one."

"Damn, the books must have laid some of the money off."

"That's my guess."

Joshua changed the topic back to the colt. "Tell me about the way he ran."

"He got knocked down at the gate, I mean slaughtered," Sam said. "He was dead last down the backside, and on the turn started to move. When Clay asked him to run...I've never seen anything like it, Josh, the colt just ran away from the field and Clay never hit him with the stick."

"The Deuce is the one, Sammy, he's the horse of a lifetime...I knew it the first time I looked into those eyes of his."

"Aye," Sam said, giving his best Irish accent. Now Sam changed the topic back to money. "He paid $34.20, so Emily will get back 1.7 million. It's not enough to bust..." Sam stopped in midsentence.

"Bust?"

"I had to do it, Josh, you know I had to do it."

"Do what? Bust who?"

An uncomfortable silence passed, then Joshua's voice dropped in tone. "Tell me what ye've been up to."

In short sentences, Sam explained what he'd done and who he'd been dealing with to get it done.

"What have ye got yerself into, Sammy?" Joshua said, the high-pitched notes of his voice telling of his disbelief. "No wonder ye didn't want Bess and Amy with ye. If Belichio, that murderer, finds out—"

"He won't."

"I pray he doesn't, because if he does, he'll hang ye up on meat hooks."

Sam cut the conversation off and said goodbye to Joshua. He'd just leaned back in his chair when the phone rang.

"Hello?"

"Good job, mac," Baker said, his voice rumbling over the phone.

"How'd you get this number?"

"Mac, I know how much you weigh, where you live, what you had for breakfast—"

"When do I get my share of the money?" Sam interrupted.

Baker acted hurt. "What? You're not going to ask how my health is, how my dog is—"

"When do I get my share?" Sam interrupted again.

Baker laughed, a series of harsh barking sounds, then his voice dropped to a growl when he said, "You'll get your money. It'll take a few days to get it together, I had to spread it thin—"

"Somebody bet heavy on my horse late."

Baker laughed again, said, "Sammy boy, I got rent to pay too."

With a click, Sam was listening to a dial tone.

25. EMILY

Emily sat in a chair by the window, her eyes glassy openings to a mind living in the past. She was waiting for William to come home from school, for Edwin to return from checking on Sudan and her new foal. She smiled over her victory in another breeding coup, there was no mistaking the diamond light in the foal's eyes. Emily brushed the sleeve of her wedding dress against the arm of the chair, and bits of lace crumbled and drifted like snowflakes to the floor. Another memory flickered in her mind, and violins and cellos played.

Then a summer breeze swept down through the oaks. Leaves turned, moss-draped branches swayed, and when this breeze billowed the curtains at her window it distracted Emily and she returned from the past. Reality came without mercy. Edwin and William were dead. Grief forced her mouth open, her eyes to roll upward and then close. Her face turned the color of ash. She stiffened in her chair, felt a grabbing in her chest, and when she put both her hands over her heart, more lace crumbled onto her lap.

The phone rang.

When the phone kept ringing, Emily wondered where Robert was and she managed to stand. It wasn't until she saw the colt's paddock empty, that she remembered why the phone would be ringing on this day, at this time in the afternoon. She hurried as best she could and put the phone to her ear.

"Is that you, Joshua?" she said, her voice frail and halting.

"The colt won, Emily," Joshua said, "he devastated the field...you were right—"

Emily hung up the phone on Joshua, she'd heard enough. She felt such joy that it seemed possible to her that she would never know sorrow again. She began to walk to the door, to call for Robert, to tell him the news, but suddenly couldn't catch her breath. She made it to her chair and sat down heavily. A huge weight was now on her chest and she began to struggle. Then came a massive jolt of pain and Emily would never know sorrow again.

26. ROBERT

Robert hurried into the kitchen with the bags of groceries. A woman had backed into Miss Emily's car in the market parking lot. It had taken the police officers forever to get there, and then even longer to take statements. But now he was home, and Robert was sure the phone call about the colt's race had already come. He placed the groceries on the table and rushed out of the kitchen. In the gloom of the great hall a chance ray of sunlight flickered among the prisms of the crystal chandelier, and Robert paused at the bottom of the staircase. His eyes widened behind the lenses of his spectacles. There was something wrong. Never had he heard a silence so heavy in the great house.

"Miss Emily!" he called out.

Robert ran up the staircase and for the first time in his life, didn't knock before entering Emily's chambers.

When Robert saw Emily in her chair, he knew she was without pulse or heartbeat. Death had freed her, she was no longer a prisoner of her sorrow. She was now part of the past, the past she'd so desperately tried to relive for so long. Grief stirred in Robert, powerful and wrenching, but as always, his control remained firm. Robert backed out of Emily's room and softly closed the door. When he returned only minutes later, he had changed back into his livery. Outside Emily's door, he brushed off the sleeves of his black jacket, straightened his white tie, tugged on his vest to remove any wrinkles. Then, after knocking, Robert opened the door, and with a measured step that would dignify a king, he presented himself one last time to the Mistress of Southern Oak.

"Go to him, Miss Emily," Robert said, "go to where Mr. Edwin waits in the shade of the oaks."

27. JOSHUA

It was the next morning and Joshua walked into his tack room with Marcy Winchell's whip in his hand. Marcy was close behind him.

"Give it back, Josh," Marcy said.

Joshua turned around, waved the whip at her, said, "No. Ye've got to stop treating horses like animals."

"Give me my whip back," Marcy insisted, and now her cheeks were pink and there was a trace of anger in her voice.

"Not a chance, young lady," Joshua said. He waved the whip at her again. "This stick is the only thing keeping ye from being a good hand. Without it, ye'll do fine, with it, ye're a terror. Now off with ye, we'll start all over again with that tough two-year-old filly in the morning."

Marcy frowned at Joshua, huffed and puffed, then turned around and stomped off down the aisle of the barn. Joshua smiled, shouted after her, "I'll make a rider of ye yet, Marcy Winchell."

"I quit," Marcy shouted back.

Joshua's nose twitched. "That's the third time this week," he shouted.

The phone rang.

"Blarney Stone Farm," Joshua answered.

"It's Robert, Mr. Joshua."

Something in Robert's voice made Joshua ask, "What's wrong?"

"I have sad tidings, Mr. Joshua, Miss Emily has passed

away."

Joshua drew a sharp breath. Sorrow, not arthritis, now twisted and bent him, and looking at the floor, he walked behind his desk and sat down. He began to suffer a pain that would never completely leave him for the rest of his life. "Emily," he said in a voice that cracked, and he could see the emerald of her eyes, the auburn of her hair.

Robert said, "I tried to call yesterday, but was unable to reach you."

"I was celebrating and having dinner with Bess and Amy, Sam Jack's wife and wee daughter."

"I understand. I know the colt won."

"Did Emily suffer?" Joshua managed, his mouth quivering.

"You called her, didn't you, to tell her about the colt's race?"

"I did."

"Then she was happy, Mr. Joshua, she was very happy."

Joshua's eyes were suddenly wet and everything around him now shimmered. He took out a handkerchief, wiped at his eyes, "You weren't with her, then? She was alone?"

"She was happy, Mr. Joshua, she was very happy. The colt meant everything to her, the colt and, of course, you."

"Me?"

"She loved you."

"What?"

"Miss Emily loved you very much."

"Then why—"

"I don't believe even God knows what's in a woman's heart. I can only tell you what I know, and that is that her father insisted that she marry Edwin. She came to love him, love him dearly, but she once told me that she loved you from the first time she saw you in the paddock at Empire State Racetrack, and that she was only sixteen."

Everything shimmered around Joshua again, and it was all he could do to keep control. His voice climbed and dropped erratically when he said, "I remember that day, 'tis the very day I gave up me own heart to her."

"You understand that the Arceneaux line is now dead, that Miss Emily has no living relatives."

"No heir?"

"Oh, there's an heir, Mr. Joshua…I'm quite familiar with the contents of Miss Emily's last Will and Testament."

Joshua said nothing, he waited for Robert to go on.

"Southern Oak and the colt are yours, Mr. Joshua. She left everything to you, everything but two *breeding shares* in the colt that she left to me."

Stunned, Joshua's vision blurred and he sat blinking. "She left everything—" He stopped, collected himself, started again: "She left the colt and the farm to me?"

"Her Charleston attorneys, Weinberg & Weinberg, will be in touch. In the meanwhile, we need to make final arrangements for her…"

Joshua and Robert talked on, with Joshua telling Robert that he'd fly down to South Carolina the next day. After Joshua hung up the phone, he quickly dialed another number. When it rang, Sam answered on the other end of the line.

"Sammy," Joshua said, a choke in his voice.

"Are you alright?" Sam asked.

"Emily has passed away."

"Oh, Josh, I know what she meant to you, I'm so very sorry."

"Thanks, Sam."

"She was a beautiful woman."

"She was."

After a short silence, Sam said, "Not to be overly practical, but do you know who owns the colt now?"

Joshua sat in his chair blinking, staggered by the answer to this simple question.

After another short silence, Sam said, "Josh?"

Joshua took a deep breath and used it to say, "I do."

"What?"

"Emily left everything to me, the farm, the colt, everything."

"Josh, that's freaking wonderful," Sam blurted.

"Wonderful, yes, but Southern Oak is buried in debt, we need that money from those monsters ye're dealing with as soon as they'll cough it up."

"I'm meeting with Baker tonight."

"Make it as public a place as possible."

"That's what I wanted, but I'm meeting him at the Atlantic Hotel, a flop house just off Maxwell Street."

Joshua put a hand to his forehead, said, "I'll never see me boy Sammy again."

"I'll be alright. Baker thinks Black Deuce was just the first of many horses I'm going to give him to bet on. I'm an investment to him."

"And when he finds out there are no others?"

"Let's talk about something else, like where I'm going to run the colt next."

Joshua said, "It's a shame we didn't get him earlier so he could run in the Triple Crown."

"Those grueling races come so early in the year. I'm going to give Emily credit for being far-sighted. The colt's so big, and she gave him all the time he needed to mature."

"Where are ye going to run him?"

"Emily has him nominated for the Windy City Derby here at Suburban."

"That's coming up soon."

"A week from this Saturday."

"It's a mile and one eighth."

"This colt's dead fit and if you could have seen what he did yesterday—"

"Yesterday he beat a field of maidens, not a good bunch of three-year-olds running for a purse of one-hundred-fifty-thousand dollars. There'll ship in from California and New York to run for that big pot."

Sam gave a quick laugh, said, "Close your eyes, Josh."

"What? Are ye daft?"

"Just close your eyes."

Joshua squeezed his lids together. "Alright then, me eyes are closed."

"Now, I want you to picture him in your mind, picture Black Deuce."

Joshua's eyes snapped open. "Aye, run the colt in the Windy City Derby, and God help those other poor horses."

28. Sam

It was just before midnight, and Sam left his truck parked around the corner from the Atlantic Hotel. He walked through the cone of white light beneath a street lamp, and in that moment felt an aloneness he'd not known since he was a boy missing his father. Vacant storefronts with broad dark windows and padlocked doors lined the block. Little gusts of wind swirled the dust and litter on the sidewalk. Sam stopped in front of the five-story brownstone building. Faded curtains blinded the rows of windows and Sam peered through the tall pane of glass framed in the front door. Jaundiced light from the lobby flushed him a sickly yellow.

Footsteps.

A woman stepped out of a dark door well to his left and Sam stepped back from her. A cheap lavender dress clung to her like paint, her heels were spiked, her makeup looked thick and sticky. Drug-dulled eyes shifted as she looked Sam up and down.

"Need a date, handsome?" she said, slurring her words.

Sam rushed through the hotel's front door.

"Didn't mean to scare you, lover," she called after him, and like a vision in a nightmare, she slowly retreated back into the darkness of the door well.

The door shut behind Sam in a glassy rattle. His eyes darted around the lobby. The plaster ceiling was a network of cracks, wallpaper roses withered on the walls, once elegant red-plush furniture smelled of damp and rot. The desk clerk was alone, snoring, his chin resting on his chest, his bald head shining in the glare of the light bulb dangling from a cord above him. Sam walked by him, his footsteps muffled by carpeting that smelled worse than the furniture. Moving down a badly lit hallway, Sam came to room seventeen. He raised his hand, but the door swung open before he could knock.

"You must have ESP," Sam said to Baker, stepping into the room.

"I just know my part of the jungle, mac," baker answered.

When Baker locked the door, there was a click. Then came the sound of a bolt sliding into place. Baker wore a vested blue suit. Draped across his vest was a gold watch chain. The nickel plate of his revolver flashed as he tucked it away in his shoulder holster. Sam looked into Baker's eyes and saw an animal looking back. Nausea came and went.

"You don't look so good, mac," Baker said, a smile stretching his face. "You alright?"

Sam swallowed, was very much on guard, said, "I'm fine."

A bare light bulb hung from the ceiling above the table, its weak glare throwing shadows into the corners of the room. Against one wall was a bed with a mattress that sagged, against another was a chest of drawers. The room reeked of the sour smell of old linen. On the table was a large army surplus duffle bag.

"Glad you're okay," Baker said as he walked over to the table. He lowered his hulking form onto a chair, and without looking away from Sam, he unzipped the duffle bag and showed Sam what was in it: bundles of one-hundred dollar bills. "Just think, mac, if you weren't okay, I'd just have to keep all this money for myself."

Just as Sam took a step toward the table, Baker turned his head quickly toward the door. In the next instant, the door flew open in a wood-splintering crash, and a huge, square-shouldered man rushed in, thrusting a long-barreled revolver before him. The man's sloping forehead and heavily boned jaw made him look like a Neanderthal, his eyes shown like polished steel.

"Guns on the floor," he said.

Baker bristled like a rabid dog, but he removed his revolver from the shoulder holster and let it drop to the carpet with a dull thud. Sam's pulse was loud in his ears.

"I don't have a gun," he said.

"Turn around and show me," the man said.

Sam did show him, holding up his hands as he slowly did a complete turn.

Satisfied, the man stepped closer to Baker, keeping the gun pointed at Baker's chest. "All clear," he said to someone waiting out in the dark hall.

A small, dark-suited man stepped into the room. After closing the broken door as best he could, he turned to face Baker and Sam. Snake eyes glittered in the shadow of a wide-brimmed hat, and Antonio Belichio's wire-thin lips tightened into a grin against his teeth.

Baker made a growling sound, and hate and fear put a pounding in Sam's head.

"Sam and Bill, what a pleasure to catch you both together," Belichio said in a hiss. Then he glanced at the table and anger altered his face, made it hard and red. "How fucking stupid do you think I am? You didn't think I'd find out about your little coup? You thought I'd let you walk away with my money?" He pulled out a nickel-plated automatic pistol, said, "Tie these nitwits up, Frankie."

"Sure thing, boss," Frankie answered. Frankie tucked his revolver in his belt, and took out a length of twine. He moved quickly around Belichio, careful not to come between the bookmaker's automatic and Baker.

"Don't get me wrong, Sam," Belichio said, "I can understand a guy trying to cash a bet, but you must have picked among the rotten fish a long time to come up with Baker for a partner. Didn't you know Bill worked for me at one time?"

Breathing heavily, Sam looked away from Belichio to stare at Baker.

"That's right, Sam," Belichio continued, "he used to take care of the people who didn't pay. How many people do you suppose you killed for me Bill? Six, maybe seven?"

Baker glowered at Belichio, and Frankie, now behind Baker, forced Baker's hands behind his back. Frankie began to loop the twine around Baker's wrists.

Pretending to contemplate, Belichio said, "At least seven now that I think of it," then he looked squarely at Sam with his mean, dark, snake eyes, "but that number doesn't include Chinamen or guys who train horses and have farms in Iowa. They're too easy, don't fight much, so they don't count." Belichio's chest jerked with laughter. "You can imagine what a kick it was to find out that Henry Jack's son and Bill Baker were gambling partners."

Sam saw the world in sharp clear focus, and rage made the arteries in his neck bulge. He threw himself at Belichio, trying to knock the gun from the old man's hand, wanting to gouge the old man's eyes out, rip his tongue from his throat. In that exact instant, Baker lunged backwards, pinning Frankie against the wall. Bellowing, struggling, he pulled his hands free, swung his elbows back with rib-breaking force, then both men grabbed for the gun stuck in Frankie's belt. Desperate and fumbling hands dropped the gun, and Baker kicked it away and reached in his coat pocket to pull out a switch blade. The blade appeared with a sharp click. Came the flashing blur of polished steel, and Baker buried the knife in Frankie's gut. Baker savagely jerked the knife back and forth, opening Frankie's abdomen, then jumped back. Frankie slid down the wall, clutching at the curls of intestines that bulged from the bloody wound. Slumped on the floor, gutted, bleeding, dying, Frankie looked up at Baker with bewildered eyes that quickly grew dim and then blank.

Sam and Belichio were sprawled and rolling on the floor. Belichio had kept a grip on his pistol. He swung it toward Sam, but Sam leaped away. It was then that Sam heard an animal sound, wild, furious, frightening, and he looked up to see Baker lunging across the room at Belichio. The air exploded, a jet of yellow flame blazed from the barrel of the automatic, and a bullet shattered Baker's jaw and mangled his neck as it exited. Blood pumped out of Baker's jugular, and before Belichio could fire again, Baker grabbed the automatic with one hand and with the other swung his switchblade and buried it in Belichio with such force that it lifted the old man off the floor. Baker kept Belichio impaled on his switchblade, holding him up in the air, and Belichio twisted and squirmed and kicked. Belichio's mouth rounded to a black hole in his face, but with Baker jerking on the switchblade, he seemed unable to gather air enough to scream. Then Belichio's strange eyes rolled in his head and he stopped struggling and went limp. Baker gave the switchblade one last hard jerk, then tossed Belichio aside. Belichio twitched there on the floor, his arms and legs left at odd angles by the indifference of death. Baker's switchblade was still in him.

Baker clutched at his neck with both hands and blood spurted between his fingers. Baker's shattered jaw sagged open and his tongue wagged in the bloody hole that was his mouth. He stumbled over to the table and sat down heavily on a chair. Giving Sam a murderous look, he smeared blood on the duffle bag and bundles of the money. Then Baker grabbed the gold chain draped across the front of his vest, yanked it free, and threw the chain and the pocket watch attached to it so it landed at Sam's feet. Sam stared at the watch. He felt a shock of recognition. He stooped down, picked up the watch. Inscribed on the back of the fine Patek Phillipe was the inscription *Silhouette, Winner of the 1953 Chicago Gold Cup.*

Baker made an odd gurgling sound, and Sam looked up to see him sputtering blood and pink froth as he tried to laugh. Then Baker was suddenly fierce again. He stood up, swung his arms wide, and took a step toward Sam. Sam felt a jolt of terror, then Baker's knees buckled and he fell heavily to the floor and was dead.

The last thing Sam remembered about room seventeen of the Atlantic Hotel was making the decision to run and not to take any of the money. The ride back to his apartment was a blur of streetlights, stop signs and expressways. When he got into his apartment, he heaved for air. It felt like he'd been holding his breath since running out the back door of the Hotel.

Then the phone rang.

29. BESS

It was that time of night when the lonely and troubled are still awake, and Bess was in the kitchen, looking out the window into the dark. She was thinking of Sam. She never stopped wanting him home, and to keep sane, she could trick herself into believing she saw him at lunch time sitting at the table with her, could make him materialize when she heard a certain song on the radio, and when she was lying in bed, she could close her eyes and hear his hot whispers, feel his body press against hers, and it was his touch, not her own, that thrilled her and made her shiver. Looking out the window into vast darkness, the feeling of being forsaken became unbearable, and she made the abrupt decision that she had to talk to Sam, that what she suddenly knew she had to say couldn't wait until morning. She finally had the courage to tell him that she could no longer tolerate the life she was living as his wife. She was tired of Sam being a phantom of her imagination.

Bess dialed the phone and Sam answered.

"I need you," Bess blurted. "Amy and I both need you."

"What?"

Bess didn't recognize Sam's voice. The voice sounded strange and high-pitched. "Sam?" she said.

"It's me. What's wrong? Are you alright? Is Amy alright?"

"No, Amy and I are not alright. I need my husband, and Amy needs her father."

"Bess, we've talked about this. Not now."

"Then when? I want to know when."

Sounding agitated in a way she'd never heard before, Sam repeated lines from other phone conversations, about how he needed to get settled in as trainer of the Keene horses and how Emily Brandt's colt needed so much of his time. He told her for the hundredth time that he didn't want Amy going to school in a place like Chicago.

A frown put delicate lines in Bess' forehead. "Sam, have you been drinking?"

"No."

"You sound so strange."

"I'm sorry, it's been..." Sam never finished the sentence.

"About Amy and school," Bess went on. "She can go to a good private school and I can drop her off and pick her up every day."

Sounding even more agitated, Sam began to repeat all the arguments he'd already made that kept Bess and Amy on the little rented farm in Iowa, and Bess started to tremble. It wasn't the tremble that came before the tears, it was a different tremble, a tremble foreign to her. Never in her life had she been so angry.

"Excuses," Bess said, and there was no sound of harps in her voice. "I'm tired of excuses. What is wrong with you? Don't you love us?"

"Bess, I love you and Amy more than anything in the world."

"No, Sam," Bess shook her head rapidly back and forth, "you don't love us more than anything in the world...you'll never love us more than you love horses."

Sam answered, but his voice was suddenly muffled and Bess held the phone tight to her ear, trying to listen and hear every word he said. When she heard Sam say something about sending her more money, Bess' anger turned into rage.

"You think I'm calling you for money?" she said, and realized she wasn't restraining her voice, that she was shouting into the phone. "Amy and I don't need more money, Sam, we need you."

Bess slammed the phone down so hard it made loud ringing

noises. Unable to stop trembling, she went into her bedroom and sat down on the bed. Next to her pillow was Sam's pillow, and on Sam's pillow was one of his shirts, one she had purposely kept and hadn't washed. There in the dark, she held the shirt to her face. Just the smell of him brought the memory of every kiss, every moment of love she and Sam had shared, and the loneliness she felt was overwhelming. It was like the night had become a dark hole she was falling into. Bess began to cry, and it was then that she became aware that someone was beside her on the bed and that little arms were hugging her and that little Amy was crying too.

30. JOSHUA

It was the next afternoon, and Joshua sat on a lawn chair out in front of his main barn. He'd talked to Sam by phone in the early hours of the morning and knew what had happened in room seventeen of the Atlantic Hotel. He also knew that Sam and Bess were having problems and that Sam had driven over to see Bess after the work under the Keene shedrow was done that morning. Joshua sat waiting and worrying about Sam, and then, just after three o'clock, Sam's truck turned up his lane.

Joshua stood, straightening slowly, and Sam parked the truck and got out. One look at Sam and Joshua looked away, cursed himself, felt a guilt that went soul-deep. Sam looked like a man who'd been through hell. Dark rings were under his eyes, and his face was gray, deeply grooved. He walked with a stumble, like a man exhausted.

"I should never have gotten ye in the middle of this," Joshua said. "I'm an old fool, I just couldn't say no to Emily."

"I'm sorry about the money," Sam said with small breaks in his voice, "and I'm sorry I let you and Emily down. I'm sorry I tried to use the colt to get justice."

Joshua's Irish eyes were hard as stone. "Justice was delivered. The men ye left in that room will all be turned away at the gates of heaven, and I'll hear no more about the money...damn the money. That ye're alright is all I care about."

Joshua opened his arms, and Sam stepped into them. The old

horseman hugged Sam strongly and Sam hugged him back. Joshua felt the relief a father feels when he knows his son has survived the threat of death. Now the two men stepped away from each other, and Sam stuck a hand into the pocket of his blue jeans. When he brought the hand back out, his father's Patek Phillipe dangled from the gold chain he held. The watch slowly turned at the end of the chain, the gold case shining. Joshua reached out and took the watch from Sam, his eyes wide with disbelief.

"Can ye imagine the coincidence of it all?" Joshua said, looking at the inscription on the back of the watch. "It boggles me mind."

Joshua pointed at the two lawn chairs.

"Let's sit," Joshua said. After they both sat down, Joshua handed the watch back to Sam, continued: "Did anyone see ye? Can they place ye at the Atlantic Hotel?"

"I didn't touch anything," Sam said. "Not the doorknob when I arrived at the room and nothing while I was there. I swung the door to the room open with my foot when I left, Belichio's—"As soon as he said that name, Sam squeezed his eyes shut. After a deep breath, he looked at Joshua explained: "The door was kicked in, the locks broken, it was easy to open with my foot."

"So no fingerprints. Did anyone see ye?"

"I don't think so. But wait—" Sam blinked, fell silent, then said, "There was a girl…out front when I went into the hotel."

"At that time of night, in front of a flop house, a working girl?"

"Yes."

"Any mention of her in the *Tribune* this morning?"

"No, and I read the article over and over."

"Even if she shows up, you committed no crime in that room."

"No, not in that room."

"We'll keep an eye on the paper, but I don't think ye've got a thing to worry about. If the police knew anything, they'd already be at yer door."

"But there was something about this morning's *Tribune*

article, Josh, something left out, something never mentioned."

"What?"

"The money, the duffle bag...no mention of all that money stuffed in the duffle bag I left on the table."

Joshua looked off into the distance and his eyes remained fixed there. Moments passed and a swallow darted through the barn's open doors and flew up into the rafters. When Joshua turned back to Sam, he said, "Someone else was there. Who else knew about yer involvement with Baker?"

Sam said, "The Deacon."

Joshua stared at Sam, twitched, looked away. "Another of the monsters," he said. When Joshua looked back at Sam, he gave him a sharp hard stare. "Ye didn't see anyone else though...ye can't place The Deacon there at the hotel?"

"No...I saw no one else."

Joshua blinked, rubbed his elbow, looked at the ground. "If The Deacon was there, and he thought ye saw him, ye'd already be dead. All he wanted was the money. This smells of a double-cross to me. The Deacon was in another of that hotel's rooms, probably right across the hall watching who was going in and out of room seventeen, just waiting for the right time to strike."

Sam processed what Joshua had just said. "He was going to kill us...The Deacon was going to kill Baker and me for the money?"

"It's what me bones tell me is true," Joshua said. "But Belichio showed up and after the smoke cleared, all The Deacon had to do was walk into the room, take the bag, and walk back out...he didn't need to kill anyone."

Sam leaned forward to rest his elbows on his knees and look at the watch he held in the palm of his right hand, then he swung his head up quickly to look at Joshua with wide glassy eyes. Sam said, "The way Baker died, the blood, and the way he killed—" Sam stopped, put a hand over his mouth, made a gasping sound.

"Ye are innocent of all that," Joshua said in his not-to-be-argued-with voice. "Those men were killers, and they died a killer's death. Now enough of being weak, put all that happened in that hotel room from yer mind. Live the rest of yer life as if it never happened." Joshua stared into Sam's eyes, and when Sam dropped his hand from his mouth and leaned back in his chair, Joshua changed the subject: "What did Bess have to say?"

Sam drew a deep breath, let it go, said, "She wouldn't see me."

"No?"

"No. Her father was there, and she talked to me through him, wouldn't even let me in the house."

Joshua scowled, leaned over, spit on the ground. "Ezra, what a piece of work...I wish him to Borneo where the cannibals can eat him up."

"He enjoyed himself, working as the go-between. You should have seen the way he grinned at me through the crack in the door."

"The bastard." Joshua spit again, then changed the subject: "What was it that Bess had to say?"

"Bess said that either we're a family, or not a family."

"There's sense in that."

Sam turned, looked at Joshua with anxiety-bright eyes. "I can't bring her and Amy to Chicago, not now. The police may be coming, and God knows who else."

"Ye couldn't tell her that, so what did ye tell her?"

"That I love her, that I love Amy, and that I'm never going to give them up."

"That's a good place to leave it for now," Joshua said, then crossed his legs, released his breath in a long sigh. "But I'm hardly the man to come to for advice on women."

"I'm sorry, Josh," Sam said, "I completely forgot to ask about Emily's funeral."

"She's at peace, she's beside Edwin in the Arceneaux family plot right there on the farm."

"How is the farm?"

"It's like a beautiful woman with a dirty face, that's how a poet might describe Southern Oak. But the good news is, I've got Robert to count on and there's nothing wrong there that can't be cured with money."

"How much money are you going to need?"

Joshua's nose twitched. "To start with, the winner's share of the Windy City Derby."

31. SAM

Sam got through the next days by spending long hours at the barn. Oscar, the night watchman, considered it part of a new nighttime routine to find Sam in the shedrow office or sitting on a bale of straw in front of Black Deuce's stall. The newspapers carried lurid articles about the killings in the Atlantic Hotel. In these articles, there was never any mention of witnesses or a duffle bag of money, and any conjectures of other parties involved were brief and without detail.

These days saw the Keene horses winning no races. Excommunicator ran third in an allowance race going a mile on the grass, Danube ran fourth against three and four-year-old fillies in a non-winners of a race other than maiden or claiming, and Evening Song, who'd been training so well, ran a disappointing sixth in a two-year-old maiden allowance. But after Evening Song ran, Sam had an idea about what had gone wrong, and the next time the filly—who'd grown so attached to Voodoo Queen—went to the post, Sam intended to make a change he thought would make all the difference in the way the filly ran.

The highlight of the week was when Black Deuce worked a mile on Sunday morning.

Sam stood at the gap, stop watch in hand, watching as Clay dropped Black Deuce over to the rail at the mile pole just before the clubhouse turn. Black Deuce accelerated with a quickness that startled Sam, and when the colt went by, every muscle in him was working in perfect rhythm with his hooves, giving him a grace that was breathtaking. Sam became concerned when the colt suddenly began to act rank under Clay, throwing his head in a temper, but then Sam understood. Two other horses were working together a good twelve lengths ahead of the colt, and the colt had seen them. At the three-eighths pole, Clay turned Black Deuce loose, and the colt accelerated, each of his strides becoming more powerful than the one before it. He was running so fast his hooves never seemed to quite touch the ground. The sight sent a thrill through Sam. At the eighth pole, Clay took the colt off the rail to go around the other two horses, and the colt easily blew by the pair to draw away at the wire. Sam's stop watch clicked and it read 1:35:4.

Sam stood there at the gap while watching Clay let the colt gallop out an extra eighth. The colt always inspired in Sam the same thought, that never in his life had he seen a horse as beautiful as Black Deuce.

Ralph Binder, a tall long-nosed man with a big mouth full of crooked teeth, walked up to Sam and put his face inches from Sam's. Binder was a *Kentucky hard boot* and trained for Green Paddock Farm, one of the oldest and most powerful breeding farms in the blue grass state. Anger flushed Binder's face. Sam arched his back, but refused to step away from Binder.

"That your black colt?" Binder said hotly.

"That is my black colt," Sam answered, and in saying this, Sam couldn't help but smile.

"That fucking rider of yours…that was a dangerous thing to do."

Sam stared back into Binder's eyes. "If I could hear Clay yelling *on the outside*, those two jocks in front of him could hear too."

Binder stomped around in a small circle. "It figures it'd be Repp, that washed up drunk."

Sam was no longer interested in Binder's tantrum, Black Deuce and Clay were coming back. The colt moved in a fast walk, raising dust with his hooves that the morning breeze quickly blew away. About him was the unmistakable look of power. Clay turned the colt to face him back toward the racetrack, then stopped him. The colt took a long moment to look out over the morning action. He worked the bit in his mouth, blinked, held his head high and took in all the sights. Then Clay turned him around and came off the track where Sam waited. Binder was there too.

"Don't you ever do that to my horses again," Binder shouted.

"Work around them?" Clay said in wonder, looking at Sam with a look of confusion, then back at Binder.

"Don't get smart with me you *has been.*"

Clay let the colt step along the pony path, he turned back in the saddle. "Mr. Binder, sir," Clay said respectfully, "if you don't want me to work around your horses, you'll just need to get faster horses."

Binder jumped as if stung by a bee. "Smart ass," he shouted. "Sam Jack, you might have Keene behind you now, but you're still a *gyp*, and you'll always be a gyp."

Sam didn't bother to answer, he was too involved in watching the colt. The colt took no bad steps, looking more like he should be on his way to the track, not on his way back to the barn. That Sam was oblivious to Binder seemed to anger Binder even more. Binder, still standing at the gap, continued to sputter and swear. Clay sat in the saddle grinning at Sam.

"Ignoring Binder is the best way to handle him, Sam."

"Only idiots argue with idiots," Sam answered.

"Training for Green Paddock sure has changed Ralph's luck," Clay said. "I remember the old days when he only trained a horse or two. The feed man would meet him at the winner's circle whenever he won a race...hoping to get paid."

Sam changed the topic, asked, "How'd Deuce feel, Clay?"

"Strong."

Sam nodded, kept watching the colt. "Any doubt he'll get the distance?"

"None," Clay answered.

As Black Deuce moved along, Sam was aware of the interest the colt provoked. Three trainers stood talking together near the pony path, and as the colt went by, they went silent and followed him with their eyes. An owner and trainer were walking behind a horse on its way to the track, but when they saw Black Deuce they stopped to look the colt over. Black Deuce caused people to pause from what they were doing and stare after him all along the pony path.

Clay suddenly squeezed his eyes closed, covered his nose and mouth with his hand, and sneezed. The colt gave a hop, began to prance with his neck bowed, and Sam came around and took hold of the reins. With Sam now leading the colt, Clay kicked his feet out of the irons and the colt settled back into a walk. Clay gave a snicker.

"You know the real reason Binder's pissed?" Clay said.

"Just his natural ornery self?"

"Well, yeah, that, but do you know who those two horses were we worked around?"

Sam shook his head that he didn't know.

"That was his good three-year-old colt, Reason Why, and working with him was his other good colt, Cryptic."

Sam did a double-take. "That was Cryptic? You and Deuce made Cryptic eat dirt?"

"That's right." Clay was smiling wide. "Deuce just blew by the colt that ran forth in the Kentucky Derby and second in the Belmont...and that's why Mr. Binder is so upset."

A smile broke across Sam's face, and for the first time since leaving room seventeen of the Atlantic Hotel, he was happy. He was even happier the next day when he read in the *Form* that Green Paddock Farm's *entry* in the Windy City Derby, Reason Why and Cryptic, was the heavy six-to-five favorite.

2

Bill Baker had Sam in his grip. Baker squeezed him so hard Sam felt ribs snap, and each time Baker tried to laugh blood blew out of his mouth in a red spray that splattered Sam's face. Sam shrieked, tried to break free, but Baker had him and wouldn't let go. In the next flash, Black Deuce was down in his stall, thrashing from the pain of a twisted gut, his legs flailing, eyes wild, and Sam wasn't there to help him, no one was there in the dark of night to help the colt.

Sam bolted upright in his bed, awakened by his nightmares. He gasped for air, he was wet with sweat. Sam stumbled around in the dark, grabbing at clothes to put on, and then he was in his truck heading for the barn. At Euclid and Gadsden Road, the intersection in front of the stable gate, Sam blew through a stop light. He didn't even see the red, he was concentrated on the image projecting in his mind, the image of the colt down in his stall.

Head lights in his review mirror, then swirls of red and blue. The police.

Sam pulled over to the side of the road, just outside the stable gate. The squad car stopped behind him. In the side mirror, Sam watched an officer in blue get out of his cruiser, then come to a stop at the back corner of the truck. A flashlight beam sliced through the night, flashing in the mirror. The officer had his hand on his holstered gun.

"Let me see your hands," the officer demanded.

Sam put both his hands out the window. "Yes, officer," he said, and the feeling of being trapped came over him.

"Keep them there," the officer said and now came up to the side window and shined the flashlight in Sam's face. Sam blinked in the harsh glare.

"I'm sorry about that, officer, that red—"

"Driver's license and registration," the officer interrupted.

After reaching into his glove compartment and taking out his wallet, Sam gave the officer what he asked for. Sam sat looking into the flashlight's bright beam, blinking, squinting, turning his head from side to side. The officer finally turned the flashlight off. He was a fit forty-year-old in a neatly pressed uniform.

"Mr. Jack, a red light means what?"

"Stop."

"Very good. Now why the big hurry?"

"My horse," Sam pointed toward the stable gate, "I had a nightmare that he was sick, and I want to check on him."

"A nightmare about a sick horse?"

"Yes, officer."

"You must really care about this horse."

"I do, and I'm worried about him."

The officer nodded, and with a steady gaze, studied Sam coldly without a trace of emotion. Then suddenly the officer relaxed, said, "I get nightmares like that too, Mr. Jack, but not about horses. I get them about my three kids...I'm always worried about my kids."

"I understand, officer. I've got a wife and little girl too, Amy's six-years-old."

The officer smiled. "Oh, kids are so much fun at that age. I wouldn't give up the memories of those years with my kids for anything."

Sam smiled, pictured Amy's little face.

The officer handed Sam his license and registration back, said, "Mr. Jack, no ticket for you tonight, but drive careful, not just for your own sake, but for your family's sake...what would Amy do without her father?"

"Thank you, officer," Sam answered.

The officer turned to walk away, but stopped, looked back. "What's your horse's name?" he asked.

"Black Deuce."

"Should I bet on him?"

"This Saturday, in the Windy City Derby, he'll run good."

The officer gave a thumbs-up sign, and smiled at Sam before walking back to his car.

Sam pulled away slowly, and took a turn into the backstretch. Some of what the police officer had said would remain forever in his thoughts. Sam pulled up to the barn, parked the truck, and got out. In the muffled stillness of the night, the sound of Sam closing the door to the truck went from barn to barn. An owl, the beat of its wings soundless, landed on the peak of barn one's roof. The owl stood out as a silhouette in the starlit sky. When the owl hooted, all the mice in the feed rooms stopped to listen. Sam walked under the shedrow, looked up the line of stalls.

"Hey, Sam," Oscar said, stepping out of a cluster of shadows. Before Sam could ask the question he always asked, Oscar reported: "The colt's fine, Sam, I just looked in at him. Coffee?"

Sam grinned. "Oscar, when have I ever turned down a cup of your coffee?"

"Cup of joe, coming right up."

With a steaming mug of coffee in his hand, Sam walked down to the last stall at the end. When he got to Black Deuce's stall, the colt was there waiting for him at his webbing. Sam flipped on the light, then rubbed the colt's neck with his free hand, and like he always did, talked to him in low mutters. The colt looked deep into Sam's eyes, pressed his muzzle against Sam's chest and nudged him gently.

Sam could hear the phone ring in his office, heard Oscar answer it, and then heard Oscar's footsteps.

"It's the wife, Sam," Oscar said.

Sam hurried down the shedrow in a half run, couldn't stop thinking that something was terribly wrong. Horses stirred in their stalls, came to their webbings, and when Sam flipped on the light in the office, pairs of eyes reflected like mirrors up and down the shedrow.

Sam picked up the phone. "What's wrong?"

"I tried calling your apartment, but there wasn't an answer and I got worried about you."

"Don't worry, I'm here."

"The sound of your voice…"

"What about my voice?"

"You sound like…you sound like yourself."

"I love you," Sam said.

"That's funny," Bess said, and there were harps in her voice, "I was calling to tell you the same thing."

"We're going to get through this."

"Time will tell," Bess said.

3

The sun had long since burned off the morning mist between the barns, and Sam stood in the office, studying the board. Only two more horses needed to track. The noise of the shedrow came through the door: the spray of a water hose, the rattle of a shank, the tap of a blacksmith's hammer. Sam stepped back out the door. A groom, flushed with work, shuffled down the row of stalls, struggling with the weight of a full water bucket, and two hotwalkers went by leading horses, one with a brisk step, the other in an easy amble. The last set of horses to come back from the track were getting their baths, and the gallop boys were in the tack room gathering tack for the last two horses. Mutineer had just come back from his gallop, and his gallop girl came out of the old gelding's stall with a saddle over one arm and holding up a bridle in her other hand. Highland Lad, a high-strung two-year-old being hotwalked, began to kick and rear, raising dust all around him, and everyone stopped what they were doing, watched until the hotwalker got him under control again, then plunged back to work.

Vance came up to stand beside Sam.

"Disappointing the way Evening Song ran the other day," Vance said.

"I've got a plan to turn that around," Sam answered.

"Bet I know what it is," Vance said.

"Tell me what you think we should do."

"The next time the filly runs, I think we should use Voodoo to pony her up to the paddock, even use Voodoo to pony the filly to the gate."

Sam nodded. "You're starting to think like me," he said. "I think it'll make all the difference in the world. It'll keep the filly calm, a lot less likely to *wash out*."

Vance looked into the office, smiled, pointed at a saucer of milk on the floor. "Still trying to make a friend of that old orange tomcat, Sam?"

"He's a sly old timer, he'll have nothing to do with me. I don't think I've gotten closer than twenty feet of him."

"Don't feel bad, he doesn't let anyone near him. I did get a good look at him once though. He's a real honest to goodness *ratter*, his face is all scared up."

"He's a big boy too," Sam said. "Bet he weighs over twenty pounds."

Sam looked to where a horse van came to a stop on the main road through the backstretch. It was a big eighteen-wheeler, a Cranston & Reeves Horse Transport van. The tractor's big diesel engine clattered, traces of black smoke puffed out of the chrome exhaust pipe mounted vertically behind the bright red cab. A side door came open and a man tossed out a suitcase and climbed down off the trailer. Once on the ground and clear, he picked up the suitcase, waved, and the van pulled away. Another man stood in the open doorway of the trailer, waving at the man that had gotten off. The big van took a turn to go down a side road toward barns twenty through twenty-eight, and the man that had gotten off the van started walking toward where Sam and Vance stood.

As soon as Sam recognized who it was, he started grinning and said, "I'll be damned, it's Moses Kent."

"Who's Moses Kent?" Vance asked.

"He's Deuce's new groom, Joshua sent for him, and he's the best *leg man* in the business." Now Sam cupped his hands to the sides of his mouth and shouted, "Moses, I'll give you a thousand dollars for your liniment recipe."

Moses looked up, saw Sam watching him and gave a cackle. "No, sir, ain't for sale, only the hosses I put these hands on get that special recipe."

Moses smiled and a gold front tooth gleamed in his black face. Moses was in his fifties, had a broad forehead and a nose wide at the nostrils. Suspenders held up loose-fitting trousers, and his old crumpled hat was sweat-stained. Moses was the kind of man who was happy only when he was around horses, and he was, without doubt, the best racehorse groom alive. If anyone wanted to argue the point, they could argue with Joshua Kincaid. Moses had worked for Joshua on and off for thirty years, and every time Joshua got a big horse, he put out the call for Moses.

Sam turned to Vance, said, "There's not a better assistant trainer on this backstretch than you, Vance, but watch what this man does with a horse and you'll learn a lot."

"Thanks, Sam," Vance answered. "I'll keep my eyes open."

Moses came to a stop in front of Sam and put the suitcase down. He took his hat off, wiped his forehead with his shirt sleeve, and put his hat back on. He smiled widely, the gold tooth shining. Like it always did, the air around Moses smelled of liniment.

"This must be *some* hoss you got, Sam, and I sure hope he's worth me coming all the way up from Lexington Downs. You know I don't much like leaving Kentucky."

"He is *some* horse," Sam assured.

"Name?"

"Black Deuce."

"Got a runner's name," Moses quipped.

"Moses, you're only going to rub one horse for me, just Black Deuce."

"Oh, I know what that means. It means we'll be doing a lot of shipping."

"We start running in the big ones this next Saturday in the Windy City, and over the coming months we'll be in California and New York, and every racetrack in between that offers the big money."

"That sounds fine," Moses said, tilting his head to look at Sam slyly, "but I'm telling you right now, if I see this hoss and don't like him, I'm going to follow after that Cranston & Reeves van and get right back on it and head back to my old Kentucky home."

Sam nodded, turned and called down the shedrow: "Mary, I know you're busy, but can you do me a favor?"

From somewhere in the stalls, a hollow-sounding voice answered, "Sure, Sam."

Mary stepped out of a stall, put aside a pitchfork, stood with her hands on her hips.

"Bring Deuce down here, please," Sam said.

Mary picked up a shank from a bale of straw and walked down the shedrow. Sam barely had time to introduce Moses to Vance and ask Moses how the trip up from Lexington was before Mary was leading Black Deuce to where Moses stood. Moses turned his eyes on the colt and kept them there as he stepped further away from the shedrow. He waved at Mary to bring the colt out. When sunshine hit the colt, blue highlights played over his polished ebony coat looking like currents of electricity. Mary brought the colt to a stop, and the colt stamped a hoof, swished his long tail, and looked at Moses with the diamond light in his eyes.

"Look at the engine on this colt," Moses said, studying the colt's quarters and back legs.

Moses walked around the colt slowly, giving the colt a close inspection, then stepped up to the colt, bent over and lifted the colt's left front leg. Moses looked down the length of the tendon, squinting, then flexed the ankle. He mumbled, "Nice medial lateral balance." Then, still bent over, he looked at the bottom of the colt's hoof, said to Sam, "Joshua shoed this horse last, I recognize his work."

Sam said nothing, only nodded.

Moses pushed on the colt's heel, pushed hard with his thumb, and while he did he looked over his shoulder to see any reaction from the colt. When the colt didn't react, Moses muttered, "Yes, sir, that's a good shock absorber." Then, again still bent over, he said to Sam, "Long striding colt, ain't he?"

Sam nodded again.

Now Moses pushed his thumb hard on the sole of the colt's hoof, muttered, "Healthy sole, nice and concave and rubbery." Moses straightened, looked over at Sam. "Joshua's a good shoer. Always liked the way he trims the toe and rolls the edge so the hoof don't crack. With Josh in Iowa, who does your shoeing here?"

"Amos Randall."

"A good man," Moses said. Then he continued: "I like the

way this colt runs, he reaches out and hits square, he don't overload on one side of his foot or t'other."

Vance said, "You've seen this colt run?"

Moses looked at Vance, gave a cackle, answered, "No, sir, but this colt's been in those shoes over two weeks and he's done some running in that time, and his foot has kept a nice balance, the wear is even. Most hosses come down on the outside of their foot when they run, then slam down on the inside, and that causes the foot to become uneven, and uneven means pressure on bones and joints where it was never meant to be, and that means, sooner or later, a sore horse. Not this colt, he throws them feets out in front of him and comes down square. Yes, sir, nice and square."

"No feet, no hoss, right, Moses?"

"You got that right, Sam," Moses said.

Moses went over the right leg and hoof just like he'd gone over the left. After Moses ran his hands up and down each of the colt's front legs, from knee to pastern, he stood up.

"When did this colt run last?"

"Day before yesterday," Sam answered.

Moses nodded, rubbed his nose, said, "That's good, if there was going to be heat anywhere in them legs, it'd be there this morning." Moses stepped back from the colt, stuck both hands in the back pockets of his trousers and studied the colt again. "I ain't seen a finer example of a racehorse since I rubbed Sinbad for Joshua back in the mid-sixties."

"Sinbad was one of Josh's best," Sam said.

Moses walked over to Mary and reached for the shank she held. Mary handed the shank over. Moses led Black Deuce back under the shedrow, and as he passed by where Sam and Vance stood, Moses said, "Put my suitcase in the tack room for me, Sam, I've got a hoss to *do up.*"

4

Fifteen minutes later, Sam sat on the bale of straw across from Black Deuce's stall, watching Moses work on the colt's front legs. Moses was on his knees in the straw. From a plastic bottle he poured a greenish liquid into his cupped hand, then applied it to the colt's left knee, shin, tendon and ankle. This sharp-smelling liquid was Moses' liniment, his own secret recipe. Using a firm, brisk, up and down motion, he rubbed in the liniment. Moses spent twenty minutes on the colt's left front, then switched over to the right front and started the process all over.

"These legs are cold as ice, Sam," Moses said.

"And you'll keep them that way," Sam answered.

The colt stood quietly at his webbing with Moses at his feet working away. The colt used his tail to chase away a troublesome fly. Now the colt lowered his head, gave a low nicker, and stretched his neck out toward Sam. Unable to coax Sam into giving him some TLC, the colt investigated exactly what it was Moses was doing. He sniffed at Moses, his nostrils twitching as he patiently stood still and watched his groom do his work.

Sam said, "I don't think I've ever seen a more intelligent horse, Moses."

Moses looked up at the colt, pulled a slipped suspender back into place, and began to rub on the colt again. "He seems interested in everything that happens around him."

"Show him how to do something once," Sam said, "and you never have to show him again."

Mary marched up, her pony tail bobbing with each step she took. She stood looking at Sam with her hands on her hips, said, "Sam, I need to talk with you." She glanced at Moses, added: "Alone."

Sam stood up. "Sure, Mary," he said.

Moses asked, "What bandages and cottons you want me to

use, Sam?"

Sam pointed at the wooden box painted in the Keene racing colors. The lidded box was sturdy enough to sit on and big enough to hold everything a groom would need, from curry combs and *vet wraps* to furisin and DMSO... it was the box where Mary kept all the things she used when grooming horses. Mary turned bright red, held her arms stiff at her side.

"So, am I fired?" she said, and there was both hurt and anger in her voice.

"No," Sam answered not hiding a smile.

"But you've taken Deuce from me and now you just gave away all my combs and brushes, and..." Mary's small face turned even brighter red when she demanded in a furious voice: "And stop smiling at me."

"What...I can't smile at my newest assistant trainer?" Sam said.

Mary gave a start, as if someone had pinched her nose. Her hands and arms relaxed and she said, "Assistant trainer?"

Moses looked up out of the colt's stall, amusement putting crinkles at the corners of his eyes. Sam's smile got wider when Mary couldn't seem to make sense out of what he'd said. The girl only frowned and looked confused.

Sam said, "It's going to be a busy summer, and with Bentley wanting to buy more horses, Vance and I are going to need some help."

Mary tipped her head, regarded Sam with eyes half-closed with suspicion. "Go on," she said.

"Well, I talked it over with Bentley, and we both decided you'd make a great assistant trainer...that is, if you want the job."

Mary's eyes burst into sparkles. She leaped at Sam, threw her arms around his neck, gave him a lip-smacking kiss on the cheek. She now held Sam at arm's length, and her face was radiant when she said, "I want the job!"

5

Joshua came in to watch the Windy City Derby with Sam on Saturday, and neither of the men could say no to Bentley when he invited them up to his box seat to watch the race. Bentley's box was on the finish wire on the outer edge of the top floor of the clubhouse, the exclusive Turf Club. There in the shade of the huge overhang roof with its immense steel I-beams, the three men returned from saddling Black Deuce. They settled into comfortable seats. Sam and Joshua were dressed alike: Khakis, polo shirts, zippered Kroop jodhpurs. Bentley sported a white Palm Beach suit and white shoes. The sound of a happy and rowdy Saturday crowd rose up from below, and in the box seats around them, a fashionable crowd flashed with jewelry and was dressed in the bright colors of summer. It was the custom on Derby day for women to wear designer hats, and the way the hats bobbed about gave the box seats the illusion of being a flower garden.

Sam looked over the railing in front of the box, down at the box seats that made up the second deck. Then he looked all the way down to the ground floor and the apron. People looked small, and the height made Sam feel dizzy. He looked over at the crowd in the grandstand, a great and noisy gathering of race fans. Now the horses came onto the racetrack to parade to the post. Cool confident riders sat atop sleek hot-blooded thoroughbreds.

"This is quite the view, Bentley," Sam said. Then his eyes found Black Deuce in the post parade and he focused on the colt. "I like coming out of the nine hole. We'll be the last one in, no waiting, and hopefully the first one out."

"I've got a lot of confidence in Clay," Joshua said, lounging back in his seat. "He rides with his wits, he's damned crafty."

After the formality of the post parade, the pony boy turned Black Deuce and Clay loose, and Clay proceeded to warm the colt up. The colt had great presence that dominated the space around him, and this presence was magnified when Clay let the colt break into a jog. There was confidence in every move the colt made, and his black coat glowed, seemed to give off light.

Bentley suddenly straightened, waved at a group of people in another box seat, said, "Gentlemen, please excuse me, I'm going to say hello to some friends, I'll be right back."

With that, Bentley was up and out of the box. On his way down the aisle, other people swung their attention Bentley's way and called out their hellos. Bentley stopped and shook several hands. The sound of Bentley's voice wishing all a good derby day joined the roll and hum of voices in the clubhouse.

"They don't make many like Bentley," Joshua said, still lounged back and now crossing his legs.

"I train for the best owner in racing," Sam said. Then Sam changed the subject: "I appreciate you trying to get Bess to come in and watch the colt run."

"Sammy, she's a fine lass, but her mind is made up, she'll have nothing to do with horses until this thing between the two of ye is settled."

"I've offered her a home in the suburbs, but when I explain about how I'll be gone so much of the summer with the colt and busy traveling to look at horses for Bentley to buy, she becomes unreasonable."

"'Tis part of a woman's job description to be unreasonable."

"And there's that other business...I still don't feel comfortable having them here, maybe exposing them to—"

"I understand," Joshua interrupted.

Now Bentley returned, and two other men entered the next box and sat down. One of the men was Rupert Fitzhugh, and the other man was his trainer, Ralph Binder. Binder looked over at Sam, wrinkled his nose as if smelling something awful, and looked away. Fitzhugh had a great shaggy mustache and eyebrows, and was dressed in gray slacks and a blue blazer that fit perfectly. Binoculars hung by a strap around his neck. Rupert Fitzhugh brought with him an imperial air. There were people afraid to even speak in Fitzhugh's dominating presence. He owned Green

Paddock Farm and his horses Cryptic and Reason Why were the entry in the Derby, 1 and 1A.

"Rupert, good afternoon," Bentley said.

Fitzhugh turned his head as if it hurt him to do so. "Bentley, how are you?" he said.

"Capital, capital," Bentley answered.

The two men stared at each other for a long moment, then as if by some secret signal, both stood up and formally shook hands. Neither man blinked, and neither man smiled. Sam and Joshua felt the tension and exchanged quick glances. The look on Bentley's face was totally unexpected, neither Sam nor Joshua had ever seen it. It was the look of a man preparing to disembowel someone he detested.

"Have you a horse in this race, Bentley?" Fitzhugh said with the slightest of smirks as he sat back down.

"You know I don't, Fitzhugh," Bentley said as he settled into his seat, "but I like the eight."

Fitzhugh put on a pair of enormous black-rimmed glasses, and opened his *Racing Form.* He tilted his head to one side as he studied the Derby's *past performance charts*, then curled his lip in scorn when he said, "The eight horse, this Black whatever, is well bred to be sure, but it appears to me he got lucky just to break his maiden, and going by his first two races, he has all the speed of a wounded turtle."

Binder's shoulders jerked, he pinched his nose with a thumb and index finger as if to keep himself from laughing out loud.

"A fine judge of horse flesh like yourself won't mind booking my bet then," Bentley said, his eyes narrowing, "after all, I'm sure you have confidence that your horses can beat a wounded turtle...or are you afraid of turtles this afternoon?"

The two men were staring at each other again.

"How much?" Fitzhugh said.

Bentley took out a small leather bound notepad, and with a Montblanc pen wrote down a number on a page of paper. He tore the page out of the notepad and handed it to Fitzhugh. Fitzhugh looked at it and Sam was sure he could hear Fitzhugh make a gulping sound.

Fitzhugh looked at Bentley, his eyes doing strange things behind the lenses of his glasses, and said, "You're covered."

"Capital," Bentley chortled, tapping his cane on the carpeted floor.

Suburban Park had a mile and one-eighth chute at the top of the backstretch, and now the horses arrived behind the gate. Sam's every nerve tingled as he watched assistant starters began to load the three-year-olds. The Green Paddock Farm entry, Cryptic and Reason Why, was the betting favorite at four-to-five. Black Deuce was a huge price at 45-to-1. Sam glanced at Joshua, Joshua looked back, then both men focused on the colt.

The voice of Phil Adams, the track announcer, now came over the speaker system. The fullness and clarity of Adam's voice demanded the attention of every race fan: "They're at the post for the running of the Windy City Derby...they're entering their stalls."

Horses walked calmly into the gate, others bounced, some threw their heads. Black Deuce, his long tail nearly sweeping the racetrack behind him, went into the gate without hesitation.

The track announcer: "They're all in...the flag is up..."

The crowd murmured, all heads were turned toward the gate. When the gate opened, the crowd in the clubhouse and grandstand roared like a single beast.

The track announcer: "And there they go!"

From the nine hole, Black Deuce sprinted to the lead.

The track announcer: "Breaking sharply is Black Deuce, Reason Why is second on the inside, Vilify is third right alongside, and spread across the track only heads apart for fourth are Oxford Junction, Tuneful, Orlando Winter, and Ripley Believes. Running as a pair in last place are Paris Spring and Cryptic."

Coming onto the main track, Clay dropped Black Deuce over to the rail. Energy and power were in the colt's every stride. The colt was now five lengths in front. The official timer on the tote board flashed its first numbers, :22 flat.

"The colt is full of himself," said Joshua.

The colt continued to lead the way to the half, and when the official timer flashed the time of 45:3, Fitzhugh, watching the race through his binoculars, said, "Your horse is beat, Bentley, he can't cut fractions like that and win going this distance."

As Black Deuce left the half mile pole behind, Clay looked like he was moving all over the colt, but wasn't. He was really sitting still, keeping his body poised over the withers, really only moving his elbows and head.

Fitzhugh misunderstood what he was seeing, said, "The jockey is already asking your horse to run, Bentley."

Joshua was grinning. "I've seen Clay do this routine on a speed horse a hundred times."

Black Deuce ran with such speed over the racetrack that his hooves were a blur, and now Clay made a change in the way he was riding the colt. He kept moving his elbows and head as if he was riding the colt hard, but he reached for the colt and tightened the reins. The colt did just what Clay asked of him, and he settled, relaxed, seemed to move effortlessly as he skipped along on the front end.

Sam looked over at Binder, and Binder turned his head and looked straight into Sam's eyes. Sam knew what Binder was thinking, he was thinking of the black colt that blew by his two good colts during a morning work, and when Phil Adams announced that Black Deuce had reached the three-quarters in 1:11:2, Sam smiled at Binder and Binder quickly turned away.

Sam called out, "That's enough of a breather, Clay, now let him run!"

Furious, Binder curled his lips back to show his crooked teeth, grabbed the railing in front of him, and shouted, "You're letting him steal it on the front end! Run at him!"

Joshua let out a whoop. "Clay backed up the pace, the boys behind him bought the head and elbow show."

The track announcer: "At the three-eighths pole, it's Black Deuce in front by three but here comes Reason Why and Oxford Junction, and on the extreme outside Cryptic is closing with ground-eating strides. Black Deuce is down to a two-length lead…a one length lead! Here comes Cryptic!"

"You're beat, Bentley," Fitzhugh said, peering through his binoculars, "here come both of my horses, I hope you brought your checkbook with you."

Clay saved the colt until he was down to a half-length lead, then finally made his move on Black Deuce. Clay threw a new cross in the reins, showed the colt the whip and begin to push. With a burst of speed, Black Deuce showed how eager he was to put more of the racetrack behind him, and in the next strides, the colt was once more three lengths in front of the field. Sam felt a shock of excitement, and as the fans in the clubhouse and grandstand came roaring to their feet, he let loose a series of shouts: "Do it, Clay! Run, Deuce!" Joshua and Bentley joined in. All three men shouted until their lungs were empty, then filled them with air, and kept right on shouting.

The track announcer: "Closing with a rush on the outside is Cryptic, the Binder trained horse, the pride of Green Paddock Farm, but Black Deuce isn't through, he kicks on, he's found another gear! It's Black Deuce again by three lengths…it's Black Deuce by five lengths!"

The colt flattened out, and with each stride he kicked up dirt so it looked like he was leaving the race track smoking behind him. Inside the eighth pole the colt showed no signs of tiring, his every move was rhythmic, graceful, beautiful to watch, and he continued to open up on the field. The other riders were moving all over their horses, pitching and bobbing and swinging their whips, but were going nowhere. Clay kept pushing, hand-riding, and again at the sixteenth pole showed the stick to the colt because the colt started to prick his ears and look up into the stands where all the noise was coming from.

The track announcer: "And down the stretch they come! Black Deuce is running away from the field, his strides are lengthening, here's yet another gear! He's six lengths in front…he's nine lengths in front…here's the wire…Black Deuce wins by eleven lengths! How can I describe this performance? There are no words!"

After the colt hit the wire, Clay stood up in the irons and pumped his fist in the air. Black Deuce left behind him a field of thoroughbreds completely destroyed.

Just as Sam, Joshua and Bentley were leaving the box happily in conversation, Bentley turned to look back at Fitzhugh. Fitzhugh's face was bright red, the gray hairs of his shaggy mustache blew in and out of his open mouth, and beside him, Binder had his eyes closed as if concentrating on how to recover.

"Not to worry, Rupert," Bentley said, "if you don't have your checkbook, your credit is good with me."

Fitzhugh refused to even look at Bentley.

Phil Adams had left his mic open and he could be heard in a background conversation: "Wow. All I saw was a black streak coming down the stretch, that colt's a runner. And look at the final time." Now he spoke into the mic again, returning to his formal deep-toned voice: "Ladies and gentlemen, may I direct your attention to the time of the race. Suburban Park has a new track record for nine furlongs: 1:46 flat."

The elevator to the winner's circle was just down the aisle. Once Sam, Joshua and Bentley were inside the elevator, the doors closed and the elevator whisked them down to track level. Bentley was bubbling.

"Poor Fitzhugh," Bentley said, "I've heard he suffers terribly from hemorrhoids and that's what makes him so surly."

When the doors of the elevator opened, the three men tumbled out of it seeming to be overcome with laughter.

6

Moses and Black Deuce had returned from the *spit barn*, and Moses was giving the colt a bath. Thad Cox, a new hotwalker Sam had hired the week before, held the colt. Thad was a tall, skinny teenager with floppy hair parted down the middle. Sam, Joshua and Bentley stood in the shade of the shedrow watching Moses as he added alcohol to the tall bucket of warm soapy bath water. After dipping a big sponge into the warm water, Moses began to swab down the colt. Soap suds soon covered Black Deuce, and he stood quietly enjoying the bath. The colt now and then would reach with his teeth, take hold of the leather shank Tod held in his hands, and give the shank a brief playful pull.

"Emily Brandt would be so proud," Bentley said. He stood in his shirtsleeves, having left his white jacket in the Rolls Royce.

"That she would," Joshua said, leaning against a support post.

"What plans have you for Southern Oak?" Bentley asked Joshua.

"The house is being cleaned up, repaired, painted and according to my man on the scene, Robert, it should be in fine shape within the month, and now that the colt has won a good purse, I can have the contractors start rebuilding the main barn. I have to plan carefully, money's an issue, I'm not made of it, but I should be ready for horses by summer's end."

"You'll sell your property in Iowa?" Bentley asked.

"It's on the market."

"You'll stand studs?"

"Of course, and the way this one"—Joshua nodded toward the colt—"is bred, and after the way he ran today, he'll be my first."

Sam swatted at a fly, missed, said, "I think what we saw today is just the beginning of great things for this colt."

"And I want to be a part of it," Bentley said.

Both Sam and Joshua turned their attention away from the colt to look at Bentley.

Bentley went on: "I have a number of broodmares at Shady Lane Ranch in Barrington and would like to send them all to Southern Oak. You know my wife is responsible for breeding both Tigress and Voodoo Queen, she's a student of bloodlines, not unlike Emily Brandt, and she tells me this colt is *the one*."

"Anything you want, you can have, Bentley," Joshua said.

Bentley stuck his cane in the ground in front of him, planted both hands on the gold handle, said, "Then sell me breeding shares to the colt, and let's do it right here and now."

Joshua looked directly into Bentley's eyes, then said, "What if the colt disappoints us in his next start? What if he's just a flash in the pan?"

Bentley smiled. "That's why you should take me up on my offer now."

"What are you suggesting?"

"As I understand it," Bentley said, "Mrs. Brandt left orders in her will that called for there to be thirty-two breeding shares in the colt. She has given two of those shares away to a long-time employee on the farm, and that leaves thirty." Bentley's chin came up, there was a sparkle in his eye. "Sell me fifteen shares at two hundred thousand a share. You see, Joshua, you may not be made of money, but I am. Let's build a breeding farm that will give Rupert Fitzhugh hemorrhoids the size of basketballs."

For a brief moment all three men rocked and swayed with laughter, but getting back to the subject of money again sobered all three.

Joshua eyed Bentley narrowly, said, "Three million then?"

"As soon as you want it."

Joshua smiled his acceptance and put his hand out and the two men exchanged firm grips.

All three men looked out where Moses had just finished using a *scraper* to partly dry the colt, and to help with the process, the colt shook himself, sending drops of water shimmering into the air. Now in one practiced motion, Moses threw a flynet over Black Deuce, and Thad, bouncing on his toes, walked toward the barn with the colt. When the colt came under the shedrow, he moved with a casual grace, and though he'd just set a new track record, he seemed undiminished by the effort, the air around him still pulsed and quivered with energy. All three men watched until the colt disappeared around the corner of the shedrow.

"Black Deuce is the pinnacle of evolution," Bentley said, turning the full light of his eyes on Sam and Joshua. "He is supremely adapted to running, and other than running, he has but two purposes on this earth. The first is to replicate himself, and the second is to be worshiped by men like us."

"Aye," Joshua said in solemn agreement.

"Aye," said Sam with a shiver in his soul.

32. ROBERT

Robert picked up the Sheffield silver bulter's tray from the kitchen counter. On it were six frosty glasses of lemonade. When he walked to the kitchen's swinging door, he glanced out the window and saw part of the scaffolding the painters had erected on the east side of the house, the last side of the house to be painted. It amazed Robert how quickly the team of painters worked. Once more the great columned house blazed white in the South Carolina sunshine. Coming to the door, Robert turned and used his hip to pushed the door open.

Now he entered the drawing room where the cleaning crew was busy. Robert purposely didn't look at the blank space above the fireplace, the space where the portrait of Camille Arceneaux should have been. But all else about the room lifted his spirit. It gleamed with the hardwoods of fine furniture, the Aubusson carpets were clean and colorful. The room would soon be ready to entertain guests after dinner. By trick of imagination, Robert could smell the fragrance of fine cigars, the bouquet of vintage wines and cognac.

When Robert set the tray down on a table, the foreman of the crew, John Trimble, a broad-chested man with a crew-cut, stopped working on the damper of the fireplace and stood up.

"Liquid Wrench, that's all it needed, Robert," John said, wiping his hands on a rag that hung perpetually from his back pocket. "And you have spoiled me and my people beyond repair these last weeks. From now on this bunch of scoundrels will want it in their contract to be served lemonade for their morning and afternoon breaks."

"There is something civilized about a frosty glass of lemonade on a hot day, Mr. Trimble," Robert answered.

The crew of men and women now gathered around the Sheffield Butler's Tray and helped themselves to the lemonade, thanking Robert as they did.

"You are all most welcome," Robert said back to them all.

Then came the pounding of the heavy knocker on the front door.

"Will you all please excuse me," Robert said, giving a small bow.

Some of the crew nodded their heads, others returned Robert's bow. In these last weeks, Robert's good manners had made an impression on them that would last a lifetime.

Robert stepped through the great hall. The chandelier glittered, the prisms flashed with light. It had taken one worker three days to clean away the years of dust and cobwebs from the fine French crystals. When Robert swung open the door, it couldn't be told by his expression, but he was shocked by who stood on the portico.

"I need to talk with you," said Josiah Krump.

"Good afternoon, Mr. Krump," Robert greeted with his customary dignity, "but guests are not yet being received at Southern Oak."

Wiping spittle from the corner of his mouth that drooped, Krump looked past Robert, into the great hall. His eyes widened at the sight of the magnificent sparkling chandelier, at the gleam of hardwood finished in the workshops of Duncan Phyfe. Five generations of Arceneauxs stared back at him from out of oil paintings.

"I should apologize for the way I behaved," Krump said.

"That is unnecessary, Mr. Krump," Robert said, standing very straight.

Krump turned his attention away from the great hall and now

looked into Robert's face. "You must think of me with hate," Krump said.

"Mr. Krump, I don't think of you at all."

Robert gazed steadily at Krump through the polished lenses of his spectacles, and Krump averted his eyes, looked down at his shoes. When Krump looked back up, he changed the topic, said, "My sympathy for your loss. Mrs. Brandt was a fine woman."

"We are all diminished by her leaving," Robert answered.

"Southern Oak's rebirth, it's all the ladies of the Charleston Historical Society can talk about. Every day there's news in the paper about the resurrection of this house. Today's sports page of the *Gazette* had an article about the last racehorse Mrs. Brandt bred. Black Deuce I believe his name is."

"He is a thoroughbred of remarkable quality," Robert said.

Then Krump said, "I want to write a book about this house, its people and its treasures, maybe even its horses."

"So that's why you've come?"

"My book on French porcelain has been well received by the art world, and my publisher is enthusiastic about the idea of a book on Southern Oak."

"I will speak to Mr. Kincaid about it," Robert said.

"With your knowledge on the subject of this great house, I was hoping you could assist me."

"I'll give it careful consideration."

"That's all I can ask."

There was a disturbance beneath the oaks, and came the sound of an automobile. Both Krump and Robert turned to see a pink Lincoln Continental pull up behind Krump's Cadillac. Krump took his breath in with a short, sharp gasp.

"For the love of Jesus, hide me," Krump said in a frantic breath. "It's that Pinkney woman."

It was too late.

"There you are, Josiah Krump," came a woman's voice.

Leola Faye Beauregard Pinkney was the president of the Charleston Historical Society, and had held that office now for over a decade. She was at the top of the social register in

Charleston and a force to be reckoned with. She'd been friends with Emily and Edwin Brandt. Blue-haired and rouged, her long legs and neck gave her a crane-like appearance. Married to Forsythe Pinkney, the Chairman of the Board and majority stock holder of the First National Bank, Leola Faye was the great-great-granddaughter of the celebrated Southern general, P.G.T. Beauregard. Beauregard had directed the bombardment on Fort Sumter to start the Civil War.

Her head held high, her purse in the crook of her arm, Leola Faye advanced on the portico and up the steps like she was leading a regiment of Confederate infantry into the heat of battle. The string of pearls that hung from her curiously long neck, swung from side to side. When she stopped in front of Robert and Krump, she tutted her tongue at the antiques dealer, then turned to Robert.

"Good day, Robert," she said. "Emily and Edwin, I miss them dreadfully."

"Good day, Miss Leola," Robert said. "It was so good of you to come to Miss Emily's funeral. Before Miss Emily passed, she spoke of you often."

Leola Faye arched a delicately plucked eyebrow at Krump, and with notes of combat in her voice said, "And why, Josiah Krump, have you been avoiding me?"

"For the same reason I always avoid you," Krump croaked.

Leola Faye ignored the offense in Krump's remark, said, "Like it or not, Josiah, you *are* going to participate in this year's *Antebellum Days.*"

"I will not participate."

"But why? Nobody knows more about the great houses of Charleston than you."

"I'm not well."

Leola Faye eyed Krump much like her great-great-grandfather had eyed Fort Sumter just before he ordered his cannons to open fire. "You're as healthy as I am," she said with a huff, "and this year I have a secret weapon, and you *will* participate...or else."

"Or else what?"

"Or else Forsythe will execute my orders and not renew that lease of yours that's about to expire."

Krump Antiques occupied the entire second floor of the First National Bank Building on the corner of Meeting Street and the Battery and had been there for thirty years. Krump's face seemed to fold in on itself, even the side that drooped. The way he now looked at Leola Faye made Robert wonder if Krump wasn't capable of murder. But this look of hostility made no impression on Leola Faye, she pressed her attack.

"You can't just put me out," Krump said horrified.

"Oh, yes I can, and oh, yes I will, Josiah Krump."

Krump hardened his hand into a fist and waved it at Leola Faye. "You're not your great-great-grandfather, you can't order people about." Now Krump began to sway, anger seeming to have robbed him of his strength. Robert reached out to steady him. "You are not a commanding general, Leola, and I will not—" a cough interrupted Krump.

"I know why you don't want to help lead the tours, Josiah," Leola Faye said. "It's because of how you look…your face, but I don't care how you look and neither does anyone else who has a heart worth more than a Confederate dollar on the day our noble General Lee surrendered to that drunkard Grant. When I was but a girl, I took care of my father when he was dying…it was cancer that killed him, cancer that started by eating away his nose."

"I remember your father," Josiah said, "we played ball in school together."

"And I remember you coming to see him, when others wouldn't. You came despite the horrors of that cancer."

"That was long ago," Krump said.

"I never forget a kindness," said Leola Faye.

Krump looked up at her then, his eyes soft, and Leola proved there was kindness behind her iron will. She reached out and took Krump's hand in hers.

"Don't you understand Josiah," Leola Faye said gently, "that Antebellum Days is a chance to have some fun."

"Fun," Josiah said, the word making a lonely rattle in his

throat.

Krump suddenly looked small and frail, and Robert thought Leola Faye had won the battle. But then Krump's eyes went so cold they seemed to frost over, becoming the eyes of a man who didn't trust kindness, and he snatched his hand from Leola's and pulled himself back together. He stomped his foot, his head bobbed about, and he croaked, "I will not participate in Antebellum Days."

"Fiddlesticks," Leola Faye said. "You might want to remain alone and a menace, Josiah, but I won't allow it, you're a much too important resource to the Historical Society."

"Leave me be, woman," Krump answered, trembling with anger.

It was then that Robert intervened, said, "Mr. Krump, if you participate in Antebellum Days, I will see to it that Mr. Kincaid gives you full access to the house and its treasures, and I will assist you in every way I can in the writing of your new book."

Krump looked at Robert, blinked, and then his head sank between his shoulders. Spittle dribbled from the slack side of his mouth and he wiped at it with a handkerchief. In a feeble voice, he said, "But—"

"There is no *but*," Robert interrupted. "Participate or I'll advise Mr. Joshua not to allow you access to this great house."

With this surprise flank attack, Krump understood he was beaten. Out flanked and exhausted, he seemed to diminish in size. There was a slur in his voice when he muttered, "Alright...I'll do what you ask of me, Leola."

Leola Faye smiled, said, "Good, and now that we've settled that, what we all need is a cup of coffee."

Robert nodded. "Of course," he said, stepping back into the house to swing wide the doors, "please come in and follow me."

The cleaning and maintenance crew was still busy in the drawing room, and there was work still to be done in the parlor and library, so Robert led the way into the dining room. He seated Krump and Leola Faye at the mahogany dining table. The flame-patterned grain of ancient trees from Honduras was highlighted by the table's French polish. Robert soon brought three cups and saucers, a sugar, a creamer, and a coffee pot on a large tray. All the pieces were part of a matching service. Robert began to serve the coffee.

"How would you like your coffee, Miss Leola?" Robert asked.

"Just two sugars, Robert," Leola Faye said brightly, "and thank you for using this lovely porcelain."

In his defeat, Krump had retreated into the safety of silence. He'd kept his head down and had said nothing since coming into the house. But with these words from Leola Faye, he looked up at the coffee service Robert had placed on the table. His eyes grew wide, he made a small sound of astonishment.

"It can't be," Krump said. He reached and picked up a cup, and when he saw the factory *mark* on the bottom he made yet another sound of astonishment. Krump read aloud in French: "Manufacture de S. M. l'Empératrice, P.L. Dagoty à Paris." Krump stared at the cup, then carefully put it back on its saucer and looked at the tray. The large tray was decorated with a magnificent painting of Napoleon on horseback surrounded by his field marshals and soldiers, victorious on the field of battle at Austerlitz.

When Krump began to breathe hard and wheeze, Leola Faye became alarmed. "Are you alright, Josiah?"

"This…" Krump swallowed hard, caught his breath. "This is part of the *Service de Austerlitz*, it was made for the Empress Josephine by the Paris porcelain factory of Pierre Louis Dagoty. Josephine gave it to Napoleon as a gift to commemorate his greatest victory." Krump swung his head up to look at Robert. "Do you have any more of the service?"

"There were originally eight hundred and nine pieces in the service," answered Robert. "Sadly, one saucer and two plates have been broken over the centuries."

Robert now pointed behind Krump. Krump turned around so quickly he nearly fell from his chair, and when Robert flipped on a switch that lit the built-in shelves that covered much of the wall, Krump let out a cry. There was the shine and glitter of fine porcelain.

"But here," Robert continued, "are the remaining seven hundred and ninty-six pieces of the service. Etienne Arceneaux bought the service in 1831 from Joseph Bonaparte, the brother of Napoleon who came to the United States soon after his brother's defeat at Waterloo."

Robert stepped back as Krump and Leola Fay stood and walked over to the shelves. Krump forgot all his anger, and he and Leola trilled and buzzed in delight over the porcelain. They pointed out to each other beautifully painted serving dishes and compotes, and fussed over fruit coolers and sauciers that would have been included with pride in the collection of the Louvre.

"I've had coffee from this service many times," Leola Faye said, "but never knew its importance."

Krump turned to look back at Robert. "This service is a book all by itself, Robert," he said. "The battle scenes on the platters and the individual portraits of Napoleon and his generals on the plates are exquisite."

"In Etienne's diary," Robert answered, "he references Joseph Bonaparte telling him the service was in use at Malmaison."

While Krump and Leola Faye continued to marvel, Robert poured himself a cup of coffee and walked over to one of the tall windows. He stood there in the bright light of day, the sunshine putting a polish on his face, and while he looked out over the white-fenced paddocks of the great farm, he sipped coffee from a cup that had once been a gift from an Empress to an Emperor.

33. SAM

Black Deuce shipped to Belle Isle Racecourse in Detroit, Michigan for his next start, the mile and a quarter Auto City Derby. A field of twelve gathered for the hundred thousand added event, and three of these runners shipped in from the east. All three, Maryland Kid, Fredericksburg and Cashtown, had been heavily campaigned and proven themselves to be thoroughbreds of great ability. Cashtown finished second in the Kentucky Derby, Maryland Kid third in the Preakness, and Fredericksburg had already beaten a good field of older horses in the prestigious Hanson Handicap at Long Island Downs in New Jersey. Black Deuce's first two races still caused gamblers to question him, and the colt was allowed to go off at nine to one.

Belle Isle raced at night, and protocol required Sam and Joshua to spend the evening seated at a table in an air-conditioned section of the clubhouse called the Derby Room. The Belle Isle Racing Association had rolled out the red carpet for everyone with a horse in the Derby, and put a great effort into serving a fine dinner. Seated around Sam and Joshua were the connections of the other three-year-olds. With diamonds on their fingers and gold jewelry dangling around their necks, Joshua referred to them as the caviar and cashmere crowd. Blazing stadium lights lit up the mile racetrack, and swans stood out in the night as they flapped their wings and sailed around the infield lake like an armada of white ships.

Now that Sam and Joshua were back from saddling the colt in the paddock, Sam sat down and gave a nervous fidget.

Joshua was finishing a story: "…and I said to Charlie Brewster, don't knock the fly off that horse, it's the only thing that makes him run." Joshua leaned forward, slapped his knee and began to laugh. When Sam didn't even smile, Joshua sobered, heaved a sigh, said, "It's easier to put socks on a crocodile than make ye laugh when ye get like this…would ye just relax."

"He's running under the lights for the first time," Sam answered, feeling the acid in his stomach burn.

"If shipping doesn't bother the colt, running at night won't."

"Good thing he doesn't mind shipping. Emily planned a campaign that has him running in five states in three months."

"Nothing bothers a good horse," Joshua said. "Moses said he looks out the window of the van most of the time, curious about all he sees." Joshua looked down through the large plate glass windows to where Moses stood out on the apron near the winner's circle, then said, "Too bad Bentley couldn't join us."

"It would have been nice."

"How is Ruth?"

"Better, but still not good," Sam said.

"A shame, the poor woman. Where did ye say Bentley was this week?"

"Bolivia. He's buying a tin mine."

Joshua chuckled, took a toothpick from a holder, picked at his teeth. "Clay's funny, isn't he?" Joshua looked to where the horses were approaching the starting gate at the top of the stretch, found the black colt with the jockey in white colors. "You told him not to worry about coming here to work the colt—"

"When I showed up at the barn yesterday morning," Sam broke in, "Clay was already there waiting. He didn't even tell me he was coming. He wants no part of letting any other rider near Deuce."

"Has he hired an agent yet?"

"Carl Billings has Clay's book."

"Billings is sharp, he'll get Clay on some stock."

"He already has. Clay won two yesterday."

"Like old times seeing Clay among the leading riders." Joshua said. Then he squinted to give Sam a sly look, added: "Did I tell ye Katie Calhoun called me?"

An image of a long-legged redhead projected in Sam's brain. Katie was the first woman to take him to that uninhibited place, a place wild with biting and scratching. But in her wildness was a tenderness too, and Sam knew Katie loved him. Sam suddenly had to clear his throat before he could ask: "How is she? What's she doing?"

"She's fine, she's hustling a jock's book, a rider by the name of Calvin Kale."

"She coming to Chicago?"

"She is and wanted to know how ye were."

When Sam didn't say anything, Joshua continued: "How many mattresses did the two of ye wear out in that tack room at Lincoln Park?"

Sam turned bright red, said, "A long time ago, I was only seventeen."

Joshua's nose twitched. "Ye two drove yer neighbors to near insanity, the two of ye yowling like happy alley cats to all hours of the night."

Sam gave Joshua a quick frown. "That was long before I met Bess."

Joshua chuckled, enjoying his fun teasing Sam.

Now the horses were being loaded into the gate, and both men fell silent. The atmosphere in the Derby Room was thick with anticipation. Sam could hear a ringing in his ears. The horses were all in.

There came a heart-stopping moment, when the gate opened and Black Deuce broke slow and Fredericksburg went right to the lead. But by the time the horses went into the first turn, Black Deuce was in front. Clay rode the colt just as he had in the Windy City Derby. He let the colt scorch the race track with a blazing half mile in 45:4, let him relax and catch his breath, then when Cashtown made a big run inside the three-eighths pole, he got belly down on Black Deuce and turned him loose.

"What a beautiful sight," Sam said, watching the colt come down the stretch.

"Aye, Sammy, what a sight," Joshua answered.

Neither Sam nor Joshua heard the groans, words of disappointment, even anger from the other owners and trainers around them. All they were aware of was the way Clay kept split-second rhythm with the colt, and the way Black Deuce gleamed under the lights, the way his long tail floated behind him, the way the colt hurled himself forward in a movement so powerful it appeared with each stride that he was about to soar into flight.

Black Deuce won the Auto City Derby by fourteen lengths, equaling the track record of two minutes flat.

2

Over the next month, Black Deuce won two more races. The Bethesda Derby at Columbia Racecourse in Silver Springs, Maryland, and the Bunker Hill Derby at Liberty Downs in Boston, Massachusetts. In both races he left behind him good fields of three-year-olds struggling and fighting it out for second place. Then, just as Emily planned, the colt was given a month off and flown to California. He ran at Malibu Park on August 29th in the Pacific Coast Classic. In his first attempt against older horses, Black Deuce smashed an eleven-horse field of the best horses in California to win by six lengths in 1:59:3, a new track record for the mile and a quarter on that racetrack. The colt was then flown back to the East coast to run in the prestigious Boardwalk Handicap at Oceanside Racecourse in Atlantic City. Black Deuce was the only three-year-old in the field running for the purse of two-hundred-fifty thousand dollars. The colt won the mile and three-eighths event by seven lengths, equaling the track record of 2:11:3 set by the legendary race mare Greek Maiden in 1923.

With all that Black Deuce had done, he still couldn't erase the first two starts on his past performance chart, two races that weren't his, and though the press and the public had fallen in love with him, the eastern racing establishment still scorned him. Only because of Bentley's connections, did Black Deuce receive an invitation to the Samuel D. Riddle Invitational Handicap run at a mile and one half on the grass at Adirondack Racecourse in Albany, New York.

It would be the greatest test yet for Black Deuce.

34. MOSES KENT

Moses had purposely waited so Black Deuce would be the last horse to leave the holding barn to go to the paddock for the Riddle Invitational. The other horses had several people accompanying each of them. Four of the horses had a veritable entourage, and Moses wanted to avoid all the hubbub these people were creating. Thad the hotwalker, the floppy-haired teenager who always walked the colt, was the only other person with Moses, and that's the way Moses liked it. No fuss.

Moses finally led the colt out of his stall and out to the pony path that would lead to the paddock. Thad trailed after them, a bounce in his step. Thad had a curiosity that tested everyone's patience, always asking questions, but because Thad was so eager to learn about horses, Moses liked him. Moses wore his big-horse-runnin' clothes: a clean blue shirt, his best wide-brimmed straw hat, and his favorite pair of red suspenders to hold up his gray baggy slacks. But even all showered and shaved, Moses still smelled of liniment, his secret recipe. Clouds were scattered and fluffy in the blue sky, but the thickening line of dark clouds coming from the west growled with thunder and flashed with lightning.

"Think we'll run before the storm, Moses?" Thad asked.

Moses glanced westward, said, "We won't get wet for a while yet."

"How long you been workin' with horses, Moses?" Thad

said.

"I was nine when I first got me a job on a farm."

"You were just a little guy, what did you do?"

"I slept in the stalls with expectin' broodmares. If they went ta havin' their babies late at night, I'd be right there with 'em so I could run and get help. I was their 911 call for emergency." Moses gave a soft cackle at the thought. "I was never so proud as when I gave my mama that first week's pay."

"How much was it?"

"Twenty dollars."

"Did you give it all to your mom?"

"Had to, every penny of it. My daddy was kilt workin' on the railroad and my mama had five kids to feed."

"Your mama still alive?"

"My sweet mama crossed the river years ago," Moses said, a softness in his voice.

"I love horses, don't you, Moses?"

Moses told few people how much he loved horses, not that he wasn't proud to be a groom, but because so few people would understand, especially people off the racetrack, and whenever he did try, he could never find the words to tell it right. That, and he didn't want people to think he was just a crazy old man who only thought and dreamed about horses, who was only really happy when he was in the stall with a horse, only happy if he could sleep at night in a tack room where horses were only steps away.

"Yes, Todd," Moses said. "I love horses too." Then Moses did that which he seldom did, he tried to explain: "I suppose if you was to look in my head, you'd only find a hoof pick, rolls of bandages, maybe a pitchfork and a rake, and for sure the recipe to my liniment."

Todd laughed as he bent down, picked up a rock from the pony path, threw it into the parking lot.

Black Deuce grabbed the leather shank with his teeth, and, like he so often did, gave it a playful pull. Moses smiled, looked into the diamond light. As the colt walked along his muscles flexed and stretched beneath his coat, and a big fly, metallic and iridescent, zipped up and landed on the colt's back. The colt swished his long tail at it, and when he couldn't reach it, Moses swept the very end of the shank at the fly to dislodge it. In response, the colt flattened his ears, and made a sound Moses had never heard him make before. It was a rumbling, and it came from deep in the colt's throat.

Moses never trusted a change in a horse's temperament. Such changes were a warning, and now Moses watched the colt closely, heeding the warning. The rumbling came again, still a distant sound, but now the colt bowed his neck and broke into a nimble prance. Sunlight flickered in blue and silver designs on the colt's ebony coat, and when the colt passed sparrows twittering and hopping along the top rail of the fence without giving them any attention, Moses became wary. Moses recognized a transformation was taking place, and the closer the colt came to the paddock, the more apparent the transformation became.

As Moses neared the entrance to the paddock, he felt what the colt was telling him through the shank, and the colt was telling him he was anxious to run. The colt suddenly kicked with both hind legs, aiming at nothing, then began to bounce as if his legs were spring-loaded. Moses jerked on the shank to settle the colt down, and the shank's chain rattled, biting into the colt's nose. The colt jerked his head up, looked at Moses, settled. But as the identifier lifted the colt's lip, Moses looked into the colt's eyes and saw nothing of diamonds. The diamond light had turned into fire.

Two steps into the paddock, the colt dropped his head and when his head came back up, the colt's front legs left the ground and he was standing on his hind legs, rearing, his front hooves slicing through the air. Moses gave the colt more shank, controlled him as much as any man can control an eleven-hundred-pound animal with fire in its eyes. Now poised in the air, towering above Moses, Black Deuce loosed a cry that thundered through the paddock. Race fans near the paddock fence flinched and stepped back, and now everyone in the paddock turned to look at the colt. There were ohs and ahs, words of praise and awe, and then came applause.

Standing where the colt would be saddled, Sam, Joshua and Bentley exchanged a quick glance, then watched as Moses led the colt around the saddling ring. Race fans watched the colt go by, and on their faces were expressions of admiration. Then the colt reared again, gave another call like thunder, and once more fans flinched and stepped back, once more there was applause.

"What happened to our kind colt?" Bentley said.

"He's become a racehorse," said Sam.

While Sam and a valet saddled the colt, Moses talked to Black Deuce, now and then rattling the shank to keep the colt's attention. When the colt did move, shifting impatiently on his hooves or giving a toss of his head, his race-hardened muscles stood out beneath his brush-polished coat to put on display the detail of his perfection. Then Sam tightened the girth. It was as if the colt was waiting for this signal that it was time to run. There came the rumbling from the colt's chest, a savage sound, and the colt released it in an explosive snort that expanded his nostrils. Moses felt the blast of hot air, like heat from a furnace, saw nothing but flames where once there were diamonds.

Sam stepped back from the colt, said, "What do you think, Moses?"

"I got this feeling in me," Moses said, "but I ain't got words to tell of it."

"Give it a try," Joshua said.

A trickle of sweat ran down Moses' nose, and he said, "I think we're gonna see something today we're gonna talk about till the day we die."

Then the jockeys were in the paddock, and the fans were delighted by the sight of racing colors, boots, whips. Delighted by the dash and swagger of top race riders. When Moses led the colt and Clay out to the track and turned them over to a pony boy, a great mutter rose up from the packed stands as people swung their attention to the horses arriving to be paraded to the post. Sports writers were calling the field of eleven a gathering of the finest handicap horses in the country, and when it was learned Black Deuce would run, those writers agreed that to run the brilliant three-year-old against the *nuts* was questionable.

A security guard stationed at the gate by the winner's circle let Moses through to the apron in front of the grandstand. Adirondack Racecourse was one of the oldest in the country, and the spires and turrets of the original 19th Century structure had been preserved. Even the original slate roof was in place. Here at Adirondack, racing was presented in all its finest traditions. Moses heard the colt's name being called out by racing fans, and saw the colt was the nine-to-five favorite. "Let them sports writers chew on that," Moses said and felt so proud of the colt that it put a knot in his chest.

Then the horses were in the gate on the main grass course.

When the gate slammed open, Moses went into something like shock. Horses on either side of the colt banged into him, then collided with each other to cut the colt off. Moses vaguely heard the massive gasp that came from the packed grandstand and clubhouse, vaguely heard the announcer make the call that the break had been a disaster for Black Deuce. With the colt throwing his head up and Clay standing in the irons, Moses felt his heart give a violent thump. When the field ran by the stands the first time, Black Deuce was dead last.

As the horses ran into the clubhouse turn, Moses began to breathe hard and fast, and a tightness squeezed at his chest, a tightness that wouldn't release. But when the field straightened out for the run down the backside the announcer's voice broke through Moses' shock again when he called that Clay Repp was already "shaking the reins" and asking Black Deuce to run. The colt began to make a sweeping power move on the outside of horses. It was a move no common young horse could make against older handicap horses. Black Deuce ran smooth over the grass, with no breaks in his action, and in Moses' head the sight of the colt running was given sound. Moses could hear the rhythm of the colt's hooves, and for Moses, those hooves made the music of the sport.

When the horses came to the far turn, Black Deuce had taken the lead and was putting daylight between himself and the field. Moses braced himself, waiting for the huge early effort to take its toll, but Black Deuce didn't appear to be losing strength, with each gigantic stride he seemed to be gaining it.

Thunder rolled across the sky, the storm had arrived, and Moses glanced upward just as lightning lit the dark tumbling clouds in bright flashes. When Moses looked back to the colt, the colt was three lengths in front of the field. Then at the quarter pole the colt was five lengths in front of the field. Then at the sixteenth pole the colt was eight lengths in front of the field, and the din of voices that rose from the stands behind Moses became a roar that made his eardrums throb. And then the colt came to the wire and Moses began to breathe easier, the tightness releasing in his chest, and Moses could hear the announcer "…at the wire it's Black Deuce, a destroyer of the competition, a glory of speed and power! Racing under the historic colors of Southern Oak, Black Deuce wins the Samuel D. Riddle by ten lengths in the record smashing time of 2:23:1!"

To get to the winner's circle, Moses had to sometimes push his way through the crowd, and after the security guard let him through the gate, he stepped out onto the racetrack and waited for Clay to bring the colt back. Grinning wide, Moses' gold tooth gleamed; he'd never felt more alert or alive. When he saw the colt, Clay was bringing him off the turf course back onto the main racetrack. The colt stepped along lightly, but was heavily lathered and still blowing. The sheet of sweat that covered the colt made the full shape of his every muscle stand out. Moses moved to meet Clay and Black Deuce, but Clay kept the colt out in the center of the track and went on by him.

"I'll be right back," Clay called out to Moses.

"I'll be waiting," Moses answered.

Clay took Black Deuce all the way down to the end of the grandstand, then turned the colt. Now he let the colt step along at a brisk walk, parading the colt before the stands, letting all the race fans see the colt. Clay raised his whip and waved it, looking up into the packed stands as he did, and from those stands came the sound of voices merging into a din of approval so loud that it was like a physical assault. When Black Deuce broke into a prance and began to rumble and snort, the din became like the roar of some ancient coliseum horde celebrating the spectacle of a gladiator's victory in battle.

As Moses watched Black Deuce come back toward him, emotion began to build and push its way up his throat, and when he attached the shank to the colt's bit to lead him into the winner's circle where Sam and everyone else waited, he was glad the rain had started. Moses didn't want people to think he was just a crazy old man, a crazy old man who couldn't find the words to explain why his eyes were flooded and his cheeks were wet.

35. SAM

Sam left that night to return to Chicago, leaving Black Deuce with Joshua, Moses and Thad. In the last months he'd been focused on the colt, but he hadn't neglected the other horses he trained. The Keene horses were having a successful meet at Suburban Downs, winning fourteen races and running eighteen seconds and twelve thirds. Voodoo Queen won the Jacqueline Hunter Handicap on the grass, and Excommunicator won the Marathon Handicap going two miles on the grass. Bentley's horses were out of the money only nine times. Vance Reed and Mary Linwood proved themselves to be worthy of the responsibilities Sam gave them and worthy of his trust. There was only one major disappointment during this time.

During the running of the Chandler Moss Memorial Handicap, Mutineer ruptured the sheath to a tendon and *bowed* in his right front. Bentley ordered him retired immediately and sent him to Joshua's farm in Iowa for the time being, intending that Mutineer's permanent retirement home would be Southern Oak. The upside of Mutineer's retirement was that it gave Joshua an idea for an additional barn on the farm in South Carolina, and the more Joshua thought of it, the bigger the idea for the barn became. Joshua and Morris Fenton, the architect in charge of rebuilding the main barn at Southern Oak, came up with the idea of a forty-stall barn. The stalls would be back to back with a shedrow all the way around, just like at the racetrack, and one side would be for horses in training, the other side for retired racehorses that needed a home. When the press publicized the building of this retirement home for thoroughbreds, Joshua started hearing from people all over the country about old horses that needed his help. But what really overwhelmed Joshua was the deluge of donations from horse lovers all over the world who wanted to support the idea that old racehorses should live out their lives with dignity.

One goal that Bentley had assigned to Sam, the buying of more horses, was left unachieved. But this was corrected when, on a sunny afternoon in September, Arthur Benedict dropped dead of a heart attack in the paddock of Malibu Park in California. Benedict's wife, Abigale, did not share Arthur's passion for horses, and their nine horses, trained by the Hall of Famer James T. Wright, were put up for sale. Sam and Joshua both flew with Bentley to California, and with Sam and Joshua's approval, Bentley made the widow Benedict an offer on all nine of the thoroughbreds. She accepted the offer, and Bentley now had thirty-two horses in training. Among the nine new horses were two mares that Bentley's wife wanted as breeding stock to breed to Black Deuce, and two top West Coast stakes horses: the four-year-old gelding Normandy Beach, and the four-year-old filly Minx.

After these nine horses arrived at Sam's barn, and Black Deuce returned from his victories on the road, Sam felt able to kick back and take a deep breath. Sam even entertained the idea of going against Bess' wishes to make a surprise visit to her and Amy. But Franklin R. Delaney, the owner of Suburban Downs, would interfere with Sam's idea of taking any deep breaths and going to see his wife and daughter.

2

Tom Bean groomed Evening Song, and the lanky boy with the over-active Adam's apple stood looking into her stall. He was beaming. The filly had just won the ninth race, her second win in a row, and done it in good fashion, easily handling the field in the non-winners of two in a life time condition. In both wins, Voodoo Queen had gone with the filly to the paddock and been used to pony the filly to the gate. Sam had just told Tom the filly's next start would be in the Miss Illinois Stakes, and the proud groom could already see himself in the winner's circle with the filly.

"She'll win it, Sam," Tom said, his Adam's apple bobbing as he talked.

Sam smiled at the boy, walked down the shedrow toward his office. "She runs like she did today, Tom, she's got a big shot," Sam said over his shoulder.

Tom looked in at the filly who had her head in her feed tub, enjoying a late dinner, then turned and started to walk away. "See you in the morning, Sam," Tom called.

"Okay, Tom," Sam answered, and without looking back, raised his hand and waved.

Black Deuce was in the first stall by the tack room office, Mutineer's old stall, and at the sound of Sam's voice the colt stuck his head out over the webbing. When the colt saw Sam, he threw his head up, making his mane flutter, then gave a lip-quivering nicker.

Sam stopped in front of the colt's stall, put a hand to the colt's velvety muzzled and rubbed. Then the colt lifted his head, and with his ears pricked, looked behind Sam. Sam turned around to find out what had interested the colt and found a man standing behind him. It was Franklin R. Delaney, the owner of Suburban Park. He looked as if he'd just stepped off the cover of *Gentleman's Quarterly*: a black Armani suit, a crisp white shirt, a blue and red striped silk tie, Italian loafers polished to a shine.

Delaney said, "When I see your horse, Sam, I always think of Buchanan's poem *Sheridan's Ride*." Delaney turned his eyes on the colt as he recited: "And there, through the flush of morning light, A steed as black as the steeds of night, Was seen to pass, as with eagle flight."

"My father's favorite poem," Sam said. "He'd quote from it while we stacked hay and straw."

"Your father was a good man, Sam, and he'd be proud of you."

Franklin R. Delaney was a man of eloquence. He loved to talk, and could praise, charm, admire, and philosophize all in the same sentence. And he didn't just like to hear himself, he also liked to listen to other people, to hear their ideas, to get to know them. Delaney loved people, and he loved horses. When Delaney was seen on the backstretch of his racetrack in the morning, even hotwalkers felt comfortable to wave and say "Good morning, Frank." He was a hugely successful businessman, especially gifted at the art of promotion. He was recognized as a brilliant chess player, and for adventure, he went on safari in Africa and had a considerable reputation as a hunter, though he hunted not with a gun. Franklin R. Delaney hunted animals with a camera.

Delaney glanced down the neat shedrow, tilted his head back, took a deep breath, said, "There's something special about places that have the flavor of oats and hay in the air."

Sam smiled, nodded, knew something was up, said, "My father read Conan Doyle to me at bedtime," he rubbed his chin, as if trying to recall something specific, "what was it Holmes so often said...*the game is afoot*?"

"The game most certainly is afoot," Delaney said, smiling, "and, by the way, Doyle borrowed that line from Shakespeare. Tell me, Sam, how many racing associations have asked you to run Black Deuce at their racetrack?"

"The Canadians want him bad for their big turf race, they call almost every day, and so many others...let's just say if I was to make them all happy, Deuce would need to run once a day for at least two weeks."

"But you'd be running against the same horses you've already beaten. Black Deuce can't enlarge his fame by beating the same horses again, there would be nothing to gain."

"Money to gain."

"Money, yes, but why do I think a horseman like you is driven by more than money?"

Sam said nothing to this, he waited, and while he did, great shafts of evening sun struck the barn and coppered his face. He watched Delaney turn back to look long at the colt. A quiet and comfortable moment passed.

"This colt has an extraordinary presence," Delaney finally said. "After he won the Riddle, when your rider paraded him before the stands…it thrilled even me."

"It was a moment racing will never forget."

Now Delaney turned back to Sam. "And I want a moment like that for my racetrack."

Again, Sam remained silent, waited.

"There's only one horse left that the colt hasn't beaten, one horse with real credentials."

"You can't be talking about any horse on this continent."

"Exactly."

"That English horse?"

"The pride of the Duke of Carlisle, the unbeaten English gelding, the European champion two years in a row…the great Death Wish."

Sam lowered his head, fell silent again.

Delaney went on: "Black Deuce won't be denied Horse of the Year, but if you defeat Death Wish, it will make your colt horse of the decade, maybe horse of the century."

"What are you proposing?"

"A two-horse match race at a flat mile."

"And the Duke is willing to come here because his horse likes this track, Death Wish won last year's Arlington International."

"That's right, and also the Duke is an arrogant man, he considers your horse a lesser horse. When I spoke with him he kept referring to your colt's first two races, and kept reminding me that Death Wish is an unbeaten champion."

Sam flinched, dropped his head, felt guilt over cheating his horse. Then he recovered, looked up, said, "Weight-for-age?"

"Yes."

"Purse?"

"One million dollars, winner take all."

Sam blinked. He and Delaney locked eyes and Delaney went for the kill.

"Death Wish is the only worthy rival left, and if you refuse my proposal, it will be said that you avoided the gelding, that you were afraid to run your colt against him. If you refuse to run, Sam, Death Wish will always stand between Black Deuce and the true meaning of the word champion."

"So you've already told the press about this?"

"Read tomorrow's *Racing Form.*"

Anger flashed in Sam's eyes. "I don't like being painted into a corner."

"I want this race."

"Let me talk to Joshua and Bentley. Bentley has a lot of money invested in this colt."

"I've already talked to them both. To run or not to run is up to you."

Sam fell silent again, looked down at his boots, and footsteps came up behind him. Moses was suddenly there. Moses nodded a greeting at Delaney, Delaney nodded back. The groom pulled at one of his suspenders, let it go so it snapped against his chest.

"This about the match race?" Moses asked.

Sam looked up at Moses, smiling in amazement, said, "How did you know?"

"It's all everyone is talking about in the track kitchen," Moses answered.

Delaney's voice was filled with humor when he said, "Nothing travels faster than news on the backstretch of a racetrack."

Sam said nothing, lost his smile, continued to think.

"Tell the man yes, Sam," Moses said. Then Moses turned to Delaney: "And, Frank, you can pass on a message to that Duke fella over there in England. Tell him Black Deuce is waitin', and Deuce is gonna beat his hoss so bad that Death Wish is gonna need to borrow money to get back home."

Sam was laughing when he shook Delaney's hand and agreed to run.

36. FRANKLIN R. DELANEY

Delaney parked his car and walked through the paddock of his racetrack. The fans had long since departed. He was headed to the elevator that would take him to Suburban Park's business offices. He stopped in the middle of the saddling ring, took a slow glance around him. The paddock was parklike with beds of flowers, trimmed boxwood hedges and tall stately elms, and in Delaney's mind he pictured what it all would look like on television. Then he looked up at the new towering grandstand and clubhouse he'd built after the old grandstand and clubhouse burned down in the fall of 1968. He could have built an adequate structure for a far lesser cost after the fire, but he wanted a showcase, and the result was a marbled and gilded palace, one of racing's most beautiful tracks. Smiling with pleasure and pride, Delaney walked on and got into the elevator. When the elevator opened, his personal staff, the staff of the racing office, and his publicity people—all totaled a group of over thirty—stood looking at him as if holding their breath. Delaney stopped, looked among the expectant faces to heighten the drama.

Then Delaney announced, "The race is on."

Everyone cheered. Staff leaped in the air, high fives were exchanged. Then everyone quieted as Delaney started to speak again.

"We are going to put on the greatest show racing has ever seen, this is our chance to shine. You all know what to do."

Delaney started to walk toward his office, and his secretary was right behind him and he said to her, "I have a list of people to call, and I want to start with the Duke of Carlisle. We're paying for all his horse's expenses, and I want Death Wish out of quarantine after his flight and here training ASAP. Next, I want Baxter Butler on the line, head of NBC, and Miss Williams, we'll be here late."

"Of course, Mr. Delaney," the secretary said. "I'll get the Duke on the line at once."

When Delaney got to the door of his office he turned to look back at the room. People were already on the phones giving prepared statements to newspapers and the sports departments of radio and television stations. Typewriters clicked as his press people prepared statements to follow those already prepared.

Delaney raised his voice above the hum of activity: "The Suburban Park Special will be a race talked about for the next century."

Within the hour the news of the match race was already being talked about on television and radio, and news of the race dominated the morning sports section headlines of every major newspaper in the country. Everyone seemed to be talking about the Suburban Park Special, and Black Deuce and Death Wish were the most talked about athletes in the world. Both horses inspired nationalism, and the *Chicago Gazette* ran a headline that read *The British Are Coming!* In turn, the *London Sun* ran the headline *The Boston Tea Party To Be Avenged!* There was so much interest in the match race, that Amtrak announced special trains would run to bring fans from all over the country. Responding to the growing estimates of race-day crowd size, Governor Francis Tillman called Delaney to offer the use of the Illinois National Guard to help keep order. Delaney gladly accepted.

Franklin R. Delaney made sure that everything that happened at Suburban Park during the next weeks happened on a grand scale.

37. SAM

It was late morning and Sam was on the phone with an *entry clerk* in the racing secretary's office. He leaned back in the chair looking at the condition book he held in his left hand.

"Is the eighth race going to *go,* the flat mile for non-winners of two *other than* since July first?"

"We want it to," the clerk answered, "it'll be the feature. There's five in there now, and if you've got a horse, that'll make six. We're going to let it go with seven."

"Good. Put Normandy Beach in there, it'll be a good prep for the Secretariat Stakes."

"Thanks, Sam," the clerk said.

Sam hung up the phone, pulled out the center drawer of the desk to put his condition book away, and when he looked up, Katie Calhoun was standing in the doorway. With long legs, the waist of a ballet dancer and big brown eyes with flecks of gold, Katie provoked calamity among men wherever she went. Her tight blue jeans followed the curves of her hips, her white blouse highlighted her sun-bronzed skin. When Sam stared at her as if he'd suddenly froze solid, Katie's red lips curled to a lovely smile. She tilted her head to make smooth waves of red hair fall over her shoulder.

"Funny how a person's memory works sometimes," she said in that breathless way she had of talking, "because I never think of you with clothes on, I always remember you naked."

During the time it took Sam to unfreeze, smile and stand up

to come around the desk, he was remembering those nights in that hot tack room at Lincoln Park with Katie, her body slippery with sweat in his hands, her slow kisses, the throb and pulse of her body, his hormones dictating that he should do things to her he'd never imagined doing before.

Katie opened her arms, and when Sam stepped into them and they hugged, she whispered, "Pant for me little doggy."

Sam laughed then, stepped back out of her arms, said, "There'll be none of that…I'm married, and the last I heard, so are you."

"*Was*, Sam, I'm divorced."

"Sorry it didn't work out."

"I thought I found Mr. Right, I just didn't know his first name was Always."

"Sit down, Katie," Sam said, motioning toward a chair before sitting back down behind his desk.

As Katie sat down, she gave the office a quick scan. "This is classy, Sam. I'm so glad to see you doing good, and that colt, Black Deuce, he's the horse of a lifetime."

"He is. Some luck finally came my way."

Settling back in the chair, Katie now attacked Sam with another smile, the invitation in it unmistakable, and Sam was remembering how he and Katie would put their bodies to furious work any time of day or night, how Katie was limber as a willow and how he could bend her any way he wanted. Once a friend of his, Ross Dwyer, was sitting in the pickup truck Joshua let him borrow any time he needed to, and Ross started to laugh. When Sam asked him why, Ross pointed upward. When Sam looked, Katie's bare footprints were all over the truck's ceiling.

Katie said, "All I'd have to do is sit down on that old iron bed and make it creak and you'd come running…my darling little puppy dog."

"I *was* a pup, only seventeen."

"I know I robbed the cradle, I was five years—"

"You were twenty-four," Sam interrupted with a grin.

"Alright, seven years older…now let's lock the door and put

that leather sofa to good use."

Katies eyes seemed to slant, becoming even sexier, and she was so beautiful Sam suddenly couldn't look at her. He glanced away, felt a tremor, but it was nowhere near his heart. The next tremor he felt *was* his heart, reminding him of Bess' perfection. Sam looked back at Katie and Katie understood the look. The light in her eyes faded.

"Not even a foot rub?" Katie said.

Sam shook his head and Katie stuck her tongue out at him, glanced away, turned the color of cherries.

"Don't be mad," Sam said.

"I was hoping to work off some anxiety," Katie answered. "Handling a jock's book isn't easy, you know."

Sam just smiled at her, waited for the pitch.

"All these good horses you train now, Sam," Katie went on, "you've got to have something for my jock, you know, for old time's sake."

"I've got a first call rider, Katie, but I'll keep your rider in mind if I ever run an entry."

Katie's brown eyes were suddenly clear and soft. "I miss you," she said in a whisper.

"We were great together…but it was a long time ago."

"Wife's name?"

"Bess."

"She must be something special."

"She is."

"And you love her?"

"I do."

"You never once told me you loved me, never once," Katie said, and gave a weary sigh. "Most men do, either to get what they want or in appreciation for getting it…but not you, never the *L* word spoken."

Sam said nothing to this, knew he couldn't do anything about the loneliness he heard in Katie's voice.

"Bess is a lucky girl," Katie went on, then suddenly playful again said, "and if you ride her like you rode me, you'll keep her happy a long time."

Sam didn't answer. A man had appeared in the doorway, and Sam was looking at him. The man had heard what Katie said, and he blinked at her wide-eyed, took in the head to toe length of her with a slow glance, then looked at Sam and blinked again.

"I think I came at a bad time," the man said.

"No, come on in," Katie said, standing up. "I'm not doing any good here at all…can't get my jock on a mount"—Katie gave Sam a smirk—"or even get myself mounted." The man's jaw opened in surprise, and Katie walked to the door. Before she left she said, "You change your mind, puppy dog, I'll be at the Belair Hotel on Cicero Avenue, room 217."

Sam shook his head slowly, said, "Don't look for me, Katie."

Then Katie was gone and the man turned around to look at Sam, and said, "Didn't Credence Clearwater Revival sing a song about her…long cool woman?"

"Credence got the temperature wrong," Sam said. Then asked: "What can I do for you?"

"I'm Detective Carson Flood," the man said. "I'm with Chicago P.D. Homicide."

The entire twenty feet of Sam's intestinal tract spasmed.

38. DETECTIVE CARSON FLOOD

Flood found nothing unusual about Sam's reaction to a homicide detective come to see him. Most men falter, hesitate, look guilty, and Sam Jack looked and acted just like most men do. If Sam had acted with an unnatural calm, this would have alerted Flood.

"Mind if I sit down, Mr. Jack?" Flood said, patting the back of the chair Katie had just been sitting in.

"Of course," Sam said.

"That was one beautiful redhead," Flood said, looking out the door as if in hope Katie would return.

Flood was a short, beefy man who appeared to have no neck. He wore his iron-gray hair in a waxed 50s-style flat top, his pushed-in face gave him the appearance of a bull dog. The enamel of his teeth was stained yellow by cigarette smoke. His clothes were rumpled, as if he'd slept in them for a week. Flood had been a detective for twenty-four years, and before that he'd been in uniform for ten. Detective Carson Flood was a remarkable man. No matter how chaotic the situation, he could remain calm, and no matter how heinous the crime, he took it in stride. Flood had been the lead detective in the North Shore Ripper case, and when he arrested Gonzo Phipps, the serial murderer who'd left the body parts of five women in dumpsters between Lake Shore Drive and Milwaukee Avenue during the summer months of 1976, he put the cuffs on him with all the emotion of a scientist peering through a microscope. Flood was unshakable, rock-solid in a crisis, and had the uncanny ability to separate good from bad, lies from truth. Once seated, Flood leveled cold gray eyes on Sam, the kind of eyes that could make even a murderer flinch.

Sam flinched.

"You like to gamble, Sam?"

"I don't gamble," Sam answered.

Flood stared at Sam, registered Sam's answer as the truth. Flood said, "Three days ago Chicago P.D., in cooperation with Berwyn P.D., executed a search warrant on a house at 2397 Oak Park Avenue. You know a man by the name of Milton Peabody, Sam?

Sam repeated the name, then said a quick, "No."

"We knew Peabody was home, and when he wouldn't answer the door, we broke it down. There was a gunfight. A Berwyn cop took one in the belly. My partner, Eddie Schultz, put a bullet in the middle of Peabody's forehead, that's why Eddie isn't here. He's temporarily assigned to desk duty…I'm sure you understand that drill."

Sam nodded.

"But you don't know Milton Peabody?"

"No."

"The Deacon, that's Peabody's name on the street."

Sam looked like a man falling off a cliff.

"So, you did know him," Flood said, and didn't wait for Sam to answer. He continued: "We searched the house, came up with blood money"—Flood stared hard into Sam's eyes—"real blood money, lots of it. The same blood all over those stacks of hundred dollar bills was on a duffle bag, or what was left of a duffle bag, in a burn barrel in Peabody's back yard."

Flood paused there, studied Sam's distress—the flexing jaw muscles, the rapid breathing—then continued: "What do you know about the Atlantic Hotel murders, Sam?"

"Nothing," Sam said.

"Did you know a man by the name of Bill Baker?"

"No."

Flood's intensity was grim, he'd registered two lies in a row.

"How about Frankie Costello, or Antonio Belichio?"

Flood felt an icy gust of anger come across the desk at him. He'd expected it, but the power of it surprised him.

"Antonio—" Sam faltered, then, as if the words burned his tongue, he said, "Antonio Belichio murdered my father."

Flood's chin went up and down in a nod of agreement. "According to Pete Bennett," he said, "that's exactly who killed your father."

Sam shifted back and forth in his seat, his eyes suddenly very bright. "I remember him, he was the detective from Chicago who came asking my mother and I questions."

"Pete remembers you too," Flood said. "He's retired now, but he remembers you and your mother really well. When I talked to him about this case he said he remembered interviewing you like it had happened just that morning. He said it was one of the hardest interviews he ever did, talking to you, a young kid who saw something no kid should ever see. You found your father's body, didn't you?"

For a brief moment Sam seemed paralyzed, then he said, "Yes...I found him in the barn."

Now Flood looked away from Sam, up at the trophies gleaming on their shelf. "There was nothing Bennett could do, it was a jurisdiction problem, and the cops in Iowa wouldn't listen to him. In those days, Joey Cassini, a left over from the Capone days, ran all of Eastern Iowa and Bennett figured that's who kept him from any information that could connect Belichio to the murder. Bennett had been after Belichio for years, he wanted to put him away, but could never pin anything on him. Bennett became obsessed. He was sure Belichio was committing murder after murder, but he could never get to him...it finally drove Pete crazy...the futility. He was forced to retire due to psych problems, the department shrink said he had to go."

"I didn't know," Sam said. "All these years I thought I was the only one who believed my dad was murdered."

Flood felt an odd pressure in his head. The pressure had become familiar as of late, usually a fleeting feeling, but this time the pressure wouldn't go away and continued to build. As a young cop he had a self-concept of himself as a hero, but all these years as a homicide detective had destroyed that self-concept. Flood felt powerless against all the evil in the world, now toward the end of his career believed that good would never triumph over it, that human beings are carnivores, that the only things constant in the human condition were greed and a taste for blood. Sitting there in the tack room office, across the desk from Sam, Flood was suddenly aware that he'd lost something, that something was spent, gone, not retrievable, and that the loss of this something had left his soul in shreds. A huge depression came over him. He looked at Sam, into the clean shine of Sam's face, and saw him as a boy finding his father murdered. Pete Bennett had told him how Sam had got down on his knees beside his dead father and frantically tried to fit his father's skull back together, had frantically tried to place all the bloody pieces of bone back where they belonged.

Flood now had a massive headache. He cleared his thoughts of the horrors by saying to himself, I'm Detective Carson Flood, I am the law, and I have a job to do. Flood gathered himself back together, got his bearings, renewed his attack on Sam.

"There was a big bet made on a horse you train, and we know that's what put Baker, Peabody, Costello and Belichio in room seventeen of the Atlantic…all that money. It's not hard to imagine a man like The Deacon to be the last man standing." The grim intensity was back in Flood's eyes. "What's hard to imagine, Sam, is a guy like you being involved with those animals. Not a man in that room didn't deserve the rough rope and the short drop."

There was a long moment of utter silence as the two men stared at each other. Then Flood began to fire questions at Sam like he was firing a .357 magnum.

"Sam Jack, did you kill Frankie Costello?"

"No."

"Sam Jack, did you kill Bill Baker?"

"No."

"Sam Jack, did you kill Antonio Belichio?"

"No."

Flood was intense, he'd registered the truth three times in a row. There was no doubt in his mind that Sam had done something, but there was also no doubt that Sam was no murderer. Murderers were all alike, they gave off a stink as pungent as dime-store aftershave. Flood took a deep breath, inflating his chest, and when he let it go he relaxed. He'd gotten the answers he came for. He looked into the swath of sunshine that came through the window behind Sam, and the massive headache was abruptly gone.

"There was a forth murder," Flood said, "or at least I think it was connected to what happened at the Atlantic. A *Jane Doe* we found stuffed in a garbage can a block away, she probably saw something she shouldn't have. A working girl in a lavender dress."

Sam made no response.

After a long silence, Flood's pushed-in face arranged itself into a tired smile and he said, "You and your wife have any kids, Sam?"

"Amy's six."

Flood nodded, stood up. "You know what I think, Sam?"

Sam shook his head.

"I think it takes a good man to love his wife and daughter so much that he'd turn down that long-legged redhead who was here when I showed up. Yes, sir, a real good man."

Sam smiled a weak smile, said nothing to this, and Flood turned and walked toward the door. Over his shoulder he said, "I'll be in touch, Sam...if I need you."

Then Flood was gone, leaving Sam sitting alone behind his desk. Relief made Sam's mouth go slack, even his eyelids to droop. It took Sam a long time to gather back his strength.

39. SAM

During the days before the match race, so many photographers and people from the press showed up at Sam's barn, barn number one, and Death Wish's barn, barn twelve, that a boundary of yellow police tape was created around both barns. No photographer or journalist was to venture past this boundary unless invited. Sam and Joshua gave interviews to the press, but it was Moses who provided the most quotable quotes, and Black Deuce's groom became a favorite of the reporters.

Moses sat on an upturned bucket in front of Black Deuce's stall rolling bandages, and Mark Schroeder of the *New York Herald* called out, "How do you see the race being run, Moses?"

Moses looked up from the bandage he was rolling, called back, "It'll happen at the quarter pole, boys, that's where Deuce'll blow by Death Wish like a pay car passes a bum."

Laughter erupted behind the yellow-tape boundary.

Sam came out of the office, and he was laughing too, and a chorus broke out among the reporters and photographers: "C'mon on, Sam, let us come take some pictures, and give us some insights into your horse."

Sam looked over at Moses. "There's only eight or nine of them this morning, Moses. You mind if I let them come under the shed for a closer look?"

"Let 'em come, Sam," Moses said. "They ain't a bad bunch, and to tell you the truth, I think Deuce likes all the attention."

Sam looked at the colt, and the colt stood with his neck stretched out over the webbing, trying to see the people making all the hub-bub. Sam looked out to those beyond the tape and waved them in. The group moved quickly toward the barn, looking like a gaggle of geese, and soon came the sound of camera shutters. Black Deuce gave them what they wanted. The colt stood at his webbing tall and handsome, a gleaming blue-black.

"Thanks, Sam," one of the reporters said, "you're a lot more friendly than Death Wish's trainer, Sir William Benchley. What do you think about running against royalty and English knights?"

"Don't see how a title can make their horse run any faster," Sam said.

"What about the title of champion, Sam? Death Wish has been the Euro champ two years in a row, and an undefeated champion at that."

"Death Wish is a remarkable horse," Sam said, "and—"

"The onlyest reason Death Wish is undefeated," Moses interrupted, "is because he ain't never run yet against Deuce." Moses pointed at the colt, said, "There's thunder in this colt's hooves, and I been told God himself is already standing in line at the fifty-dollar window waitin' to bet on him."

Smiling broadly at Moses, Sam revealed his even white teeth, and more laughter came from the reporters.

Now Moses looked up at Sam, said, "Tell 'em, Sam, tell these fellas what the jock said about Deuce, go on now, tell 'em."

"What did Clay Repp say, Sam?" chorused the crowd of reporters and photographers.

Sam looked over at the colt, drew a long breath, then looked back at the reporters. "Clay told me he's never really let this colt run, that even with all the races the colt has won, that the colt has other gears he's never shifted into, and that—"

Sam went silent in midsentence, kicked at the ground, looked at the colt.

"And that what, Sam?" two reporters said together, sounding like a duet.

Sam looked back at the reporters, said, "And Clay said that

he dreams about the day he asks this colt for everything he's got…and that the thought of it thrills him, but the thought of it scares him too. Clay told me on the day this colt gives everything he's got, the earth will move."

"The earth will move," repeated Mark Schroeder of the *New York Herald*. "That's my headline for tomorrow. Thanks, Sam."

"About this undefeated thing—" Sam stopped himself, looked at all the faces around him, and in that moment wanted to tell the real story, about how the colt had never been beaten, about how a frightened and confused Emily Brandt did what she thought she had to do to save her farm, and how he and Joshua had followed her instructions and shouldn't have, how he and Joshua had helped cheat the colt, how he knew what happened in room seventeen of the Atlantic Hotel. Guilt came over Sam, and it weighed him down, came across his shoulders like a giant boulder. And now Sam was thinking of two other people he'd cheated, he was thinking of Bess and Amy.

Sam stood in a suspended silence, and it seemed to him the Patek Philippe he carried in his pocket ticked loud enough to be heard by everyone there. It was Moses who broke the silence.

"You okay, Sam?" he said.

This brought Sam back, and he blinked at the groom, then looked at the photographers and reporters and said, "That's all for today, guys."

The group voiced their appreciation to Sam and Moses, then slowly moved back behind the yellow-tape barrier.

40. SIR WILLIAM BENCHLEY

In Sir William's younger years, he'd been a jockey, but as a middle-aged man he'd swelled up into the shape of a pear. Bloated and bejowled, his yellowish eyes were set in pink sockets and his fat lower lip seemed to flop as he talked. He walked in the manner of a bowling pin indecisively teetering between falling and standing. A man of savage temper, his wrath was easily provoked. Those who knew him best said his heart didn't pump blood, rather, it pumped bile.

Sir William had grudgingly allowed reporters and photographers to visit his horse. It angered him to be in the company of those who didn't understand just how important he was, and as if to punish them all, he launched into a rambling narrative about his unequaled ability to get the most out of a thoroughbred. When Sir William began to repeat himself, one of the reporters cleared his throat in an exaggerated manner, and the other reporters and photographers began to exchange sly glances and roll their eyes. This made Sir William furious. Understanding that no reporter was interested in any of his wisdoms and philosophies, that nothing of what he was saying was being written down, he glowered contempt. From behind his webbing, so did Death Wish.

The gray gelding was a behemoth. Standing at eighteen hands and weighing over twelve hundred pounds, he barely fit into a starting gate. He was far from a sleek and beautiful racehorse. His symmetry was all wrong because of a shoulder so heavy he appeared hump-backed, and because of a huge set of hindquarters constructed of freakishly thick slabs of muscle. His mane was stiff and bristling, his tail short and scrubby, and he was walleyed. His eyes were a bluish white, and always seemed to be wide and staring in a way people found unsettling.

"Get any closer and you'll be sorry for it," Sir William said in an English accent to a photographer.

The photographer was standing near the gelding, looking to get a close-up of one of the gelding's staring eyes.

"Death Wish will take a chunk out of you," Sir William went on, "and if you don't believe me, have Pinky show you his ear."

Pinky, Death Wish's groom—a bright little man who hopped around like a jaybird—cocked his head so everyone could see that half his ear was gone. "He chomped it right off me head he did, when I weren't looking," Pinky explained in a heavy accent.

"I didn't think horses were carnivores," said one reporter.

"This one is," Sir William said, "and he's going to chew Black Deuce up and spit him out just like he did Pinky's ear."

"Catching Black Deuce to do all that might be a problem for your horse," a reporter said.

A chuckle went through the gathering, and anger made the lids of Sir William's eyes flutter. He wasn't accustomed to being laughed at.

"When the gate opens, Death Wish will make Black Deuce look like an elephant in a ballroom," Sir William said. "No horse foaled can stay with Death Wish once he goes into his drive."

"Is that your strategy, Sir William, to send your horse right from the gate?" a reporter asked.

"You'll just have to wait and see," Sir William snarled.

"Will Aiden Bishop be here to ride Death Wish?" asked a reporter.

"Bishop will be here," Sir William said, "and he'd be more than pleased to give out autographs to your jockey colony. Bishop is a real race rider, not a cowboy...who is this Clay Repp? What riding title has he ever won that was worth winning? Bishop is

Europe's leading rider. He won more races last week than Clay Repp has won all year."

"Clay Repp has the best hands of any jockey I know," said Frank Wilson, a writer for the *Racing Form*.

Sir William raised his eyebrows as he laughed. "Before today, I've never heard of Clay Repp, or this Sam Jack, and you, Frank Wilson, must have a weakness for lost causes."

"Your horse looks like he shipped in good order," said a reporter.

"Didn't turn a hair," Sir William said, "and he's already proven he likes this racecourse. It should be fun to humiliate America's champion on his home court."

"You sound as if you've already won," said a reporter.

When Sir William replied, something in his voice made everyone there stop and really listen to him for the first time. "Death Wish runs like a lion on the hunt," he said, "and when he gives Black Deuce the stare with those eyes of his, Black Deuce will be nothing more than prey."

41. SAM

Both horses were scheduled to blow out for the race on the Friday before. The racetrack would be closed following the morning break, harrowed, then Death Wish would be given the track for half an hour. After Death Wish, the track would be harrowed again, and then Black Deuce would be given his half an hour. The track would be reopened for regular training after Black Deuce was off the racetrack.

Delaney made sure the event was well-publicized.

Clay and Sam stood outside the colt's stall, looking off toward the racetrack. The parking lot was full, the grandstand and clubhouse packed with people, and on the morning breeze was the low hum of thousands of voices.

"There's more people here this morning, than on a regular Saturday," Clay said with wonder in his voice.

There wasn't a photographer or reporter standing behind the yellow tape, they were all following behind Death Wish, recording all he did, and recording, with some editing, all Sir William said.

"Have you seen Death Wish?" Sam asked.

"He's a monster," Clay said. "His withers are like a big hump, I don't know how they get a saddle on him. I've heard they have to have his girths special-made."

"I watched him gallop…like you say, he's a monster."

A snort came from the colt's stall, and it didn't come from Black Deuce, it came from Moses.

"Monsters?" came Moses voice. "What is this Halloween? Now if you two are done tellin' boogieman stories, I'm ready here."

Moses dropped the colt's webbing, and led the colt out of the stall. Just then the low hum of voices began to rise until it reached a peak of sound that shook the air. Sam, Clay, Moses, and Black Deuce looked off toward the racetrack.

"I'd say Death Wish has just broke off to work," Sam said. Then to Moses: "Take the colt once around, Moses."

When Moses brought the colt back around, Sam gave Clay a leg up.

"I like the way you do rundowns, Moses," Clay said as he tied a knot in the reins, "The red tape on the white bandages makes Deuce look spiffy."

"Got to make my big hoss look dapper, jock," Moses said.

"Around again, Moses," Sam said, "and I'll meet you at the end of the barn. By the time we get up to the gap, they should be done with the harrow."

Because barn twelve was behind the grandstand, Death Wish went to and from the racetrack by a route that took him through the paddock and out around the winner's circle. When the colt left the barn by the route that took him to the gap, a loud applause rose up in the distance from the crowd gathered in the stands.

"Death Wish must be stepping off the track," Sam said.

"The fans seem to really like him," Clay said.

"Nothin' wrong with appreciatin' a good hoss," Moses said.

But if Sam, Clay and Moses thought the fans liked and appreciated Death Wish, what waited for Black Deuce went far beyond that. Once Black Deuce was on the pony path, a swarm of reporters and photographers arrived to follow after him. They asked more questions, took more pictures, and as soon as the colt stepped out onto the racetrack, the low hum coming from the stands was replaced by fans giving in to their excitement. The appreciation the crowd had shown Death Wish was one thing, but here was the home town favorite, America's horse, and the fans held nothing back. A massive sound came from the fan-packed clubhouse and grandstand, a sound of shouting and cheering and applause. Sam felt a swelling in his chest as he watched the colt jog the wrong way up the racetrack.

That morning, Death Wish worked in 35:1. Black Deuce in 35:4.

Everything was set for the running of the Suburban Park Special.

2

It was late morning, and Sam was on the phone with Bess and Amy. It was one of those rare phone conversations when both his wife and daughter were the ones who wanted to talk about horses, one horse in particular, Black Deuce, and they were excited about the race. Sam wanted them to come, but Bess refused, she and Amy would watch the race on TV. Sam listened to Bess tell him about the cakes she'd made for the St. Mark's bake sale, and he laughed out loud when Amy told him how hard it was to keep her fingers out of the frosting, that the cakes looked so yummy. Amy also told Sam about the fun she was having in Bible School. After the I love yous, Sam hung up the phone, leaned back in his chair, put his hands behind his head, and shut his eyes. The long phone conversations he had with Bess had become a daily event, and he looked forward to them so much he understood something was happening. Exactly what this something was, he wasn't sure. All he knew for sure was that he hadn't seen Bess or Amy for over two months, yet loved them more every day. So often, even when he was working under the shedrow, he caught himself not thinking about horses, instead thinking about what Bess and Amy might be doing.

Vance and Moses had been having a conversation in front of Black Deuce's stall, and when their voices stopped, Sam opened his eyes. He wasn't alone.

A woman in a blue summer dress and sandled feet was

standing just outside the office door, looking in at him. Her short blond hair came to points over her cheeks, and her long-lashed eyes were brilliantly blue in her lovely face. She was in her forties, but there was still a fineness to her slender figure that had caused Vance and Moses to go silent and stare at her. When her eyes met Sam's, pink pastels flushed her cheeks.

Sam brought his hands from behind his head, leaned forward, placed his hands on the desk and asked, "Can I help you?"

The woman opened her mouth to speak, her teeth flashing white between the red of her lips, but she only made a choking sound.

Sam smiled, puzzled, then as he studied her, his smile disappeared. Now staring into her eyes, a tremor ran through him.

"May I come in?" the woman finally managed.

Sam said nothing, his stare now intense.

The woman stepped into the office, said, "The last time I saw you, you were mostly legs."

"Who are you?" Sam said, his voice cold and deliberate.

"Look how handsome you've become," the woman said, ignoring the question. "When you were a boy, you were almost too beautiful to even be a boy."

"I said, who are you?"

The woman said, "I'm your mother, Sam."

Sam saw it clearly then, what he'd suspected, in her face, the reflection of his own, and the room seemed to rise and fall, and Sam felt so off balance, that he held onto the desk. The next moment was the kind that has nothing to do with the seconds and minutes ticked off by a clock, and in the silence of that moment, Sam looked at his mother with eyes that doubted she was real. Then a sudden blaze of emotion engulfed Sam, a combustible mixture of new anger and old sorrows. He wanted to scream at her, release how he felt in wild sounds, but when he opened his mouth, there was none of that, only an icy quality to his voice.

"I forgot you even existed," Sam said.

All color left his mother's face, and when Lauren spoke, she couldn't keep her voice steady: "Your father was my strength, without him, I didn't know how to be strong. I was helpless, didn't know how to help you or even help myself."

"But all the years that have gone by, and now you come to see me?"

Sam's mother faltered, struggled, said, "Sam, after you ran away, I spent almost a year in Dubuque, in the mental hospital."

"Excuses? You've come to give me excuses?" There was no pity in Sam. "I was only a boy, and you didn't even try to find me...do you know how many times I woke up at night needing you?"

His mother's voice hit an aching note: "But I did find you, and you were working for Joshua Kincaid, and I knew you were where you needed to be, where you wanted to be, and I didn't want to ruin it for you."

"Ruin it for me?" Sam said, putting in his voice all the anger he was capable of. "What have you really come here today for? Is it money? Have you finally come to see me because you need money?"

"No..." His mother put a trembling hand to her mouth, then took it away, said, "I haven't come for money. I remarried, and he's a good man...he can never replace your father, no one will ever do that in my heart, but he's a good man, a Federal Judge, and we have a comfortable life." Misery twisted at his mother's face, and her voice trembled: "I've been coming to watch you race your horses for months. I was within twenty feet of you when you ran Black Deuce in the Windy City Derby, you were coming out of the winner's circle. I wanted so to talk to you then, but now I'm glad I didn't, because now, talking to you here, I know you still hate me, Sam, that you still blame me for everything...losing the farm, somehow your father's death...everything."

And Sam always had, and still did, blame her for everything, and in the confusion of the moment he was remembering how he would wake at night as a boy wanting to hear her voice, but how he hated her too, that the day she gave up the farm, the farm his father had loved, was one of those bitter memories that could ambush and destroy any moment of happiness he might have. Sam turned away from his mother, his jaw tight with anger. Then and there, all he could think about was how much he blamed her for all that had happened, and how much he missed and loved his father.

And then it happened.

From out of a hiding place in his head came an image, a memory from his boyhood. He was four-years-old, sitting on a chair in the middle of the kitchen, a white towel around his shoulders, and he could hear his mother's voice, she was pleading with his father not to cut the long blond hair that fell to his shoulders, that it was too beautiful to cut and that she couldn't bear to watch. And after his first haircut, Sam could see his mother standing in the kitchen, holding the cuttings of his long hair in her hands, and that her eyes were flooded with tears. And other memories came out of their hiding places: his mother was holding him up so he could put the star on the top of a Christmas tree, and she was sitting on the side of his bed and he held tight his raggedy teddy bear, the one with the button eyes, as she read to him about *Jack and the Bean Stalk.* And it was the memory of the sweetness in his mother's voice as she read to him that now haunted Sam's ears, and he understood that not all memories can be trusted, that for years he'd blamed her for everything, and that she was blameless, that she was a victim too, and that now he had to do what was right, and that in so doing a door would be closed, finally, and that another would open.

Forgiveness came suddenly, and Sam turned to look at his mother. In that moment, love stirred violently in him, and the next sound Sam heard was a beautiful sound, it was his mother's voice and she was saying his name.

"Sam?"

Sam stood up slowly from the chair, and afraid if he said one word, he'd lose control, he walked over to his mother and touched her cheek with his fingertips. A great tenderness came over him, and he put his arms around her, held her close. His mother clutched at him then, squeezed him, and both made the small sounds of great emotions, and both felt a feeling of closure and joy.

Then Sam became aware of a man standing in the doorway.

Silver-haired and with eyes that were lively and clear, there was authority in his presence, about him a compelling look of intelligence. Keeping an arm around his mother, Sam wiped at his eyes.

"Is everything alright, Lauren?" the man said.

Through the tears that spilled over her lashes and down her cheeks, Sam's mother turned to look at the man, a glowing smile on her face. She still clutched possessively at Sam.

"Bertie," she said happily, "I want you to meet my son Sam."

3

It was after ten o'clock that night and Sam sat in a lawn chair outside the shedrow office. He'd gone out to dinner with his mother and her husband, Bertrand Chase, and had a pleasant time. Old memories were stirred, some painful, but in the recalling of times that seemed to him from another life, what he remembered about his mother caused a new bond to grow. Sam found *Bertie* to be of good humor and likable, and that Bertie loved his mother was without doubt.

After dinner, Sam had gone to his apartment and tried to get some sleep. Impossible. There in the dark, staring at the ceiling, every nerve in him twitched as he thought of the post time that would bring Black Deuce and Death Wish together. When Sam couldn't sleep, he always ended up at the barn.

The moon tinted the clouds silver, and Sam sat in the dark sipping at a big cup of Oscar's coffee, listening to the soft sounds of a horse barn at night. A mouse scampered out of one stall and into another, a bird roosting in the rafters gave one sleepy chirp, and somewhere a horse nickered through a dream. Black Deuce was in the back of his stall asleep, and Oscar was on the other side of the barn, checking on horses and keeping a watch over the night. A June bug came whirring by the stalls, seemed to aim itself right at Sam, and when it bumped into his shoulder the whirring stopped and the beetle lay on its back in the dirt, its legs twitching in the air. Sam reached down, flipped the June bug right side up, and off it whirred into the dark.

Headlights bounced on the road, casting glowing circles on the blacktop. A truck appeared, and when it turned in to park in front of the barn, light from the headlights floated briefly on Sam's face before going out. Sam smiled. It was Joshua. Came the sound of the truck's door opening and closing, and now footsteps.

"I'm hoping that coffee tastes as good as it smells," Joshua said.

"It does," Sam answered. "You know where to find it. There's a clean cup on my desk in the office, and another lawn chair behind the door."

Joshua walked by Sam, opened the office door, flipped on the lights.

"I haven't seen this before," Joshua said.

"What?"

Joshua stood in the doorway holding up a framed picture of Bess and Amy. Bright smiles did something beautiful to both faces. Sam turned and looked at the picture.

"Oh, that," Sam said. "It just looks right on my desk."

"That it does."

"It's a good picture of them, isn't it?"

"It is, Sammy, and I'm glad to have found it where I did."

Joshua put the picture back on the desk and was soon sitting in a lawn chair beside Sam, sipping at a steaming cup of Oscar's finest.

Sam said, "I knew you couldn't wait until tomorrow, that you'd be here tonight."

"Ye know me well," Joshua answered. He peered toward the stall, said, "Asleep?"

"He's lying down, dead to the world."

Joshua only nodded. Both men sat in the silence friends are so comfortable with. There was a movement in the dark, and the old orange tomcat leaped up on a railing. He looked Sam and Joshua's way and lowered his head, watching them in the sly way cats do.

"The old boy is out courting," Joshua said.

"He's the barn *ratter*," Sam answered. "You should see the scars on that old face of his."

"Fought many a battle has he, for love and a snack?"

The cat leaped from the railing, disappeared into the shadows. Crickets played their nighttime ballads. Joshua leaned forward, gripping the cup with both hands, then leaned back, looked at Sam.

"Heard anything from that detective?"

"No."

"Good," Joshua said, then took a drink of coffee. He changed the subject: "Like we've talked, the colt is done with running after tomorrow, he's nothing left to prove. It's to the breeding shed with him."

Sam nodded, thought about life under the shedrow without the colt, said, "I'll miss him." Then Sam changed the subject, said, "I had a visitor today."

"Who?"

"My mother."

Joshua uttered a small sound of surprise, said, "How much money did she ask for?"

"It's not like that, I had dinner with her and her husband Bertrand. He's a judge and a nice man."

"Just a coincidence that she finally showed up when yer pockets are full?"

"No talk of money."

"Then box seats for tomorrow's race?"

"Nope. She'll be here tomorrow, but she doesn't want to get in the way. She and Bertrand have tickets for the infield. They said they'd cheer Deuce on from there."

Joshua gave a grunt, shifted in the aluminum lawn chair to make it creak. There was another long silence, one not so comfortable. Joshua briefly rubbed his elbow, then said, "I've a favor to ask."

"Anything."

"When I ship Deuce, I want you to drive along with me down to the farm."

"Why?"

Joshua shifted again to make the chair creak, and remained silent.

"Josh, I asked why?"

"I haven't been..." Joshua's voice trailed away.

"You haven't been what?" Sam said, now sitting up straight. Concern was in Sam's voice: "Are you alright?"

"I've been to a doctor..."

Concern became alarm. "What's wrong?" Sam asked.

"They need to run more tests," Joshua said, looking away from Sam.

"What do they think it is?"

"Ye know how doctors are, they make being sick miserable...they aren't sure what's wrong...and all I know is that I have these spells..."

"Spells?"

"I haven't felt well for a long while, Sammy...and I don't trust meself to make that long drive with the colt, not with anyone else but ye to keep watch over he and I."

"I'll be glad to."

Joshua reached over and tapped Sam's arm. "I appreciate it, Sammy, but I want no one else to know about me health...no one, understand? And let's drop the subject, I don't want to dwell on it and spoil the sport of tomorrow."

"Sure," Sam said.

Nearby, one shadow separated itself from the others.

"Our visitor is back," Joshua said.

In the next instant, the orange tomcat was in Joshua's lap. Joshua cupped his hand over the cat's head and rubbed, and the cat looked straight up into Joshua's eyes, blinked long and slow, and invited Joshua into friendship. The cat began kneading with his front paws, then making half a turn, settled comfortably on Joshua's lap. He began to purr, sounding like a small outboard motor.

"Just look at that face," Joshua said, running his fingers through the tomcat's fur to make him purr louder. "Only an old pirate would have a face with such battle scars."

"I've never seen that cat let anyone else near him," Sam said, "let alone touch him."

"He's taking a wee break from pursuing the feline beauties," Joshua said, "and maybe feeling a bit mellow and in need of some understanding."

Sam grinned, said, "The understanding of one old pirate for another?"

The cat's eyes glowed like gold fluorescent lamps in the night, and Joshua talked to the old tomcat, his voice soft, caring, weaving tenderness into the things he said, and Sam understood why animals loved Joshua so much, and why he did too.

Then Sam changed the subject: "What's Robert down on the farm have to say?"

"Everything is spic and span. The house is as it should be, and the main barn is all but finished. The contractor knows how to build a barn, I'll give him that, it's like a palace, the main barn is. The two new barns should go up quickly."

"I thought there was only one new barn."

"I decided on two forty stall barns, instead of just one."

"Will you need that kind of room?"

"And more," Joshua said. "Old friends up East have already been in touch about wintering horses with me, and the other project...I can't believe all the inquiries."

"A lot of old horses looking for a home?"

"So many, Sammy. I had to add stalls...and even then, I'll have to turn away some."

Straw snapped under hooves, and Black Deuce came to stand at his webbing. The colt worked his ears and smelled the night air with dilated nostrils. A chance beam of moonlight caught in his eyes and made them gleam. Sam and Joshua sat looking at him. It was Joshua who broke the silence.

"I don't remember much about me mother, she went to her reward during the influenza epidemic of 1924. But I do remember how she liked to read to me when I was but a wee lad, and not stories of wizards and goblins, mind you, but stories of great men, like Napoleon, Cromwell, and that ancient one Alexander." Joshua gave a short laugh. "She was so sure I was going to grow up to be a great man, that she wanted me to get some learning on the subject."

"Did you learn anything?"

"I didn't give a hoot about those great men of hers," Joshua said, stroking the old tomcat's fur to make him keep purring. "What difference was it to me that Napoleon stubbed his toe at Waterloo? But I'll tell ye what did fascinate me about all those men…the one thing they all had in common."

Sam tipped his head, curious.

"Horses, Sammy," Joshua said. "Every one of those great men met their greatness seated on the back of a horse."

Sam uttered agreement.

"Now ye take us, the two of us, where would ye and I be without Black Deuce? We'd be cleaning out stalls somewhere, just living and dying among the shedrows without anyone remembering whether the doctor slapped our behinds to start us breathing or not. But now, in a hundred years, even two hundred, because we're standing in this colt's win photos, people will remember us. But we'll only be an afterthought, Sammy, only an afterthought." Joshua looked up at the colt, the whites of his eyes showing in the moonlight. "When people look at the win photos, their first thought will always be the same, and down through the years they'll speak the truth of it when they say, look at this, this is Black Deuce, the greatest racehorse ever to leave hoof prints on a racetrack."

Joshua turned to look at Sam. "Do ye understand? Understand that ye and I will only be remembered because we stood in the shadow of the great black horse?"

42. THE SUBURBAN PARK SPECIAL

Race day arrived, and as Delaney planned, it arrived with a fanfare that had few equals in the annals of racing history. People converged on Suburban Park in bustling hordes, coming by train, by car, by bus, even by foot. There were so many lined up at the turnstiles before the track was officially open, that Delaney opened the track at 7:30, an hour ahead of schedule. By eleven o'clock acre after acre of the racetrack's parking lot was filled with cars, and when the sprawling lot could hold no more, the property owners for blocks all around the racetrack began to sell parking spaces in their driveways and even in their front yards. All this traffic had no effect on the trains, they continued to arrive at regular intervals at the Arlington Metra station, but it was said more than one bus driver lost his temper over the heavy traffic that congested all roads leading to the north-side track. By noon, over eighty thousand people had swarmed into the clubhouse and grandstand, and the infield, with tents and temporary box seats and bleachers, took on a rowdy but happy circus atmosphere. Fans ate burgers, hot dogs, studied *Racing forms,* checked out tips sheets, drank beer and soda pop. And there was plenty of entertainment for the huge crowd. Five different rock bands took their turn on the temporary stage in the infield. Ten hot-air balloons, bobbing in the sky like brightly colored bubbles, raced across the city of Chicago toward the Suburban Park finish wire. And six ostriches with jockeys on their backs, were raced down the stretch. Laughter burst from the crowd when one of the six ostriches kept running in circles with Dean Kruz, Suburban Park's leading jockey, shouting for "Help!" and screaming "I'm never riding anything with feathers again!"

By post time for the first race, over one hundred twenty thousand people had jammed into Suburban Park, and the trains and buses kept adding more people to the throng. Everyone came expecting to witness one of the most dramatic sporting events of the twentieth century. Black Deuce and Death Wish weren't going to disappoint them.

2

There were two other stake races scheduled that day on Suburban Park's nine-race program, and Minx, one of Bentley's California purchases, had run a good second in the Black Dahlia, a sprint for fillies and mares. Minx was beaten only a length in the *racehorse time* of 1:08:4. To the glee of Rupert Fitzhugh, Green Paddock Farm's Insomniac had won the event, ridden by Aiden Bishop, Death Wish's regular rider. Bishop *picked up* the mount when Sir William asked Ralph Binder to put Bishop on a horse so that the English rider could get a familiarizing trip over the racetrack before the match race. Binder was more than happy to give Bishop a leg up on one of his horses, especially if it meant helping to get Black Deuce beat. Binder and Fitzhugh were still bitter over the colt winning the Windy City Derby.

In Suburban Park's Jock's Room, there was an atmosphere of tension and strain from the moment Clay and Bishop set eyes on each other. When Bishop walked back into the jock's room after his victory in the Black Dahlia, Rudy the valet kept an eye on Clay. Rudy recognized the expression that compressed Clay's face into hard lines, and was ready to stop any violence Clay had in mind...and there *was* violence on Clay's mind. When Bishop went by him inside the sixteenth pole on Insomniac, Bishop had been busy with his whip and had hit Clay across the right hand, leaving a stinging welt that had swelled to a bright red.

"Don't do anything stupid," Rudy said to Clay.

Clay glared across the room at Bishop. "This was no mistake," Clay said, rubbing his hand, "he meant to hit me."

Rudy stepped sideways to block Clay's view of Bishop. "Yeah, so what? Don't be a fucking cry baby. Now promise me you aren't going to go bonkers on that Brit."

Clay scowled, nodded and sat down still rubbing his hand.

Rudy went back to the business of being a valet. He knew Bishop's reputation as a brawler, but doubted Bishop understood that Clay was fully capable of sending him back to England in a full-body cast.

Clay and Bishop now stared at each other across the room.

Bishop was tall for a jockey, and at five foot ten he was rail-thin. But like all hardened race riders, there was great strength in the sinewy muscles across his shoulders and in his legs. Without a shirt, all Bishop's ribs could be seen, and because his cheeks were deep hollows, a dark shadow ran beneath his cheekbones, giving his mouth an odd muzzle-like appearance. All this gave Aiden Bishop the look of a famished wolf. Strangely long canine teeth furthered this wolfish look. Bishop seldom smiled, and when he did, he used it as a warning, a warning that devils and demons possessed him. Aiden Bishop's smile was all it took to set alarms off in other riders, putting in them a need to give Bishop all the room he wanted on and off the track. With just a smile, Bishop could destroy an ordinary jockey's self-confidence, could make most riders feel inferior and uncertain of their talents.

Aiden Bishop started to come across the room…and he was smiling.

Clay stood up to meet him, and all the noise and bluster of the jock's room ceased. All the other riders and valets stopped what they were doing to watch the confrontation play out. So complete was the silence, everyone heard when Clay muttered through gritted teeth, "Just give me an excuse."

Bishop stopped on the other side of a long table where Rudy

had saddles and other equipment arranged. Bishop looked at Clay's hand and spoke in a heavy accent: "Did I do that, old boy?"

"Go fuck yourself," Clay answered, anger turning his cheeks red.

Bishop's smile widened. "Black Deuce is going to make the earth move today? Is that the quote you gave the papers?"

Clay took a step to go around the table to get at Bishop. Rudy blocked Clay's way. Rudy looked at Bishop, his eyes steady into Bishop's, said, "Don't let your battleship mouth get your canoe ass in trouble here, jock."

Bishop threw his head back and laughed a harsh, unnatural laugh. "Oh, I say, that's rich...I'll use that one day." He stopped laughing, tilted his head to look around Rudy at Clay. "I do hope you won't have to take off the rest of the day because of that hand...it looks to me like you're going to have trouble holding on to your stick." Now Bishop smiled so wide his pointed canines were fully exposed. He continued: "But if what I saw earlier is an example of your ability to hit a horse...well, let's just say the girly boys of Soho hit harder with their feathered boas."

Bishop rolled his eyes, turned around and laughed on his way back across the room.

"Limey prick," Clay said.

Now the other valets and riders went back to their own business. Noisy talk resumed, the sound of tack being cleaned and readied could be heard.

Rudy got Clay to sit back down. He changed the subject: "Are Doris and Tommy coming today?"

This was the only topic that could instantly change Clay's mood. He smiled at Rudy, said, "Yep, they're out there."

"Doris is a swell gal, I'm so happy she's letting you have visits with Tommy."

"It's gotten to be more than just visits, Rudy. I think Doris and I are going to get back together. She and I and Tommy are going to be a family again."

Rudy made a sound of surprise, said, "That is just great news, jock!"

Clay was beaming, looking at the pictures of Tommy and Doris he had taped to the inside walls of his cubical. One picture in particular held his gaze. It'd been taken at Great America just last week. Clay stood with his arm around Doris, and standing in front of them, grinning a little-boy grin for the camera, was Tommy. He held balloons in one hand, and a stuffed panda in the other.

"Nothing more important than family," Rudy said.

And with these words, Clay wasn't smiling anymore. He was remembering what the swing of Bishop's whip had done to him, and it wasn't the pain he was remembering. He was remembering that for an instant he wasn't focused on riding Minx and getting the filly to the wire first, that for an instant he'd felt himself in danger and in that instant he wasn't race riding but thinking about Doris and Tommy, his family, that for an instant he'd lost his concentration and wasn't any more use than a sack of potatoes in the saddle. And Clay was remembering that races are won or lost in an instant.

"You're right about that, Rudy," Clay said distantly, "there's nothing more important than family."

Now Clay glanced at the bottle of Scope Rudy kept handy and wished it to be Seagram's.

3

Sam had left Joshua and Bentley in the clubhouse, and now followed behind the colt as Moses brought him up to the paddock along the pony path. Sam wore a new blue blazer, tan slacks and oxblood loafers. The *outfit,* as Sam called it, was a gift from Bentley, purchased at the Ralph Lauren store on Michigan Avenue. The colt stepped along gracefully, his musculature standing out clearly defined beneath a brush-polished coat that shined and glimmered in the sunshine. The colt pulled on the shank just enough to make sweat bubble out across Moses' forehead. When the colt began to pull hard enough to make Moses break into a jog,

Moses yanked on the shank to make the chain rattle.

"Take it easy on me, Deuce," Moses said as the colt slowed back down to a nimble, bouncing walk. Moses looked over his shoulder at Sam. "He's in one of his moods, Sam...one of his runnin' moods."

Halfway to the paddock, cameramen with TV cameras balanced on their shoulders began to follow Black Deuce. The NBC logo could be seen. The race was being televised live across the country, and in a little farm house in Iowa, Amy gave an excited "There's Daddy!" to make Bess come running back into the living room, and in the servant's quarters of Southern Oak, Robert leaned closer to his TV marveling how Black Deuce had grown into a full-fledged racehorse. An NBC sports reporter, Chris Collins, a middle-aged man with graying blond hair and a handsome face meant for television, now walked beside Sam, talking into the microphone he held.

"Your horse looks magnificent, Mr. Jack," Collins said, then began the routine of swinging the microphone between himself and Sam as he and the horseman talked.

"Thank you," Sam answered.

"By all reports, Black Deuce has come up to the race in fine condition."

"He's never been better."

"Black Deuce has been running hard these last months," Collins said as they walked along, "has it taken anything out of him? Will the grueling schedule he's kept affect his effort today?"

Sam glanced over at Collins, hid his irritation, said, "I wouldn't run the colt if he wasn't right."

"I followed Death Wish into the paddock just moments ago," Collins said, "and I have to say, he's one impressive thoroughbred. In all my years of following horses for NBC, I've never seen such a Goliath."

"Death Wish is a runner," was all Sam said.

"There have been great changes in your life these last months, Sam. You were an unknown, then came out of obscurity to take over the Keene Racing Stable, and now comes this marvelous racehorse Black Deuce. The future must look very bright to you."

"I don't like to look too far ahead," Sam said, then gave a well-used racetrack quote: "In this sport, it's chicken today, feathers tomorrow."

Collins gave a quick laugh, then once again became serious. "America has become infatuated with Black Deuce, he's a legend in the making, and yet not until his last two starts has he been the betting favorite. The handicappers I know blame Black Deuce's first two races. How do you explain the colt being beaten so badly in his first two starts?"

"I discovered the colt had a minor problem and sent him to Joshua Kincaid for some time off. Joshua worked his magic and sent the colt back to me perfectly sound."

"Kincaid, now there's a top horseman."

"None better. What my father didn't teach me about horses, Joshua did."

"I have to ask you about your choice of riders, Sam. Clay Repp is an old timer by jockey standards, and he's had his problems, that DT episode in the jock's room really tarnished his reputation."

Sam stopped walking to turn and look squarely at Collins. A frown put grooves in his forehead. "I won't listen to you bad-mouth Clay. He's had his problems, but he's the best race rider I know."

Collins pressed the issue. "You've never been tempted to change riders? I know jockey agents representing the leading riders in the country have been on the phone to you trying to get the mount on this colt."

"I get calls all the time from agents," Sam said, leaning forward to talk directly into the microphone so everyone listening could hear him clearly and not misinterpret his words, "but Clay has my full confidence, and I've never thought of replacing him."

There was something in Sam's tone that caused Collins to become wary and change the subject: "What about running a three-year-old against an older horse like Death Wish?"

"It's late in the year and Deuce has already beaten older

horses," Sam said, starting to walk along the pony path again, "I don't see age as a factor."

"Sportswriters disagree with you, Mr. Jack," Collins said, following Sam. "They say this is a mistake, that a veteran racehorse like Death Wish, a horse with a perfect record of twenty-seven starts and twenty-seven wins, can ruin a young horse, can take the heart right out of him."

"The sportswriters are wrong...that may be true about some horses, but not my horse."

"But one prominent sportswriter has even used the words malpractice and incompetence to describe your allowing your three-year-old—"

Sam put his hand up to stop Collins in midsentence. He reminded himself he was on national television, then said, "Mr. Collins, it's time I give my horse my full attention, so you'll need to excuse me." Sam walked on and Collins didn't follow after him. Just as Collins began to talk into the camera to all the TV viewers, Sam turned back, said, "One more thing, Chris."

Collins was smiling when he held out the microphone toward the horseman and said, "Yes, Mr. Jack?"

Sam looked into the camera lens, a smile widened his mouth, and into the microphone said, "Hi, Amy and Bess!"

There were squeals of delight in the little farm house in Iowa.

Sam followed after the colt and Moses. The low, heavy mutter of a huge crowd was on the air, and rising against the sky was the vast glass and steel grandstand and clubhouse of Suburban Downs. Up ahead, waiting in the green and flowered paddock, was the competition, Death Wish and his connections. Sam felt a wonderful thrill.

When Black Deuce entered the paddock the voices of waiting fans rose up, sharp with notes of excitement. Sam enjoyed the effect the colt's arrival had on the crowd. People bumped into each other as they pushed forward to stare at and admire the colt, and all around the paddock there was movement as the dense crowd shifted back and forth to try and get a better look at both Black Deuce and Death Wish. There was something wild in the crowd's delight over the two horses, and there was one moment when Sam became alarmed about how the colt might react to fans who seemed on the verge of going out of control as they pressed against the paddock fence. But Black Deuce tolerated the crowd, and as he walked beside Moses, he responded to all the commotion by stopping now and then to prick his ears and hold his head high while he curiously examined the noisy throng.

Under the spreading branches of one of the paddock's elm trees, Desmond Fairchild, the NBC anchor, waited for Chris Collins to turn the TV audience back to him. Fairchild was a tall, silvery man with a perfect tan. As was his trademark, he was dressed in formal evening wear, and in the satin lapel of his white jacket was a red carnation. He was the master of NBC sports, a man whose oratory could make the scene of a church sewing circle seem a cataclysmic confrontation between yards of violently uncooperative material and stout-hearted housewives armed with weapons of threaded needles. Waiting for his cue, Fairchild calmly watched the paddock scene, and suddenly there the cue was, and he was *live.*

"Race fans! This is Desmond Fairchild, and this is NBC Sports, live from beautiful Suburban Park in Chicago, bringing to you The Suburban Park Special, the match race of all match races, a race between two titans of the turf, two heroes of the harrowed loam. Not since Jesse Owens put it to the Nazis in Berlin have I seen such tension and excitement. Not since Babe Ruth left the dugout to take his last stand at bat have I seen such anticipation."

Moses and Black Deuce went by where Fairchild was announcing, and as if on cue the colt began to prance and snort.

"Here's the brave three-year-old now, race fans!" Fairchild announced. "Sleek, honed, and unbelievably handsome! It's a mystery to this sportscaster how those slender legs can take the concussion of running at nearly forty miles an hour. Believe it, race fans, nearly forty miles an hour." From across the paddock came voices shrill with alarm, and Fairchild turned his attention to where NBC cameras were catching the sight of people dodging and ducking away from the paddock fence.

"The crowd around Death Wish seems to be running for cover," Fairchild explained into his microphone. "There, I see why now…the gray is in the air. He's on his hind legs. One of the men holding Death Wish is off the ground, dangling by a shank. Look at the size of Death Wish, he dwarfs Black Deuce, he towers above everything in the paddock, and the stare of those eyes is enough to send even your anchorman running for cover."

In the servant's quarters of the great columned house, Robert leaned toward the television, his eyes wide and blinking behind the lenses of his spectacles, and in the little farm house in Iowa, Bess and Amy looked into the television screen barely able to breathe, seeming to expect the giant gray gelding to kick his way out of the television and devour them instantly.

Fairchild went on: "I'm now recalling the brilliant colt Hastings, winner of last year's British Derby, and how Hastings has failed to win another race after matching strides with Death Wish in the Tower of London Stakes earlier this year. It's said that at the eighth pole, when Death Wish looked at Hastings with those staring eyes of his, that it broke the colt's heart. Can it be true? Can one look from those walleyes destroy Black Deuce? Is trainer Sam Jack sending a kitten out to face a lion today? A cub out to face a grizzly?" Fairchild was given a cue, and he said: "And for more insights, let me turn you back over to Chris Collins who's with Sir William Benchley, Death Wish's trainer."

Chris Collins stood not far from where Death Wish was back under control. The huge gelding's muscles swelled beneath his gray coat, muscles hardened by training and hard-run races, and he swung his head from side to side as he was led away, looking as if he was ready to bite. The gelding flicked his stubby tail back and forth.

Chris Collins said, "Sir William, it's disappointing that the Duke couldn't be here today."

"The Duke has a heart condition," Sir William said, "and at the last minute was unable to make the trip."

"We wish him a speedy recovery," Collins said. Then he changed the topic back to the race: "Your horse seems battle-ready, Sir William."

"He's always battle-ready," said Sir William, talking into the microphone Collins had swung his way. "He's the best racehorse in the world, he's already proved that twenty-seven times."

"His last start, the Irish Handicap," Collins said, "Death Wish broke the world record for the mile and one quarter, running it in—"

"1:57:3," Sir William interrupted, "and no three-year-old can hope to equal such an effort."

"You've been talking all week like this is a *walk over*, that Black Deuce has no hope to beat your horse."

"When that gate opens, there's no horse, past or present, who can match strides with Death Wish. They should save time and award the Duke the gold trophy and the million-dollar purse right now."

"Black Deuce has compiled a brilliant record of performances, beating the best horses in the United States and doing it in near record breaking and track record breaking time."

"Black Deuce proved what he is in his first two starts," said Sir William. "Great racehorses don't get humiliated, not even in their first two starts...no more questions." Sir William gave a flip of his hand as if to dismiss Collins. "Here come the valets, I need to saddle my horse."

Collins looked into the camera lens, said, "Thank you, Sir William, and with that, Desmond, why don't we switch over to Everett Daily in the winner's circle, where two Pinkerton detectives and four national guardsmen are watching over the trophy awaiting the winner of today's Suburban Park Special."

To the delight of the crowd that surrounded the winner's circle, Everett Daily, a retired jockey, began to talk into the camera. From 1965 thru 1969, Daily had been the nation's leading rider. During his long career in the irons, he was recognized as a rider's rider, and now he was an exceptional horse racing analyst for NBC. Balding and with a small-featured face, he was still trim and fit. People behind him peeked over his shoulders and started grinning and waving into the camera.

"Thank you, Chris Collins," said Daily, standing in front of a table where a large trophy and three smaller trophies were being watched over by detectives and uniformed national guardsmen. The large trophy was gold and finely decorated with bands of laurel leaves, handles in the shape of horseshoes, and a detailed rendering of a thoroughbred in full racing tack on top. The smaller trophies were exact copies of the larger trophy, only in silver. "I'm standing here beside the trophy to be awarded to today's winner, and I must say it is exquisite. Crafted by Tiffany, this trophy is reportedly made with over fifty ounces of gold. The scrolled cartouche on front of the trophy is waiting to be engraved with the winning horse's name. There are also three smaller trophies, one for the winning jockey, for the winning trainer, and the breeder of the winner."

Daily kept talking as he walked out of the winner's circle, the cameras following after him.

Leaning over the fence in front of Daily was a big man, a football player-type. "Jockeys aren't real athletes," he called out to Daily, "all they do is ride a horse in a circle." The man grinned wide at Daily, seeming glad to have interrupted the analyst and gotten himself on TV.

Daily stopped talking into the camera, gave the man a swift glance, then looked back into the camera. Daily's festive attitude changed dramatically. When he began to speak again, his voice was slow and deliberate: "Of course jockeys aren't real athletes." Daily said. "All it takes to be a jockey is the balance of a gymnast, the hands of a concert pianist, the strength of an Olympic athlete, the ability to keep time in your head with the accuracy of a Swiss watch, and have the courage to put all that to work while on the back of a thousand-pound animal running at top speed."

Daily looked back at the big man, fixed him with intense eyes, and the man lost his smile, was suddenly unsure of himself, and with people applauding Daily's comments, he seemed to shrink in size like a scolded child. Now Daily was smiling at the supportive crowd and he turned back to the cameras.

"I only hope I just did justice to all jockeys everywhere with

my reply, and I hope I made a real racing fan out of that man"—
Daily looked for the man, but he was gone in the crowd—"who
doesn't understand, like I do, like the millions of people watching
NBC's broadcast of this match race do, that jockeys are hundred
pound daredevils and that thoroughbred racing is the greatest sport
on earth."

The crowd burst into applause, and Daily, smiling broadly
and with a spring to his step, continued on toward the paddock. He
talked into the microphone, giving his analysis of the coming race
as he moved along.

When Aiden Bishop left the jock's room to walk out to the
fence-lined path that led to the paddock, he worked the rubber
bands on his wrists that kept the sleeve openings of the silks
closed. He repeatedly wound his finger on the inside of the bands,
stretching the bands before letting them snap back against his
wrist. This habit was the only indication he showed of being
nervous, all else about him was normal: he was stiff, arrogant,
unsmiling. Then he saw a woman standing next to the fence, and
his eyes widened with interest. Raven-haired, she had olive skin
and fine dark eyes. There was a soft loveliness to her that made her
seem nothing less than a miracle of nature. Bishop had just stopped
to say something to her when a voice came from behind him.

"That's my girl, Bishop," Clay said, his face burning with
pride as he walked up to stand between the English rider and the
fence where Doris stood, "so just keep moving."

Startled, Bishop snapped a rubber band against his wrist, and
kept walking.

Clay turned to Doris and smiled. Just to look at her made him
pleasantly short of breath. "You're so beautiful today," he said,
"and you and Tommy make me so proud."

"Daddy! Daddy!" said Tommy standing beside Doris. Apple-
cheeked and grinning happily, he reached out to hold onto Clay's
leg. "Mommy bet two dollars on your horse for me, Daddy. I hope
I win lots of money!"

Doris smiled a lovely smile. "I had to bet on you, Clay, just
for luck."

Clay leaned over the fence and put his hand to the side of Tommy's face, and Tommy held onto the hand with both of his, his little face bright with the kind of smile an adoring little boy reserves for his father. Clay said, "I hope you win Lots of money too, Tommy, so you can take your poor old dad out to dinner tonight."

"Alright, Daddy, if we win I'll buy you and momma dinner tonight...pizza!"

Clay turned to Doris grinning. He looked into the luster of her face, into her fine dark eyes, and a feeling of love filled him up. Then his grin disappeared and he said, "You and Tommy mean everything to me, but I've got to do something, and I need your permission to do it."

Doris frowned, said, "Clay?"

"I need you to tell me it's alright, that when that gate opens I can forget I even know you, forget that Tommy was ever born."

"Why?"

"Because to be the rider I want to be I need to risk everything, and if I'm thinking about how much I love you and Tommy, about how much you both mean to me, I'll hesitate when I shouldn't."

"You need my permission?" Doris said.

Clay briefly closed his eyes, took a deep breath, said, "Yes, because I feel so guilty about doing it, and I need you to tell me it's okay."

Clay stood tense, waiting, and Doris gave Clay a sweet smile that lifted his heart. Doris said, "It's okay...from the gate to the wire it's only you and your horse."

Clay leaned over the fence and kissed Doris, a brief touch of the lips, then turned on his boot heels to go into the paddock.

"Ride the race of your life, Clay," Doris called.

"For the three of us," Clay called back.

Then Everett Daily was there with Doris, and the cameras were on she and Tommy. It wasn't until Daily started to talk into his microphone and a chorus of voices rose up around she and Tommy that Doris realized what had taken place wasn't a private conversation between she and Clay, that the entire NBC audience had heard and watched the scene play out, that all the racing fans around them had heard and been watching.

"And this is the untold story of dedication," Daily said with emotion as he spoke to the audience of millions beyond the camera lens. "This is what it takes to be a jockey, what it takes to be the family of a jockey, and I can't add to the eloquence of what we've all just witnessed." Daily turned to Doris and Tommy, said, "Good luck to Clay, and God bless you and your little boy, Doris."

Now Daily called after Clay, and when Clay turned around just inside the paddock, Daily and his Cameraman caught up with him. Clay looked into the camera, then at Daily, and at that moment Rudy walked by and handed Clay his whip.

"And that's what I want to talk to you about, Clay," Daily said, "about the whip and Black Deuce."

"Ask away," said Clay.

"Everyone knows you've seldom touched the colt with the stick, that the colt's always given you all he had to give without being hit."

"I've tapped him on the shoulder before," Clay said, "and in California, in the Pacific Coast Classic, he got so far in front he began to look around…he was more interested in the crowd in the grandstand than he was in running, and I had to uncock my stick and reach back and hit him once."

"I've watched the replay of that race several times, after you hit him he took off like an artillery shell from a howitzer."

"He was mad at me over that," Clay said, grinning. "For a week he pinned his ears whenever I came around him."

"You broke the track record that day by three ticks, was that the best the colt has?"

"No, it still wasn't his best," Clay answered, shaking his head. "Even on that day he left me feeling that there was more in the tank."

"In my opinion, Clay," Daily said, "you're going to need to ask the colt for everything he's got to beat this European Champion."

"Death Wish is a great horse," Clay said, "there's no doubting that, but if I need to use my stick today, every racing fan watching will have something to tell their grandkids about."

"Just one more thing before I let you go, Clay," Daily said. "Years ago you were a leading rider in Chicago, and I want to congratulate you and tell you how glad I am that you've overcome so many problems to make this great comeback."

"I couldn't have done it without the support of Bentley Keene and Sam Jack, I owe those two men everything."

"And of course, Doris and little Tommy."

"Doris and Tommy are who I live for."

"Good luck today, Clay, and thanks for talking with me."

Clay nodded, smiled into the camera, and walked away. Now Daily walked over to where Aiden Bishop stood off to the side watching Death Wish being saddled. The gelding was giving his handlers fits, acting more like a hump-shouldered beast than a thoroughbred racehorse. When the girth was finally tightened, the gray dropped his head, made a bellowing sound like a bull might make at the sight of a matador, and kicked out with both hind legs.

"What's it like to ride this great racehorse, Aiden?" Daily asked.

"Like riding a bolt of lightning," Aiden replied, standing tall and stiff with his arms crossed over his chest. He held his stick in his right hand.

Moses was walking Black Deuce around the paddock, and Death Wish, with two men on shanks, was also being walked. The presence of both horses was superb there under the paddock elms. Daily glanced at the thoroughbreds. Black Deuce walked beside Moses with cool grace. Death Wish gave another bull-like rumble.

Daily said, "These two horses remind me of prize fighters, eyeing each other across the ring."

"That's what Harry Wilkinson, the editor of *Racing Today,* wrote about Death Wish," Bishop said, "that he's like a prize fighter who enjoys pounding his competition into the ground."

"Is that the plan, to pound Black Deuce into the ground?"

"That's the plan," Bishop said, smiling at Daily to show his pointed canines. "You can look for Black Deuce at the quarter pole after the race...he'll be the black spot on the track, that's all that's going to be left of him."

Sir William was waving Bishop over, and Bishop gave the camera a nod, Daily a nod, and walked over to join the trainer. Daily and his cameraman now took up a position where they could get a good shot of the horses leaving the paddock. Sir William stood with Ralph Binder and Fitzhugh. After Bishop won on Insomniac, Sir William had invited them to join him while he saddled his horse.

Bishop shook hands with all three men, said, "I appreciate you putting me on that good filly, Mr. Binder and Mr. Fitzhugh."

"You rode her perfect," Fitzhugh said.

Bishop looked over where Clay was just joining Sam. "I about had a row with Black Deuce's rider after we were back in the room. It seems he didn't appreciate the good whack I gave him with my stick."

This pleased Binder and Fitzhugh, and both men looked over at Sam and Clay. Binder glared, and Fitzhugh put his head back and looked down his nose, said, "Six months ago Sam Jack couldn't afford a ham sandwich."

Bishop, Sir William, and Binder all laughed.

The paddock crowd's fascination with both horses seemed to intensify as the minutes ticked by. Heads moved back and forth between the two horses as if everyone was watching a tennis match.

Clay now stood with Sam, Joshua, and the assistant trainers, Mary and Vance. He'd kept his eyes locked on Black Deuce as he'd come across the paddock. Like all riders who know the thrill of riding a good horse, he was greedy for the rush of that moment when he asked Black Deuce to run. Clay put his arm out and first shook Sam's hand, and then everyone else's. Now Clay stood with his chin up, holding his stick in one hand, the other hand on his hip, and because he had confidence in himself, confidence in Black Deuce, he had about him the indisputable presence of a winner.

Joshua noticed Clay's right hand, the swelling caused by

Bishop's whip. "I saw that happen," Joshua said. "Does it bother you?"

Clay held his hand up, flexed it, said, "Not at all." Then he looked around. "Where's Bentley?"

"He left right after Minx ran," Sam said. "I'm not sure..." Sam paused, pointed across the paddock. "Here he comes."

Everyone turned to look, and understood exactly why Bentley had disappeared for several races. He came toward them moving not at his customary rapid pace, but much slower, and this because he had a lady on his arm. She was a small woman, straight and slender, and she moved with slow aristocratic grace. She was dressed in autumn tweeds, and under the wide brim of her fashionable hat, her heart-shaped face was delicately boned, her eyes sparkling like that of a little wren. It was Ruth, Bentley's wife, finally come to the races.

Now standing by Sam, Joshua and everyone, Bentley said, "Sam, Joshua and Clay, you've never met my wife...with great pleasure, let me introduce you to Ruth."

The three men made their greetings, as did Vance and Mary. Everyone agreed that it was wonderful to see Ruth.

"I hope, gentlemen," the notes of Ruth's voice chimed sweetly, "that you don't mind that I've come to meet you on such an important day."

"Not at all," the three men assured her.

"Hearts can be a miserable organ," Ruth explained, "and mine has kept me from the races for far too long."

Just then the noise from the crowd swelled and Ruth gave a small gasp, looked about in alarm. For months, Ruth had been helpless in the grief of losing her only child and was still extremely fragile. She clutched at Bentley's arm and in the shadow of her brimmed hat her eyelashes fluttered like the wings of a frightened little bird.

Bentley assured her: "All is well, my dear, the fans are just excited to see the two horses."

Moses came by leading Black Deuce, and Ruth saw the colt and was no longer afraid. "My, isn't he debonair," she said. "He seems an equine cross between Cary Grant and Fred Astaire."

Everyone smiled, nodded, agreed, but Sam, turning his attention back to business, gave a nervous fidget. "Excuse Clay and I for just a minute," he said to the group, "we'll be right back."

The five understood. Bentley and Ruth, Vance, Mary and Joshua watched Sam and Clay walk out of hearing range. Clay followed Sam back toward the stalls used for saddling during bad weather. It was quiet there and they were away from everyone else. Sam stood with his back to the crowd, and Clay tipped his head to look up into Sam's face.

Sam said, "I didn't think I needed to say this, but here at the last minute I think I have to. There's something I want you to know." Sam glanced over his shoulder, spotted Daily and his camera crew far across the paddock, then went on: "Remember the first morning you worked Deuce in the fog, the way you looked at Deuce and then looked at me like you had a question?"

"I remember."

Sam's eyes narrowed, hardened. "Then you know he's perfection, that he's never come off the racetrack beaten."

Clay nodded, said, "Of course I know…those first two races aren't his, since that morning in the fog, I've always known they couldn't possibly be his."

Sam nodded, rubbed his chin, looked around him at the closest people still far enough away not to hear what he was saying. "Heart will win this race, the horse with the biggest heart, the horse that can take the pain and punishment, the horse that won't give up."

"In a match race, if you're not first, you're last."

"That's right," Sam answered. "From the gate to the wire, you never stop riding this horse, you get to the front and do what it takes to stay there." Sam took in a breath, drawing in a lungful of cool autumn air. Then he said, "Racing might be the sport of kings, but match races are the sport of madmen, and today our *crazy* has to be bigger than theirs."

The paddock judge, a man with stiff short black hair and black-rimmed glasses, called out his command: "Riders up!"

The noise from the crowd swelled, excitement was crisp in the air, and Sam and Clay returned to where Moses had Black Deuce standing and waiting. Both riders were now in the saddle, and being the number two horse, Bishop should have waited for Clay and Black Deuce to lead the post parade. He didn't. Bishop gave Pinky, Death Wish's groom, a tap with his stick, and the jaybird-like groom gave a hop and led Death Wish out of the paddock despite the protestations of the paddock judge. Bishop looked back over his shoulder at Clay. He pulled his lips back against his teeth in the kind of wolfish grin only he could give.

"Get accustomed to being second," Bishop said.

Clay flushed red, but when he opened his mouth to answer Bishop, Sam reached out and took hold of his boot. Clay looked down at Sam.

"Don't take the bait," Sam said. "Just give that jock no mercy."

The exchange delighted the crowd. Voices climbed in volume, there were shouts and sharp whistles, and as Bishop turned back around and looked out over the humanity packed into the paddock, his grinning expression shifted rapidly back to no expression at all. As the horses left the paddock, so did the crowd, and thousands of race fans began to make their way back to their seats or to the mutual windows, looking like a sea of bobbing heads.

Desmond Fairchild was talking into his microphone: "Race fans, it seems the entire population of the Midwest has squeezed onto the grounds of Suburban Downs. Traffic jams, packed trains, and parking lots filled to capacity are the order of the day. I'm told the crowd is now bigger than the crowd that watched Seabiscuit and War Admiral, and now that the horses are leaving the paddock the crowd has really come alive. You should hear this noise."

In the little farm house in Iowa, Bess and Amy were staring at the TV set, both nibbling their nails, and in the servant quarters at Southern Oak, Robert was leaned forward in his chair, gazing at the TV, and didn't give the tall glass of lemonade beside him a second thought.

When the red-jacketed bugler in his black top hat played *Call to the Post,* the sounds coming from the Grandstand, clubhouse and infield increased in volume. The occasional sneeze or cough of an individual was drowned out by the rising mumble and mutter of tens of thousands of racing fans. Then as the bugler's cheeks swelled and he blasted out *The Horses are on the Track* and the two thoroughbreds appeared, there came a surge of voices as people swung their heads to watch the horses parade to the post.

Sam didn't get into the elevator with everyone else to go up to Bentley's box in the Turf Club.

"I hope you all don't mind," he said, "but I want to watch from the fence."

Vance took a step toward Sam, said, "I'll come with you, Sam."

Joshua grabbed Vance by the arm, held him back. "I think the man wants to be alone with his horse," Joshua said with a wink.

Everyone understood, and the elevator doors closed and up they went to the Turf Club.

A security guard let Sam step through a gate onto the grandstand apron. All around Sam there was motion as people bumped against one another, trying to see the horses, and Sam felt helpless at times as he found himself trying to stand in the middle of the shifting multitude. When the horses went by, a mass of upturned faces slowly turned as the fans followed Black Deuce and Death Wish to the gate.

Desmond Fairchild: "The weather is beautiful, sunny and in the seventies, and the track is fast. The horses are heading for the gate, and the fans have made their choice. Death Wish is going off the favorite at two-to-five, and Black Deuce is two-to-one. I agree with the bettors, I can't get by the first two races Black Deuce ran, not in the face of the unbeaten and older horse Death Wish. Who are you betting on today, Chris Collins?"

Chris Collins was in the winner's circle, and Collins looked into the camera, said, "I've got to go with Death Wish. He's the older horse, has proven himself twenty-seven times in a row. What about you, Daily?"

Daily was still in the paddock, and he answered: "Up until minutes ago, I was giving Death Wish the edge, a big edge, but I was within feet of the colt when he left the paddock, and it was like...it was like he radiated a force field, some unseen power, and it made me change my mind. I'm backing the colt...Black Deuce to the wire first."

"There you have it, race fans," said Desmond Fairchild. "it's two to one for Death Wish. And now that the horses are nearing the gate I'm turning you over to the Eclipse Award winning track announcer, Phil Adams, for the call of the race."

Phil Adams, the voice of Chicago racing, could now be heard over the public-address system: "The horses are nearing the post for the Suburban Park Special."

Mathew James, the starter at Suburban Downs, watched the two horses come up the mile chute toward the gate. James was a short, stocky man who was known for the *Open Road* Stetson hat he was never without. A pair of sharp blue eyes were set in his weather-burned face. Few riders had ever dared to argue when the sharp blue eyes focused on them. James was already in the starter's stand, and when Clay and Bishop came by him, he stood polishing the lenses of his gold-rimmed glasses.

"You boys listen up here," James said in a quick shout, and both riders looked up at him. "You get *tied on,* and you stay tied on...you won't be in that gate long enough to spit."

In answer, both riders said, "Yes, sir."

Now James put on his glasses, focused sharp eyes on the process behind the gate. He held the long electrical cord with the red button on the end with a steady hand.

Once behind the gate, Bishop reached back and slapped the gray on the quarters with his open hand. He was provoking Death Wish, rousing him for the task ahead. Death Wish gave a loud snort and began to bounce alongside the lead pony. Not satisfied with this reaction, Bishop swung his whip and hit the gray a sharp, stinging blow on the belly. Now Bishop got what he wanted. Infuriated, the gray leaped in the air and bellowed like a bull. The pony boy had just unsnapped the lead shank from the gray's bit when an assistant starter reached for the gray to begin leading him into the gate. But the gray turned on the assistant starter with a vengeance. As the assistant starter's hand came near him, Death Wish struck, biting the assistant starter's hand. There was a brittle snap, and the assistant starter jerked his hand back, cried out, and hurried away from the gelding holding his hand against his chest.

Bishop pulled on the reins to make the gray bow his head, and the gelding's walleyes glared their stare as Bishop shouted, "The gray runs best when he's hungry!"

Phil Adams announced: "They're entering their stalls."

Black Deuce went into the gate without incident, and when Death Wish entered the stall next to him, the assistant starter had just gotten the doors closed behind him when the bell rang and the gate slammed open.

Phil Adams: "And they're off in the Suburban Park Special!"

In that first lunge, quarters dropped, rear hooves pushed, the horse's heads came up and then down again as both riders sent their horses into a drive right out of the gate. Bishop's whip cracked as he hit Death Wish, and both riders shouted and reins slapped. The horses began to cover ground in bounding strides, their hooves coming down on the track, then refusing the track with such speed that the sound made seemed to come from the hooves of other horses running lengths behind.

Phil Adams: "And the horses break from the gate as a matched team!"

A roar composed of tens of thousands of voices came from the crowd in the stands and infield.

Both horses glided over the track, slipped through the air, *leveled off* as if the finish wire was just ahead. Hooves dug into the racetrack, *toe grabs* caught their grip, and with tremendous force both horses launched themselves forward. They set a scorching pace that would have hammered a lesser horse's bones to dust.

Phil Adams: "The first quarter reached in a blazing 21:2! The horses are nose to nose, Black Deuce on the inside, Death Wish on the outside!"

The chests of the two thoroughbreds expanded and

contracted, faster now, as their breathing quickened to keep time with their hooves. Both horses defied science, both horses pushed themselves beyond what flesh and bone could tolerate, and both riders felt the bond of gravity loosen…and both riders asked their horses for more.

Phil Adams: "The half in 43:1! It's a pitched battle! Black Deuce skims the rail, Death Wish right alongside! The lead changes with each stride, with each nod of the head!"

Clay was belly down, had his face in the colt's mane, and beneath him he could feel Black Deuce straining as he ran, could hear the colt pulling air into his lungs in great drafts and releasing it in blasts. And Clay was in perfect rhythm with Black Deuce, timing himself, sensing as only a race rider can that micro-second when he should be pushing on Black Deuce, and at the three-eighths pole, when Clay was in that intense, narrow world where only he and Black Deuce mattered, Bishop and Death Wish bumped him and the colt hard.

Both horses fishtailed, their hooves scattering dirt as they quickly recovered.

Clay looked over at Bishop, the wind whipping Black Deuce's mane in his face, and he could see Bishop moving on his horse, bent forward, swinging his whip in wide arcs to hit Death Wish punishing blows. Reason seemed to have left Bishop, he was screaming words that sounded like no language, screaming like someone who'd lost their mind.

Phil Adams: "Three quarters in 1:07:3! Raw speed! Raw power! Both horses are pouring it on!" Now Adams raised his voice over the loud speakers, and to the thrill of racing fans, his voice shook when he called, "And down the stretch they come!"

Now Clay brought Black Deuce out away from the rail, doing it in answer to Bishop and Death Wish coming over to crowd he and the colt and make the rail tight, and with this the horses bumped hard a second time. Both horses fishtailed again, their plated hooves scrambling for footing. Then Black Deuce and Death Wish, in the exact same moment, turned their heads and both tried to *savage* the other. Teeth flashed, bits clacked, eyes rolled to white, and Clay twirled his whip, waved it at the colt to make him turn his head forward again, and Death Wish *lugged out* and away. Clay gathered up his sweat-slick reins, threw a new cross, and put his head back down and once more began to push. The colt responded by flattening out, reaching out still further with his hooves, and Clay was instantly back in that intense, narrow world where only he and Black Deuce mattered. It was then that Clay heard the call, the call all great riders and horses have heard down through the centuries of racing, the call clear and ringing above the thunder of hooves, the roar of the crowd…the call of the finish wire.

Phil Adams: "We're down to the last furlong! Both horses are in a desperate drive! They're scorching the racetrack! Neither horse will give an inch! This is the most spectacular stretch duel ever seen on any race track!"

The over one-hundred-fifty thousand fans that crowded Suburban Park were no longer a civilized gathering. The sound of their cheering voices had been rising, growing steadily since the two horses left the gate, and now at the eighth pole the crowd held nothing back, erupting like an out of control mob, their voices swelling to a volume that deafened.

Approaching the sixteenth pole, Black Deuce's legs still flashed with speed, but his lungs burned, every muscle in him ached. Extreme exertion caused lights to explode in the colt's head like miniature suns. Clay felt the colt giving way. It was then that the giant gray gelding put his head in front.

Clay's answer was the whip.

Clay switched his stick to his left hand, and when he swung his whip, he put behind it all the strength he was capable of. Clay hit the colt only once on the quarters and it sounded like a gunshot. The crack of the whip was so loud it caused Bishop to look back over his shoulder.

Phil George: "The gray has taken the lead! Clay Repp has gone to the whip!"

The colt's response to the whip and being *headed* was immediate. He hurled his entire weight forward against the bit with a ferocity that nearly pulled the reins from Clay's grip, and each time a hoof touched the racetrack, it came down with such force that Clay felt an earthquake come up through the irons. Blood surged through the colt, his lungs heaved and bellowed, and beneath his lathered coat, muscle and tendons stretched and pulled as if they might tear away from the bone. With just yards to the wire, when the pain should have been violent and unrelenting, Black Deuce's great spirit rose up in a fury that blinded him to the agonies of his exertion, blinded him so that the only thing he could feel was the pounding of his heart.

Phil Adams: "Black Deuce isn't done! He has more run! This is un-be-liev-a-ble! We're witnessing one of the greatest performances in racing history! An exhibition of sheer determination and power! Black Deuce has come back on the rail!"

The thundering roar from the fans shook the very concrete and steel foundations of the grandstand and clubhouse. When Black Deuce drew back even with Death Wish, the colt looked into the stare of Death Wish's walleye, and it was then that the giant gray gelding blinked.

Phil Adams: "Death Wish has no answer to the colt's rally! Here's the wire…"

Sam had been shouting since the quarter pole and now as he watched the colt drive for the finish he shouted so hard his throat seized up and he began to choke.

Phil Adams: "…the great Death Wish is beaten!" Adams' voice detonated above the roar coming from the infield, the clubhouse, the grandstand: "The Suburban Park Special, the race of the century, won by a horse for the ages…it's Black Deuce on the inside by half a length!"

In the excitement of the moment, people waved their arms, their programs, their *Racing Forms*. People were cheering, calling out the colt's name, and some people were overwhelmed and stood with open mouths, stunned by the spectacle. And some fans were crying. Everyone there at Suburban Downs would remember this day, the day they witnessed one of the greatest moments in all of sports.

In Bentley's box seat everyone was hugging one another, pumping their fists in the air, and in the little farm house in Iowa, Bess and Amy were jumping up and down in front of the TV, and at Southern Oak, so was Robert.

Sam struggled to get air back into his lungs, and now had the feeling he would spend the rest of his life trying to catch his breath. He headed toward the winner's circle, trying to get through the crowd, the many faces around him coming and going, and Moses was just steps behind him with tears running down his face. Sam said, "Please, people, let me get to my horse." And people turned to look at Sam and understood, recognized him, began to shake his hand, congratulate him, pat him on the back. "Thank you," Sam kept repeating as he worked his way through the crowd.

Franklin R. Delaney stood in the turf club, looking down at his racetrack. He was so excited his hands were trembling, and now as Black Deuce came back around the clubhouse turn to return to the winner's circle, he watched as a racing fan leaped over the grass course rail, ran across the grass course, then leaped over the outside rail of the grass course and the rail of the main track. Hundreds, and then thousands of people in the infield followed him. Soon people from the clubhouse and grandstand apron were jumping over the outside fence, and now a huge crowd was out on the racetrack. National guardsmen were trying to keep order, but it was an impossible task.

"The national guard, they were only for show," Delaney said, watching the scene spellbound. "I never dreamed we'd really need them."

As Clay approached on Black Deuce, the crowd split, giving him a fan-lined avenue leading to the winner's circle. The shouting and cheering of the fans made a scrambled sound, only a stray syllable or word could be understood. When Clay saw Sam waiting up ahead, he shouted to him, "The earth moved, Sam!"

Phil Adams: "And returning to the winner's circle is Black Deuce! The best of the best! And, ladies and gentlemen, let me direct your attention to the time of the race. Black Deuce has set a new world record for the mile. 1:32 flat!"

When the colt stepped into the winner's circle he was lathered, dripping sweat and still blowing, his nostrils flaring wide and red with each breath. And when the track photographer took the win photo, Black Deuce looked into the camera lens, and the diamond light was in his eyes.

43. Oscar Holley

It was late, and the horses were asleep in their stalls, the birds quiet in the rafters, and the old orange tomcat played the eternal contest with the mice in the feed room. The excitement of Black Deuce's victorious return to the barn was long over, and there in the dark, Oscar stood leaning a shoulder against one of the barn's support columns, enjoying the unusually warm autumn night. Oscar was retired, had taught United States history in the Chicago public schools for thirty-two years. He'd brought his family out to watch the match race that afternoon and had brought them back to the barn after it was over. It was so nice of Sam to insist that a photo of Oscar and his family be taken with the colt. Oscar could still hear the happy and excited voices of his wife, Beatrice, his son and daughter-in-law, Walter and Donna, and his four grandchildren, as they gathered around the colt for the snapshot. Sam Jack, Oscar thought to himself, is a nice man.

Oscar looked up into the deep purple of the cloudless sky and stars reflected in his eyes. He liked his night watchman job, and what he liked most about it was quiet moments like the present. He could stand there in the dark knowing that his wife, his son and daughter-in-law, and his grandkids were all healthy and safely in their homes and in their beds. No worries. Everyone safe in good homes. Oscar let out a long sigh of contentment. Life is a wonderful thing, thought Oscar.

A truck pulled up to the barn, and before Sam even opened

the truck's door to get out, Oscar turned and walked to the tack room and turned on the light. The smell of burnt coffee. Oscar picked up the coffee pot and the black brew at the bottom looked like crude oil.

"Sam'll like this pot," Oscar said with a smile.

Oscar took a carton of cream out of the refrigerator and put a splash in the pot. Now Oscar moved the pot in a slow circular motion and, with a swirl, the white of the cream dissolved into the black of the burnt coffee. Oscar then went about the ritual of making a fresh pot to add to the old stock, and when he heard another truck pull up outside the barn, he knew it was Joshua, and he kept scooping Columbian roast into the filter compartment of the coffee maker. The last ingredient Oscar added came from a baggie he carried in the pocket of his jacket. In the baggie was the real secret to his coffee. From the baggie Oscar scooped out two heaping scoops of chicory.

When Oscar stepped out of the tack room, he had in his hands two mugs of coffee: one with two sugars, one with one sugar. By this time, Oscar knew how everyone associated with the barn liked their coffee. Sam and Joshua had just sat down in lawn chairs across from the colt's stall. Oscar handed them their coffees, and both men nodded their appreciation. Oscar nodded back, understanding the reason for the silence: Black Deuce was sleeping.

In the next moments Bentley's white Rolls Royce pulled up next to where Sam and Joshua's trucks were parked. The sound of a car door and footsteps, and Bentley walked under the barn. Sam and Joshua, visible in the faint glow of the security light, held an index finger in front of their lips. Bentley understood, and by the time Bentley set up a third lawn chair and sat down, Oscar handed him a mug of coffee: half coffee, half cream. While the three men sat drinking Oscar's brew, making an occasional humming sound of appreciation, what seemed a little ghost came down the shedrow. The little ghost was the old tomcat, and he was soon settling comfortably into Joshua's lap, purring with contentment as Joshua stroked his long fur.

Now Moses came down the shedrow. Oscar saw him coming, and as Moses joined everyone and sat down on a bale of straw across from the colt's stall, Oscar handed Moses a mug of coffee: black, no cream, no sugar. Moses smiled, nodded, and Oscar smiled and nodded back.

Oscar walked out to the Rolls Royce and gave Randolph, Bentley's chauffeur, a mug of coffee: four sugars. When Oscar walked back under the shedrow, headlights shown in the night and because Oscar knew the rattles and clatter of Sam's old truck, he knew without looking that Clay Repp had arrived. Oscar went into the tack room, and when he came back out, Clay was sitting on the bale of straw next to Moses. Oscar handed him a mug of coffee: one sugar, light cream. Oscar had brought the coffee pot with him this time, and arms extended mugs in his direction. He topped everyone's mug off.

After Oscar made another pot of his brew, it was time to check water buckets, and he walked to the other side of the barn, leaving the five men there in front of the colt's stall, all five men still respectfully silent. Then, half way down the backside of the barn, Oscar heard the five men make a sound, all in unison, like they'd just seen a meteor flash across the night sky...and Oscar knew that Black Deuce had waked up and had come to his webbing.

44. SAM

Black Deuce was leaving for Southern Oak and his new career at stud on the next Friday. Joshua insisted they start the trip around six in the evening, Sam didn't argue, and it was estimated they'd arrive at Southern Oak at noon on Saturday. They had an extra passenger: Moses had decided it was time to retire to farm life, that, and he admitted he couldn't bring himself to say goodbye to the colt. Joshua was pleased Moses was coming along.

News of the departure spread through the backstretch, and by two o'clock a crowd began to gather. They came singly, in twos and threes, and in groups, the people of the backstretch: grooms, hot walkers, trainers, owners, exercise riders, feed men, track kitchen workers, shoers, racing office personnel, tack shop people, Veterinarians and jockeys. Even the racing stewards and Mr. Delaney were there. Everyone wanted to get a glimpse of their hero before he left. Many of the people brought their children, and repeatedly these children were told to remember what they were seeing, that they were witnessing history and that one day they could tell their own children that they had actually seen the great black horse.

Just before noon, Moses dropped Black Deuce's webbing, signaling an end to his life at the track, and led him out of his stall. His legs were wrapped in cottons, his coat brush-burnished to a sleek gloss, and when Moses brought him out from under the shedrow there were oohs and ahhs and words of worship from the crowd. Non-racetrackers would call the send-off subdued, but these people saying their goodbyes were people of the backstretch, and they didn't want to excite a horse that had far to travel. One look at all the faces told the story of their emotion.

Just before the ramp was put away, Joshua stood looking back at the shedrow. After looking for several long moments he said, "Well, are ye coming, then?" No one understood who he was talking to, then growing impatient, Joshua called, "There's many a feline beauty on the farm, ye old pirate," and with that the orange tomcat came darting out of a stall, ran by where Joshua stood, and was up the ramp and into the horse van. This prompted a ripple of laughter to go through the send-off gathering.

When Joshua pulled the van away from the barn, he and Sam waved at the crowd, and so did Moses from a window in the back. Black Deuce gazed out the window with Moses and as the van went by the stable gate the colt gave one long, nostril-quivering call, then settled quietly.

Joshua was behind the wheel, and once on Interstate 80, Sam said, "Let me know when you need a break."

"It'll be a while," Joshua answered, sounding relaxed.

"I ordered a video copy of the race," Sam said.

"Get me one?"

"I did, I ordered two."

"Waiting for the stewards to make their call on the bumping and savaging put some hard miles on me old heart."

"Death Wish bumped Deuce first."

"And the two horses went to savaging each other in the same instant."

"What a horse race," Sam said.

Sam looked out the window. Off in the distance was a two-story farm house with a vegetable garden in the back and a big well-kept barn. In the paddock where horses grazed, the grass rippled, performing at the summons of the wind.

Joshua said, "I enjoyed having dinner with yer mother and her new husband."

"They said the same thing about you," Sam said. Then with

humor in his voice added: "I liked that crack Bertie made about seeing you someday in his court room."

Joshua put his head back, gave a burst of laughter. "If they haven't caught me by now, they never will." Then he sobered, said, "I misjudged yer dear mother, she isn't evil, she was just hurt and broken."

Sam nodded, smiled at the thought of the woman who read *Jack and the Beanstalk* to him. "I spent a lot of time with her this last week, long, long talks."

"Is she why you were late to the paddock to saddle Evening Song in the Miss Illinois Stakes?"

"No. I was on the phone with Bess and Amy and just lost track of time, but Vance and Mary had me covered, and it didn't seem to bother the filly, she ran a big second."

"Vance dropped out of Dental school?"

"I knew he would," Sam said.

"How so?"

"Because he loves horses the same way you and I do."

"Aye," Joshua said with a nod. "I've watched the boy, he'll be a fine trainer when given the chance." Then Joshua changed the subject, went on: "And, oh, I haven't told ye about the conversation I had with Robert yesterday."

"Nothing wrong at the farm, I hope."

"No, all is well, he asked me about his two breeding shares in the colt."

"Does he understand how it works?"

"I explained it, and when I told him what those two shares were worth he was speechless." Joshua's nose twitched, he gave a chuckle. "He was thrilled with such a sum of money, but when I told him that he would receive such a sum every year for as long as the colt can breed, I thought I killed the poor man...I never thought I'd hear Robert lose it, but he did, and he kept saying 'Oh, Mr. Joshua, God bless Miss Emily, and I do pray Black Deuce lives a long, long life.'"

Sam and Joshua laughed together, and the van's tires hummed on the asphalt. Sam looked down into the ditch that ran along the roadside. There was a blur of green, the glint of an aluminum can. Then Sam brought up a topic that had been plaguing him with worry. "So how are you feeling, Josh? And tell me the truth."

"I'll survive."

"Have you heard from your doctors? What did the test results say?"

"We'll talk about it, but not now, let's enjoy the drive."

Sam watched Joshua for a long moment, put aside his worry and changed subjects by saying, "I think back at how stupid we were. You were blinded by your feelings for Emily, I was blinded by hate."

Joshua looked over at Sam, said, "Ye do know how to destroy a fine drive."

"It's just that we cheated him, Josh," Sam said. "Black Deuce is perfect and the world should know it."

"Put it from yer mind. There's nothing we can do about it."

"Maybe not, but somehow, some way, I've got to make it up to the colt."

"Knowing ye, ye'll come up with a way to let the world know…but hopefully not get us both put in prison."

Sam retreated into silence, brooded for several miles, then brought up a new topic, said, "I'm happy Ruth is doing so much better."

"I am too."

"She's a lovely woman.

"And knows a bit about the blood of thoroughbreds, I like the mares she's picked out to breed to Deuce."

Sam switched to yet another new topic: "I'm happy for Clay and Doris."

Joshua grinned. "Clay was more nervous on the day he asked that girl to remarry him than he was before any race I've ever seen him ride…including the match race."

Sam nodded, grinned too. "Quite the idea for the ceremony to be held at the farm in the aisle of the stud barn, right in front of the colt's stall."

"Clay says he owes the colt everything, that every time he thought of taking a drink, he thought of being taken off Deuce and that helped keep him sober…that and all the support Doris gave him."

"That little boy of his is something too," Sam said. "What wouldn't a father do for a little boy like that?"

Joshua gave Sam a quick glance, his Irish eyes looking straight into Sam's, then he looked back out the windshield again at the eighteen-wheeler many car lengths in front of them. Sam understood the glance, the reference to himself and his family, and wasn't in the mood to talk about it. Now that the colt was done racing, there were decisions to be made and though logic and reason dominated Sam's decisions when it came to horses, logic and reason deserted him when it came to his family. To avoid the talk he knew Joshua wanted to have, Sam reached for the unread *Chicago Tribune* on the dashboard. He opened it and began to finger his way through the pages. The flutter and snap of newspaper pages being turned suddenly stopped and Sam made a small sound, abruptly brought the paper near his face. He began to hoot a laughter that had more relief in it than mirth.

"Are ye having some sort of seizure?" Joshua asked him.

Sam said nothing, he just grinned at Joshua and held the paper up so Joshua could see the bold headlines on the third page. The headline read: *Case Closed in the Atlantic Hotel Triple Homicide.*

2

"I've never seen anything like them," Sam said, craning his neck to look up at the bronze horse heads that sat atop the brick columns of the great iron double-swing gate that led into Southern Oak. "They're just a glimpse of what waits to be seen," Joshua said as the truck entered the avenue of oaks. "Ye've never seen such a place as this farm."

Leafy branches tangled overhead, and shawls of Spanish moss, swaying lazily, draped the oaks. As Joshua and Sam came to the end of the avenue, the ancients seemed like curtains being drawn back to reveal the great house in all its majesty.

"What a show place," Sam said.

Sam moved his head this way and that as Joshua drove the van past the house. The massive columns soared upward, tall windows gave glimpses into an elegant interior. Joshua brought the truck to a stop in front of the stallion barn. Ivy covered much of the nineteenth century red-brick barn. Sam jumped out of the truck, stood with his hands in his back pockets looking out over the farm. The breeze ruffled his blond hair and he was smiling. Horses already populated the white-fenced paddocks, and he had the odd feeling that he was dreaming, that he'd slipped from one world into another.

"What's that house over there, Josh?" Sam said, pointing at a small cottage tucked between two giant live oaks.

"That's where I'm going to live," Joshua answered coming around the truck.

"You're not going to live in the big house?"

"Such a house as the *big* house is meant for a family," Joshua answered.

With that, Sam eyed Joshua and his defenses came up, but Joshua said no more.

Moses was standing in the doorway of the van, and with Sam and Joshua helping, the colt was soon coming down the ramp. People began to arrive, and Joshua introduced Sam and Moses to those who were already working on the farm. They were a bright-eyed, bright-faced group who made a great fuss over the colt.

"We've got his stall ready for him, Joshua," a young man said coming out of the barn.

"As I knew ye would Christopher," Joshua said, "ye're always a step ahead of me."

Joshua took a moment to introduced Christopher Markham, a slim black-haired man in his early thirties. Joshua introduced him as the assistant farm manager.

With the colt settled in his stall, and Moses with his suitcase moving into a tack room, Sam and Joshua walked out of the barn.

"Let's take a walk," Joshua said, "I want to show ye the house."

Sam and Joshua walked down the road and were soon walking up the steps to the portico.

"These columns are massive," Sam said, putting a hand on the one nearest to him.

"Give the door a knock," Joshua said. "I want ye to see firsthand Southern hospitality."

Sam took hold of a heavy bronze ring held in the mouth of a lion and used it to knock. Came footsteps and one of the doors opened. Robert stood in his livery, light reflecting off the lens of his spectacles.

"Mr. Sam, welcome to Southern Oak," Robert said, and with a slight bow he stepped back and swung both doors wide.

Sam stepped into the great hall, his boots sounding on the marble floor. He was momentarily speechless. He saw the glitter of the Baccarat chandelier, the gleam of fine hardwood furniture, and felt the gaze of generations of Arceneuxs.

"Nice to meet you, Robert," Sam finally said, extending his hand.

Robert shook it, and when he smiled, his teeth were very white in his dark polished face. "And you too, Mr. Sam," Robert said.

Sam stepped further into the house. The library doors stood open, the dark wood polished to shine like mirrors, and Sam peered into the room where books lined the shelves of glass-doored mahogany bookcases that reached to the twelve-foot ceiling. "Look at this place," he said, dazzled.

Joshua stood at Sam's side and said, "One day, all I have will be yours. All of it."

The two men stood looking at each other, eyes locked.

Sam said, "You haven't even been to a doctor. You're not sick at all, are you?"

Joshua smiled. "Not even a wee bit. Aside for the kink in me back, I feel like a two-year old colt in a paddock of green."

"Then tell me why you got me down here."

Just then there came a disturbance beneath the oaks. A yellow cab drove up and parked at the bottom of the stairs. A cabbie, a spry old man with a bald head, got out. He opened the cab's back door, then moved quickly to open the cab's trunk. Bess and Amy got out of the back seat, and both looked around them seeming spellbound.

"What is this place, Mommy?" Amy said. She wore a pretty blue dress and had red ribbons in her hair.

Bess blinked rapidly, looked confused, said, "I don't know, Joshua just said that I needed to trust him and do what he told me to do, and now we're here and I just don't know what's happening—" Bess stopped abruptly, looked around her as if she was lost.

"A wee bit early, they are," Joshua quipped, "but understanding the complications that could have transpired, I think the plan has worked nicely."

"*Plan*?" Sam said.

Joshua didn't respond, he hurried toward the kitchen, taking Robert with him. Over his shoulder he said, "This fine house comes rent free with the job of farm manager." Then just before he and Robert disappeared into the kitchen, Joshua said, "But it is only a house, it's up to the new farm manager and his family to make a home of it."

Now alone in the great hall, a sense of panic came over Sam, and he looked out the open doors to where Bess and Amy stood. Bess with her long black hair shining, Amy with her red ribbons. Sam's panic increased. It was decision time. Sam's impulse was to find a horse to hide behind.

And then it happened.

The universe seemed to stand still, the planets in their orbit, the horses in their paddocks. With nowhere to hide, Sam waited for the pain to start, the pain of a murdered father and an uncaring mother, the pain that always came to destroy any moment of happiness. But closure had come, justice delivered, and once more he couldn't think of his mother without a feeling of warmth coming over him. When Sam took a step toward Bess and Amy, the universe began moving again, and the pain in his heart, the pain he had carried there so long was suddenly gone. And without the pain the rhythm of Sam's heart changed. Suddenly, Sam wanted to grow old in this house, he and Bess together, and along the way to give Amy brothers and sisters, and when he thought of hearing the bright voices of his happy grandchildren in the great hall, the joy he felt overwhelmed him.

Now Bess saw him.

"Sam," she called.

Sam felt a thrill just hearing Bess say his name, and now he was moving quickly out the door and onto the portico. Amy had seen him and began to run up the steps.

"Daddy!" she cried.

Now Sam reached down and picked Amy up and his little girl hugged him around the neck, and Bess was there, and Sam put an arm around her, pulled her close, kissed her in a way he never had before. And then Sam was looking down at Bess, into her lovely upturned face, into the violet of her eyes, and Sam said, "Welcome home."

45. BLACK DEUCE

The colt stirred from his nap. Through a deep bed of straw, he walked over and put his head out over the closed bottom half of his stall door. He looked up and down the aisle, drew in a deep draft of the sweet-smelling breeze that came through the barn, then began to carefully check the four corners of his stall for toads. He snorted a warning as he searched. He didn't like toads. As a yearling, he'd discovered a toad living in one of the corners of his stall and was happy to share his stall with him…until he was horrified by how badly the toad treated a cricket. He'd stomped his hooves at the toad, snorted his outrage, and when the toad finally left in awkward hops, he was very proud of himself.

Above the colt's head there was a flurry of wings, and he stretched his neck to look up at three sparrows sitting all in a row on the rafter. Aside from their little arguments, not once had he ever seen a sparrow do a mean thing. He loved sparrows, even though at times he was jealous of them. Then he heard familiar footsteps and Moses was there attaching a shank to his bridle.

"You should see this one, Deuce," Moses said, leading the colt out of his stall and down the aisle toward the open double-wide doors. "She's the most beautiful bay roan mare I think I've ever seen. Mr. and Mrs. Keene sent her to you…her name is Tigress."

The colt liked the happy ring in Moses' voice and he reached and gave his groom's shirtsleeve a playful tug. Now he and Moses were on the path to the breeding shed, walking together in the bright yellow haze of the sun. The colt missed the hurry and stir of life under a shedrow, but here on this farm is where he belonged, this was home. The colt looked up ahead and was pleased to see Sam and Joshua waiting for him. Robert was there too, his oldest friend. Now the colt swung his head and looked back at the great house, up at the windows of Emily's room. Somehow, he knew Emily was gone forever, that she would never again sit by the window and be his companion during long afternoons, and this caused the strange trembling in his heart to come. He didn't like the trembling, and he wanted Moses to make it go away. When the colt swung his head back toward Moses, Moses did make the trembling go away by talking to him once again with the happy ring in his voice.

And then the colt stopped, lifted his head. The breeze fluttered his mane and tail. He'd caught the scent of the mare, and now the colt bowed his neck and began to prance. A rumbling started in his chest, and his throat pulsed and flexed when he released this rumble in a thundering call.

And when Black Deuce saw her, the beautiful bay roan, and Tigress looked back at him with lovely eyes of amber, the colt thought how glad he was to be a thoroughbred, and not to be a sparrow.

Antebellum Days is a busy week at Southern Oak. Buses arrive and Robert and Josiah Krump give tours of the great columned house. Amy Jack, along with her two brothers Joshua and Henry, and her sister Emily, serve refreshments to all the guests. The ice-cold lemonade is a favorite. Southern Oak's open house is a much-anticipated event by those who love history, art and horses. The tours always begin in the drawing room where Josiah talks of the artist Adrienne Saxon White and how he came to America to paint Camille Arceneaux, Southern Oak's founder. Everyone is fascinated by the painting and the story of how Krump came to own it for a short time only to return it to its rightful place. Visitors are moved when they hear how this painting became the focal point of a great friendship between Josiah Krump and Robert Todd, the authors of the much celebrated book *This Great House.* The book tells the story of Southern Oak in people, horses and treasures.

Not just during Antebellum Days is Southern Oak busy with visitors. Visitors come throughout the year to see the horse that is the foundation sire of a thoroughbred dynasty. They come to see Black Deuce. Black Deuce has passed on his speed and stamina, is a sire of champions, and visitors come to watch in awe as he races across his paddock in a show of grace and power.

From the leggy foals romping alongside their dams, to the retired racehorses lounging in the comfort of their very own barn and paddocks, there is so much to see at Southern Oak. But there is one attraction that stands out above the rest, even competing with the great horse himself. This attraction is a bronze plaque mounted on the front of Black Deuce's stall. This plaque has inspired writers and the curious to ask many questions of Sam Jack and Joshua Kincaid, but no matter how many times they are asked to explain the meaning of the plaque, neither Sam nor Joshua offer any explanation. Sam and Joshua answer all questions about the plaque in the same way, they answer the questions with silence and a smile. This, of course, only fuels curiosity, only fuels the debate that has raged for years among historians of the turf, for on that bronze plaque, just below the name Black Deuce, are two words: Undefeated Champion.

THE END

About the Author

Stan D. Jensen received his bachelor's degree in history and his
master's degree in education from the University of Northern
Iowa. He has owned racehorses, and spent the 1980s as a jockey's
agent. His short stories have been published in the magazine "The
Backtretch." *Black Deuce* is his third novel. Mr. Jensen lives in
Clinton, Iowa, and continues to write.

Also by Stan D. Jensen

Red Otter
Ethan's Peach Tree